FI
PRAYER

BOOKS BY KATHRYN CASEY

The Fallen Girls

THE SARAH ARMSTRONG MYSTERY SERIES
Singularity
Blood Lines
The Killing Storm
The Buried

TRUE CRIME
Evil Beside Her
She Wanted It All
A Warrant to Kill
Die, My Love
Shattered
A Descent Into Hell
Deadly Little Secrets
Murder, I Write
Possessed
Deliver Us
In Plain Sight

Kathryn Casey

HER FINAL PRAYER

bookouture

Published by Bookouture in 2020

An imprint of Storyfire Ltd.
Carmelite House
50 Victoria Embankment
London EC4Y 0DZ

www.bookouture.com

Written by Kathryn Casey

ISBN: 978-1-80019-036-8
eBook ISBN: 978-1-80019-035-1

For Elaine Larson, my beloved aunt, who has set such an inspiring example on how to age with style and grace.

CHAPTER ONE

"I'm late," Naomi muttered. She turned right out of the trailer park and heard a faint grinding coming from the white van. She wondered about the health of the wheel bearings, or if the brakes needed repair. Before Abe died, he kept the family's vehicles in top condition. Back then, in addition to the van all three sister-wives had their own cars. Now the family had only the aging van. Naomi glanced at the odometer: 148,692 miles, most of it on mountain roads. How long would it last?

A little more than a year since Abe's passing, their world had become infinitely harder, and Naomi had begun to think of her life as before and after. Before, they had the big house in town. Mornings were busy but manageable. A calming force, Abe circulated and gave each child a kiss on the forehead and encouraged them to study hard and make him proud.

After? Naomi pulled back an errant strand of her brown hair—just beginning to fade at forty-five—and deftly tucked it back into her topknot. She could think of only one word: chaos.

This morning, a Monday, was a perfect example. Up before sunrise, the women rushed about in the cramped double-wide trailer, surrounded by sixteen of their jostling and complaining offspring. Too many bodies in a small space bred confusion. While Sariah flipped pancakes, Ardeth fulfilled her status as first wife and head of the family by shouting orders: "Sit down at the table! Eat! Get dressed! Don't forget to collect your homework!"

Meanwhile, Naomi tried in vain to quiet the storm for a brief morning prayer. She had finally calmed the other children when Kaylynn clamped on to her leg and held tight, scrunching her eyes shut in rebellion and screaming that she wouldn't go to pre-kindergarten. Not that morning. Not ever.

"Child, let go!" Naomi had shouted. She didn't like raising her voice with the little ones, but everyone had a limit, and the girl had found hers. "Kaylynn, I insist you be still. You will obey me. I am your mother."

In spite of the confusion, by the time the sun came up, the children had eaten and dressed. The girls in their long prairie dresses and the boys in khaki pants and button-down shirts rifled through the dozens of hand-me-down winter jackets that hung from hooks. At the last possible moment, they all, including Kaylynn, ran out the door to catch the school bus.

Yet the hubbub delayed Naomi's departure. Forty minutes later than she'd planned, she left the trailer to work the hives.

Winters in Utah's high valleys could be hard, and she had to prepare the bees. The first hard freeze was expected that night, and snow already dusted the mountaintops surrounding the small town of Alber. If her hives were to live through the frigid months to come, Naomi had to make preparations. A lot to accomplish—she had little time to spare. In three hours, Naomi had to return the van to the trailer so Ardeth could do the family's bi-weekly grocery shopping.

Considering the time crunch, Naomi wondered if she should have made the promise the day before. Heading southeast, she glanced over at the metal and plastic object wrapped in a plastic bag that sat on the seat beside her.

At Sunday's church service, Naomi had had a long conversation with Laurel Johansson about her baby, Jeremy. "I'm afraid he's not getting enough nourishment," Laurel had confided. "Two months old and he's not much over his birth weight."

Saying she understood the young woman's concerns, Naomi explained the benefits of using a breast pump. In fact, Naomi said she had one Laurel could use. "I'll drop it off in the morning."

A big, handsome man with shaggy dark blond hair and laser-like blue eyes, Laurel's husband, Jacob, had stood beside them, listening intently. "That would be kind of you, Naomi. What time will you arrive?"

Giving Jacob a broad smile, Naomi vowed, "I'll be there at seven thirty, no later."

A first-time mother, Laurel had been so grateful that she threw her arms around Naomi and hugged her.

Naomi turned off the highway, passing the Johansson family's bison grazing in the surrounding fields. Naomi wondered if Laurel realized how lucky she was to be Jacob's second wife. He came from a respected family, one with a business that funded all their needs. More than a thousand head roamed the Johanssons' 300 acres. Skilled marketers, they sold to high-end meat markets where big-city folk paid premium prices.

"Envy is the devil's cauldron," Naomi mumbled, reminding herself to be grateful for all she did have and not resent the good fortune of others.

Yet she did envy. And what had convinced Naomi to keep her promise, even though she was running late, was the opportunity to tell Jacob good morning. As she drove, Naomi thought about Jacob's two young wives: Laurel and his first wife, Anna, and their three children. Naomi wondered what it would be like to be in Ardeth's position as the most senior woman in a family.

A short drive and she reached the gate, with MRJ RANCH in wrought iron at its crest. She looked beyond it in appreciation of the wide columns at the front of the impressive house, the vast maze of corrals that led to a massive barn. Naomi couldn't help but compare it to the run-down double-wide she lived in, when she suddenly noticed something that appeared out of place.

Pulling onto the driveway, she eyed a stark white shape that lay on the ground, the breeze billowing its sides and corners. It looked like a fallen sail, but that struck her as ridiculous. Alber lay far from anywhere anyone could use such a boat.

Normally, Naomi would have driven up to the house and parked near the front door, but something—she wasn't sure what—so bothered her about the scene that she stopped a hundred feet back, close to the barn. For a moment, she hesitated, uneasy. Then, scolding herself for being silly, Naomi plopped the visor down and took a last look at her light brown hair. She ran her tongue over her teeth and pinched her cheeks.

She grabbed the bag holding the breast pump with one hand as she grasped the door handle with the other. Then, again, she froze. Staring out at the strange object, she decided it looked like a bedsheet. She considered the outline and spotted three distinct areas where something appeared to be hidden beneath it: one long, flat bulge, two smaller and shorter ones.

Maybe they planted fall flowers they want to protect from the freeze, Naomi thought, readjusting her wire-rimmed glasses on her long, thin nose.

Fighting a sense of dread, she flung the door open and slid down onto the driveway. The breast pump tucked against her middle, the flowing skirt of her denim dress rippling in the breeze, she approached the house. As she did, she walked closer to the sheet. Not far away, newly hung wash flapped on a clothesline. A basket holding more laundry sat below it. Naomi considered the sheet spread across the ground and wondered if it could have blown out of the basket or off the line. No, she decided. It was laid out too precisely. As she thought through the possibilities, she stopped and stared at the white cotton fabric. Her eyes settled on scattered bright red spots near all three of the mounds.

Above her, a bird let out a raspy squawk. Startled, Naomi followed the sound to the bare, gnarled branches of a thick-trunked oak. Three vultures so black their feathers showed blue stared down at her. One huffed, as if expressing annoyance at her arrival. Naomi looked again at the sheet, again at the red stains, again at the vultures in the tree. Her heartbeat hastened.

"Dear God," she whispered.

A sharp breeze ruffled the last remaining leaves, and in the tree one of the vultures beat the air with its muscular wings. As the gust trailed along the ground, it snagged a corner of the sheet. It flew up, executed a pirouette, and as it fell folded back into a twisted triangle. Twice Naomi blinked, trying to make sense of what the wind had uncovered: smooth, pale flesh exposed between the hem of a pair of blue corduroy pants and a white athletic sock that ended in a toddler-size tennis shoe.

"A child," she whispered. Bending down, her heart fluttered as if one of the gloomy birds had flown from its perch and roosted in her chest. She picked up the sheet ever so slightly and peeked beneath it. Naomi gagged back a scream at what she saw: a motionless boy, his hair matted with something thick, across his forehead a trail of drying blood.

"Benjamin," Naomi whispered.

Her hand trembling, Naomi dropped the sheet and stood erect. Her pulse pounded in her ears as she scanned the yard. Empty. Her eyes traveled over the house, the porch where three empty chairs lazily rocked in the breeze, surrounded by scattered children's toys. She gazed up at the dark windows and saw no one staring down. Turning back to the body, her eyes migrated to the other two shapes hidden beneath the sheet. Feeling suddenly ill, she reconsidered the bright red stains.

Naomi reached into her pocket and realized that in the morning's haste she'd left the family's lone cell phone at home. Looking again at the Johanssons' house, she listened for any sound out of place. Far off in the field, the bison bellowed, letting loose short grunts and deep throaty roars. Above her the vultures shuffled in the tree, impatient. What she feared hearing, she didn't: Something human.

Swallowing a growing panic, Naomi drew closer to the house, the van's keys in her hand in case anything convinced her to turn and run. Up the steps, onto the porch, she hesitated at the door. Her heart felt as if it were a separate being trapped inside her, one that pounded against the cage of her chest, demanding to be let out. Ever so cautiously, she edged the screen door open and turned the handle on the unlocked inner wooden door.

At first, she saw no signs of a disturbance. A well-furnished house, comfortable-looking, a living room, dining room. She stopped at the base of the staircase, pausing long enough to confirm the silence. A few feet farther in, she came to an abrupt stop.

Just inside the kitchen, two thick legs clothed in jeans splayed out across an off-white tile floor. Before she rounded the corner, Naomi heard the sound—a rhythmic gurgling. She peeked around the corner. A man lay there, his chest heaving, struggling to breathe. Blood bubbled from the front of his neck.

"Dear Lord, Jacob!" Naomi called out. She ran to him and knelt beside him.

Jacob Johansson's eyes fluttered, opened, found her, and locked on to her face. Naomi sensed a slight smile, then his lids drifted down. She put her hand on his chest and felt the rise and fall of life. "Please, don't die," she whispered. She scanned the room. An old-fashioned Trimline phone hung near the stove. She rushed to it, grasped the handset and pushed three buttons. She looked down and realized that blood stained the front of her skirt.

"Nine-one-one. What's your emergency?"

Naomi tried but couldn't speak.

"Who's calling? What's your emergency?" The operator sounded impatient, perhaps wondering if the silent caller could be a child pulling a prank.

Naomi cleared her throat, trying to free her ensnared vocal cords. "I'm... I'm... at the Johansson ranch southeast of Alber. Send an ambulance. Send the police. Quick. He's dying."

"Who's dying? Ma'am, who are you?" the dispatcher demanded. "Are you in danger?"

"I-I'm... Just send help. I saw a body, a little boy, Benjamin. I think there are more. Jacob is bleeding on the kitchen floor," she stuttered. Her hands shook so that the phone threatened to drop from her grasp. Then, from somewhere above her in the house, she heard a long, shrill cry. *The baby.*

CHAPTER TWO

Crack. The metal made a high-pitched sound as it hit rock. In response, I moved a foot to the right and started over, pressing my boot down on the spade, struggling to force the blade into the cold earth. Three months earlier, a monster had made this land his hunting ground. After ten years as a Dallas cop, I'd returned to stop him. I'd planned to go back to Texas. Instead I signed on as my hometown's police chief. Yet my relationship with Alber, Utah, came with bad memories, the kind that too often woke me up at night wondering if I'd made a foolhardy decision.

Although we'd closed the case, the prospect of undiscovered victims pricked at my conscience. At least one young woman remained unaccounted for. Her family hoped for answers, and I felt responsible. If I didn't find her, who would? So, when I drove streets and highways, I watched for areas where the ground appeared recently disturbed. And on mornings like this one, when I roused early and couldn't fall back asleep, I threw on old clothes and grabbed my shovel.

This particular patch of earth caught my attention because of a pile of rocks that looked like it might be discards from someone else's dig. Nearby I noticed a patch of disturbed dirt. Big enough for a woman's body? Maybe.

The November sky was still dark, and the morning air brought a definite nip. Our valley had had a light snowfall the week before, blanketing the town at dawn with flurries of less than an inch. By noon it all melted, except for the bright white caps that topped the surrounding mountains and the rooftops. I wondered if the spirits of our ancestors, in local lore said to live atop our highest mountain, Samuel's Peak, watched me conduct my fruitless searches. What must they think of me, of the fact that I stayed in a town doing all I could to protect people who at every opportunity made it clear they didn't want me?

The shovel heavy, I threw its contents onto the growing mound of dirt beside me. Most of the trees were bare, only the pines stubbornly holding onto their green, and as I dug, their scent surrounded me. The rising sun painted the horizon gold and pink.

The rhythm of the dig occupied my body and freed my mind. I thought about the prior Saturday evening, my weekly dinner with Max. We'd fallen into a pattern. The relationship felt comfortable, and that bothered me. I knew he wanted more than friendship; I wasn't ready to take that step. At times, there was a heavy silence between us, and much remained unsaid. I had issues I wasn't ready to face. Max had buried a wife he loved. Every time Miriam came up, his lips clenched and no words escaped. He felt guilty. I sensed it. But why? A couple of times he appeared to be considering explaining, then stayed silent.

We both had so much baggage, our pasts unsettled.

Damaged, that was the word for Max, and for me. We weren't as we'd once been, a boy and a girl who yearned for each other. I first noticed Max in grade school, our desks three apart in fourth grade. In my home-sewn prairie dresses, my hair in dark braids, I was a somber child, silent much of the time, perhaps too introspective. I followed orders and listened to my parents; I hid in my books and never let anything pull me away from my homework. As good a student, Max had a bit of the imp about him. We were still children when he started passing me little notes, silly, childish jokes printed on notebook paper with pencil. When I read them, I shot him a grin, and Max erupted in giggles. I loved his laugh. More often than not, the teacher hauled him up to the front of the classroom.

I felt embarrassed, as if we'd made ourselves a spectacle, but Max never seemed to mind. By sixth grade, he picked me daisies in the summer and left them on our family's front porch.

But that was all in the past. In the intervening years, life had thrown us to the curb and left us broken.

"Clara, how about dinner Monday, at my house?" Max had asked as he walked me from the restaurant to my SUV on Saturday evening. "Brooke can join us, and I'll make a pot of chili."

"I'd love that, sure," I'd said. Then I had misgivings about including his daughter. "But, Max, maybe Brooke will get the wrong idea about us?"

Max had clenched his lips tight and stared at me as he reached over and opened the door. I'd seen the disappointment in his eyes. "Would that be the worst thing?" he asked. "If we were more than we are?"

"I-I don't…" I had started, but then fell silent.

Disarming my qualms, Max had smiled, and images flooded me from that same smile so many years ago. "You've always been so serious, Clara," he'd whispered as he moved closer. "Can't you find a way to let your mind rest?"

I'd taken a deep breath and tried to quiet my pulse as he ran his hand along my shoulder. I'd stared into Max's eyes, the softest of browns speckled with gold and dark green. I'd reached up and tousled his light brown hair, caressed the dark stubble that covered his dimpled chin. My body had responded, my nerve endings tingling and my heart opening. For a moment, I'd hesitated, but then I forced myself to pull away.

"Clara, please…" Max had frowned and looked at me as if pleading. "Can't we—"

"I need to go," I'd blurted out. "It's late and I have a lot to do, work waiting for me."

Max's eyes settled on mine, and I'd instinctively understood that he knew I lied. I had nothing I had to do that night. I sensed that he understood that our closeness frightened me. I'd felt vulner-able. My reaction to his touch had made it clear that, someplace deep inside of me, I hadn't given up on us. In that moment, all I'd yearned for was to nestle against him. But I didn't say any of that. Instead, I'd turned to leave.

As I'd closed the SUV's door, Max had shouted, "No strings attached, just a bowl of my special chili and a little time for you to get to know Brooke."

I'd started to shake my head no, but then, despite my misgiv-ings, I'd nodded.

Now Monday had arrived, and this evening would be my first real time with Brooke. And I wondered again: Is this something we should do?

Crack. I hit another rock, relocated a bit to my right and pushed Max from my mind.

Two hours on, the sun rose ever higher into the sky and, despite autumn's chill, sweat formed on my neck and under my parka. I pulled it off, hung it on a branch, and focused on my work. A foot or so down, the pine-scented air became impregnated with the thick, rancid odor that I recognized as death. I considered calling for assistance but decided I had to know for sure. To filter the stench, I untied the red bandana from my neck and knotted it in the back to cover my mouth and nose, then got down on my knees and began pushing the dirt away with my hands.

The loose ground gave way easily, which I interpreted as a sign that I was right, that this patch of earth had been recently dug up. With each swipe of my hands, I removed another thin layer of dirt, getting closer to something rotting not far below the surface. My anticipation built as the foul smell grew heavier. I pulled on a pair of latex gloves from my pocket. Ready, I sat back on my heels and looked into the two-foot-wide hole I'd dug. I scooped out a couple more handfuls and threw the dirt to the side. I saw strands of hair, red and wispy, streaked with gold.

I wondered again if I should stop, but I kept going, pulling out handfuls of earth.

Adrenaline rushed through me as I worked ever faster, brushing away the earth. A few more swipes and I stared at the placid face of a fairly recently deceased Irish setter.

I had found a grave, but not a human one.

For a brief moment, I hesitated, thinking about how obsessed I'd become that I would spend my morning digging up a dog's grave in hopes of finding a young woman's body. Then I stood and methodically shoveled the coarse dirt back into the hole, restoring the canine to his peaceful rest. Once finished, I removed the gloves and brushed off my clothes and boots. I was filthy. I looked at my watch: 8.15. I had just enough time to swing by my room at Heaven's Mercy to clean up before I drove to the office. My friend Hannah Jessop ran the shelter, housing women and children who had nowhere to live or weren't safe at home. Since I debated about whether or not I'd stay in Alber, she'd agreed to rent me a room while I made up my mind.

I threw the shovel in the back of the black Chevy Suburban that I'd inherited from the prior chief and pushed the button to lower the liftgate. Then I pulled out my phone to check my email. The symbol in the left corner indicated a missed phone call. Somehow, I'd turned the ringer off. A message asked me to call my office ASAP.

"Chief, we have a situation at the Johansson bison farm." Stephanie Jonas sounded wired. Until a month earlier, she'd been Alber PD's day dispatcher. When I took over as chief, I hired a replacement, got Stef licensed, and promoted her to rookie cop. Once she finished her classes and became certified as a full-fledged forensic officer, I planned to make her the department's crime scene officer. As a small police department in a town of a bit more than 4,000 souls, we didn't have any. I knew Stef would be good at it. She had a knack for detail.

"What kind of situation?" I asked.

"The sheriff's department called. Chief Deputy Max Anderson has been dispatched to the scene with backup, but the ranch is within Alber city limits, so it's ours," Stef said. "An unidentified woman called nine-one-one and reported multiple fatalities."

"The Johansson ranch?" I verified.

"Yes," Stef confirmed. I felt a chill rush through me when she said, "Chief, it sounds like a massacre."

CHAPTER THREE

Max led the caravan off the main road in his Smith County Sheriff car and turned under the MRJ logo onto the Johansson ranch. Behind him trailed two squads and an ambulance. He drove deliberately, eyes scanning the pastures, the bison, and the driveway. Everything looked ordinary, until he noticed a white object on the ground up ahead. As he passed a parked van with tinted windows, a woman ran from the house clutching something wrapped in a blanket to her chest. Was she the one who called in the report? Max frowned. Why did she hang up on 911? The dispatcher had only sketchy information to give him, and that made Max nervous. All he knew was that a nameless woman claimed someone needed medical assistance and that there were dead bodies.

The woman looked frazzled. As his car approached, she ran erratically, weaving back and forth. Max worried about what she might have hidden in the blanket she carried. He watched her hands warily for signs she might drop it and expose a gun. Then he recognized her.

"Naomi Jefferies," Max whispered. "What's she doing here?"

Max considered bumping Stef on the radio and asking her to tell Clara that one of her mothers was on the scene. Instead, he slammed on his brakes as Naomi made a sharp turn and jumped nearly in front of the car. The car jerked to an abrupt stop, and he lowered his window. As she bent toward him, he realized she had a crying baby bundled in the blanket, one who looked small enough to be a newborn.

"Naomi, what the heck is going on here?" Max asked.

"They're dead!" Naomi shouted over the baby's screams. Her eyes bulged with fear, and her lips quivered. "Everyone but the baby. And Jacob, but he could be dead by now, too. Please, help him. Please, Max! Hurry!"

"How did they die?" he asked. When Naomi stared at him as if she didn't understand, he explained, "What did you see?"

"Blood. Lots of blood." Indicating the white object that Max now realized was a bedsheet, she screamed, "A child dead under there, and I'm pretty sure there are others. I think that Jacob's throat has been cut."

Max pointed at the squad's back seat. "Get in!" he shouted. "Now!"

"Why... no... no... Drive up there. Help Jacob. He's..." She pointed at the house again, her hair fanned wildly out around her face and her eyes bright red from crying. Max noticed what appeared to be blood on the front of her skirt.

"Quick! Get in my car, before you get us both shot." When she didn't move, he shouted, "Naomi, now!"

"He's gone," she said. "There's no one..."

"Who's gone?"

"Whoever did this. Max, there's no one on this ranch alive but the baby and Jacob," she said, sobbing. "And he could be dying while we're out here arguing."

"Get in." For the third time he shouted, "Now!"

Finally, Naomi did as he instructed, scurrying into the back seat. Once she slammed the door, Max pulled forward and parked. The ambulance stayed at the gate, per protocol, while the other squads moved in behind Max in the lead car.

"Aren't the paramedics coming to help Jacob?" Naomi asked, swiveling to look out the back window. "He's—"

"They don't go in until after we clear the scene. Someone could be hiding," he said. She turned back around and stared at him as he explained, "Naomi, if you hear shots, you duck. And you don't get out of this car, not for any reason, until I tell you it's safe. Understand?"

Naomi's face contorted and Max thought that perhaps she finally comprehended that they could all be in danger. Instead of answering, she gave him a quick nod. He looked out and scanned the sheet, seeing for the first time a section folded over, exposing two small legs. A fist tightening in his chest, Max bumped dispatch on his radio.

"We potentially have a live scene. Send more backup. Alert the medical examiner and the CSI unit," he said, and then he slipped his gun from his holster and warily opened the door.

The four deputies backing him up stayed low and made their way toward him as Max clambered out of his car. Once they reached him, he jerked his head to the right then the left. "One takes the front, the other around back. Two of you stay with me," he snapped. "I'm going to make sure that no one is hiding under that sheet, and then we'll head inside."

As instructed, one deputy ran to surveil the back door, while his partner positioned himself with a view of the grand house to his right and the barn off to his left. Meanwhile, Max led the other two officers over to the sheet. He bent over and pulled it back, exposing the boy's body. The child's dark hair glistened in the sunlight, wet with something thick, Max assumed blood. A trail of dark red began at an angry black hole just above the boy's eyebrows, streaked his pale skin until it dripped off his face onto the ground. Max had seen similar wounds over the years. Shot in the back of the head, Max figured. Exit wound in the forehead.

"Keep watch, especially the house," Max said to the two deputies beside him. "Someone could have a gun on us."

Once the deputies focused on the surrounding area, Max got down on one knee and lifted the sheet higher. He didn't want to disturb any potential evidence, but he needed to know what it concealed. A short distance from the toddler boy, near the center of the sheet, was a young girl, maybe five or six, wearing a tan-and-pink-flowered prairie dress. Like the boy's, the girl's black hair glistened with something dark. He saw no signs of life.

Dead bodies had always made Max uneasy, but he'd found them harder to tolerate since his wife's death. Bloody scenes brought up images of Miriam squeezed between the steering wheel and seat, unable to breathe. The children's bodies, frozen by death, made it that much worse. An image of his young daughter, Brooke, unconscious and bleeding in the back seat, her body twisted like a sapling caught in a tornado, flashed before him.

Taking measured steps, his eyes shuttling all around him, Max walked to the other side of the sheet. As he approached, something emitted a sharp cawing sound above him. He looked up to see a committee of vultures, pitch-black with pale, wrinkled bald heads, hovering in a nearby oak, glaring angrily at him. Ignoring them, Max focused on the larger mound under the sheet. As Max shuffled closer, a particularly thick-bodied vulture hopped off a tree limb and landed ten feet away. Max looked into the bird's beady black eyes and thought it jeered at him, as if daring him to approach.

"Scram! Take off!" he yelled, marching toward the bird. It shuffled back two feet, stopped, and stood its ground.

"Damn thing," Max murmured.

Max returned his attention to the sheet. Once there, he realized the vultures had been pecking at the bodies, their beaks tearing small holes in the sheet, ones ringed in bright red blood. Again, he knelt. He held out his gun, his finger on the trigger, as he lifted the white cloth, and a gust billowed beneath it, forming a tent over the sprawled body of a woman. Her dark hair flared around her head, and she lay flat on her stomach, face down on the ground. Creeping closer, he placed two fingers on her neck. No pulse. Max stood and turned to the deputy assigned to keep watch on the house and barn. "Three vics, one woman, two kids. Looks like all three have been shot. Radio headquarters and notify them," Max said. "And keep the birds off the bodies. We're going in."

A bob of the deputy's head, and Max turned to verify that Naomi was following orders. In the car's back seat, she had her head bowed over her lap, as if trying to comfort the baby.

Drawing a deep breath, Max marched toward the house, the remaining two deputies tracking behind him. Their heads rotated side to side, watching, waiting for someone to charge out of the shadows, for a shot to ring out from an upstairs window. Their heavy boots pounded on the cement steps as they ran up onto the porch, swung the door open, and entered the house.

Following the route Naomi had taken, they cleared the living room, then the dining room. Max stationed one deputy at the foot of the stairs to make sure no one came charging down to take them by surprise. Then he and the fourth deputy made their way toward the kitchen.

Before he entered, Max heard a strange sucking noise. He hurried into the kitchen, careful to avoid a pool of blood near the head of a tall, bulky man sprawled legs akimbo on the floor. Max hadn't seen Jacob Johansson since high school, and he wouldn't have recognized him even if blood didn't cover his neck and his skin wasn't dead pale. Jacob struggled to take in each breath, and with every attempt the wound in his neck gurgled up foaming blood. The sound reminded Max of a death rattle.

"Should I stay with him?" the deputy beside Max asked.

"No. Follow procedure. Clear the house fast and we'll get medical in here," Max said. "Let's go. Hurry."

From the kitchen, they rushed through the mudroom and pantry, then downstairs and did a once-over of the cellar, shelves filled with the typical gallon-size glass jars of canned fruit and vegetables fanning out around them. In Alber, nearly all the families stored at least a year's worth of supplies. As he scanned the rows, Max worried about Jacob, intent on getting care to him as quickly as possible.

When they rejoined the officer at the foot of the stairs, Max and the two deputies ran upstairs and did a swift search, going room to room. Nothing appeared out of the ordinary in the nursery with the crib, or the children's room with two single beds, a framed fairy princess picture over one and a Buzz Lightyear poster over the other. A moan caught in his throat as Max glanced at two sets of pajamas discarded on the floor, and he thought again of the small, lifeless bodies under the sheet. One set of PJs had purple flowers and the other cartoon fire engines.

The next bedroom had a king-size bed, two nightstands, a dresser, and a three-foot-high vase on a corner table that held oversized artificial pussy willows and cattails. The quilt spread across the unmade bed reminded Max of one his mother had made, a double wedding-ring pattern, light peach and yellow on a white background. No one hid behind the shower curtain in the attached bathroom, and they turned and walked out.

They quickly cleared a second bathroom, one with a basket of Fisher Price figures in the tub, two-inch-tall plastic girls in skirts and boys in trousers, along with cheerful, smiling yellow rubber ducks.

That left a single room to search, and Max wondered why that particular one had the door closed. The others had all been open.

His gun raised and ready, the two deputies behind him, Max cautiously cracked the door open. The drapes were closed, and the room had only dim light coming in from the hallway. But Max could see into the closet gaping open, clothes hanging haphazardly from a wooden rod, boxes piled up on the shelf. He felt around on the wall to his left and found a switch.

The ceiling light flicked on. The room looked normal; the large dresser had a mirror, and a fluffy duvet, the blue of a pale morning sky, was pulled up to the headboard's wooden spindles. But the more he looked at it, the more unnatural the bed appeared. It had a bulge on the far-right side. Pointing his gun at the bump, Max circled the bed and let his eyes trail down the bedside. A delicate wrist and hand peeked out from beneath the bedding.

Max held his breath, inched over to the bed, and picked up the corner of the duvet. Slowly, he pulled it back. A woman in a cotton nightgown covered with cheerful flowers lay spread-eagled on her back beneath it, her hand dangling down. Blood saturated the sheet beneath her in a pattern that resembled a Rorschach turtle. Her light brown hair encircled her head on the pillow, and her open pale eyes were unseeing. In life, he thought she must have been beautiful: finely chiseled features, an alabaster complexion.

Yet his attention kept being drawn to her mouth, where someone had taken lipstick and pushed hard to paint a thick red oval around her lips, one as dark as the smears of drying blood that marked the deep slash across her throat.

"That's Laurel Johansson," the deputy at his side whispered. Max wondered why that name sounded familiar, then felt his heart lodge in his throat when the guy said, "You know, one of Mullins' kids."

"Jeff Mullins?" Max asked, hoping the deputy meant someone else, not Alber PD's veteran officer. "The detective?"

"Yeah," the deputy said. "That Jeff Mullins."

Max's stomach churned thinking that someone would have to call Mullins. That wasn't a call he wanted to make and no one wanted to receive. But first they needed to take care of the man bleeding on the kitchen floor. Max tapped his shoulder mic. "Send in the EMTs. We have two additional vics inside, one alive, one dead. Tell the paramedics that their patient is on the first floor, the kitchen, throat cut. The house is clear. We're on our way downstairs."

To the two deputies who'd searched the house with him, Max said, "Go outside. Help the others clear the barn and any outbuildings. Additional backup is on the way. Tell headquarters to dispatch the CSI unit and the ME."

The deputies sprinted off, following orders.

Alone in the room, Max took another look at Laurel Johansson, thinking again about the painful moment Jeff Mullins would face when he heard his daughter was dead. Max focused on the angry red slit across Laurel's neck, ear to ear, and thought about Jacob on the kitchen floor, still alive but his throat cut as well. It struck Max as nearly biblical to kill in such a fashion.

In contrast, from the look of it, the woman and children under the sheet had all been shot.

As Max walked down the stairs, he realized that the sheer carnage rivaled anything he'd witnessed in all his years in law enforcement, the bulk of it spent not working for a rural sheriff's office but Salt Lake PD. As a big-city cop, Max had investigated gang killings and been part of major drug busts. Despite its squeaky-clean image, Salt Lake shared the problems common to all cities: robberies, sex crimes, gun violence and murders. Yet never had Max walked into such a shocking scene. The bodies of the woman and two children under the sheet sickened him. And Max had a hard time wrapping his mind around the scene in the upstairs bedroom.

Two EMTs rushed in nearly simultaneously as Max reached the first floor. "Did you assess the victims outside?" he asked. "Under the sheet."

"All three dead," an EMT confirmed as they hurtled toward the kitchen.

Max walked outside to check on Naomi in the car and saw that she'd disobeyed him and gotten out. She still held the baby, but now she talked to a new arrival. Naomi appeared deep in conversation, bouncing the baby nervously on her hip. He approached, his eyes fixed on the newcomer's black hair, pulled into a familiar bun at the nape of her neck.

When Clara turned toward him, Max looked into her wide, dark eyes, the deep brown of strong coffee. He noticed her mud-caked jeans, her dirt-covered boots and immediately understood where she had been—out digging, looking for bodies in the woods. Once again, he thought about how this was a woman who didn't understand the concept of ever giving up.

"Chief Jefferies," Max said. He thought about how eager he'd been to see her again, but not this way. Never this way. "You got our message?"

"I did." All business, she asked, "What do we know?"

CHAPTER FOUR

Mother Naomi jumped out of Max's squad car and came running toward me the moment I climbed out of the black Suburban. I put my hand on her shoulder, hoping to calm her. The baby let loose a torrent of screams from within his blue blanket, I thought perhaps picking up on Naomi's agitation as she fidgeted while she tried to quiet him. "You're frightening the child," I said, trying to be as soothing as I could. "Mother Naomi, you need to calm down and tell me what's happened."

Our family lost one mother, Constance, years earlier to breast cancer. Of my three surviving mothers, Naomi had always been the most excitable. During prayer service, she was the one who more often than not shouted praise to the heavens as her face glowed with an exuberant love. Emotions rarely bottled up inside her, since she so enjoyed releasing them out into the world. When she didn't stop juddering the child, I put my hand on her cheek and looked into her eyes as I ordered, "Stop bouncing. Please."

Gradually, she reined her emotions in. The terror drained from her face and she stilled. As she did, the baby quieted. "That's better," I said. "Now tell me, what's going on here?"

"Someone's killed them all," Naomi said, each word drawn out like a full sentence.

"Killed who?"

"The Johanssons. All dead, I think, except Jeremy and maybe Jacob."

I remembered Jacob, the oldest of Michael and Reba Johansson's sons, from my childhood. I'd lost touch with everyone during the ten years I lived in Dallas, where I trained to become a cop, eventually working homicides. But I'd heard that Jacob had left Alber not long after I did and only returned about a year earlier to take over the bison ranch so his father could retire. Once Jacob and his family moved onto the ranch, the elder Johanssons had taken up residence in a house not far off Main Street in the center of town. The other person Naomi referred to I didn't know. "Jeremy?"

"This is Jeremy," Naomi said, looking down at the infant, a tiny one with a sparse fringe of light blond hair and bright blue eyes, rosy cheeks. Naomi looked up from her small charge, took a deep breath and pointed at something white spread out across the ground. "There's blood, Clara. On that sheet over there, on the face of the dead boy under it, and all around Jacob on the floor."

"Did you see how it happened?" I asked. Naomi shook her head. "Why are you here?" I asked.

At that moment, her attention shifted to something or someone over my shoulder. I turned and saw Max trudging toward us. I felt uneasy about my physical response, the way my pulse kicked up at the sight of him. I thought of the way my body reacted when he touched my shoulder just two nights ago. He walked over and his eyes settled on my muddy jeans. I knew he guessed what I'd been up to. I'd confessed my obsession and my morning forays with my shovel over dinner a few weeks earlier. When I looked at his face, though, I realized that Naomi's description must not have been an exaggeration. This was a bad scene, I knew, simply from the dour look Max wore as he came to a stop beside me.

When I asked what he knew, Max gave me a rundown. "The men are still checking the outbuildings, but the count so far is four dead, two women and two children," he said. Beside us, Naomi gasped, as if starved for air. At that, Max appeared upset with himself for talking in front of her, and he sighed. "Naomi, we need answers." Then he asked the question I had just moments earlier, "First off, what brought you here this morning?"

"That," Naomi said, pointing at a clear plastic bag with something inside made out of white plastic, shiny metal, and plastic tubing. It lay on the ground not far from where we stood. "I was delivering that breast pump to Laurel for Jeremy. I promised her and Jacob that I would when we talked at services yesterday."

"Did you see anyone when you arrived?" I asked, and Naomi shook her head. "But you went inside?"

"I went in the house to find a phone after I saw the little boy, Benjamin, dead under the sheet. I needed to call nine-one-one." Naomi shrugged as if slightly embarrassed. "We only have one cell phone at the trailer, Clara, and I forgot it when I left to go to the hives this morning. I had to go inside the Johanssons' house to call for help."

"Laurel was expecting you?" Max asked.

"Yes," Naomi said. "She and Jacob both were. But I was running maybe half an hour late, a little bit more. There was a lot of commotion at the trailer getting the young ones off to school this morning, and I didn't get out the door as early as I planned."

"When you saw Jacob, did he say anything?" Max asked.

Naomi shook her head. "Nothing. He was awake when I walked in, his eyes open. I had the feeling he felt relieved to see me. As soon as he did, his eyes closed. It was like he drifted off and went to sleep."

Max looked at me, and I shot him a glance that signaled agreement. We both knew where this was going. "Mother Naomi, we need you to go to police headquarters," I said. "I'm going to have one of the deputies drive you there, and I'll ask Detective Mullins to take your statement."

I noticed that Max grimaced when I mentioned Jeff Mullins. I wondered why and was just about to question him on it when Naomi interrupted me.

"Oh, I can't give an official statement. I *can't* do that," she protested. A fundamentalist Mormon town that adhered to the principle of plural marriage, Alber had an uncomfortable relationship with civil authorities. Hence cooperation wasn't always easy for those of us in law enforcement to get, so I shouldn't have been surprised at Naomi's reaction. Plus there was my frigid relationship with my family, which despite my best attempts hadn't thawed. Still, there were four dead bodies on the property and a man who, according to Naomi, appeared to be dying. I'd hoped she'd step up. "I just told you everything I know," she said. "There's no reason for more. I'll just get some things for Jeremy, clothes and such, and take him home and care for him. Clara, you and Max can go off and solve this. You don't need me."

I squeezed my eyes nearly shut, lowered my head and gave her a firm headshake. "Mother Naomi, you are going to the police station. Once there, you'll give a full and complete statement to Detective Mullins," I repeated. Again, Max bristled at the mention of Mullins' name. This time he signaled me that we needed to talk. I nodded but first wanted to finish with Naomi. "Right now, you're going to sit in my vehicle and wait to be transported into town," I told her. "I'll collect a few things for Jeremy, to take with you."

"Clara, as one of your mothers, I must protest and point out that—"

"Naomi Jefferies, I said get in the Suburban," I ordered. "Chief Deputy Anderson and I don't have time for this. We need to check on Jacob."

Used to having motherly sway over me, Naomi crumpled her mouth into a peeved bow the way I remember her doing when I was a child and I or one of my siblings disappointed her. Once upon a time, that look would have sent me straight to my room. But I wasn't a child any longer. Instead, I wore a badge, this was a murder scene, and Naomi needed to listen to me. Perhaps she understood that, because she didn't argue. "You'll get some of Jeremy's things for me to take, though?"

"I will," I said.

Reluctantly, she slunk over to my Suburban and Max raised his hand to one of the deputies from a squad that had just pulled in with more backup. "Stay with her," he told her. "I'm going to give Chief Jefferies a walk-through."

As we turned toward the house, the CSI's mobile unit, converted out of an old horse trailer, pulled into the driveway. Max acknowledged the driver, then turned back to me. "We need to talk about Mullins. He can't work this case."

"Why not?" I asked. "He's my lead detective. He's got the most experience of—"

"Clara, Mullins is related to one of the victims," Max blurted out. I gave him a questioning glance and he explained. "He's the father of the woman upstairs, Laurel Johansson, one of Jacob's two wives."

"And she's…?" I knew, but, on some level, I needed to hear it.

"Dead," Max said. "Her throat's cut."

I couldn't think of anything to say. The grisly scene suddenly felt even more tragic.

The CSI unit began their work, focusing on the bodies under the sheet. Before we entered the house, Max and I stood for just a moment and watched while they photographed the sheet and the uncovered boy's body. The child looked perfect, like he'd gone out to play and lay down on the grass. But this child would never get up. He'd never start school, never play softball or soccer, never have a first date or hold his first-born child. I felt sickened by the raw exit wound above his eyebrow.

Once they had him documented, CSI officers got on all sides and raised the bedsheet. They walked away from the bodies, holding the sheet high, and then folded it into two rectangles, into quarters, then eighths. They laid the bloody sheet on top of a paper evidence wrapper, folded the paper over it, secured it and dated it, wrote the case number assigned to this outrage across it.

As they worked, Max and I examined what we could of the bodies. Max had learned the victims' names from a deputy who knew the family, and he said the dark-haired woman was Anna, Jacob's first wife. She looked as if she'd tripped and fallen face down in the yellowed winter grass. I could only see her long dark hair and her back, the soles of her slippers. I couldn't walk closer and risk contaminating the evidence field, so I stood back, but it was easy to see the bloody holes that stood out on the white terry cloth. The laundry basket sat nearby, and it appeared as if she'd been outside hanging clothes when someone came up behind and shot her. It bothered me that Anna had her robe on. *Why hadn't she changed before coming outside?* I wondered. *She must have been cold wearing that. It's chilly out here.*

The children's motionless bodies punched a fist into my heart. The little girl, Sybille, age six, lay in a fetal position on her left side, her dark hair half fallen out of a loose ponytail. Like her brother, she had so much ahead of her that she would miss: reading her first book, learning how to add and subtract, picnics and playdays. She'd never marry or have children, and never grow old and hold her grandchildren on her lap. The girl's jacket was bunched up around her, and I wondered if she'd been sitting when someone fired a bullet into her head. She looked as if she might have been and tipped over.

Benjamin, age three, lay on his side, his face turned toward the ground. It appeared that someone had repositioned him, because the gunshot was barely visible, not more than an inch above ground level. It seemed an awkward position to fall into.

The medical examiner was on his way, and the bodies wouldn't be moved until he arrived, but the CSI folks were taking lots of photos and putting out numbered plastic tents to tag pieces of evidence. This would happen throughout the yard, the house, anywhere they found anything they thought should be collected. There were four bright yellow markers scattered in the yard when Max and I went inside to find out about the condition of the lone adult survivor.

On the kitchen floor, EMTs worked on Jacob. The pool of blood on the floor next to him looked substantial.

A small patch of it was smeared and I wondered if the medics had done that—they usually tried to avoid blood on a scene—or if Naomi might have. Earlier I'd noticed blood on her dress. She must have knelt close to Jacob, perhaps to try to help him. A short distance off, in the blood, I noticed what looked like a faint print from the toe or heel of a shoe. The print, just a few inches long, had enough detail to make out the sole's pattern. It looked like it had deep grooves, perhaps from some kind of tennis shoe or a work boot. Someone had put a kitchen chair over it to keep anyone from stepping on it. I stared at it for a moment. The blood had an odd arrangement of small crosses inside a semicircle of what looked like bowling pins. I took out my cell phone and snapped a photo.

"Does your office have access to a good shoe man?" I asked Max, pointing at it. In Dallas, we had experts in the lab on nearly every aspect of criminology, from blood pattern analysts to those who catalogued fiber sources and diagnosed insect evidence. When it came to shoe print tracing, we had a guy with access to a database like those used to compare fingerprints. The system matched sole designs to manufacturers and styles. Working in the sticks, specialists didn't always fit into my slim budget.

"That's not someone we've used in my time here, so I don't think so," he said. "We can try to find someone. Unless you know anyone?"

"I do," I said.

With that, I tapped on the photo I'd taken and attached it to a text and sent it to a friend in the lab in Dallas. *Can you match this for me?* A minute later, I got a response: *No problem. Have it for you late today.* I would have liked it sooner, but beggars can't be choosers. The guy was doing me a favor. "Taken care of," I told Max. "I'll let you know when I have any info."

Although the EMTs had spent a substantial amount of time attempting to stabilize him, in truth there wasn't much they could do for Jacob on the scene. As long as he kept breathing through the opening in his throat, and so far he'd been able to do that, they wouldn't try to bind it and bag him. His right hand had a gash that looked like a defensive wound, as if he'd attempted to grab the assailant's knife away from him. A heart monitor beeped while a paramedic cleaned the blood off Jacob's neck, assessing the wound. When a gauze pad filled with blood, he threw it to the side. Jacob's eyes were closed, his body eerily still except for his struggle to breathe.

"This is so weird," the medic muttered.

"What is?" Max asked.

"This guy got really lucky," he said. "Whoever did this was in a hurry. He didn't stay around to make sure the guy died—he cut this guy's trachea but he missed the carotids. If the attacker had sliced through one or both of the arteries, this guy would have bled out in no time."

"Can he talk to us?" I asked.

"Unconscious," the medic answered, then to my disappointment he added, "He was out cold when we got here. Hasn't said a word. But even if he were awake, he wouldn't be able to talk. Not with his throat in that condition."

"Why haven't you moved him?" I asked.

Even when patients are comatose, medical personnel are acutely aware that they may be able to hear, so we followed him into the mudroom to get out of earshot.

"He's lost a lot of blood," the medic said. "We're trying to administer fluids and stabilize him before we load him on the ambulance. Without that, it's doubtful he'd survive the ride."

"Okay," Max said. "Got it."

Jacob, of course, wouldn't be able to get a transfusion until they got him to the hospital; ambulances didn't carry blood because of its short shelf life, and the fact that it has to be warmed before being administered. Instead the EMTs were attempting to hook up a saline IV to replenish his lost fluids. The problem: heavy blood loss had dehydrated Jacob and constricted his veins; the medic in charge was having a hard time inserting a needle into his patient's arm.

Unconscious, struggling to breathe, Jacob had bloody foam bubbling from his cut throat with each gasp for air. Assessing his dire condition, I found it impossible to think of him as lucky.

"What are his odds?" Max asked.

The medic shook his head. "Not good. If we'd gotten here even a bit earlier... But he's got a chance."

We had no way to help Jacob or to make any headway on the case simply waiting, so I said, "Max, I should call Mullins."

He shot me a concerned look but nodded. With that, Max and the medic walked back into the kitchen, while I lagged behind in the mudroom. On my cell phone, I hit the listing for the station house. Stef answered: "Alber PD."

"What are you doing on the desk?" I asked.

"Just relieving Kellie," she explained. I'd hired Kellie Ryland to work the dispatch desk, but Stef was still training her. "What's it like out there?"

"Bad," I said. "Really bad."

"Shoot," she said.

"Listen, as soon as Kellie returns, head over here and watch the CSI unit work. It would be good for you to see how a case like this is handled first hand."

"You bet. She's walking over to the desk now. I'll be right there. Anything else?"

"I need to talk to Mullins," I said.

"He's not in yet. Called in about half an hour ago and said he might be late. He had a report to take on a break-in at a house in town. Someone got into the garage and stole the homeowner's tool box. Had some valuable stuff in there to work on cars."

"Hmm." I took a deep breath. Those were more the types of crimes I was used to in Alber. Not quadruple murders. I thought about Mullins and considered calling him directly, but decided against it. I didn't want to deliver this kind of bad news over the phone. "When Mullins gets there, ask Kellie to instruct him to wait for me. Tell her to give me a heads-up, and I'll drive into town. I need to talk to him in person."

"Something up?" she asked.

"Nothing we can talk about now," I said. "Just ask him to wait there for me."

"Will do," Stef said.

I hung up and trekked back into the kitchen. Max was still watching the medics work on Jacob. One had finally gotten an IV started and he held a bag while the other two monitored their patient's vitals.

"Did you get in touch with Mullins?" Max asked.

"He's not in," I said. "I'll head in to talk to him once he arrives."

Max shook his head. "Poor guy."

"Yeah," I said. Determined to put the time to good use, I asked, "So where's Laurel?"

CHAPTER FIVE

"What do you make of the lipstick?" I asked Max.

"Not sure. It's odd, isn't it?" he said.

We were holding up the pale blue duvet, doing our best not to disturb the scene, looking at Laurel's body. She had on a sweet cotton nightgown covered with flowers, one that reminded me of the type a little girl might wear. It struck me as a stark contrast to the angry red lipstick encircling her mouth. From the copious amount of blood saturating the sheets beneath her, it appeared evident that this time the killer hadn't spared the knife; the gash was longer than the one on Jacob. Whoever murdered Laurel had made sure that she died.

"It's so strange," I said. Max gave me a questioning look and I explained, "Anna and her two children were shot to death outside, and Laurel and Jacob had their throats cut in the house. That's an odd set of circumstances. Why did the killer change weapons? Why didn't he shoot them all? So much quicker, easier."

"And less personal," Max said.

I nodded. "Maybe that's precisely what he wanted."

"What do you mean?"

"Maybe Anna and her children were collateral damage, simply murdered because they were here when it happened. I wonder why they were covered with the sheet."

"The killer didn't want to see them?" Max speculated.

"It could be. Maybe the killer was ashamed and wanted to hide their bodies," I ventured. "If you're proud of something, you show it off. If you're not, you're more likely to hide it. Their deaths, the shootings, are different."

"What do you mean?" Max asked. "Something in addition to the type of weapon?"

"The killer took more time with Laurel and Jacob. My guess is that they were the primary victims."

Max gave me a questioning glance. "In at least one way, Laurel's killing is the same. She was covered, too."

"Shame again?" I speculated.

"And Jacob?"

"That's different. There was no attempt to hide his body," I said. "But if he didn't matter to the killer, if he was simply collateral damage like Anna and her children, why didn't the killer just shoot him?"

"It all seems pretty bizarre," Max said. "Any chance we could have two killers?"

I thought about that. "Possible," I said. "At this point, anything's possible. We might find that the killer is a man, a woman, or multiple people."

While we talked, I looked about Laurel's room. My instincts guessed that we weren't looking for a gang of killers, at the most one or two. The scenes were all fairly small, concise. Nothing appeared disturbed; I saw no evidence of a struggle. Laurel had an antique silver brush and comb set, like one my mother had, precisely arranged on the dresser. As a child, I snuck into Mother's bedroom just to use it, delighted by the soft bristles. The painting over Laurel's bed was perfectly straight and was of a spray of delicate white and yellow flowers on a beige background. Looking down at her face frozen by death, I figured she couldn't be older than nineteen or twenty.

"I bet the killer surprised her," I said. "Attacked her while she was asleep, or she woke up on the bed during the attack."

"Because there's no sign of a scuffle?" Max said.

"Yes, because she didn't try to fight him off," I confirmed. "Maybe she was lucky in a way, too."

"What do you mean?"

"Because she didn't see it coming," I said.

Max and I paused our conversation and looked at the body again, each lost to our own thoughts. I wondered about the order of the killings. I wondered which of the victims was the last one to die. How horrible to have watched the others murdered knowing the killer would soon turn his attention to you. I thought about how loud a gunshot is.

"All that considered, what's the lipstick for?" Max asked. "To make her look cartoonish?"

"Perhaps," I offered. "Maybe to humiliate her, but there's something else."

"What?"

"Red lipstick is considered overtly sexual around here. It isn't worn by the women. Perhaps painting her with it was like leaving an explanation for this one killing. Labeling her a tainted woman," I said.

The conversation faded, and my mind picked up where it left off, calculating the sound of the gunshots outside and wondering if it would have carried into the house. Was it possible that Laurel slept through the first three murders? Perhaps even the attack on Jacob? I thought about what Naomi had said, that Laurel and Jacob were expecting her to arrive early that morning. It seemed odd that Laurel would still be in bed sleeping. Although a new mother with a tiny infant is often up well into the night.

Max gently lowered his side of the duvet so that it fell back in place, and I followed suit, covering Laurel's face and body. We walked toward the door. "How sure are you of all this? Your thoughts on how this unfolded?" he asked from behind me.

I turned and looked at him. "Not sure at all."

*

The three medics were loading Jacob to transport him to the hospital when we walked into the kitchen. They'd bandaged the cut in his hand and placed gauze under his neck to collect the still-seeping blood. They eased him onto the stretcher and then, one at the head and another at the foot, snapped it into place. As they turned to wheel him out, Jacob suddenly stirred, thrashed about, but they had him strapped down. He let out a deep guttural sound, and his eyes opened.

"Stop!" I shouted.

"We've got to get him to the hospital," the lead medic protested, indicating the others had to keep moving. "Come on, let's load him on the ambulance."

"Owww," Jacob moaned. His head turned, and he looked directly at me.

I wondered if he'd die on the way to the hospital. Looking at him, it seemed likely. With no time to think, I seized what might be my one opportunity to talk to the only witness. Before I even knew what I was doing, I had thrust my foot under the front wheel and grabbed the gurney's frame. Max latched on at the back and held it steady.

"We've gotta get him loaded," the medic in charge wailed. "You two let go."

We were determined to try to get any information we could from Jacob, and Max held tight, while I leaned over Jacob and thrust my face close to his. "Who did this to you and your family?" I asked. "Jacob, tell me—who did this?"

Jacob's eyes grew rounder, and he nodded ever so slightly at me. He searched my face and his lips moved a touch. I felt certain that he was trying to talk. But then, as he strained to take yet another breath, the sucking sound coming from his throat built and that awful rattle returned. All hope evaporated as his eyelids drifted down and locked closed. The monitor attached to his chest kept beeping.

"He's out again," the medic shouted. "We're moving. Now!"

Max and I stood back as the EMTs pushed the gurney toward the front door. We followed and stood on the porch as they loaded him into the back of the ambulance.

"For a moment, I thought maybe he'd at least try to talk," Max said, visibly disappointed. "Maybe mouth something so we had a name."

"No such luck," I said.

It took seconds to secure the gurney into place inside the ambulance. "You think we'll ever be able to talk to him?" I asked.

Max shrugged again. "I hope so, but it's no better than a toss-up."

"We'll, of course, keep our fingers crossed that he makes it, but we need to work this like we'll never be able to ask him a single question," I said, and Max gave me a raised eyebrow that signaled agreement.

CHAPTER SIX

As the ambulance pulled onto the open road, the air filled with the wailing of the siren. I thought about Mullins, about the fact that he still didn't know about his daughter, and pulled out my phone yet again, hoping to see I'd missed a call. Disappointed, I slipped my phone back into my pocket as an Alber PD squad pulled into the driveway. Rookie officer Stef Jonas got out. Her skin a deep copper, her eyes the darkest of browns. Hair in her usual cornrows that fanned out around her face, she wore a uniform that pulled a bit too tight across the middle. Stef looked at my dirty clothes and said, "Out digging?"

We'd gotten fairly close over the past few months. Stef had helped in the investigation that pulled me back to Alber. She knew about my extracurricular activities, too. Perhaps I should have kept it more of a secret. I gave her a half-hearted smile and said, "I couldn't sleep."

A short sigh that seemed to mix amusement and resignation, and Stef looked about at the CSI officers documenting the first location, the bodies found under the sheet. She appeared intrigued, and I knew that she ached to get into the mix.

I hadn't noticed that George Wiley MD, the internist from Wilbur who served as the county's medical examiner, had shown up, but he was hard at work, inspecting the sad body of little Benjamin. I walked over with Stef and Max, stopping a way back. Doc Wiley sauntered over to us. His white hair disheveled, his clip-on bowtie crooked, he wore a lab coat with his name embroidered on the chest.

"Clara, Max, I had my assistant cancel my appointments and rushed right over. Did you just get here? I didn't see you."

"We've been in the house." I motioned at the newest arrival. "All except Stef, she's studying forensics and is here to learn. Can you show her, all of us, what you know so far?"

"Sure. A lot of it you've probably already figured out," Doc said. With our lack of specialists in the county, Doc tended to go beyond the normal ME duties. "We'll have to double-check all this once I get to the lab and have my equipment. I need to put their clothes and skin under magnification, get a better look at the powder marks and wounds. But first glance, it looks like the children were shot from a short distance, maybe two or three feet away, based on visible powder residue on their clothes."

"And their mother?" Max asked.

"At least five or six feet away," Doc said. "Maybe more. All three were standing when they were shot."

I'd been wrong about the little girl, Sybille, it appeared. I thought perhaps she'd been sitting. "How do you know?" I asked.

"The blood patterns. I found drops not far from each of the bodies that I think were initial impact." Doc pulled out a pencil, held it in his gloved hand and pointed at a spot on a dried leaf just behind Benjamin that had an evidence marker next to it. "They're round, as if the blood fell straight down."

"All shot from behind," I said. "The kids in their heads, and Anna Johansson in her back."

"That's right," Doc said. "I think Anna may have been shot first. I think she was hanging the laundry when it happened."

"How do you know that?" Max asked.

"Blood spatter," Doc said, pointing at the clothes pinned onto the line. "There's a fine mist on a few of the pieces near where she fell."

"Were the bodies moved?" I asked, wondering about my hunch about Benjamin.

"It appears the boy was rolled over," Doc said. "I think he was initially standing, tottered, stumbled and fell after the bullet hit him and landed on his back. I checked his neck, above his shirt, and he has mild lividity on his back, but it's darker on the side he's lying on."

When the heart stops, gravity pools blood at the body's lowest point and causes lividity, a purplish tone to the skin that resembles bruising. I thought about what Max and I had just been debating, why the killer covered the bodies. This might be more evidence that he did it out of shame. Rolling Benjamin off his back and onto his side kept the kid's blank eyes from staring up at the killer. "I'd noticed the angle of the shot seemed off for him to have fallen in that position," I said. "It makes sense that he initially fell on his back."

"I'll know more when I open them up and chart the trajectories of their wounds," Doc said. "But, yes, I think you're right about the boy. The woman and girl, however, I'm guessing simply fell and were left in those positions."

"Time frame?" I asked.

"Rigor mortis has begun to set in, but it's early in the process. I'd say this happened two to three hours ago," he said, adjusting his wire-rimmed glasses. "From what I hear, Jacob Johansson was bleeding out pretty badly in the kitchen. That right?"

"It is," I said. "Throat was cut but not carotids. Some blood on his shirt. A moderate pool near the neck when the EMTs arrived and started an IV."

"That type of blood loss, it's lucky he survived that long," Doc said. "Anyway, looking at the condition of Anna's body and those of the children, I believe they died early this morning. My guess is roughly about seven a.m. or so. But we'll do a liver temp to check cooling as soon as I get them to the morgue. That should tell us more. Although none of this is precise, always an estimate."

"Anything about the weapon?" Max asked.

"Not from the bodies, but I think the CSI folks have information for you," Doc said. "I may find fragments during autopsy that could help, but we're not there yet."

"Thanks, Doc," I said.

The old man shook his head and his lips melted into a deep frown. "Gotta be one of the saddest things I've ever seen, Clara, and I've seen a lot," Doc said. "What the hell's wrong with people that someone would do this?"

None of us had a good answer, so we didn't even try to explain the tragedy surrounding us.

"When are the autopsies?" Max asked. Doc said he'd start on them that afternoon, and we thanked him and excused ourselves, then made our way over to Craig Mueller, the Smith County sheriff's lieutenant in charge of the CSI unit. There'd only been a handful of evidence markers when Max and I left to go inside, but now they spread across the grass and one was off fairly far into a grove of trees. Stef's eyes had grown rounder, and she appeared excited. I remembered my first few murder scenes, the excitement of being involved in an investigation. It might change Stef's attitude if she knew that one of the victims was Mullins' daughter.

"What have you got?" I asked Mueller.

"We found the murder weapon," he said. "At least, I'm guessing it's the murder weapon."

"Where is it?" Max said. "Show it to us."

Mueller started to respond, but I cut in. "No, Lieutenant, take us through how you think this unfolded," I said. "I want to see it the way it happened, assuming you have a theory on sequencing?"

"Yeah," Mueller said. A tall, gangly guy with an angular face and a prominent Adam's apple that bobbed up and down with each word, he seemed more arms and legs than body. He led us over to a point about six feet back from where Anna Johansson lay. "It started here," he said, pointing at a few discharged cartridges on the ground.

While Max and I understood Mueller's inference, I asked, "Explain what we're looking at for Stef. She's a new officer, and she's taking forensic classes at the community college."

Mueller shot our CSI-officer-to-be a supportive glance, and then pointed down at the cartridges. Nearby someone had perched a yellow plastic evidence tent with the number six on it. "We believe the gun's a nine-millimeter semi-automatic with an extended magazine," he said. "We found one dropped or thrown in the trees. We'll work our way there. We think the shooting started here with the woman."

"Anna Johansson," I interjected. Mueller looked at me. "I like to use names. It reminds me that these were real people. Helps keep it human."

"Sure, Chief, good idea," Mueller said. "Out here, surrounded by all this death, it's hard to think of them as…"

"Alive?" I suggested.

For a moment, Mueller didn't talk, and then he nodded and swallowed hard. He pointed at a shirt hanging half on, half off the clothesline. "I think Anna may not have realized what was about to happen. It looks like she had her back turned to the shooter, hanging that shirt up. She still has a clothespin in one hand. There's blood spatter on the shirt. When the first bullet hit, Anna probably turned slightly, away from the clothesline. He kept firing, and she staggered and fell face down. The kids were hanging out, maybe running around playing with each other and watching her, is my guess, because they were right behind her, not far away."

I pictured it. A calm, sunny morning, winter right around the corner. Everyone just up from bed, getting a start on the day. Maybe Anna gave Sybille and Benjamin breakfast, but maybe not. No dishes in the kitchen waiting to be washed, and Laurel, if she was still alive, was upstairs in bed, maybe after a late night with the baby. She hadn't made her way down yet. If there'd been a lot of kitchen noise, it might have awakened her. Someone walks up and stands behind Anna, pointing a 9mm handgun at her back. I could almost hear the bang of the first shot when I envisioned a finger pulling the trigger.

"You know the killer stood here when he killed Anna because of those cartridges," I said, pointing at the three on the ground.

"Yeah," Mueller said. He turned to Stef, indicated a spot on the ground and continued, "Based on the position of Anna's body and the point where we found the cartridges, the gunman had to be standing approximately here when he shot her. With each shot, the gun ejected an empty cartridge to the right. Anna was shot three times and we have three cartridges."

Bang. Bang. Bang. The reports went off in my head. Anna tottered and then fell. Internal organs burst open, ruptured. I wondered if on some level she questioned what was happening to her, or did she know? Did she try to turn to look for her son and daughter? Maybe not. In seconds, it was possible that she was dead.

"Then the gunman turned on the children. You can see that he moved to get behind them. Maybe they were trying to run away." Mueller pointed at two more evidence markers. "Both of those mark where we found cartridges. They were ejected when the kids were killed. He shot one, then the other, one shot each, back of their heads, and he was done."

We stood there for a moment, allowing all we'd learned to imprint on our memories. I looked down at the small bodies lying on the ground and wondered who could be so cold. *Who shot you?* I wondered. *Who committed this unspeakable evil?*

"What did he do next?" I asked.

"I'm not sure," Mueller said. "Either he then turned, went in the house, accosted Jacob in the kitchen and went upstairs to murder Laurel, or they were attacked first, before the killer shot

Anna and the children. What happened first, these three killings or the knifings inside the house, that I don't know."

Max sucked in a deep breath and let it out slowly, I figured trying to calm the anger he felt looking at the scene. As a cop, you can't become emotionally involved, you have to step back, but that was hard in this case. I understood. Looking at the children made my heart ache.

Stef, on the other hand, appeared simply intrigued. Her eyes glistened with interest, and I knew she absorbed Mueller's words as if her textbooks had come alive.

"Okay, so our gunman either turns and walks into the kitchen, or he flees?" I said.

"Yeah," Max agreed. "But at some point, he must have stood here for a few moments, looked at the children and the mother and became uncomfortable enough to take the sheet and cover the bodies."

I thought about that. "Where's the gun?" I asked.

"Over there," Mueller said. We followed behind him and walked maybe thirty feet off into a grove of pine trees, not far from the barn. There it lay, with evidence marker number eleven beside it, a black 9mm handgun with an extended magazine.

"Bullets in it?" I asked, wondering if maybe the killer cut the throats of the victims inside the house because the gun ran out of ammo.

"Not sure," Mueller said. "We haven't touched it yet to check. After the state lab finishes processing the gun for prints, DNA and such, they'll take a look and let us know."

"I'm sure they do this routinely, but the lab will check for a serial number, try to ID the owner, of course," I said, mostly to Stef, and Mueller nodded.

"Any thoughts on what happened with the two victims inside the house?" Max asked.

"Not yet. All we've done so far is mark that bloody shoe print on the floor and take photos of Jacob. We backed off while the EMTs worked on him." Mueller again went into more detail than he normally would have, to explain the procedures for our new officer. "We didn't want to get in their way. Now that they're gone, I'll send a couple of techs inside and we'll start with a video, follow with placing evidence markers, looking for fingerprints, fibers, hairs and such, and taking photos."

"Is it okay if Officer Jonas shadows you for the rest of this?" I asked Mueller, pointing at Stef. "She could use the real-world experience."

"Sure," he said. "I'm grabbing a couple of the techs and moving them inside next. I'll assign one of them to watch over the newbie."

Stef laughed, and I thought again about how her mood would change when she learned that the woman upstairs was Mullins' daughter. This would suddenly become all too real. I hesitated to tell her until Mullins knew, and I thought again about trying to reach him.

"I'm going to check in with the office," I said, pulling out my phone.

"Are you still trying to get in touch with Mullins?" Stef asked.

"Yes, do you know where he—" Max started.

"I forgot. Kellie called me on my way over here and mentioned that Mullins is following a lead in this case. He heard about the murders and had some kind of a theory," she said, looking sheepish. "Sorry, Chief, but I was just so wound up about seeing the scene, I forgot."

That Mullins worked a lead without checking in with me seemed odd. I didn't even know that he'd been told about the killings. Perhaps when he heard the location and the homicide references, he immediately realized that one of the victims was Laurel. "A theory on the case?"

"Yeah," Stef said. "I didn't talk to him, but Kellie said he had someone he wanted to check whereabouts on."

"I'm going to call Mullins," I said, shooting Max a worried glance. I walked off a short distance.

The phone rang six times before voicemail picked up: "This is Alber PD Detective Jeff Mullins, please leave a message."

"Mullins, it's Chief Jefferies," I started. "I need to—"

Before I finished, another call beeped in, this time from the station. "Hey, Chief," Kellie said. The girl had kind of a singsong voice. I'm not always the most cheerful person, and it was one of the reasons I hired her. Alber PD's new dispatcher seemed to be in a perpetually good mood.

"Where's Mullins?" I asked.

"That's why I'm getting in touch," she said. "Mullins called in a little while ago and asked where you were. As soon as I told him you'd gone to the Johansson bison ranch, that there were casualties, two women and some children, he got super-agitated. Said he had a lead to follow up on. He didn't tell me what kind of lead."

"Okay," I said.

"Well, now I've got Carl Shipley on the nine-one-one line. Says he's got a problem. Chief, he needs someone out there at his place ASAP."

One thing I still had to teach Kellie was how to zero in on the most important information. "What's he asking for?" I prompted.

"Police assistance," she said. "He claims that Detective Mullins has him pinned down inside his trailer out near Old Sawyer Creek, a few miles from the ranch."

"Wait. Mullins has him pinned down?" I repeated.

"Yeah," Kellie confirmed. "The guy says that Mullins is threatening to break down the door and kill him."

CHAPTER SEVEN

Max saw Clara storming toward him. "You know a Carl Shipley? Mullins is at his place with a gun, has him trapped in his trailer. Any idea what's going on?" she asked.

"Not a clue," Max said. "I don't know much about Carl, just that he and Jacob both lived in Mexico for a while and came back together. I hear that they're inseparable. Carl moved into a trailer down the road about the same time Jacob took over the ranch. I can get us there. It's close. Follow me."

"I'm right behind you." As they sprinted to their vehicles, Clara shouted at one deputy to get Mother Naomi out of the Suburban and watch over her until she returned. Then Clara ordered Stef: "Stay with the lieutenant. We'll be back."

Max took the lead and Clara followed. He felt unsettled, anxious, and he couldn't really decide why. He'd seen grisly murder scenes before. But the flashbacks had started as soon as he'd reached the house and saw Anna and the children. All three were so young, and he couldn't wipe away the images. But it was Laurel he felt drawn to. Miriam was ten years older when she died, but Laurel looked remarkably like her. They had the same light hair, patrician features. Vital-looking women—left with blank, dead eyes.

Miriam had been gone for nearly two years, but the vision of her caught in the car, bleeding from a gash in her forehead, the steering wheel pushed into her rib cage? Max had been fighting it for a very long time, he realized, willing himself not to see it.

I never should have let Miriam drive, he thought for the thousandth time. *It was my fault. All of it my fault.*

He tried to wipe the memory from his mind, and instead thought of the sound of Jacob struggling to suck in a breath of air through his damaged trachea, of the blood foaming and seeping out from the cut. Max decided he'd seen more than his share of blood in his lifetime. At times, being a cop seemed overwhelming. Imagine all the folks who went to work every day and didn't have to worry about ending up on a murder scene.

Why did the killer murder the children? Max decided it had to be that the kids saw whoever did it kill their mother, and allowing them to live would have meant leaving behind witnesses. When they caught the SOB, Max vowed he'd make sure that the killer understood just how wrong that had been. *I'll make him regret it. Every day of his sorry life.*

Now it appeared Mullins had gone rogue. Max wondered what they were walking into at Carl Shipley's trailer. How dangerous was it? Had Carl pulled a gun on Mullins? Threatened him? Why would Mullins go after Carl? But then, Max had heard rumors about Carl, that he was something of a bad seed, in trouble from his earliest years. Whatever was unfolding at Carl's place, Max figured Mullins must have a reason.

At a bend in the road, Max glanced in the rearview mirror and saw Clara's SUV directly behind him. He wondered if she remembered that they had a dinner date that evening at his house. He hoped so. Brooke had been planning it for days. She'd gotten up early that morning to set the table with her mother's good china. Clara had agreed; certainly, she'd come.

Still, Max recognized this wasn't something Clara felt comfortable with. Her reaction wasn't unusual. In fact, each time they made plans, Clara agreed and then he suspected she had to fight her instincts, which told her to call it off. She struggled, he sensed, with trusting anyone, even him.

Despite his mounting impatience with her, Max couldn't give up.

Somewhere hidden inside Clara, he felt certain, waited the girl she'd once been. He remembered those early years, when they became schoolfriends. He thought of how she'd looked back then; a strong girl, a bookworm who was also a bit of a tomboy, who ran faster than most of the boys. When did he first realize that she was becoming special to him? He couldn't remember. "Maybe she was always special," he whispered, thinking of the sparkle in her eyes when he whispered in her ear, how she wrinkled up her nose when she laughed, how serious she became poring over a math assignment.

It was her courage that turned the friendship to love.

In junior high, the school bully shoved another girl on the playground and broke her glasses. The girl cried, and Clara jumped the boy, pushed him to the ground and held him down, plastering his face against the asphalt until he apologized. Max stood among a throng of kids watching, impressed by her bravery. Afterward the rowdy kids kept a watch for Clara, not wanting to start trouble while she was around.

We found each other while so young, Max thought. *But our road hasn't been a smooth one.*

The world hadn't treated her well. She'd been hurt. He didn't know what, but something terrible had happened to her, and she was wary. He understood. He'd been hurt, too. But if he just didn't give up, eventually...

Anything seemed possible.

On the final stretch, Max took a rickety wooden bridge over a bone-dry ditch. In heavy rains and during the spring thaw, water off the mountainside turned the gully into a stream. Beside it a crooked sign dangling from a frame read: OLD SAWYER CREEK. Up ahead, Max saw a beat-up pickup and an Alber PD squad parked crossways near a travel trailer that looked worse for wear. Max sped up. Behind him, Clara did the same.

CHAPTER EIGHT

Off a bumpy asphalt road onto a dirt driveway, we drove until I saw a clearing ahead strewn with piles of broken bricks. Stacks of unused roofing shingles that had been discarded for so long that weeds grew up high between them and much of their cardboard casings had weathered away. A decomposing brown leather recliner sat at one end of the travel trailer with an open, stained beige patio umbrella over it, apparently Carl Shipley's only outdoor furniture.

I parked directly behind Mullins' squad, and Max pulled up just a short distance away. We kept low and had our guns drawn as we slunk over to join Mullins, who had taken shelter behind his car. He had an AR-15 pointed at the trailer, and his attention was focused on the door and windows.

"What's going on here, Detective Mullins?" The long scar on his cheek had turned purple, a sign, I'd come to recognize during my brief months back in Alber, that the detective's blood pressure was at its upper limits. Squat with faded blue eyes, his salt-and-pepper hair receding at the crown, Mullins looked like the neighbor nobody approached on the street because he always wore a sour expression.

"Chief, I've got that POS where I want him. I'm gonna show him what happens when he kills someone. Anyone." Mullins looked over at me. His eyes were red and watery, and I could tell he'd been crying. "That waste of oxygen murdered my daughter. My Laurel."

"Okay, slow down here, Mullins," I said. "Fill in the blanks for us."

Mullins pinched his mouth shut, as if debating whether or not he'd talk to me. The two of us had a rather strained relationship. It hadn't started out well during our first case together. I'd sometimes wondered if he was working with me or against me. Things only got worse when I took the chief's job, one he'd assumed his seniority at Alber PD meant he'd claim. At weekly department meetings, Mullins habitually sat at the back, usually one foot up on the chair in front of him, and stared at me as if daring me to say something he could jump on. I tended to ignore him.

Despite all that, I didn't want to lose him. While we weren't the best of friends, Mullins was a pretty good cop. He did what he was told, if not with a smile. Our police force was small, and he had more experience than any of the other officers on my staff. Perhaps more importantly, Mullins had access. People talked to him because he was part of the old guard, a member in good standing with Elijah's People, our reclusive town's fundamentalist Mormon settlers. While I'd fled and disavowed its teachings, including the practice of polygamy, Jeff Mullins was a member in good standing. In Alber, that meant everything.

"Listen, Mullins," I said. "Max and I need to know what's happened here. Did Carl Shipley threaten you? Did he pull a gun on you?"

Mullins turned his head side to side while keeping his eyes trained on the travel trailer. "Carl refused to come out when I told him to, and that was enough," Mullins finally said. "I know he killed my little girl. No doubt about it, but this proves it. If he didn't kill her, he'd be out here jabbering away, answering all my questions."

"Did you knock on the door and ask him to come out?" Max inquired.

At that, Mullins' flush turned a raging red. "Nah, but I stood out here and shouted, told him to get his sorry ass out here and tell me why he killed my daughter."

"Why are you so sure he killed Laurel and the others?" I asked. Mullins glared at me for a few moments and didn't answer, so I pressed the issue. "Detective, you need to explain what the hell is going on here. And you need to do it now."

At that, Mullins pulled his lips tight, furious. He looked at me, looked at the trailer, looked at me again. "Dammit, Chief," he seethed. "There's not an ounce of doubt in my mind that the piece of shit in that trailer murdered Laurel because she wouldn't have him. Didn't want anything to do with him. Even though he followed her around like a sick puppy dog."

"And you know this because—"

"Laurel told me, the last time I talked to her, just a few days ago, that she was scared of Carl, that he was paying too much attention to her, always trying to get close to her," Mullins said. "Now she's dead. They're all dead. My little baby, first grandson, dead. Jacob hurt bad, I heard." Mullins pointed at the trailer, his finger trembling with rage. "And that man in there, he's gonna pay for it. I promise you that."

"Jeremy's alive," I said. Mullins stared at me like he didn't believe me, so I went on. "One of my mothers, Naomi, was bringing something to the ranch for Laurel this morning. She found the bodies and called in the killings. Naomi has Jeremy at the ranch. She's taking care of him while we sort this out."

With that, Mullins took one step back from the squad car and let the rifle barrel drop. "I thought they said this monster murdered the children."

"Benjamin and Sybille, but not Jeremy," I said.

Mullins shook his head. "Those two beautiful kids, good kids. Anna was a wonderful woman. And my Laurel. My sweet, innocent Laurel." He paused, choking up. "But Jeremy, you're not lying to me, he's okay?"

"In Naomi's arms as we speak, most likely being cuddled and cooed to," I said. "I promise you."

That seemed to change things for Mullins. I figured he didn't care what happened to him when he thought they were both dead, but now he had second thoughts. Maybe he saw there was something that made it worth not throwing his job away, something to fight for. "You going to stand back now and let us do our jobs the right way?" I asked.

Mullins agreed with a jerk of his head.

"I'm going to talk to Carl," Max said. "Clara, cover me. You two stay here."

"You be careful, Max," Mullins growled, again pointing at the house. "That man... he's a killer. Don't trust him."

Max gave Mullins a sympathetic look, and then took a few steps out into the open, walking around Mullins' squad toward the trailer. "Carl Shipley, can you hear me?" he shouted. "This is Chief Deputy Max Anderson. I have Police Chief Clara Jefferies with me. We need to talk to you."

The voice that came from the trailer was surly, condescending, and I thought I heard fear hidden deep within it. Maybe Mullins' threats had hit their mark. "Did that deranged cop put his rifle away?" Carl asked.

Mullins stared at the trailer door, and I saw his rifle edging higher, on its way to his initial position. I put my hand on top of the barrel. At first, Mullins resisted, but then he allowed me to gradually push it down until the barrel pointed at the ground. "Give it to me," I ordered. Mullins held tight but shrank back, as I said, "I'm sorry about Laurel. If it's Carl, we'll get him. But right now, give me your weapon."

"You better keep your eyes on that man," Mullins warned. "You and Max can't trust him."

"We'll watch him," I said. "Now, give me your rifle."

Mullins hesitated, but then handed it over. I put my gun in my holster and held the rifle up, aimed it at the door. When I did,

Mullins turned away from me, I hoped satisfied that we were in control. He again glued his attention on the trailer.

"Detective Mullins has relinquished his rifle," Max said. "Now it's your turn. Carl, if you're holding a weapon, put it down. Come out slow and easy, hands in the air."

"I don't have any gun. I know the damn drill," Carl shouted. I felt a bit of surprise that he'd volunteer the next bit of information. "Shit, I've done this before."

"Then you ought to be good at it," Max called out. "Follow instructions and come out here. We need to talk to you."

For a moment, silence, then the thin metal door cracked open. The man who stood in the doorway was a big, bulky guy with messy dark brown hair and a broad face, a high forehead and a stunted chin. His heavy work boots rattled the trailer's tinny drop-down steps as he made his way to the ground, hands empty and held high.

The moment Carl's feet touched earth, Mullins rushed forward.

"Detective Mullins, stop!" I shouted. Max and I ran after him, but not quickly enough. Mullins, a foot or so shorter, gripped Carl by the collar of his plaid flannel shirt and started twisting it as if to strangle him. Carl grabbed at Mullins' hands, attempting to peel them off, but Mullins was surprisingly strong. I held the rifle on the two of them and ordered, "Detective Mullins, move back!"

Mullins had a death lock on that shirt collar, tightening it like a noose, while Carl took one of his massive hands and pulled it back, preparing to deliver a blow to Mullins' face. I shouted again. "Carl, stop. Don't hit him! Mullins, damn it, I ordered you to move back!"

Carl appeared ready to strike, but Mullins finally did as I instructed and let go. He looked as if something deep inside him had taken control, something that wanted more than anything to kill the man before him. But he did as I'd demanded and took two steps back. "Goddamn it, Chief, this guy killed my daughter, I'm telling you. Killed my Laurel."

Carl was coughing and pulling his shirt down, straightening his collar, the color of his face starting to slowly return to normal. A deadpan look on his face, Carl said, "Laurel's dead?"

"Hands up, Carl," I ordered. "Get them back up."

"What about the others?" His voice hoarse from the choking, he appeared stunned but slowly raised his hands above his head. "Jacob? Anna? The kids? Are they okay?"

"Where were you this morning?" I asked.

"Here at the trailer," he said. "I was just getting up when this—"

"Anyone see you here? Anyone here with you?" Max asked.

Carl appeared confused, looked from one to the other of us. "Shit, no. I live here alone. You think I did this?"

That, apparently, was more than Mullins could tolerate, because he jumped forward, tackled Carl, and they fell to the ground. I held the rifle on them, while Max shouted at the top of his lungs, "Mullins, get the hell off that man!"

They rolled, Mullins on top. Carl on top. Another turn around, one up, the other down, and Max put his boot on Mullins' leg and pushed hard, until he screamed.

"Damn it!" Max shouted. "Mullins, cut it—"

It happened in a single heartbeat. Carl's hand came up holding a 9mm, one I surmised Mullins must have had tucked into his pants or a hidden holster. In a split-second, single move, Carl pointed the gun at Mullins' head. Max and I aimed our weapons at Carl, ready to shoot, but only if we had to. "Now whoa, there," Carl said. "I'm not the bad guy here. He attacked me."

"Put the gun on the ground and we'll talk," I said. "Now!"

Carl kept the handgun where he had it, pointed straight at my lead detective's cranium. In response, all the blood appeared to drain from Mullins' face, turning everything but that scar of his to ash.

"Shit, I…" Carl started, but then he stopped. He looked at the two of us. "I'm not getting a fair shake here. Not with my history. Not with this crazy-as-a-loon cop convinced I did it."

"Didn't you do it?" I asked.

"Hell, no!" he shouted. "I didn't do shit. I was home sleeping. I told you."

"Well, if you didn't do it, you don't have anything to worry about," I said. "Let Detective Mullins go. Put down the gun. We'll talk and clear this up."

"Damn it, I…" Carl started. Then, it appeared, he'd made up his mind. "You two put your guns down, and then we'll talk."

"Not until you let the detective go and put your gun down," Max said, his voice steel. "That's the only way this works."

"Hell, you think I'm a fool?" Carl yelled. "I told you to put your guns down, and when you do, I'll let him go."

"We're not putting anything down," I said. "Let. Him. Go."

Carl had the handgun pressed so tight against Mullins' skull it must have hurt. I bit the inside of my lip and tasted something metallic—blood. I couldn't take my eyes off Carl to look at Max, but I sensed that he was creeping farther to the right. Carl swiveled to get a better look at Max. "Stay where you are or I'll shoot the man," he threatened. "Move back, closer to the chief!"

Max did as Carl said and inched toward me. We both still had our firearms aimed at the men on the ground. I noticed Mullins' hand tremble.

"We're going to get up now, this guy and me, and when we're standing, we'll talk about this," Carl said. "You two okay with that?"

In truth, we didn't have a lot of good options. "Yeah," I said. "We're okay with that."

Max and I backed up a couple of feet to give them room, and Carl lumbered up, his left hand pulling Mullins along with him by his collar, his right hand holding the gun's barrel in place. Once they made it up, we all stared at each other, except for Mullins, who kept his eyes focused on the ground. Carl kept low, trying to shelter behind his shorter hostage. Max and I had our guns pointed but had no opportunity to shoot without most likely killing both of them. Plus, this seemed like a situation we could talk to a conclusion.

"Now what?" I asked. "You ready to put that gun down so we can clear this up?"

"You gonna arrest me for holding this guy hostage?" he asked. "He jumped me. You both saw it. But I know how you cops stick together. How's this gonna come down?"

Mullins' face pinched tight, displeased I knew, when I answered, "No. The detective didn't follow procedures. He was out of line. We won't pursue you for fighting him off."

Max looked over at me, questioning.

Carl stared at both of us, unsure. "This wouldn't be the first time I've been lied to by a cop."

"I'm not lying," I countered. "We will not arrest you for assaulting a police officer. Detective Mullins made the first move."

I sensed that Carl weighed his choices. Should he run, take Mullins with him as his hostage? Should he believe me and drop the gun? Maybe he thought he could kill Max and me, then shoot Mullins and escape?

"I've got priors," Carl said. "I want you to know that, so if it figures in you can tell me now."

"What kind of priors?" I asked.

Carl focused on me. "Lots of juvie stuff, nothing big. But I beat up a guy pretty bad. Bar fight. Put him in the hospital."

"Assault?" I asked.

"Yeah, that's what they called it at first, but they whittled it down to a lesser charge. I only served six months."

I kept quiet. I could feel Max beside me, the tension radiating off all four of us. The sun had made its way higher than the treetops and I felt it on my back. "The guy must not have been hurt too bad," I said.

"I got him good," Carl said. "But the DA figured out that the other guy provoked the fight, so they went light on me. We were both drunk and in sorry moods."

I nodded. "Okay, if everything you've told me is true, we won't pursue charges for the altercation with Detective Mullins, if, right now, you let him go and drop that gun."

Carl kept his eyes on me and his left hand, which had been clenched in a death grip on Mullins, opened up. Mullins gulped hard and darted away, until he stood at my right. As ordered, Carl lowered his arms. We watched for any sign he could rear up at us, any indication he might shoot. That didn't happen. Instead, he crouched down and placed the gun on the dirt. Once he did, he stood again and followed instructions, hands up in the air.

Max grabbed the gun, and Mullins shouted, "Now you're done, you SOB." His face flushed so red it seemed to swell with anger as he shouted, "You're going down for this, for all of it!"

I turned to Mullins and ordered, "Cool it. This part of it is done."

"Chief, I…" he started. I shot him a look that warned I'd heard enough. He moved back, irritated.

"We're going to take you to the station," I said to Carl.

"You promised—"

"We're not booking you for what happened between you and the detective. I'm keeping my word. But we need to talk to you about Jacob Johansson and his family," I said. "We have four murders to solve."

CHAPTER NINE

Max offered to drive Carl Shipley to the police station, and I ordered Mullins to report there and sit tight, to not interact with anyone but Max until we had time to talk. I had to drive back to the bison ranch to collect Naomi. Despite her turndown, I intended to get a statement out of her.

When I arrived, I had to park on the road. The forensic folks had expanded the crime scene, and yellow and black tape hung all the way back to the end of the driveway, encircling the family van Naomi arrived in. I could tell she was agitated as soon as I saw her. She rushed me, baby Jeremy in her arms, as I climbed out of the Suburban.

"Clara, they won't let me take the van," she said. "How will I get to my hives? And Ardeth needs it to do the family grocery shopping. By now, she's screaming to the heavens about me. You know how your mother gets when she's angry." Naomi wasn't exaggerating; my mother, Ardeth, was the first of father's wives and as such had a tight grip on all that went on in the family. She was such a stubborn woman, such a strong force, that in my months home, even I'd been unable to buck her. Despite my attempts, she'd successfully kept me at arm's length from my family. Yet while I understood, even identified with Naomi's angst, I couldn't let anyone, not even Mother, prevent me from getting what I needed.

"Mother Naomi," I said, trying to calm her. "I'll do something for you. But you need to do something for me."

She gave me a twisted frown that signaled that her suspicions were building. "Do what for you?" she asked.

"You need to come to the station and give an official statement," I said. "I'll call my mother and explain the situation. When we're done, I'll drive you back here and get them to release the van, so you can drive it home."

"No," she said, as if that ended the matter. "I won't do that. I won't give an interview. I told you everything."

"How do you know?" I asked.

She gave me a confused glance. "What do you mean, how do I know?"

"How do you know what I'll ask?" I said. "Don't you want to help find the person who murdered Laurel? Anna and her children?"

Naomi muttered something I couldn't hear most of, nothing except my name, which wasn't said in the kindest tone. I let her sputter, and eventually she turned to me. "Before we leave here, I need to know that when you bring me back, I'll be able to take the van. Or I won't go."

"What will you do?" I asked, wanting to make sure that she understood she had little choice. "As far as I know the family just has that one vehicle. You don't have a cell phone, and the Johanssons' house is a crime scene. They won't let you inside to use the kitchen phone again. Who will come for you? How will you get the van?"

Naomi glared at me. I nearly smiled thinking of the days I'd quaked under that look. But I simply waited, expressionless, until she said, "All right, Clara. If I must, I'll go with you. Just make sure I can get the van later. Or your mother will wake the dead with her fury."

Agreeing, I left Naomi and walked over to talk to Lieutenant Mueller. When I pulled him to the side and explained the situation, he offered to let us take the van right then if we wanted, but I stopped him. "No, keep it where it is for now. We'll be back in a few hours," I said. "But first, I'm going in the house to get a few things for the baby."

"Sure, but be careful," he said. "You know the drill."

I nodded, then I waved at Naomi and shouted, "Everything's all set. I'll get Jeremy's supplies. Be right back."

As I walked past the bodies, I saw that Doc had Benjamin and Sybille in body bags, and he and one of his assistants had a third laid out next to Anna. I thought of what Carl had said, that she was a good woman. I looked at the small figures of the two children encased in black vinyl. This was the kind of case that strains the heart. The kind that can turn a cop inside out trying to solve it. I thought about Carl at the station house, waiting to be interviewed. Mullins insisted that Carl was the killer, but was he?

Inside the house, the blood on the kitchen floor marked where the medics had worked on Jacob. I walked to the side. The white refrigerator had sooty fingerprint dust all over it. I thought about opening it to look for formula, but then remembered that Laurel was breastfeeding and didn't have a pump, since that's why Naomi was here. It seemed unlikely that Laurel had formula for the baby. Rather than take a chance that the fingerprinting wasn't done and I'd contaminate the area, I decided to send someone to the grocery store.

Skirting around the blood, I spotted a yellow marker under the breakfast table a dozen feet away. I hunched down and saw a knife with a curved, bloodstained blade under the table, the kind used to gut deer during hunting season. The second murder weapon? How strange. The gun was outside. Neither of the weapons had been removed from the scene. The killer didn't take either one with him. I wondered if he brought the weapons, or if whoever had done this found the gun and knife at the house.

Then I noticed a couple of markers that appeared to designate nothing in particular. They sat on the floor between the blood pool and the knife. I crouched farther down and looked back at where Jacob had been found. That was when I noticed something on the floor: a few faint streaks of blood.

As I got up, Stef walked in with one of the CSI techs.

"What do you make of those?" I asked. They both shot me questioning looks. "The blood smears you marked."

"Oh, those," the tech said. He nodded at Stef. "You want to tell her?"

"Yeah. If it's okay with you?" she asked. The guy nodded and Stef grinned. "Well, Chief, what we think is that Jacob and his assailant wrestled some, and that they ended up down on the floor, and that's when he cut Jacob's throat. The reason is that if Jacob had been standing when it happened, we would expect to see round drops of blood somewhere on the floor, the type that form when liquid, in this case blood, falls straight down from an elevated position. There aren't any."

"Interesting," I said, seeing the excitement in her eyes. I, of course, knew all of this. I've been on my fair share of murder scenes. But I wanted to give Stef an opportunity to explain it, to be able to display all she'd learned. "Go on."

"Well, then, once the attacker finished with Jacob, it looks like he threw the knife under the table. It skidded across the floor leaving those bloodstains."

At that, Stef flung out her right arm, as if she'd thrown away the knife.

I thought about what that might mean. "So, you're suggesting that the killer was most likely a man and someone powerfully built? Jacob's a big guy. He wouldn't be easy to overpower."

"That's the way it looks," the tech said, and Stef nodded in agreement.

"Interesting theory," I said. "But what if it was a woman, and she had a gun? Remember, the outside victims were shot and we found a gun in the woods."

They looked at each other, and Stef shook her head. "Guess it could be?"

"Guns give folks a lot of power. She could have forced Jacob to get down on the floor," I explained. "Your theory has potential. But a word of caution: don't read too much into one piece of evidence. You have to look at the whole picture. But good job, you two. Those blood smears could have easily been missed."

"Thanks, Chief," Stef said, then she motioned toward the tech guy beside her. "We did it together."

"You're done in the nursery? I need to get a few things for the baby, diapers, clothes and such."

"Yup, the room's all clear," the tech said. "We didn't find anything to indicate it was part of the crime scene."

As I turned to leave, Stef stopped me by asking, "Chief, why do you think he did that?"

"What?"

"The lipstick on the woman. Why would someone do that?"

"Stef, the woman on the bed upstairs has a name. Laurel Johansson. Let's use it," I suggested. "And whoever did it to her wanted to send some kind of message. I have a theory, but we won't know until we get further into this if it holds up."

"Laurel?" Stef asked. Her spine arched back in surprise. "That's not Detective Mullins' Laurel, is it? His daughter?"

In my insistence that we treat the victims as individuals, I hadn't handled this well. I should have known that Mullins might have mentioned his daughter at the station, that Stef might be aware of her. "It's—"

"It is her," Stef said. The exhilaration she'd had since arriving on the scene drained from her eyes, and she appeared shaken. "I didn't recognize her, but I met her once, not long after I first started in the department. I didn't remember that she was married to Jacob Johansson. I just knew her as Mullins' daughter. She stopped in while she was in town grocery shopping, to say hi to him. She was so nice. Just the sweetest…"

My budding CSI officer, our rookie who until that moment thought the crime scene was all textbooks and mystery novels, dropped her head and closed her eyes. I knew that she was experiencing something we all have to at some point if we're going to be good at our jobs and also retain our humanity: from this moment on, Stef would understand that murder victims aren't bodies or remains; they're people. Real people. And that's why all of it matters.

I considered consoling Stef, but I knew she wouldn't want that. She needed to have room to process her feelings, so I turned to the crime scene tech, who stood back tongue-tied and watched his young charge learn a tough lesson. "You want to come with me upstairs, make sure I don't disturb anything while I'm getting what I need?" I asked.

"Sure," he said.

As we walked off, I noticed Stef rub her eyes, wiping away a tear.

CHAPTER TEN

In the nursery, the tech helped me shuffle through Jeremy's tiny clothes, onesies with trains and trucks, soft blue blanket sleepers with teddy bears on the chest. I held a pair of pajamas in my hands, heartbreakingly small, decorated with miniature dinosaurs, and a wave of remorse flowed through me as I thought of the children I'd never had. I considered, not for the first time, that my marriage had no upside. I bore the scars of that unholy union. The man my parents forced me to marry was as desolate as the alfalfa fields around town in the dead of winter.

When I got to the Suburban, I threw the bag packed tight with diapers and clothes into the back. We should have had a car seat for Jeremy, but I hadn't been able to find one. "Let's go," I said.

The baby cuddled to her chest, Naomi shot me a peeved look. "I can't believe you're making me do this. You're going to have to call Ardeth as you said you would. I'm not going to do it."

As promised, on the way to the station I had Naomi dial the house landline. "It's Clara, Mother. Naomi is with me. I assume you've heard what's happened at the Johanssons' ranch?" In Alber, bad news spread faster than maple syrup on hot flapjacks.

"Yes, well, I did hear, and—" Mother started.

"I'm sure you understand then that we need Naomi down at the station to file a report. And the van is tied up inside the crime scene tape for the time being, so she won't be able to drive it home for at least a couple of hours."

"No!" Mother snapped. "Put her on the phone! Now!"

I glanced over at Naomi, who gulped. I guessed she'd heard Mother and was having a hard time holding down her breakfast.

"Naomi can't talk to you right now. She's busy taking care of a baby we found alive at the scene," I said. "You'll have to talk to me."

I could feel Mother's anger build even over the phone. "Clara, I need the van within the hour. And I don't want Naomi talking to any police. I'm grateful for what you did, that you helped us last summer when we needed it, but I can't have you around the family."

"Mother, Naomi is a witness in a quadruple murder case," I pointed out. "Of course she has to talk to the police. And I am Alber's police chief. So that means she has to talk to me."

The phone went quiet. My greatest regret was that while I'd left Alber to save my own life, not to separate myself from those I loved, that had been the painful consequence.

I'd returned out of love to help my family, but Mother still barred me from spending time with my siblings. More than anything else, Mother feared the outside world, and I had become part of it. I was no longer bound by the strictures of Elijah's People, and she worried that my brothers and sisters would see how I lived and question their own place in the sect. As much as I hoped for an opportunity to build a bridge over the crater between Mother and I, she simply wouldn't have it. Perhaps that was the reason I'd yet to put down any permanent roots in Alber. Or maybe the town just held too many bad memories.

Rather than acknowledge that what I'd said was true, Mother remained silent, seething, I suspected. Eventually, her voice gravel, she said, "And how will I get the shopping done? I need to drive to Walmart in Pine City. We are nearly out of milk for the children."

"I'm sorry, but I'm sure it will work out. Right now, there's nothing to be done." I then said goodbye and hung up before she had time to object.

*

At PD headquarters, Naomi and I bustled in, she carrying the baby, me my shoulder bag and the diaper bag slung over my arm. Jeremy was fussy and kept nuzzling toward Naomi's chest, I assumed anticipating lunch. I looked in between the blanket folds and saw his tiny nose, the sparse lashes that framed his blue eyes. The little guy had been surprisingly patient. Kellie manned the desk. She was petite with curly sunflower-yellow hair cut short, and had a habit of twitching her nose when she got nervous—something she did as she jumped up as soon as I walked in. "You need to go on a supply run," I said. "The grocery store."

"Yes, Chief, what do you—"

"Baby formula, bottles, for this little one. Ask one of the clerks, an older woman who looks like she has a bunch of kids, what type of formula is good for a newborn who has been nursing." I opened my bag and pulled a couple of twenties out of my wallet. "Save the receipt and you can reimburse me out of petty cash."

"Maybe more diapers, too," Naomi suggested.

I thought about the dozen or so I had in the diaper bag, all I found in the nursery. Laurel must have had more stashed somewhere, but I didn't see them. Naomi was probably right. I took out a third twenty, pretty much all the cash I had, handed it over and said, "Kellie, where's Detective Mullins? Where's Carl Shipley?"

"Detective Mullins is in the conference room with Chief Deputy Anderson," she said, a deep frown on her usually smiling face. "I heard that one of the victims is the detective's daughter. He came in pretty upset and started to go after Mr. Shipley. A couple of the guys got in between and separated them."

It appeared that we were going to continue to have fires to put out. "And Carl Shipley?"

"He's in interview room number one," she said. "Chief, he's been making noises about calling a lawyer but he hasn't actually asked for one yet. Something must have happened out at his house?

He mumbled that you lied to him and you're going to charge him for holding a gun on Detective Mullins?"

"Don't worry about it. I'll handle it," I said. "I'll get someone to take over the desk for you. Just hurry and get those baby supplies."

As ordered, Kellie headed for the door, and I called over to Officer Bill Conroy to cover reception—he was one of our up-and-comers, a young guy who'd been showing some good instincts since I arrived. "Is it true what we heard, that Detective Mullins' daughter Laurel is among the dead?" Conroy asked.

"Yes," I thought the kid looked like he might have been crying. His winter-blue eyes clouded over with the confirmation. Conroy and Mullins were close. I'd heard that they sometimes palled around after work. "Unfortunately, that is true."

"I'm gonna have to go home after this then," Conroy said. "I need to tell the family."

"Mullins will probably want to break the news to his—" I began to explain.

"Chief, one of my moms is Mullins' half-sister," Conroy explained. "And my grandpa, Mullins' dad, is gonna need to be told. He's old and not in good shape. This is going to shake him."

That's the thing about plural marriage; lots of moms coming from the same families in a small town. It made it hard to keep track of who was related to whom. Conroy ran his hand through his shock of dark blond hair. "I don't know if anyone's told you yet," he said. "But Anna and Laurel, they were really great people, the kind that would help anyone in a jam. Both of them as kind as the sun is bright. I can't think why anyone would do this to them."

I nodded. "I've heard. Sure, take an hour off to get with your family. I'm sorry, but then I'll need you to head back here. I wish you could have longer, but we need you to work this. We'll be chasing leads, I hope."

"You bet," he said, for the first time looking pleased. "Nothing I'd like better than to find the guy responsible."

"Me either," I said. "Listen, while you're on the desk, call the county family services office and get a social worker out here. We need to place the baby."

Naomi's antennae rose up and she insisted, "I'll care for Jeremy."

I put my hand up to stop her. "It has to go through channels. There are regulations. And my guess is that Jeremy will be placed with a relative for now, an aunt most likely."

"Well, if you must." Naomi scowled at me, plainly disappointed. It struck me as odd when she asked, "Will Jacob be told that I helped with the child?"

I stared at her a moment and wondered why she'd asked that. "I'm sure he'll appreciate all you've done, calling for help, looking after the baby."

Naomi seemed pleased by that, but then pointed out, "If he lives."

"Yes, if Jacob lives," I agreed.

That settled, I shepherded Naomi past the officers' cubicles and down the hall to interview room number two. "Wait here," I said. "Kellie will bring you the formula as soon as she gets back."

I started to walk away when she shouted after me. "Clara, I need that." When I didn't answer, she said, "The diaper bag."

"Of course you do." I unslung it from my shoulder and put it on the table. "It'll be an hour, maybe a little more, but I'll be back. Don't leave."

Naomi gave me another of her frowns, which I was getting pretty good at ignoring. On my way out of the room, I closed the door. Before I interrogated Carl, I had questions to ask my head detective, who it appeared had a hard time holding his temper.

"You went after Carl again?" I charged as I walked into the conference room.

The blinds were closed, making the room dim, and Mullins had his face buried in his hands. It was one of those you-could-cut-the-tension-with-a-knife atmospheres. It looked like Mullins had been crying, and Max had his hand on one of his shoulders, trying to console him. As soon as I said it, I regretted not starting out the conversation with a bit of empathy instead of an attack. But we had four dead bodies, two were children, and a guy with a cut throat. I couldn't have anyone, not even a victim's dad and my lead detective, undercutting the investigation. "Mullins, I am sincerely sorry for your loss, for your daughter's death."

"Yeah, I know. Everyone's sorry," he said from between his fingers. "You're all sad that the monster down the hall murdered my daughter. I've got it."

Frowning at him, I was trying to decide what to say when Max spoke up. "The chief is trying to help, Mullins. You know that. We want to find out who murdered Laurel, Anna and the children."

Mullins remained silent, maybe assuming that wasn't something he had to remark on.

"How are we supposed to solve this case, Mullins, if you continue to interfere and put the man you peg as the main suspect on guard?" I asked. "You know that's not a good thing. We need to convince him to talk to us."

Mullins dropped his hands and looked up at me. "You can't blame me, Chief. That man killed my girl."

He had a point, if Carl was truly guilty. But as far as I knew, we didn't have any evidence against the guy. "Let's back it up," I said. "Start at the beginning. Give us some context about all this. When did Laurel marry Jacob?"

For half an hour or so, Max and I listened while Mullins talked. Some of what he said we already knew, for instance that for years Jacob and Carl lived in Mexico, high in a mountain town, with a splinter group of Elijah's People. While my hometown had never been welcoming to strangers, always a cultish place, wary of unfamiliar faces, El Pueblo de Elijah sounded even more reclusive. According to Mullins, armed guards working for the sect's hierarchy patrolled the roads leading into the town. Strangers weren't allowed in.

As Mullins talked, he detailed the similarities between the folks I'd grown up with in Alber and the ones in El Pueblo de Elijah. They shared the faith's belief in plural marriage, revered as the Divine Principle. The Mexican branch followed the same prophet folks in Alber did: Emil Barstow. An octogenarian, he'd controlled the town with an iron hand until he was sentenced to years in a federal prison for marrying off underage girls to older men.

It was in Mexico that Jacob met and married Anna, a Mexican national who came from a neighboring village. Their two children, Sybille and Benjamin, were born there. Then, Jacob's parents asked him to return to Alber to take over the bison ranch. Aging, Michael and Reba couldn't keep up with the grueling schedule the vast operation required. Jacob agreed with two stipulations: that he was given a second wife and that his pal, Carl, be allowed to return with him.

"Carl was *allowed* to return home?" I questioned. "Mullins, you're saying Carl was driven out?"

"Yeah, he was. After he was convicted and served time on that assault charge, the prophet had ordered Carl to leave Alber. He was the reason Jacob moved to Mexico, to be with him. They've always been close, those two."

"And when did Laurel and Jacob get together?" Max asked.

"Right after Jacob returned. He saw Laurel on the street and asked about her, told his father that he wanted to marry her. Jacob's father, Michael, sent a message to the prophet in prison, asked him for Laurel for his boy. The prophet issued an edict, said he'd had a holy revelation and my girl was to marry Jacob. They were married a few weeks later."

At that, Mullins concealed his face behind his hands again, I sensed not wanting to show either of us his pain. I sat next to him. "It's okay, Jeff." I didn't often address my detective by his first name, and Mullins looked over at me, perhaps surprised. "Max and I understand that this is hard. You're a grieving father right now, not a cop. We're working this, not you. You don't need your game face on. Okay?"

Mullins twisted into a painful grimace and dropped his head. A tear traced the scar down his cheek and fell onto his folded hands.

"What was the marriage like?" I asked.

"I don't think we should talk, I mean, personal stuff like—" he started, as if he planned to protest.

"These are the same questions you'd ask a family member if you were investigating this case, right?" I pointed out.

Mullins paused. "Right."

"Tell us about the marriage," I said again.

"Not particularly happy," Mullins said. "Laurel didn't want to marry Jacob. She had other ideas. But when she got pregnant right away, she settled in some. And when Jeremy showed up, well, she fell in love with the child like he was the sun and the moon."

I thought of Laurel in her sweet nightgown, her mouth inflamed with the bright red lipstick ring. "Is there any reason anyone would want to hurt her? Or anyone in the family that you know of?"

"No," Mullins said. "The only trouble I know of involved Carl."

"Now tell us about him," Max said.

At that, Mullins began kneading his hands, one into the other. As he talked, he pushed harder, as if working the words out through his motions. "From the beginning, Laurel didn't like Carl, didn't want anything to do with him. She's complained all along that he seemed too interested in her," Mullins said. "She and Anna both told Jacob they didn't want him at the house unless Jacob was home. But Jacob said Carl could come whenever he wanted. He ordered the women to be hospitable to him. I talked to Jacob about that. I didn't like it, making the women put up with a guy like that. Jacob told me to mind my own business."

"When was that?" I asked.

"Maybe a month ago. Not long after Jeremy was born." I could see Mullins' anger. "Last week, Laurel called me upset and said Carl walked in the nursery while she was nursing the baby. She covered up and told him to leave. He refused. Laurel didn't like the way Carl looked at her."

"Did he ever threaten her? Did he ever do anything to actually hurt her?" I asked.

"Not that I know of." Mullins shook his head. "And I didn't dream that... I didn't ever think it would go this far."

"Maybe it's time to talk to the judge, get a warrant for Carl's trailer?" Max said, looking over at me. "There might be clothes, maybe shoes linking him to the scene? We have that one print."

"Sure, when we're done here, you can go talk to Judge Crockett," I agreed.

After the briefest silence, Mullins said, "I need to go home." He looked over at me, as if asking permission. I'd been thinking about his family, his two wives and more than a dozen other children. He had devastating news for them. "I've gotta tell everyone about Laurel," he said. "This is gonna break their hearts."

As he got up, I noticed his shoulders slump. He looked beaten when he turned back and said, "Oh, you know, what I forgot to mention is what I've heard about those folks in Mexico. The reason right away when I heard about the killings, I knew it had to be Carl."

"What's that?" I asked.

"In El Pueblo de Elijah, they believe in Old Testament vengeance, including blood atonement."

As soon as Mullins said it, I remembered hearing rumors about the Mexican branch over the years, that they were more likely to settle disputes with violence. In blood atonement, believers professed that God alone didn't have the right to punish sinners. Instead, men were entitled to spill blood as reparations for misdeeds.

"That fits with Laurel's and Jacob's… injuries," I said, not going into specifics to shield Mullins from the gory details.

It quickly became apparent, however, that my caution wasn't necessary. Laurel's father had obviously already heard the horror of her death. "Yeah. Exactly." Mullins stared at me, as if determined to make his point. "That's the way blood atonement is usually done. Cutting a throat."

CHAPTER ELEVEN

Max left to talk to the judge about the search warrant, and I peeked in on Mother Naomi and Jeremy. The morning must have been exhausting for her, because she had her head on the table, her glasses off and her eyes closed. A nearly drained baby's bottle with a smattering of formula ringing the bottom sat next to her elbow. She didn't stir when I walked in, and I realized she'd fallen asleep. She looked peaceful, and beautiful. All my mothers were attractive women, but Naomi had the classic features of a cameo and her hair, just beginning to gray at the temples, spilled out in soft, light brown curls from her topknot. Someone had brought her a large file box, and she'd lined it with Jeremy's blanket. Napping as tranquilly as his babysitter, the little guy was curled up contentedly in a ball inside his cardboard cradle, his eyes closed and his lips sucking on an imaginary pacifier.

"You are a sweet one." Pausing for just a moment, I watched him, thinking about his innocence and that he had no idea of the tragedy that had befallen him. I rubbed the back of my fingers against his satiny cheek, and I whispered, "Jeremy, I will find out who murdered your mothers, your brother and sister, who tried to kill your father. Whatever it takes. I promise."

A short distance down the hall, I stood outside the interview room with a big numeral one on the outside. I glimpsed Carl through the one-way window, sprawled in a chair beside a metal table, his chin propped up on his right fist. He looked miserable and angry. I pressed the button that started the video equipment rolling and popped the door open. He jumped up. "It's about time," he charged. "You gonna keep me here all day, with my *amigo* dying maybe, and his family dead? What the—"

"You need to sit down," I ordered. "We're going to keep you here as long as we need you."

"Need me for what?" he challenged. "So that damn detective of yours can—"

"Need you to answer questions," I explained as I sat down and waited. He hesitated but then plopped down across from me. Once he did, I suggested, "First, let's rewind to yesterday. Tell me what you did. Where you went."

Carl gave me a perturbed headshake and a frown so deep it furrowed his cheeks. "It was just a normal day," he said. "I hung around the trailer in the morning, split some tree trunks for firewood and cut up fallen branches to burn this winter. When I finished, I threw it all on the woodpile out back."

"What else did you do?" I asked.

He eyed my jeans and my old shirt, dirty from my morning's dig. "Well, I looked pretty much like you do now when I finished, a real mess, sweaty and dirty," he said with a sheepish grin. "I went inside, showered and got dressed. It being Sunday, all the stores were closed in Alber. So, I drove over to Pine City to pick up supplies at the grocery and a few things I needed at the hardware store."

"What time was all that?" I had a pad on the table between us and I made notes.

"Got up about six, maybe seven, finished work and showered at eleven or so, then went right into town. I think I got home from the hardware store about three. Jacob had invited me over for dinner, so I was back in the truck at five driving to the bison ranch."

"When did he invite you?"

"The day before," Carl said. "He called me in the afternoon, said he wanted to have a little talk."

"About what?" I asked.

"Hell if I know," Carl said with a shrug. "Jacob and I talked a lot. He just said he had something to discuss. Not sure what, but I assumed something to do with the family or the ranch. He liked to run things by me, get my opinion on things. We were close that way. He knew that I looked out for him."

"Didn't you make it to the house?"

"Yeah, but I was there maybe ten minutes when all hell broke loose between Jacob, Anna and Laurel over the noise the kids were making, running around playing. There was a lot of shouting going on, and the baby, Jeremy, kept crying. It was louder than a train station. Jacob told me there was no sense in my staying, that it was too loud to hear ourselves think. He said he'd call me and we'd have to talk another time. I didn't even get dinner. Although Anna packed up a piece of pie and a loaf of homemade bread for me to take."

"You're telling me that you have no idea what Jacob had on his mind?"

"Not really. Probably just normal stuff. He wanted to complain about having to work so hard at the ranch, or the wives were upsetting him. Normal married people stuff." Something about Carl pricked at me: the constant challenge in his eyes, as if he wasn't offering anything I didn't specifically ask. Four dead, women and children, a best friend perhaps mortally wounded, and I had the sense that he considered it my job, not his to figure this out. He wasn't acting as if he cared to help.

"So, everything was fine, and then Jacob became angry over the children making too much noise?" I asked.

"Yeah, that's pretty much it. Jacob and me talked a little while, the women were cooking, but then it got loud and I left," Carl spread

apart his lips, revealing a gap in his front teeth where he'd lost one.
"Maybe they were a little tense when I got there. Laurel seemed
out of sorts. She gave me a nasty look when I walked in the door."

"Why would she do that?" I asked.

Carl squirmed in the chair, sat up from his sprawl and leaned
toward me. "I think she was just in a foul mood. Laurel could
get moody like that." I didn't say anything, just fixed my eyes on
him and stared. Pretty soon he shrugged and relaxed back into
his original position, putting some distance between us while he
mumbled, "It wasn't like anyone told me something was wrong.
I just picked up on the vibes."

I stared at him a minute and didn't talk, waited to see if he'd
jump in and fill the silence. He seemed content to stare off into
space. "What's this I hear about Anna and Laurel not liking you
all that much?" I asked, watching him carefully for his reaction.
I thought he'd be insulted, but he shrugged it off as if it were
unrelated and unimportant.

"Shit, who told you that?" he asked. "That hillbilly detective,
I bet. Why he—"

"Just give me your version of events, why your best friend's
wives would complain about you."

"I guess you could say I'm playful." A smile spread across Carl's
lean face, and I thought how odd it was that he'd be amused talking
about two women who hours earlier had been brutally murdered.
Max had apparently filled him in on a little bit of what we'd
found at the ranch on the drive into town, so he knew Jacob was
at the hospital in tough shape, that he might not pull through. I
wondered why Carl wasn't pushing me for more information on
his pal's condition. Instead, Carl seemed a bit proud when he said,
"People, especially women, don't always know how to take me."

"Why do you think that is?" I asked.

"No clue. I think I'm a pretty amusing kind of guy," he said.
"Anna and Laurel never really got my brand of humor."

I gave him a sympathetic nod, then suggested, "So you knew that they'd talked to Jacob about you, asked that you be told not to come to the house when Jacob wasn't home. Maybe that explains the tension when you were invited for dinner? Maybe it wasn't about the noise the kids were making? Maybe it was about having you as a dinner guest?"

Carl appeared to consider that. "Could be, but then I think Jacob would have told me if that was the problem. Silly thing for those women to feel like that."

"Did Jacob explain why the women were upset?"

"Nah," he said. "They had their own dramas going on is all I can think of."

"Like what?" I asked.

Carl gave me a conspiratorial look and leaned forward again, as if he planned to divulge the deepest of secrets. "Laurel never really wanted Jacob," he said. "She'd promised herself to some guy she went to school with. If it hadn't been for her father telling her she had to, Laurel most likely would have refused to follow the prophet's orders."

"And you know all this because?"

"Jacob told me," he said.

I let that sit for just a moment and thought it over. I had a timeline building in my notebook for Carl, one I could use to compare with what I'd learn from others.

"Did anyone see you yesterday?" I asked. "Can anyone confirm your story?"

"Lots of people at the grocery and hardware stores," he said.

"And what about this morning?" Thinking about the most likely time of the killings based on what Doc had said at the scene, I narrowed it down a bit. "From five this morning, until Detective Mullins knocked on your door."

"He didn't knock," Carl corrected. "That guy stood outside my trailer and shouted at me that I killed his daughter, demanded I come outside. I recognized his voice, knew he was Laurel's dad and a cop, but he didn't even ID himself. I dialed nine-one-one and—"

I stopped him. "Just tell me where you were last night and this morning beginning at five a.m., and the names of anyone who can corroborate it."

Carl smirked, like I'd lost my senses. "I was in bed, alone. I live way the hell out in the woods in that trailer. Who'd see me?"

At that, I tried an old investigator's trick, rephrased a few questions to see if I could confuse him and get different answers. "So, explain to me why Laurel told her father that she was afraid of you."

His sneer still planted across his face, he seemed to relish what he said next. "Anna and Laurel were good-looking women. I enjoyed being around them. They were easy on the eye."

"I heard that recently you walked in on Laurel nursing Jeremy, and you refused to leave," I said.

"It was beautiful. She was beautiful," Carl said, his voice defiant. "I didn't do anything wrong. I just wanted to watch."

"What did Jacob have to say about that?"

"You know, he never did seem to mind when I paid attention to his wives," Carl said. "I think he enjoyed having me appreciate them. I think that made him proud."

"Did you kill Anna and Laurel, Sybille and Benjamin?"

"I told you that already. I know nothing about the murders," he said, sitting up straighter, bristling with contempt. "You said at the trailer that you were bringing me here to answer questions, not 'cause you suspect I did it."

"Did you kill them?" I asked again.

"No." He locked his eyes onto mine and didn't back off.

"Did you attack Jacob and cut his throat?"

"No," he said again. He hesitated and then added, "I admit I'm not the world's best man, and it could be true that I cross lines off and on. But I didn't kill those women, those little kids. And I love Jacob. I never would have done anything to hurt him."

*

Max was waiting outside the door when I walked out of the interview room. "Anything?" he asked.

We stood at the window looking in at Carl and I shook my head. "Not really. Except that Anna, Laurel and Jacob argued the night before the killings. Carl says it was about the noise the kids were making," I said. "Carl's a strange guy."

"How so?" Max asked.

"Odd reactions. He doesn't respond emotionally the way you'd think he should." Max nodded as if he'd seen it too, and I asked, "Did the judge give us the go-ahead?"

Max held up the paperwork. "Yup. The search warrant is signed. I've got the forensic team heading out to Carl's trailer now. We can meet them there."

I turned away from the window and said, "Good. Let's go."

"What about talking to Jacob's parents first?" Max asked. "Maybe they can weigh in on what they saw out at the ranch."

I'd considered that. I knew Michael and Reba Johansson had already been told about the killings. Max's boss, Sheriff Virgil Holmes, had offered to notify the next of kin. He'd have to track down Anna's family in Mexico. Bad news coming from far away was going to be tough to deliver and, of course, even harder to take. Every violent death sent out shockwaves and ripples of sadness.

"My guess is that the Johanssons are at the hospital with Jacob by now," I said. "Let's see what Carl has out at the trailer, find out if there's any actual evidence tying him to all this, before we talk to Jacob's parents."

"Since our prime suspect is their son's best friend that's probably a good idea. They may be relatively resistant if we have no evidence," Max agreed.

"We're a long way from considering Carl our prime suspect," I countered.

Max shrugged. "True, but then we don't really have a list either. At the moment, he's our only suspect."

He had a point there.

"What about Naomi?" Max asked. "You want to take her statement before we head to Carl's?"

"The social worker should be here any minute to take the baby," I said. "Conroy will be back soon. Once that happens, he can drive Naomi out to the ranch to get the van. I'll get with her and take her statement later, but not here. The more I've thought about this, as resistant as she is Naomi may talk more easily in a more familiar setting."

A plan in place, I stuck my head back in the interview room and Carl looked up at me. "You're free to go," I said. "But Judge Crockett signed a warrant to search your place. Want to see it?"

Carl scowled. "Nah, I believe you."

"We'll get you a copy to take with you. If you don't want to be there, I suggest you take a few hours and do something else before you head home."

I watched for a reaction, wondering if he'd protest. "I'm pretty sure I left it unlocked when you dragged me down here," he said, as if none of it worried him. "You have at it. I ain't got a thing to hide."

"Good," I said. "If we need anything else, I'll be in touch. Don't leave the county, okay?"

"I'm not going anywhere except to head over to the hospital to check on Jacob." With that, Carl stood and lumbered over to us. "Either one of you know any more about his condition?"

"He's unconscious," Max said. "They've got him in the ICU."

Carl didn't seem to react one way or the other to that, showing no alarm.

"One last thing," I said, and he gave me a quizzical look. "Show me the sole of one of your boots."

Carl blinked hard and gave his head an exasperated shake, but he picked up one leg and displayed his boot, the sole side up. I took my phone out and pulled up the photo I'd taken of the blood stain from the ranch. The patterns didn't match. "Okay, like I said, don't go far," I reminded him.

At that, Carl sauntered toward the reception area and the door.

After he was out of earshot, I asked Max if Jacob had awakened at any point, if he'd said anything to the doctors or nurses. The news wasn't good.

"Not a word."

CHAPTER TWELVE

Officer Conroy drove the squad car, Naomi seated beside him. She hadn't wanted to leave Jeremy at the police station, but the pushy blonde at the dispatch desk had refused to let her take him. Kellie promised that the social worker would be there any minute, and that one of Jacob's sisters and her husband was on her way to pick up the baby. Naomi considered arguing the point. Since she'd been the one to rescue Jeremy, she thought she should be the one to watch over him. But then Naomi worried that Officer Conroy and that Kellie woman might think her insistence odd. Maybe odd enough to mention her strange behavior to Clara. Naomi didn't want that. *I just want Jacob to know I was there for him and his baby boy,* she thought.

As the car snaked through Alber, Naomi looked out the window at the sprawling houses where the townsfolk had lived before the big shake-up, when the feds came in and made arrests prompting many of the men to flee out of fear that they, too, might be arrested. Before that, Alber had been a good place to live; they had good lives. Naomi, when she allowed herself to think about it, held the prophet responsible for what had happened. It was considered a sin to criticize their religious leader. Emil Barstow ruled, by the teaching of Elijah's People, through revelations from God. But Naomi suspected that the prophet had become too old and susceptible to manipulation. The men in town who coveted young, underage brides used their influence with him to get what they wanted, and it had ruined them all.

"I'm sorry you had to see what you did out there at the ranch today, Mrs. Jefferies," Officer Conroy said, his thin lips pulled in a straight line. The young man looked pale, as if the coming winter had already faded him. "Seeing what you did? That must have been pretty terrible."

Naomi thought about the bodies at the Johanssons': Little Benjamin, his head covered in blood; the two bumps under the sheet that were Anna and Sybille. Blood. Blood on the sheet. And all around Jacob on the kitchen floor, his throat cut. She shuddered slightly when she recalled the raspy sound of his breathing, the air sucking in through the slit in his throat, the red foam that came out when he exhaled.

"It was awful, Officer Conroy," Naomi agreed. "It was like... Well... It's something I'll never forget."

Suddenly, Naomi couldn't go on. She could feel Conroy look over at her sympathetically, expecting her to continue, but she stopped talking. She gave him a weary smile and turned away.

A few minutes in the car and they were on the highway, heading to the ranch. She tried to think of something to say to the young officer, just innocent conversation, but couldn't. Instead, as they drew closer, she watched the bison grazing in the fields, the mammoth, lumbering animals with their thick hides and curved horns. The bison had their shaggy, dark brown winter coats on their backs and shoulders.

"You know, there's a frost coming tonight," Conroy remarked.

"Yes," Naomi answered. "In fact, I raise bees, and I was supposed to winterize my hives this morning. I still need to do that."

"Bees, huh?" he asked. "I bet that's interesting."

Naomi looked at the small silver watch on her wrist, a tenth anniversary gift from Abe. It was shortly before noon.

"May I use your phone, Officer Conroy?" she asked.

"Sure." He picked it up from the console between them and handed it to her.

Naomi entered the number to the family's landline. "Ardeth, one of the officers allowed me to use his cell," she said, when the oldest of her sister-wives answered. "I wanted to make sure that Clara explained to you what happened at the Johansson spread, and that I'll be late. Did she?"

"Yes, Naomi, Clara told me. And I've heard from others what you walked into. It sounds dreadful. Poor Anna and Laurel, those beautiful children. A terrible tragedy," Ardeth said, yet Naomi heard annoyance in the way the family matriarch clicked her tongue. "But are you on your way home now? I have my list ready. And I'm dressed to go grocery shopping."

"No, not yet." The less Naomi said, she decided, the better. Ardeth would simply assume that Naomi was tied up for the afternoon with the police. "I won't be home for at least a few more hours. Perhaps not until late this afternoon. Ardeth, the circumstances what they are, you'll have to do the shopping a day later this week."

Quiet, while Naomi assumed Ardeth stewed.

"Oh, all right," Ardeth finally said, just as Officer Conroy pulled into the MRJ ranch's long driveway and Naomi saw the grand house ahead, so imposing. It had to be one of the most beautiful homes in Alber.

"I'm sorry," Naomi said, not feeling at all regretful. "But I will be there when I can."

Naomi hung up the phone and placed it back on the console. "Thank you," she said.

Officer Conroy smiled over at her. He seemed like such a nice young man. "No problem."

Thanks to that phone call, Naomi had the van for as long as she wanted it. Considering her options, she wondered how quickly she could get the bees situated. She couldn't leave them out to freeze, but she had other priorities to take care of. As she considered her options, she decided that rather than see to the bees first, she'd go to the hospital to check on Jacob. His family would be there.

"Dear Lord, they'll be so grateful, won't they?" Naomi whispered.

Officer Conroy gave her a strained look. "Did you say something?" he asked as he pulled over and parked.

"No, no. Nothing important."

He looked over at her and his eyes settled on the front of her dress. "You're not going to go home and change?" he asked. "You have——"

"Jacob's blood, yes, I know." She took a clean piece of the skirt in her hand and straightened it. "I would, but I have some things to do." At that, she smiled over at him.

Naomi popped open the door and slipped out of the car. She scanned the scene, the crime scene tape and the yellow tented markers. Anna's and the children's bodies were gone, taken off in hearses to the county morgue. But Naomi noticed that the vultures remained, planted in the tree above where the bloody sheet had billowed in the breeze earlier. The ghoulish birds were watching, waiting. Shuddering, she wondered if they hoped to find scraps for dinner.

"Are you sure you're okay? You didn't say anything?" Officer Conroy said, appearing genuinely concerned about her well-being.

"Oh, it was nothing," she said with a warm smile. "I was praising the Lord, expressing my wishes for Jacob to recover."

"Well, okay," Conroy said. "Let's just get your van, then."

As he escorted her to her vehicle, Naomi suddenly stopped and stared at the impressive house. She turned her head to take in the vast fields and the lumbering bison that constituted the Johansson family fortune.

"It's such a blessing, a heaven-sent twist of fate, isn't it?" she whispered.

"What?" he asked.

Her smile grew wider. "That I was the one who saved Jacob's life."

CHAPTER THIRTEEN

The land around Carl Shipley's trailer could have passed for a dump with the piles of broken bricks scattered about. The trailer was anchored in place by more bricks stacked on either side of the wheels. "What's Carl do for a living?" I asked.

"Works at the bison ranch part-time and for a construction company part-time," Max said. "Looks like he brings the discards home."

"Maybe he's a part-time artist, too, and he considers it yard art?" I said, pointing at the discarded shingles with their frayed wrappers. Max raised one appreciative eyebrow at my sarcasm. I chuckled, but then, looking at him, I thought again about my promise to have dinner at his house that evening with Brooke. My head filled with all the reasons that wasn't a good idea. *Too much, too soon,* I worried. *Maybe I'm not ready.*

I pegged the trailer at about twenty feet long by eight feet wide. The stairs were down, and the hitch protruded up front. Instead of inspecting it on site, we could have hauled it to the crime lab, but that didn't make any sense unless we found something. I stopped and got a better look at the brown leather recliner near the trailer door, its footrest hanging askew, barely attached on one side. The umbrella overhead had a slit at the back that appeared to be the result of the fabric rotting. Based on all that, I had little hope for the condition of the trailer inside.

Instead, I walked through the door into a well-kept interior. A small table with benches on one wall, a galley kitchen with pots neatly stacked by size on shelves over the stove, a cubbyhole bathroom that doubled as a shower with a drain in the center of the floor, and a bed at the far back, the sheets and quilt pushed to the side as if someone had just crawled out.

"Are we sure Carl lives here?" I asked. "It's pretty neat."

"Rather a surprise," Max replied. "I wouldn't have pegged Carl as a good housekeeper."

A spick-and-span trailer, of course, wasn't what we wanted. We needed the down and dirty; we were looking for evidence of four grisly murders and an attempted murder. We weren't judging his housekeeping skills but his guilt or innocence. I caught a whiff of something. "Do you smell bleach?"

"I was just about to ask you the same question," Max said. "What do you think prompted him to clean this morning, to get the place sparkling?"

"Mullins?" I said.

Max understood. I was suggesting that while Mullins was outside shouting, Carl could have been inside destroying evidence. I shook my head at the thought that if my lead detective had followed procedures, if he'd called in his hunch so we could join him, we might have gotten here in time to surprise Carl and preserve any evidence.

Skimming over the trailer's insides, the place looked normal. A pair of cotton boxers lay on the unmade bed, as if Carl had thrown them there when he dressed that morning. Otherwise, nothing looked out of place. I saw a washing machine and a dryer behind a slatted door and swung it open. I put my hand on the outside of the dryer. It felt vaguely warm. I popped the door open and saw faded jeans and a white T-shirt, white athletic socks and white jockey shorts.

"Looks like he's been washing clothes, too," I said.

Max gave me a sideways grimace.

"Not to worry. They always miss something," I said. As hard as folks try to get out stains, blood is hard to hide. It seeps into carpeting, splatters and spreads, drips down into pipes. I once had a case in Dallas where the guy even put new carpet in his living room, pad and all, and we found traces of his next-door neighbor's blood on the cement underneath.

"You'll take out the drains and look for blood residue in the sinks and the shower, right?" I asked Lieutenant Mueller, when he joined us inside. There was only enough room for the three of us, so his techs were searching the area surrounding the trailer. Mueller had the CSI unit's base parked slightly up the hill.

"Of course," Mueller said. "We'll get right on it. What's covered by the warrant? What can we take?"

"It's pretty narrow. We're looking for shoes that match that print in the kitchen, any bloody clothes," Max said, handing him a copy. "Any kind of knife or gun. I know we found both at the ranch, and those are probably the murder weapons, but at this stage, before ballistics and the autopsies, we can't be sure. Anything that looks like it may have blood on it or any possible murder weapon should be logged in."

"Lieutenant Mueller," I said, and he turned from Max toward me. "Also watch for anything that could be tied to the victims, Jacob and his family. It could help us with motive."

"Got it," Mueller said. "Now how about you two go outside and let my guys take over in here. We haven't got a lot of room to work in."

Max and I did as the lieutenant asked, and once we stepped outside the videographer took our place inside, intent on doing his job and recording the interior as we found it.

On the edge of the clearing, a few folks in the unit had set up a table with supplies. They had stacks of markers, bags and labels to hold and document any evidence. One of the techs had a bottle of luminol waiting to spray anything that looked suspiciously like blood. I thought about that bleach smell again and hoped I was right and Carl wasn't able to wipe everything away.

Max and I stood close together, watching. My mind kept circling back to the ranch and the bodies. "You know, those little kids shot like that…" I started, but then I felt vaguely sick and instead of finishing the thought muttered, "I hate cases like this."

Max gave me a sad look.

Just then, one of the forensic techs shouted, "There's something you need to see back here."

Max and I followed her voice. We walked behind the trailer and into the woods. After we passed a small corral, we saw an aging mare tied up to the side of a shed munching on what appeared to be the last of a bale of hay. Carl's horse looked unkempt, like it had been through a war and hadn't come out the better for it. The mare eyed us suspiciously but didn't react, just kept eating.

We continued on and found the crime scene tech who'd called out waiting for us at the base of an oak, its fallen leaves forming a brittle, brown carpet beneath it. Not a massive tree, it stood maybe fifteen or twenty feet. Its branches stretched out in all directions, a bony circle of gnarled wood. Someone had taken rough, dark tan twine, hundreds of feet of it, and cinched it from branch to branch, tying one to the other. It looked as if someone had tried to crochet a dandelion top or a spider web onto the tree.

"What the hell—" Max started.

"No clue," I answered.

Making it even more mysterious, tucked on a smattering of the branches, hanging by hooks and crooked arms, sitting on twigs, taped to knobby limbs, were garish wooden ornaments: skeletons and devilish-looking figurines, skulls painted white and black with menacing grins wearing sombreros, skeleton women in brightly colored frocks and mantillas.

"*Día de Muertos* symbols," I whispered.

Max nodded. "You've seen an altar like this before? My experience is mainly limited to the occasional Mexican-American house or restaurant decorations."

"Nothing exactly like this, not on a tree. But I saw altars all the time in Texas, especially this time of year. The Day of the Dead is celebrated at the beginning of November, just a couple of weeks ago."

We stood and looked, thinking. "Why would he do this?" Max asked. "What does it mean?"

"I don't know," I said. "But I intend to ask him." I wondered if it had to be Carl's handiwork. Maybe someone else who lived in the woods had decorated the oak? I skimmed through the trees, searching for a house, a shack, a path that appeared to lead anywhere, but saw nothing.

We wove our way back to check on the search, and I noticed that the grass was worn away in front of us, as if someone routinely traveled between Carl's trailer and the macabre tree display. *It's his,* I thought. *It has to be his.*

Lieutenant Mueller was standing at the supply table wearing latex gloves and flipping through a black binder. He didn't acknowledge us when we approached, seemingly absorbed in whatever he was looking at. Max and I stopped directly across from him and watched as the lieutenant turned one page then another.

Photographs. An album of photographs; stark, black-and-white images displayed in clear plastic covers. Some had a slightly grainy appearance, as if they'd been taken from a distance with a telephoto lens. In one, Laurel and Anna played with the children in the yard. In another, taken through a downstairs window, Laurel leaned over the kitchen table. In a third, she sat in a chair in the upstairs nursery, looking content and happy, while Jeremy suckled at her breast. I wondered how Carl shot that one. He had to be elevated on something to get that angle.

"Where did you find these?" I asked.

Mueller shook his head as if he'd come to, the album's spell broken. "Inside a slit in the mattress, covered by a piece of duct tape. At first, we thought he'd repaired an old mattress. But then we found the folder pushed inside the foam, along with something else."

"What?" Max asked.

"This," Mueller said, as he reached over and picked up a plastic evidence bag holding a white enamel flower rimmed in gold attached to a chain. "A necklace."

"Page back a bit," I requested, and Mueller did, flipping through until I said, "Stop there."

The book lay open at the photo where Laurel bent over the kitchen table. Her arms extended, she appeared to be kneading dough, probably for bread. Dangling from her neck was the chain with the pendant. "Did you find a camera?" I asked. Given the album was discovered hidden in Carl's trailer, ownership would be assumed. But having the camera that took the photos would further tie him to the strange collection.

"Yeah, in the closet up on a shelf. It's going in for fingerprinting," Mueller said.

"Did you find anything else?" I asked.

"No boots or shoes with matching soles. Nothing linked to the case," Mueller said. "The trailer came up clean. No traces of blood. If there was any on the clothes in the dryer, it's gone now. The luminol didn't light up anything. We're sending the shirt and jeans to the lab, but I'm not thinking we'll find anything. That's where the smell came from. He used bleach on the laundry."

"On a pair of blue jeans?" I asked.

"Yeah." Mueller's voice laced with sarcasm, he added, "Maybe the guy needs a laundry lesson?"

He didn't expect an answer, and we didn't give him one.

"What do we think?" Max asked.

"I think that at the very least Mullins got part of this right," I said.

"The part where Carl Shipley murdered his best friend's wives and two of his children, then left said friend for dead?" Max speculated.

"We've got a way to go before we book this guy on a murder charge," I admitted. "But we can certainly say that Carl was obsessed with Laurel. In fact, he was stalking her."

CHAPTER FOURTEEN

Max and I had a difference of opinions walking to our cars. He wanted to head back to the ranch to see how things were coming with processing the scene. While Lieutenant Mueller oversaw the search of Carl's trailer, a few techs remained at the house scouring for any evidence we may have missed. I had a different agenda in mind. I wanted to go directly to the hospital, splinter Michael and Reba Johansson away from their son's bedside and start asking questions. We split up: Max back to the MRJ Ranch, while I drove to Smith County Memorial Hospital in Pine City.

My trip was longer, so I was still driving when Max arrived back at the scene and called. "Bad news. Just talked to Doc Wiley and no autopsy results until tomorrow."

"I thought he'd at least get to the children, maybe Laurel or Anna today," I complained, but then Max reminded me of the realities of working in the sticks. Doc Wiley wasn't just the medical examiner; he was one of only two general practitioners in the county.

"Doc got called in by one of the midwives to deliver a baby that's coming breech," Max said. "Unfortunate, but it can't be helped."

Inclined as I was to grumble, it was more important for Doc to do what he could to help the mom and her baby, even though that would slow the investigation down for the day. There were other avenues that might yield some leads. "What about hair and fiber evidence?" I asked. "When can we get that?"

"I requested a rush, but if we're lucky it will be a couple of days," Max explained. "The samples haven't even gotten to the state crime lab in Cedar City yet. When they arrive, they'll be logged into the queue, but it won't be immediate."

This wasn't the first time since returning to Alber that I missed the resources I had available in Dallas, where the PD had its own lab and the county medical examiner jumped on a case like this, one where we had a killer on the loose. "Anything we can do to push ballistics on the gun found at the scene?" I didn't give Max time to answer before I added, "What about the DNA from the blood on the knife? Fingerprint analysis? How long do you think that will take?"

A long sigh from the other end of the phone. "Clara, you work for a town of four thousand residents. I'm with a sheriff's department that oversees a rural county. Neither one of us has a lot of resources available. We rely on the state lab." Max paused before pointing out, "What we can do today is follow leads, but the forensic stuff takes time in the boondocks."

"Damn it, I…" Then I stopped. It wasn't Max's fault, and it made no sense to beat him up over the realities of our jobs. It got me nowhere to complain. "You're right, of course. Anything new I should know about the scene? Did they find anything else that might help?"

"Just from the photo album," Max said. "I brought it along and lined up the shots. What we speculated appears true. That photo of Lauren nursing the baby?"

"I know the one," I confirmed.

"It had to have been taken through the window. To do that, Carl had to be high up, off the ground. Our guess is that he climbed one of the trees near the barn."

"Do any match the perspective in the photo?" I asked.

"We think so," he answered. "I finally chased away those blasted vultures. The oak they perched in has a scar from a branch that's been cut off. Right now, the whole tree's bare. But when it's covered with leaves, it's probably pretty full. Looks like a good place to hide, and removing the branch opened up a hole in the foliage big enough to aim a telephoto through to get a shot inside the nursery."

"Take a photo of the tree, a close-up of the gap," I said. "Text it to me. It might come in handy."

"You've got it," he said.

The hospital wasn't much by Dallas standards either, but it was all we had in our area—four stories high, redbrick with a portico out front. I parked my Suburban in the lot closest to the ER. The triage nurse behind the desk gave my muddy clothes a once-over and frowned. I should have made it a point to circle back to my room to shower and change into a uniform, but it had been a busy morning.

"Police Chief Clara Jefferies from Alber." I flipped my wallet open to show her my ID. "I'm here to check on a patient brought in by ambulance, Jacob Johansson."

The woman skimmed my photo and appeared to read the fine print as if she didn't quite believe it. "You don't look like your picture," she said.

"Not the best photo, but maybe this will help," I said, and I smiled.

"Well, I guess," she said. "Let me look for his room number."

Minutes later, I departed the elevator on the second floor and sought out the surgery department. I thought perhaps that meant that they had Jacob in an operating room repairing his severed trachea. Instead, I followed the signs to his room number, which also led to the ICU. I stopped at the nurses' station, where I again had to pull out my ID to introduce myself. From there, I passed through double glass doors into the intensive care unit.

"Mr. Johansson!" I called out when I saw Jacob's dad, Michael, walking down the hall. He glanced at me, and I thought I saw him mentally debating whether to turn and walk away. Instead, he frowned and waited.

"How's Jacob?" I asked.

He shrugged, as if he wasn't sure, but said nothing.

When I was growing up in Alber, Michael Johansson was among our small town's elite, high up in the church hierarchy as bishop of one of Alber's three wards. As such, he knew the rules, including the prophet's decree that those in good standing should shun, should not even talk to those like me, apostates who left the faith. Still, Michael, despite the way I was dressed, also undoubtedly knew that I was Alber PD's chief and the lead on the investigation into the tragedy his family had suffered.

The old man's eyes were bloodshot, the only color in his long face and thin white hair. He grimaced slightly and chewed on his lower lip. Then, I guessed this was a time when it didn't take him long to decide that secular laws and personal heartbreak overrode religious dictates.

"Clara, I mean… Chief Jefferies," he said with an emotional catch in his voice. "It's good of you to…"

He stopped, I figured not sure what to say. "Michael, it's okay. It's never good to see a cop when this is the situation," I said. "I'm incredibly sorry for you and your family."

At that, the old man's head drooped and he took a long, shuddering breath. He pulled a white cotton handkerchief out of his pocket and covered his eyes. I spied a bank of four chairs across the hall. I put my hand on his arm and suggested, "Let's go over there and sit down." He followed me, and I gave him a few minutes to wrestle back his composure.

"It's been… It's so unreal that…" he started. Then he wept, and I waited. When he finally looked up at me, he pointed at my dirty jeans and changed the subject. "Were you out digging again?"

'How did you know I—"

Michael smiled, ever so slightly. "Clara Jefferies, you grew up in Alber. Things are different here, sure, but not that different. People still see. They still talk. Everyone knows about your digging. It's gossiped about among the women. I think they find it strange."

All those times, I'd never noticed anyone, but they'd kept tabs on me. "Okay," I said. "Then this will make it easy. If they're monitoring me, they watch others as well. What rumors have you heard? What do you know?"

"You're talking about…?"

"Who do you think did this?"

Michael drew in a ragged breath. "I can't say that I know who could be responsible for this kind of evil," he said. "I've been asking myself that all day long, ever since the sheriff rang our doorbell and told Reba and me what happened at the ranch. Who would murder my sweet granddaughter, Sybille? And little Benjamin, just learning to ride his tricycle? Laurel and Anna, the kind of women who were always doing for others?"

"You must have theories?"

"I…" he started and I thought he might say something helpful, give me a name, but then he gulped down his words. "I don't know. I'm sorry."

"Okay, but we all have people who don't like us. I'm sure Jacob had some enemies," I suggested. "Who are they?"

Michael shook his head, the tears rolled again, and he tried to brush them away, but the saturated handkerchief left shiny streaks. "Jacob and Carl were gone from Alber for years, so I don't know of any troubles they might have had. They've only been home a year or so," he said. "I never heard of any hard feelings in town or any altercations with others, certainly nothing so serious that anyone would do this horri…"

His voice broke on the last few words.

"You must have some possibilities in mind," I pushed. "I need to know what you know about your son, especially who might have any reason to—"

"Michael, tell her about Myles Thompkins." Reba, Michael's first wife and Jacob's mother, blurted out. She'd walked out of the glassed-in ICU room immediately to our left and stood beside her husband in her long prairie dress.

"We've known that boy his whole life, Reba. Myles wouldn't…" Michael objected. "Don't say such things. Myles has never been anything but kind to us. He'd never do something so evil."

"How do you know?" she said, jeering at her husband. "What makes you think he wouldn't be angry enough to try to kill our son? To slaughter Anna and our grandchildren? To take revenge against Laurel?"

"Woman, be still," Michael ordered. "We know his people, and they're a good, faithful family. Casting aspersions on others, Reba, is beneath you."

The Thompkins family was one of Alber's oldest. Half the town was either related to one of the Thompkins by blood or marriage. I remembered Myles from my years as a teacher at the grade school in town. An unusually shy kid with shiny dark hair and intelligent blue eyes, Myles was razor-sharp. In second grade, he tutored third and fourth graders in math. In junior high, he snuck into the high school's chemistry lab to try out a liquid nitrogen experiment that ended up shattering a wall of windows.

"Myles Thompkins?" I inquired. "Why would he hurt—"

"Because he loved Laurel, and she loved him," Reba said, casting an angry look at her husband. An angular woman, she had her gray hair anchored in a French twist in the back and it swung in an S-curve in the front, where bobby pins kept it out of her eyes. "The whole town knew those two were smitten with one another. All through high school, they planned to be together, and I wish that had happened. Myles was madder than a castrated bull when Laurel became betrothed to Jacob. I wish that girl had never wed our son."

"Reba, don't say such things," Michael objected. "Laurel was a good wife to Jacob."

"A reluctant wife," Reba corrected. "Jacob asked the prophet for Laurel's hand, and what our son got was a wife who loved another."

At that, Michael dropped his head and the tears came again. "Laurel was a good woman," he whispered. "She did what the prophet instructed. She was obedient, kind, and—"

"And probably got Jacob near killed, Anna and our beautiful grandkids dead!" Reba shouted. A doctor writing in a chart at the nurses' station looked up as if wondering what the hubbub was about. He put his finger to his lips to hush us.

"Did Jacob ever tell you that he had trouble with Myles?" I said softly. "Had Myles made any threats?"

"No," Michael insisted. "Laurel was a virtuous wife to our son, Clara. She was—"

"Trouble," Reba said, finishing her husband's sentence.

"How trouble?" I asked.

"I don't know how, but she was," she insisted. "When you have a man who loves a woman like Myles Thompkins loved Laurel, and she marries another, there's bound to be bad blood."

"Reba, please!" her husband begged. "Gossip is the devil's work."

"This isn't gossip, Michael," I explained. "If I'm going to solve this case, I need to know everything you and Reba can tell me that might lead me to the killer."

"But it's not true," Michael pleaded. "Laurel would never have kept up a relationship with another man. Any other man. The murders have nothing to do with that."

"How do we know?" his wife pushed, her voice coarse with emotion and her lips curling in anger. "We weren't there to see what happened, were we?"

"We know because that wasn't our daughter-in-law," Michael said. "Laurel did nothing to bring this terrible event to bear."

I wondered what to think, who to believe, and then Reba Johansson said, "If Myles and Laurel weren't still involved with each other, why were they together just two days ago? On Saturday."

"Myles and Laurel were together? On Saturday?" I repeated.

"We have no first-hand knowledge of this, but, yes, that's what we heard," Michael conceded.

"Heard from whom?" I asked.

"One of your mothers, Clara. Naomi Jefferies saw them together. She told us," Reba said. "You just missed her. She was here to check on Jacob. She only left fifteen minutes or so ago to go work at her hives."

"Naomi was here?" I asked, wondering why she would come to the hospital when she'd been in such a hurry to return the van to my mother.

"Yes, she was," Michael said. "She still had Jacob's blood on her dress. She didn't even go home to change, because she was so worried about our son. We were glad to be able to express our gratitude when she explained how she'd saved his life."

"And she just left how long ago?" I asked.

"A short time ago," Reba confirmed. "You're lucky to have her as one of your mothers, Clara. Naomi is a righteous woman."

I felt uncertain. Why would Naomi have come to the hospital? It seemed like an odd thing to do under the circumstances, and to not have even taken time to change out of her bloody dress.

At that moment, Carl Shipley angled his head out of the doorway and fixed his eyes on Reba. "Jacob moaned," Carl said. "I think he's coming out of it."

"Oh!" Reba released a small cry, and we all jumped up and rushed into the room. The doctor saw us and followed us in. I stood off to the side, out of the way but close enough to hear anything Jacob might say. His eyes remained closed. Monitors tracked his oxygen, his heartbeat, his pulse. The slit in his trachea had been cleaned up, the edges bandaged, but it remained open, and he made the same horrible gasping sound with each breath.

"What did he do that you thought he might be coming out of it?" the doctor asked.

"A noise kind of like this," Carl said, imitating a long, drawn-out groan. "I said his name, and, I'm not sure, but I thought that his eyes moved behind the lids. There was kind of a flutter."

The doctor took a penlight from the pocket of his blue scrubs, flicked it on, and then pried open Jacob's eyelids and assessed his pupils. He moved the light from one eye to the other to see if Jacob's eyes reacted. Whatever the doctor saw, it made his frown grow. He turned off the light and slipped it back into his pocket. "The sound he made was probably just a muscular reaction," he said. "He's still unconscious."

"Is it a good sign, that he made some kind of a noise?" Reba asked. She'd moved over to stand next to Carl, and they had their arms protectively around one another, like a mother might with a son.

"It's too early to tell how much damage your son has suffered," the doctor said. "Jacob lost a lot of blood."

"Oh, dear Lord! Our boy. Our boy," Michael cried, and rushed from the room.

"Husband," Reba called out, letting go of Carl and trailing after him. "Don't run off. Jacob needs us. Come here."

After they left, I took out my ID and showed it to the physician. "Has Jacob been conscious at all? Has he said anything, maybe on the ambulance? Or here in the room, to one of the nurses, to anyone on the staff?"

"No," the doctor said. "Although even if he did regain consciousness, speaking would be impossible with the injury to his trachea. We can't repair it until we're sure he didn't suffer damage to his airway. Right now, that opening is keeping him alive."

"But has he communicated or tried to communicate in any way?" I asked.

"Not that I know of," the doctor said. "My understanding is that he's been unconscious since shortly after he was found."

I thanked him, the doctor left, and I was suddenly alone with Carl, who held his friend's hand and stared down at him with a forlorn look.

"Tell me about the tree and the ornaments," I said. "A bit unusual in these parts, don't you think?"

At first Carl gave me a suspicious glance, as if he wasn't sure how to respond, but then let loose a rousing laugh that seemed out of place with his best friend beside him, hovering somewhere between life and death. "That's what you want to know?" he jeered. "Really, Chief. You're worried about my little bit of fun in the woods?"

"It's rather an odd thing to run into while executing a search warrant," I said. "And yes, I'm curious. Why did you do it? What does it represent?"

Carl snickered and stood straighter, ignoring the bursts of foaming blood bubbling from Jacob's throat each time he took a breath. "So what? I brought a few mementoes from Mexico, and I like having fun, enjoy the idea that someone might see it and wonder, what the heck," he said. "Jacob and me lived there a long time, and Anna, too. I got into the culture. They aren't as afraid of death as we are. I admire that."

"That's all?" I asked. He nodded and I added, "Looks fairly fresh, not like it's been there for a long time. I'd guess that you just put it up in the past few weeks?"

"A couple of weeks ago," he said. "Around *Día de Muertos*. Why?"

"No reason," I said. "But it seems like an odd coincidence to cover a tree with skeletons and skulls just before your friend's family is slaughtered."

At that, Carl swallowed, hard, and this time he didn't laugh. "Listen, you're making a molehill into a mountain. It's nothing," he said. "Just a little fun."

I nodded and took out my phone, checked to make sure I had Max's text. Watching his face, I asked, "Then let's move on, Carl. Did Jacob know that you were stalking Laurel?"

Except for squeezing Jacob's hand tighter, Carl didn't react. Instead he leaned over, rubbed his other hand over the dark blond stubble on Jacob's cheek and said, "I didn't do any such thing. I respected Laurel. She was Jacob's wife."

"Did you take pictures of her?" I asked.

He glanced over at me, and I saw a flash of anger in his eyes. "Yes," he said, his voice defiant. "I like to take photos. I take a lot of them. Of a lot of people. And I did take some of her."

"You have an entire album of photographs of Laurel, most of which look like she didn't know you were taking them." I turned my phone around and showed him the screen with the photo of Laurel nursing Jeremy.

"It's a beautiful photo." If he was shocked that we'd found the album hidden in his trailer, he didn't show it. "Why wouldn't I take that?"

"You climbed a tree, cut down a limb and took this one through the window," I pointed out, as I flipped to the photo of the tree with the missing branch. "Why would you do that?"

Carl turned away from the image on my phone and stared down at Jacob's expressionless face, then glanced over at me and sneered. "Because I wanted to, and because I knew Jacob wouldn't mind. We did everything together," he said. "We were closer than blood. Closer than brothers. He knew I would do anything for him. And he always backed me up. He was always there for me."

"You two are that close?" I asked. "Tell me about what he did for you, how he backed you up."

Carl didn't answer, and his expression became unreadable, a mask of composure. "If you need to talk to me about this any more, I'll have to get a lawyer," he said. "Not because I did anything wrong, but because I don't like your questions."

CHAPTER FIFTEEN

The afternoon sun climbing higher, I took the road that ran west of town. On the way, I thought of Naomi's oldest, Sadie, and how she'd loved working on the hives. Her diary was filled with illustrations of bees flying, collecting pollen, bees that looked like cartoon characters dancing. This time of year, the bees would be huddled together to keep warm. Inside each hive, the queen would be in the center, while the workers and drones gathered around, their bodies shivering to generate energy.

As I pulled in, I saw Naomi working on the first hive. She did this every winter, relocating the aging wooden crates with drawers her grandfather had made decades ago, ones that had come down through her family. In the summers, the colonies flourished in the shade, but with winter coming, the bees needed full afternoon sun and shelter from the winds. The land surrounding the bee shack was winter brown, the mountains in the background, and I felt a chill when I climbed out of the SUV. Naomi looked up as I approached, glowering at me. I wasn't a welcome sight.

"We still need to talk," I said. "I have questions."

"Then you'll have to help," she answered. "I have eighteen hives to move. We're expecting a freeze tonight."

I didn't take long to agree. Pitching in seemed like a good idea; it might put Naomi at ease. "Okay," I said. "It'll be like old times, Mother Naomi, like it was when I helped you as a girl. Let's get to it."

We carefully eased the first hive onto the hand truck, and its aging joints groaned as we slipped it onto the platform. I bent down and wrapped the orange strap around it, anchoring it in place, and then we gently tilted the hive ever so slightly, hoping not to disturb the colony.

We took our time, inching the hive forward to a warmer spot, one where the sun beat down on it. Once we had the hive in place, we jiggled it softly to dislodge it from the hand truck, and then I helped Naomi straighten it so that the hive sat facing west.

That done, we returned for the next hive. As we worked, Naomi gave me a once-over. "You've been out digging again," she said. "I noticed it at the ranch, the mud on your clothes."

"Yes, well…" I started, feeling vaguely uneasy, wondering why I needed to defend myself, but old habits die harder than I'd like. I was going on seven when my father married Naomi, and she was seventeen, just barely of age. Not much older than my oldest sister, my new mother had a hard time convincing some of us that she was in charge, and she and I butted heads often, especially the summer I'd wanted a horse. I stirred up my brothers and sisters, insisting that we could care for one. My father appeared to warm to the idea at first, but Mother Naomi objected. As hard as I tried, she convinced him to see it her way.

As if she could read my thoughts, she said, "Clara, you have too much of your father in you. Your stubbornness and determination are sometimes to a fault."

I gave her a questioning glance. "A lot of folks consider those good traits."

"Yes, in moderation," she said. "But knowing you? You'll let your life pass by while you're looking for that girl's bones. You may never find her, but you'll never give up. Even as a girl, you couldn't abandon any battle, even long after it was clear that the war was lost."

I let it go. I hadn't come to talk about old times. "Mother Naomi, I need to know what you saw when you arrived at the ranch," I said. "While I help, you need to walk me through it, slowly, including all the details."

"But I already told you—" Naomi began to protest. I shook my head to stop her.

"You will tell me everything," I insisted. "Four people are dead. Jacob is severely injured. You owe them that, Mother Naomi. Don't you?"

Naomi paused and then nodded.

For the next hour, Naomi talked, beginning with her encounter with Laurel and Jacob at services the day before and the promise to come first thing, early, and deliver the breast pump. From there, she described the chaos at the double-wide, the children refusing to cooperate, getting a late start, and what she saw as she pulled onto the MRJ driveway: the patch of white on the ground that hid so much tragedy. She shivered when she recounted seeing little Benjamin's still legs extending from beneath the cloth. Inside the house, Jacob struggled for every breath. Naomi called 911 and then heard the baby.

As her account ended, Naomi and I moved the last hive in place, forming three rows of six. I thought of Jacob and wondered about Naomi's interest in the man. She still had his blood on the front of her skirt, and I sensed that Naomi saw it as a badge of honor. The afternoon unfolded in the late fall air, the scent of dust blowing in the fields, and a chill that carried with it the promise of that night's expected freeze.

"You were supposed to be there earlier?" I verified.

"Yes, as I said," Naomi answered, an eyebrow arched in irritation. "I promised them that I would be at the ranch first thing, so I was maybe half an hour or so later than they expected me."

I paused and considered that. "Why didn't you go into Laurel's room to check on her?"

"Why would I?" Naomi responded, her voice shrill. "I only went upstairs because the baby cried. The nursery door was open, and I went in and found him, brought him downstairs to wait for the ambulance."

"Why didn't you stay on the phone with the emergency dispatcher? You shouldn't have hung up, Mother Naomi. What if—" I challenged.

"I am one of your mothers, Clara." Naomi's posture stiffened. "I am not to be questioned like a—"

"Like a witness?" I gave her a stern glare. "Mother Naomi, at this moment, right now, you are exactly that, a witness."

Naomi pressed her lips tight and then asked, "What else would you have me tell you, before you leave me? I have work to do."

The hives all relocated, I said, "Let's get the wraps."

Naomi grimaced but didn't object, and we walked together to the shed. There, folded and piled on a wooden shelf against a back wall, were the eighteen quilts made from old blankets that Naomi used to insulate the hives. We each gathered armfuls and carried them back outside. I helped Naomi bundle the first around a hive and strap it in place with two thick belts. So much about all this felt familiar, comforting.

"I remember when I did this with you as a girl," I said. "You and me, and Sadie. It was always Sadie who would help us. She was so young then, still in elementary school." There were good times in Alber, I thought. There were good memories as well as the bad. That was something I had to work harder to remember.

"Sadie loved the hives," Naomi said, and I heard anger in each word. "Sadie would have inherited them, if she'd lived. She would be here with me, today. If that monster hadn't…"

Naomi's words trailed off into an abyss of sadness, and I thought of Sadie's grave, the loneliness of the town cemetery. Soon Laurel and Anna, Benjamin and Sybille would be buried there. I'd made Sadie's killer pay for his crimes. He'd been held accountable. *I have to do the same for the Johanssons,* I thought. *I made Jeremy a promise.*

The questioning continued until I felt certain I understood the events as they'd unfolded at the ranch that morning. Then I turned the conversation around to her encounter with Jacob's parents. "Mother Naomi, why did you go to the hospital?"

Naomi paused, and when I looked back at her, I saw annoyance flicker across her eyes. Her voice defiant, she said: "Why would I not? After all, I was the one who found Jacob. I was interested in how he fared. I went to check on his condition."

"Fair enough," I said, although something about the situation still needled at me. "But what seems odd is that you didn't tell me something that Reba mentioned."

"And that was?" Naomi asked, her manner peeved.

"That at some point on Saturday you saw Laurel with Myles Thompkins," I said.

Pursing her lips, Naomi appeared even more displeased. "I shouldn't have told Jacob's parents that. They, not so much Michael but Reba, seemed upset by it."

"Tell me what you saw," I ordered, as she finished buckling a belt around one of the hives. Naomi scrunched her lips tighter, visibly annoyed. "The sooner you talk, the sooner I leave."

Naomi remained silent.

"Help me find out who murdered them," I insisted. Her scowl hadn't faded. "Don't you want to help me hold the person responsible?"

Naomi took a deep breath. "Yes. Of course," she said, but her words dripped with reluctance. "But to gossip, to spread rumor about the dead, is to violate their memory. The prophet says that to do so is a sin against—"

"Tell me," I ordered again.

Naomi bent over, picked up another quilt and wrapped it around the next hive in the line. I wasn't sure what to expect, but then she began talking. As she explained it, she'd been driving on the highway with her three youngest children, taking them to visit her parents on their spread in a neighboring town, when two-year-old Kyle shouted that he needed to pee.

"We're potty-training," Naomi explained. "He's still at the point where it's always an emergency."

I nodded. "Then what happened?"

"We were near the narrow road that leads to the river, where the young people go when they sneak out to be together," Naomi said.

I didn't need specifics. I knew the spot well. When I was a teenager, that was where Max and I shared our first kiss, one disturbed by my father storming toward us. It was a kiss that had changed both our lives. Naomi knew that, of course, so she didn't offer to give any more information on its location.

"Did you stop?" I asked.

"Yes," Naomi answered. "I pulled onto that dirt road and parked. When I did, I saw a red pickup and a silver van a short distance away and two people: a man, and a woman holding a baby. I didn't recognize them at first, but then I did, and it was Myles Thompkins and Laurel holding Jeremy."

"What were they doing?" I asked.

Again, Naomi seemed loath to answer. She finished fastening the final belt on the hive, then gave it a tug to be sure it would hold secure when the winter winds swept down from the mountains. She went to get another quilt, and I put my hand on it, held it and looked into her eyes, stopping her. She breathed in a long sigh, then said, "Myles and Laurel were talking. I couldn't hear what was said, but Laurel appeared upset. She kept backing away from him, and he kept walking toward her. Then Laurel turned and saw me."

"What did she do?"

"I had Kyle at one of the trees, allowing him to do what we'd stopped for," Naomi said. "At first Laurel looked surprised to see me and upset that we were there, but then she smiled and waved as if nothing were wrong. She said something to Myles, and then rushed to the van. I was putting Kyle back into his car seat when she sped by."

"Did she stop and talk to you?"

"No," Naomi said, and her lips formed the slightest knowing smile. "Laurel must have been in an incredible hurry, because she hadn't taken the time to strap the baby into his seat. She held Jeremy up to her chest with her right hand and steered the van with her left."

We stood motionless for a few moments, neither of us picking up the next quilt or the belts to anchor it in place. I pictured that afternoon, Laurel hurrying away, upset, after she'd been seen with Myles Thompkins. What were they discussing? What were they hiding?

"And when was this?"

"Saturday, early afternoon," Naomi said. "Two days ago."

"Anything else?" I asked. Naomi had a petulant look and didn't answer. "Mother Naomi, do you know anything else?"

"No, nothing." Naomi snipped off each word. "Laurel drove away. I never saw her again."

CHAPTER SIXTEEN

"Do you know Myles Thompkins?" I asked Max.

"Why?" His voice on speaker filled the Suburban as I took the main road into town. Far in the distance, on the mountainside, long lines were etched where trees had been removed. A consortium of investors was in the process of building a ski lodge and constructing runs. Although it would be another year before they opened, the town was already gearing up. In the past few months, a hamburger joint had begun construction on the highway and a ski shop had leased an old storefront on Main Street. When I grew up in Alber, strangers were kept out. So much had changed. Moving vans had become common sights, as families from Salt Lake and St. George, lured by foreclosures, bought abandoned homes at rock-bottom prices. Investors picked up the biggest of the houses to turn into B&Bs that would cater to winter skiers and summer hikers.

At the farthest east section of the mountains, Samuel's Peak jutted up, where I'd been told since childhood that the spirits of our ancestors lived and watched over our community. Elijah's People revered that precipice and counted on it to protect us. I wondered if the faithful now questioned that legend, since the ancestors on the mountaintop remained quiet when the feds moved in and made arrests.

"How does Myles enter into the Johansson murders?" Max asked. "Did someone mention him?"

"Two days ago, Saturday afternoon, Naomi saw Myles and Laurel together near the river road," I explained. "It appears that Myles may have been one of the last to talk to Laurel before the murders. And Reba Johansson believes he may have been angry enough to kill Laurel and the family. I'll explain why when we get together."

"Well, I know of him," Max said, "but not a lot about him. I'd recognize him on the street, but we've never talked. Myles is a recluse. He lives in a cabin west of town."

"Can you find his place?" I asked. "We need to interview him."

Max said he could, and I suggested that he meet me at Heaven's Mercy, the shelter where I rented my room. I wanted to shower, throw on a uniform, and to talk to Hannah. With a parade of women and children coming and going, moving in and out of the shelter, Hannah often heard the town gossip.

I parked near the front gate and as I walked up saw a man high on a ladder around the side of the house. The rambling mansion had once been the home of the town prophet, Emil Barstow, his dozens of wives and their more than a hundred children. Wondering what the guy on the ladder was up to, I took a short segue and found Hannah watching him. It turned out that she'd hired a painter to cover up the command old man Barstow had bricked in white on the mansion's side: OBEY AND BE REDEEMED.

"Finally getting rid of that?" I asked. "About time."

The painter had already covered the first two words with a red that matched the brick and was working on the 'E' in 'BE.'

Hannah turned toward me, grinning. "I should have done this as soon as the foundation bought the place," she said. "I didn't realize how freeing it would be to have old man Barstow wiped off the face of this building."

"Glad to see it go, but if you're not needed here, do you have time to talk?" I asked. "I have some questions."

"About the Johanssons? I heard what happened out at the bison ranch." At the mention of the murders, Hannah appeared visibly shaken. She shook her head, took a long breath as if to steady herself, and frowned. "Clara, the whole town is talking about it. How is this possible? It's horrible. Just horrible."

"Yes, it is. I'm not surprised you heard. It seems that the folks in Alber talk about everything," I mused. "You didn't tell me they were watching me dig."

Hannah sighed. "I didn't think you'd have to be told. What made you think your activities wouldn't be noticed?"

I thought about that and shrugged. "You're right. I should have known better," I said. "Well, Max is on his way. We have work to do. First, I have to get these muddy clothes off, but walk me inside so we can talk."

We headed in the door, just as a group of Hannah's residents in their long dresses and bulky sweaters walked out. Like me, Hannah had on jeans and a T-shirt, topped by an oversize wool jacket. Unlike the women with their long tresses in elaborate twists and knots, Hannah's graying blond hair was cut to within an inch of her head and she had it spiked straight up.

"Have you heard any speculation about who killed the Johanssons?" I whispered as the others ambled by.

"Oh, Clara, it's…" Again, Hannah shook her head, harder, as if trying to wipe away terrible images. "It's all so dreadful. But no. I haven't heard anything. Which is odd. Usually rumors float, but not this time. At least, not yet. I don't know of anyone who had a grudge against any of them."

"What about Jacob's friend, Carl? Do you know him?" I asked.

"Not well. Just to see around town." She hesitated, as if considering what to say next. "I didn't particularly care for him though, and I think others felt the same way."

"What was it about Carl?"

"Nothing I can put my finger on," she said. "He's just always made me uneasy. I used to see him sometimes, watching women out on the street. He's always seemed odd."

"What about the women?" I asked.

"Anna and Laurel?" I nodded, and she continued. "Anna's like the men—she just got here a year or so ago, and I don't know much about her. I don't know her people or anything that happened before she arrived. But she was friendly, always a smile on her face. I had the impression that she was dedicated to her family. You could tell when you saw her with Benjamin and Sybille that she loved those little ones."

"And Laurel?"

Hannah's eyes teared up, her emotions heavy. "Laurel I watched grow up. She was a responsible kid, one who seemed more worried about others than herself. Thoughtful in lots of ways. As a teenager, she used to shop off and on for some of the shut-ins in town, just to help out. I don't know of anyone who didn't like her."

We were nearly to the stairway, and I was about to leave Hannah to head to my room when I asked, "What about Myles Thompkins?"

Hannah stopped and turned to me. "Who told you about Myles and Laurel? I mean, people knew, sure, but folks didn't talk about it. Not after she married Jacob. Did someone bring up Myles?"

"Didn't talk about what?" I asked.

"That they were in love," Hannah said. "That they'd always been in love."

We stood huddled together, whispering so the women and children filtering past us wouldn't hear. Hannah told me how everyone in town had always assumed that one day Laurel and Myles would be together. A little more than a year ago, Myles had asked the prophet for Laurel's hand, but a week later Jacob's father sent a message to the prophet, saying Jacob wanted her as his second wife. "The Johanssons have more money and influence, so it's not surprising that Laurel was given to Jacob. She took it hard. I heard that the wedding had to be delayed because she refused to eat and locked herself in her room."

Listening to Hannah, I realized that Laurel's story reminded me of my own past.

I was sixteen when Max was run out of town. I grieved for him, waited for him to return. When he didn't, I came up with a plan. One more year, and I'd finish high school. Going away to college was unheard of for an Alber girl, but I had a shot at a scholarship. If I convinced Mother and Father, I would be able to be on my own, without anyone watching over me. Once that happened, I decided that I would look for Max, find him and marry him. By the time Mother and Father knew, it would be too late.

Of course, that didn't happen. Instead, halfway through my senior year, Father and Mother ordered me into his study for what they said would be "a little talk." When I walked out of that room, my world had changed forever.

Mullins and his wife had done the same to Laurel, and now she was dead. I wondered if my lead detective felt at all responsible for his daughter's demise. I wondered if my own father had any doubts after I fled Alber in fear for my life. I'd never know, since he'd died before I returned. Did Mother have any regrets?

"What did Myles do after Laurel married?" I asked Hannah.

Her brow furrowed, and Hannah appeared troubled by what had happened to the two young lovers. "In the year since Laurel and Jacob married, Myles has become a shadow of the young man he once was. He lives near the mountain, alone, and he comes into town every few months for an hour or two, just long enough to buy a few supplies. I've heard that he has a small spread where he raises hunting dogs and sells just enough to pay for supplies. They're well-bred, well-trained, and I understand much in demand."

"Myles hasn't married?" I asked.

"No. He hasn't. I'm sure he still mourns for Laurel." Hannah's expression changed and she suddenly looked alarmed. "You don't think he's involved in this, do you? Myles would never... he's not the kind of man to do something violent. And why would Myles—"

"I've gotta go change," I said, dodging the question. "If you hear anything that might help me—"

Hannah gave me a strained smile. "I will, of course, call."

The dirt clung to my ankles and feet. The washcloth foaming, I scrubbed my arms, looking at my lone tattoo, the eagle on my arm. Such proud birds, so beautiful. But like vultures, eagles foraged for carrion. I thought again of the grisly scene at the ranch and the heavy-shouldered scavengers in the tree intent on their feast. I shuddered.

Once dry, I grabbed a uniform and boots from the closet. Dressed, I threw my soiled clothes in the bulging bag holding my laundry. I'd never been good with housework, not when I was married, not when I was a Dallas cop, and that hadn't changed when I moved back to Alber. I do little until I have no other choice.

Max was waiting for me in the downstairs parlor in the center of a clutch of women. Single men were rare in this town where girls are raised to be wives and mothers, so I understood why a guy like Max would get a lot of attention. The women asked about his health, and a couple offered to cook him dinners. I chuckled when one asked him if he wanted to have more children. He shot me a panicky look and didn't answer.

"Is your daughter's condition improving?" a woman who appeared to be in her mid-twenties or so inquired. She bounced a small one on her hip. Hannah had introduced the young mother to me when they'd moved in and explained that she'd been the fifth wife of an abusive husband. "Do the doctors think Brooke will ever be able to walk again?"

"Well, she's…" Max stammered, and I knew he felt uncomfortable talking about his daughter's condition. I could have interrupted and rescued him, but I waited. These were questions I'd wanted to ask but hadn't, and I hoped he'd answer. "She's… Brooke is… doing as well as can be expected with the extent of her injuries. We really don't know what the future holds."

The women effused sympathy, and I stepped forward.

"Ladies, the chief and I need to be on our way," Max said, looking relieved as we turned and rushed out the door. I glanced back and saw a few of the women frowning at me.

We drove through Alber in his squad, out to the highway, took a right outside town and set a course toward the mountains. "Thanks for getting me out of that," Max said.

I played dumb. "What are you talking about?"

"The women surrounding me, asking me…" He glanced over, saw me smile and realized that I'd known exactly what he'd meant. Turning his attention back to the road, he chuckled and then asked, "You are coming for dinner tonight, right? I told Brooke you'll be there. She's been excited all week. She spent yesterday evening helping me make the chili."

I took a deep breath, and Max frowned, as if he knew what I was about to say. "I don't know, Max," I said. "I mean, I know I said I'd come, but…"

I noticed his jaw set. He wasn't happy. "Clara, why not?"

"Because…" I started, but then couldn't really find a way to continue.

"Brooke would love it," Max said, his voice weary. "I'd love it. You know that, right?"

"I do, but…"

He glanced at me again, his brow furrowed. "There's no 'but' here. No one stands in our way. Nothing prevents us from being together anymore. Not your father. Not your mother. Not old man Barstow rotting in a prison cell. Clara, there's only one thing in our way: your fears."

I didn't answer. He was right, but I still felt conflicted. Yet I had no good response.

Max glanced over at me and pleaded, "Clara, don't do this to us. I know there's something special between us. There always has been. The other night..." For a moment, silence, then he said, "I know, deep down, you want this as much as I do."

I said nothing, inside my chest a tug of war raging. A tear formed in my eye, and I quickly brushed it away, hoping he wouldn't see.

We drove on, the scenery flowing past, and I changed the subject to a safer one. Max knew what I was doing, gave me a regretful glance but didn't stop me. "This isn't the time to talk about other things. We need to focus on the case," I said. With that, I explained everything I'd heard from Mother Naomi and from Hannah. "It appears that Laurel and Myles were kind of a thing, and they expected to marry. Until the prophet issued other orders."

As it had for me, Myles and Laurel's story apparently brought back memories for Max. Again, he glanced over at me, and I felt the conversation take another turn, from my perspective a dangerous one. "Rather like what happened with us," he said, as he turned onto a road that veered farther west. "Clara, we both know that if the prophet and your parents hadn't interfered, we would have—"

I didn't let him finish. "Alber's past is undoubtedly littered with stories like ours," I said.

"Yes, well..." he muttered.

"Again, let's go back to Laurel and Myles," I suggested. "We have four murders to solve, remember."

Max bristled, but didn't argue. "Okay, but I'm not sure how what you've learned ties into what we saw at the ranch. How it's germane, considering what the killer did to Laurel."

"I don't know that it is," I admitted. "Although the murders did seem to all be about her, so it's reasonable to think that she has some kind of a tie to the killer."

Down a long, winding driveway, a small log cabin came into view, with a barn beside it. "Clara, if Myles loved—maybe still loves—Laurel, how does it make sense that he'd want to first kill her and secondly shame her like that?" Max asked. "If he loved her, why didn't he kill the others and take her?"

"I don't know," I said. "But love doesn't always mean happiness or safety, after all. We've both, I'm sure, worked many cases where love turned to hate, the ardent suitor who murdered the woman who turned him down. A husband who promised love but delivered violence. The wife who murders rather than allow a man to leave. Even parents who murder their own children."

"Yeah, but…" he started, and then stopped.

I stayed quiet for a moment, considering my own past, the violence that spurred me to run from Alber. But then again, that was completely different. In the case of my marriage, love had never been part of the equation.

"But what?" I asked, and I heard the edge to my voice, the anger at memories I tried to keep hidden. "We don't know what they were talking about on Saturday, out there alone on that road. Maybe Laurel and Myles argued. Maybe Myles blamed Laurel for deserting him and with this morning's killings, he took revenge."

Max sighed, and then said, "I guess it really is an old story, isn't it?"

"Unfortunately, it's also a frequent one," I said.

Max looked uncertain. "To me, Carl's still the more likely suspect. Those photos he took of Laurel suggest an obsession."

"Absolutely. Carl's still on the list," I said. "What we need is something to pop up in the lab reports that points to someone, that clears up the confusion, or for Jacob to wake up and tell us what he knows."

"Yeah," Max said. "But somehow I'm wondering if either of those possibilities will come together. When I think of Jacob breathing like he was, all the blood he lost. What are the odds he'll live?"

"It doesn't seem likely." We pulled up to the house and parked the car. "I'll take the front. You cover the back door."

Looking at the lonely setting, Max mused, "Maybe we should have brought backup?"

"We're just here to talk," I said.

Moments later, my hand on my holstered gun, I stood outside Myles Thompkins' front door. From the barn off to the side, a cacophony of barking dogs should have alerted their owner to our arrival, but I waited a few moments for Max to get in place, and then I knocked. No answer. I knocked again. Still no answer. "Mr. Thompkins, Chief of Police Clara Jefferies and Chief Deputy Max Anderson here. We'd like to talk to you. Please open up."

The dogs yapped ever louder. No answer from inside the house. Max walked back around to the front. "I peeked in the windows. I don't think he's home," he said.

"Let's take a look around the outside," I suggested.

Off to the side sat an aging fire-engine-red Ford pickup, no one inside. I put my hand on the hood. It was cold. The cabin wasn't large, but it looked well-built; the timbers had been notched and joined using hand tools. I walked around and peered in the windows. The interior appeared warm, comforting, rustic and inviting. Myles had an old desk in front of an entire wall of shelves crowded with books. A heavy, vibrantly colored wool shawl with fringe covered a table, resembling one I'd bought at a Navajo pawn shop years ago. Myles had mounted a steer's skull over his fireplace.

As Max and I walked toward the barn, the barking got louder. Inside, there were two empty horse stalls on the right, and on the left a large fenced pen filled with all sizes of bloodhounds, the hunting dogs Hannah had mentioned. The pack trailed over to greet Max. He put his hand up to the metal link cage, and they sniffed it. With that, tails began wagging and the barking abated.

"You're right. Myles isn't here." I glanced inside the stalls and noticed evidence that a horse lived inside one of them: a full water trough, an oat bucket, and a pile of drying dung in the corner. "He must be off somewhere on his horse."

"I guess so," Max agreed. "What do you want to do?"

"Nothing for us to do here. Head back to town," I said. "Let's have someone watch the place, to let us know when he returns."

"Sure. I'll put a deputy on it." Max looked at his watch. It was going on five thirty, and the sun dipped ever lower in the sky. Late November, the days grew short.

"No, it's okay," I said. "I'll get Bill Conroy out here for the evening, have them put one of the night officers on later to relieve him. This is an Alber case, after all."

"If you'd rather, that's fine," Max said. "You know, you still haven't told me what you've decided about dinner."

"Well, we have work to do. I don't——" I started.

Max jumped in, not letting me finish. "Clara, we can't do anything until we get lab results and the autopsy in tomorrow. Myles isn't here, and our only other lead is Carl, who isn't talking except through a lawyer, right?"

"All that's true, but I still don't think——"

"Why not? Why wouldn't you come? By now Brooke is waiting for us," Max said, looking not angry but hurt. "If for no other reason than to not disappoint her, why not drop in and have a quick dinner with her, with us? Your father isn't in control now. Remember: it's only us in charge. Why can't we?"

Max gave me a hopeful look.

He was right. Everything he'd said was true. This was my problem, not his; the reluctance, the fear of being pulled in too quickly and too far. "Okay, as long as I leave right after dinner," I said, hoping I didn't sound as conflicted as I felt. "I want to stop back at the hospital to check on Jacob."

"Didn't the doctor say the hospital would notify us if he comes out of it? If Jacob can talk to us?" Max asked, although we both knew the answer.

"Yes, but you know how it is, doctors get busy and they forget." I knew that Max assumed I was simply making an excuse, and I couldn't deny that having a reason to cut dinner short appealed to me. Getting to know eight-year-old Brooke better felt like a big step forward in a relationship I wasn't sure I was ready for. I didn't want to admit it, but part of me worried that I'd never be ready. I had an uneasy relationship with all men, going back to my father. As certain as I felt that I could trust Max, the prospect of attaching myself to another human being, especially a male one, frightened me.

But that wasn't all. There was another reason.

Max was right, and I was probably wasting my time. But while we'd followed all the day's leads, I couldn't get the crime scene out of my head. I kept seeing the bodies of Anna and her sweet children under the bloody sheet, and Laurel on the bed, her face stained with the blood-red lipstick. I had no choice: I had to figure out the puzzle. I'd made Jeremy a promise.

CHAPTER SEVENTEEN

Max dropped me at Heaven's Mercy, and I followed him in the Suburban to his house in Pine City, not far from the sheriff's department offices. The setting sun sent streaks of rose through the sky, and the mountains had a pewter cast that made them shimmer in the diminishing light. The mountain air smelled fresh, and I could feel the increasing chill of the coming frost.

A two-story, white-frame bungalow on a quiet street, Max's house had an oak in the front yard so big I knew without trying that I wouldn't be able to stretch my arms halfway around the trunk. The roof extended over a wide front porch, and the curtains were pinned back. Lamps lit, the inside glowed. A wooden ramp covered one side of the front steps and a short one formed a low bump over the front door's threshold to accommodate Brooke's wheelchair.

"Clara!" she shouted, from her perch on the edge of the porch. "You came!"

I immediately felt guilty for not having wanted to. My reluctance had nothing to do with Brooke, who I'd spent only fleeting moments with but who struck me as a remarkable young girl. I took in a deep breath and smiled. "Hmm. I smell garlic and tomatoes. Chili, I hear!"

"Dad's a super-good cook." Her strawberry blond hair cascading over her shoulders, Brook giggled, and Max bent down and wrapped his arms around her, lingering ever so slightly. When he let go, he turned Brooke's wheelchair and pushed her inside.

"And what did you do today?" he asked her.

Brooke screwed up her nose and grinned at him. "Well, it was a pretty cool day."

"What was so cool about it?" I asked. The girl had the most inquisitive hazel eyes, fringed in thick lashes.

"After school, Aunt Alice took me to the park and put me on a swing," she said. "The physical therapist suggested it. I couldn't pump with my legs, but I swung my body weight and pulled with my arms, and Aunt Alice helped, and I got high. Really high. So high that Aunt Alice got scared." Brooke's grin grew wider, and she mimicked her aunt. "'Brooke, you'll give me a heart attack,' she shouted. And I think I almost did. Her face was nearly purple."

Teasing, Max put his hands on his hips and pretended to be upset. "You laugh about nearly sending your aunt into cardiac arrest?"

"It was super-fun," Brooke said. "She said we can do it again tomorrow. And maybe the day after, too. I'm gonna try to convince her."

I chuckled. Max shrugged and said, "Looks like I'm outnumbered."

We ate our dinner at the kitchen table. The chili was a heavy, spicy mixture served with bread to cut the burn. Max offered to open a bottle of wine, but I reminded him that I had work to do before the day ended. Watching Brooke, I thought about my four years as an elementary school teacher in Alber, the children I'd known. Since I'd returned, I'd run into a few off and on, now all teenagers. Some turned away, mindful that as an apostate I was to be spurned. But once in a while, one stopped to talk, and when that happened, I remembered the softness of young hands in mine, the joy of seeing an idea take hold, a first word read, an addition problem solved. Throughout those terrible years, ones when I constantly feared for my life, the children I taught sustained me. I thought about how my world had changed and how my work had become so much darker.

Yet I no longer felt owned, like a possession.

While we ate, Brooke chatted happily, describing her paperweight collection. "My mom had it," she said. "And now it's mine. And sometimes Dad and me go to rummage sales and antique stores and find more."

"I'd love to see it," I said.

After dinner, Max insisted he didn't need help with the dishes, and Brooke and I went to her room. The paperweights were displayed on shelves lining one wall, dozens of them: heavy glass with flowers, ships, abstract designs and figures inside. The only one on the ground floor, the room must have been intended to be the main bedroom. Max undoubtedly gave it to Brooke to make it easier with her chair. A charming blue-lavender, it smelled of fresh paint. When I said I liked the color, Brooke explained, "I copied it from the flowers in the book."

"What book?" I asked, and she dug around in her nightstand drawer and pulled out the volume of Jane Austen's *Sense and Sensibility* I'd given her a few months earlier, the first time we met. She opened it and pointed at the label with the printed name of the girl who'd once owned it, surrounded by forget-me-nots. The paint in the room matched the flowers perfectly.

"Remember how Dad said these were my mom's favorite?" Brooke asked.

"I do remember," I said. I looked around the room at the framed pictures of unicorns and princesses, and I wished Max's late wife, Miriam, had been able to see it, to tuck her daughter into bed each night. "I bet your mom would love that you painted your room this beautiful color."

"I think so, too," she said.

Brooke wheeling beside me, Max was drying the chili pot when we reached the kitchen. "I need to go. I have that stop at the hospital to make," I said.

Although Max looked disappointed, he didn't argue, just dried his hands on the towel and turned to Brooke. "I'll escort Clara out."

I hugged Brooke goodnight, and as we walked out, she wheeled over to sit in front of the television. Remote in hand, she began surfing through the stations. "Homework?" Max asked.

"Just a little," she answered.

"Better get to it," he warned. "Bedtime in an hour."

Max walked me to my vehicle, both of us hidden in the shadows. "I think she likes you," he said.

"You're trying too hard," I countered, and he shrugged.

"I'm glad you came. It meant a lot to… both of us," he said.

"I enjoyed it," I admitted. "Brooke's a great kid."

"Yeah, I think so, too," he said. For a moment, we were quiet, and then Max said, "I'll put in a call to Doc Wiley and the lab first thing in the morning. Anything I can do tonight, for the case?"

There was something I'd been considering: "Max, do you think there are records in the secret files that might help?" While working my first case in Alber, I'd found a locked room at the station filled with file cabinets bulging with paperwork. The cases went back decades, and had everything from assaults, missing persons and domestic violence, to thefts and allegations of harassment. It appeared none of them had ever been investigated or cleared—all swept under the carpet by my predecessor to protect prominent members of the sect. I'd been working my way through them gradually, organizing and figuring out which ones to pursue. I didn't remember seeing anything on Myles, Carl, or anyone involved, but I wasn't halfway through them yet, and I worried that I might have missed something.

"Maybe," Max said. "Why don't you ask a couple of the nightshift guys to sift through and double-check?"

"Sure," I said. "Good idea."

"Back to what I can do," Max said. "Brooke will be in bed soon, and I'll have time."

"You can look up both Carl and Myles on NCIC, see what the feds have on file about them, any convictions or lawsuits," I suggested. "I'll give you a call when I leave the hospital to see what you've got and fill you in on Jacob's condition."

"Okay. I'll also put some feelers out in Mexico, email a guy I know with the sect down there, see what I can find out about Carl and Jacob," Max said.

"Good idea." My phone buzzed, and I slipped it out of my pocket. A text.

"Something on the case?" Max asked.

"My friend in Dallas says that the shoe print in the kitchen came from a pair of boots made by the Wilderness Shoe Company. It's a pair called the Steel Ranger." I held the phone up so Max could see the photo. The boots were high-tops with laces, thick stitching across the toe.

"That should make it easier to track," Max said. "They can't sell too many of those around here. I'll email the DA's office and ask them to send a subpoena to Wilderness Shoe ordering them to turn over any information on anyone who has purchased those boots who lives in this part of Utah, local stores who stock them too."

"They might have to work on that. It may take a while," I groused. "It seems like corporate requests always take days or weeks, not hours."

"Clara, it's a start," Max said. "We'll find the killer. Wait and see."

"Sure." With that, I turned to open the door.

"Clara, I…" Max said, and then stopped talking.

I turned back toward him, and he brushed his hand across my cheek.

I hesitated, but Max moved slowly forward, and our lips met. His were warm and soft, the kiss both exciting and comforting. I breathed him in and felt my body respond. I drew closer, and he wrapped me in his arms. For a few brief moments, I had a place where I truly belonged.

I felt wanted.

Then the war inside me started anew, my mind warning me to be careful, not to open myself up to being hurt, while every instinct I had urged me to fold myself into Max and to hold on to him forever. Instead, I pulled away.

On the drive to the hospital, I mulled over that kiss, our first in nineteen years. Last time I'd been a teenage girl who knew what she wanted: him. This time I felt conflicted, confused, and worried. I thought about how disappointed Max looked when I turned to leave. At thirty-five, my life was unfolding and the road ahead looked lonely. What was wrong with me that I couldn't let myself be happy? Why couldn't I reach out to Max as he was reaching out to me? Somewhere deep inside me, my past had drawn a line, one that I didn't know how to cross. Formed of my pain, of my fears, it separated me from any hope of love.

I could still feel the warmth of Max's lips on mine when I walked into the ICU and tracked over to Jacob's room. The drapes on the corridor window were pulled back, and the lights inside glared. I'd thought that perhaps I'd see Jacob's parents waiting in the hallway, but Michael and Reba weren't there. I assumed they were inside Jacob's room, but when I looked in, I saw a woman standing on the far side of the bed. It took me a moment to realize that it was Naomi.

The scene unfolding inside the ICU room looked intimate, as if something very personal were transpiring. I stood and watched as Naomi stared down affectionately at Jacob. His face was turned toward her. I couldn't be sure from where I stood, but I had the impression that he might be awake. Watching from outside the window, I felt like an interloper.

Then Naomi looked up and saw me. She frowned, and her lips moved. I couldn't hear her, but I thought she whispered, "Clara's here."

Thinking she was alerting Jacob to my arrival, I gave her a slight wave and entered the room. As I did, Jacob's head rolled lazily back to the center of the pillow. "Is he awake?" I said, but he didn't respond. His eyes were closed, his expression blank, and the only sounds were the beeping machines and his harsh breaths pulling through the slice in his throat.

"No, no," Naomi said. "Why would you think that? He's not conscious."

"But you were just talking to him," I said. "I saw you. You told him I was here."

Naomi smiled at me, just a bit condescending. "Oh, Clara, no. I was talking, but he's not awake. They say you should talk to those who are unconscious, to let them know that you are with them. I was telling him that I hoped he will wake soon, and that I pray for him."

I walked over and stood beside Naomi. "So, he hasn't come to?"

"No," she said. "There's been no sign of that."

"Why are you here again?" I asked.

"I'm covering for his parents while they have a little dinner and freshen up. Then I'll go home."

"Did they say if he woke up at any other point today?" I asked.

"If he did, they didn't mention it, and as I said, he hasn't shown any inclination toward waking while I've been here."

I said nothing more, just stared at Naomi and thought about how something didn't seem right. I had such an odd feeling, the sense that something was very wrong. I looked into the eyes of a woman who'd been one of my mothers since I was a young girl, a woman I grew up loving, part of my family, and I didn't believe her. But why would she lie?

On my way out, I stopped at the nurses' station. The woman on duty had only come on half an hour earlier, but she checked the file and said no one noted that Jacob had shown any signs of regaining consciousness. "Would you be able to tell from the monitors you have on him if he's woken up at any point?" I asked.

"No, they're just tracking his blood pressure, oxygen, and heart rate," she said. "He's not hooked up to anything that monitors brainwave activity."

"And you didn't see anything happening in the room, like Jacob interacting with Naomi Jefferies or his parents, that would suggest he'd come out of the coma?" I asked.

The woman looked frustrated, as if my questions were an annoyance. "No. I haven't seen anything unusual in that room at all. No one has told me that he's woken up." She pulled out a file and looked over at me. "Now if you'll excuse me, I have work to do."

"I would have sworn that Naomi was talking to him. And she was whispering, which seemed strange. Don't you think that's odd?" I told Max on the phone. I was driving back to Alber for the night from the hospital in Pine City. It had been a long day; I was tired and disappointed. I wanted to keep working the case, but I couldn't think of anything to be done until the morning, and maybe nothing until the reports came in. We needed more information.

I guessed Max must have been considering what I'd told him, because for a few moments he said nothing. Then he said, "We both want Jacob to wake up. Maybe you just saw what you wanted to see, Clara. We do that sometimes. When you thought you saw Naomi talking to him, you assumed that your wish had come true."

"I don't…" I started, but then I didn't go any further. Max had to be right. Naomi had no reason to hide anything from me. Why would she? "Well, maybe. I guess that could be. I don't read lips or anything. It was just what I thought I saw."

"Looks can be deceiving," Max said. "I don't know of any reason Naomi wouldn't tell you the truth. Maybe what's going on here is that you're being influenced by your trust issues with your family, your strained relationships with your mothers?"

That hit a nerve. Maybe Max was right. Rather than answer, I changed the subject and asked, "Anything interesting pop up on NCIC?"

"Just a couple of things," Max said. "There's a little more info on Carl's stint in prison. Pretty much like he described it, a barroom altercation. But he really went off on the guy, nearly killed him. They supposedly put him through anger management group sessions in prison, but you know what those are like."

"In Texas prisons, it was a group of inmates sitting around complaining about how they got a raw deal," I said. "I'm assuming the same here?"

"Pretty much," he said. "It's one of those things you hope works but doesn't seem to very often."

"What about your contact in Mexico?"

"I sent the email but haven't heard back yet," he answered. "Probably won't until the morning. I don't have a working phone number for the guy. If he doesn't get in touch, I'll reach out to the local cops down there and ask them for any information they can rustle up."

"What about Myles, his past?" I asked.

"Nothing," he answered. "The guy's invisible. No arrests, no problems. The only thing I noticed was that he hasn't renewed his registration for the pickup and it expires in a few days."

"That's odd."

"What is?" Max asked.

"Well, admittedly we just peeked in the windows, but it looked like Myles has his cabin and the barn organized, so well that the entire place could be a model home," I said. "He doesn't seem like the kind of guy who'd wait until the last minute to get his registration renewed."

"Hmm." Max got quiet. Thinking, I guessed. "Well, no, he doesn't."

"I'm going to drive out to Myles's place, check in with Conroy," I said. "I want to take another look around."

"I'll get Alice here for Brooke and meet you there," Max offered.

"Not necessary. Stay home and enjoy your evening with her," I said.

Then I brought up something that had occurred to me as we talked. "Max, I've been assuming that Jeremy wasn't murdered like the rest of the family because he was too young to be a threat to the killer, unable to tell what happened," I said. "But what if the killer didn't know Jeremy was there? What if he knows now, and the baby is in danger?"

Max thought about that for a moment. "I guess it's possible," Max said. "Tell you what, just to be careful, I'll make a few calls, find out who has the baby, and we'll put surveillance on the house, keep watch."

"No, I'll put one of my men on that, too. This is our case, remember," I said. "How worried do you think we have to be?"

"Not sure," Max said. "We still have no idea why the others were murdered."

CHAPTER EIGHTEEN

Against the night sky, the mountains looked like deep waves of shadow. It was going on eight thirty as I approached Myles Thompkins' place, and I started thinking that Conroy had put in a long, hard day. Maybe I was asking too much of the kid. I called dispatch. "Conroy's still out at the Thompkins place, right?"

"Yup," the night dispatcher said. "You want me to bump him on the radio for you?"

"No, that's okay," I said. "You have someone relieving him soon?"

"Regular time, Chief. Within the hour."

"That's fine," I said. "I'm on my way out there, just to look around a bit. I'll let him leave, and I'll stand watch until the night shift arrives."

"Got it," she said.

The road to the cabin wound through the woods, and I worried about wolves, coyotes, bears, other animals barreling out in front of me from the darkness. I came upon a car ahead, a squad, and I pulled to the shoulder and parked behind it. "Conroy!" I shouted. "You there? It's the chief."

No answer.

Something felt off. I took my Colt out of my holster and kept walking toward the squad. I shined my flashlight inside. No sign of Conroy. The door was unlocked. I stuck my head in and grabbed the mic. The dispatcher answered. "Conroy's car is here, but I don't see him. Have you heard from him?"

"No. Nothing. Should I send someone out there quick, or wait on his replacement?"

I hesitated, unsure. "Yes. Let's do it. A backup squad. You know where we are?"

"I'll trace it on Conroy's GPS and give them the location."

"Thanks," I said. "I'm going to look around, try to find him."

"Stay safe," she said.

I closed the squad's door and shined my flashlight into the woods, skimmed between the trees, seeing nothing out of place at first, but then something moved. In the distance, in the shadows, something paced. I stayed half-hidden behind the car, scanning between the tree trunks. I had my Colt in my right hand, braced on the top of the car, ready. I watched. Nothing. No one. Something flickered through the trees. I waited, trigger finger ready, and then it emerged from behind a stand of trees, my flashlight lighting up a dark eye.

"A deer," I whispered. "Spooked by a deer."

The animal stared at me, turned and ran. My thoughts returned to my young officer. *Where was Conroy?*

I left the road and walked down the winding driveway. The cabin lay a hundred feet or so ahead. I saw nothing unusual as I stepped onto the gravel, my boots making a grinding sound as I picked my way forward, my flashlight leading the way, my Colt ready.

The cabin's front door was open, lights beaming from inside. I continued on, careful, watching, moving forward knowing that someone could come at me out of the darkness at any moment, from any direction. I heard the dogs barking, and I saw a horse tied up to a railing in front of the house. Then, off to the side, two men stood close together, talking, one of them dangling a flashlight at his side, throwing a splash of light onto the ground.

I walked faster, and as I approached, the man with the flashlight aimed the beam at me. Nearly blinded, I had my finger hovering over the trigger. I was ready. "Police Chief Clara Jefferies here. Who's there?" I shouted. "Identify yourselves."

"Chief, it's Conroy," he said. "What're you doing here?"

"You okay, Conroy?" I asked.

"Yeah, sorry. Just here talking to someone."

"No problem, but next time let dispatch know you're getting out of the car," I said, slipping my gun back in the holster. "Who are you talking to? Is that Myles Thompkins?"

"No, one of his neighbors," Conroy said. He'd aimed the flashlight at the ground again. There was enough lamplight glowing from inside the house so that as I got closer, I could see Conroy in his uniform. The guy beside him I didn't recognize.

"What's going on?" I asked.

Conroy introduced me to a short, stout guy with dark brown sideburns who wore a silver belt buckle the size of a saucer on his jeans. His name was Scotty and he lived about half a mile down the road. "What are you doing here?" I asked.

Scotty frowned. "I was just asking the officer that. What the heck are you two doing here?"

"We're looking for Myles Thompkins. We need to talk to him," I motioned at the front door. "He's home, inside?"

"Nope. I opened the door," Scotty said. "I rode over to check on things for him, feed and water the dogs."

"He left you in charge?" I asked, and Scotty nodded, said that Myles often asked him to watch over the place while he was gone. "Where is Myles, and when do you expect him back?"

"Didn't say when he'd be coming home, but he texted me late, really late last night and said he was going to be gone for a while. He's hunting up in the mountains," Scotty said. The guy looked like he'd been smoking a little weed. His eyes were just a little off, and I could smell it on him. "What do you want to talk to him about?"

"A case we hope he might have some information on," I said. "Nothing we can really discuss at this point."

"It doesn't have anything to do with those killings this morning, does it?" the man asked. Conroy gave me a questioning glance.

"You've heard about those?" I said. "What did you hear?"

"That somebody murdered the family that lives on the bison farm," Scotty said. "Murdered all of them, except the dad's bad off in the hospital and the baby's okay."

"You heard that from whom?" I asked.

"Folks at the hardware store in town," he said. "Everybody was talking about it. I thought it was particularly sad 'cause I've seen that lady, Laurel, off and on. Pretty lady."

"Where?" I asked.

"When I was fishing in the river, near the place where the kids go to spoon," he said. "You know that place?"

"Yes, I know it." I thought about how as a teenager I believed that Max and I were safe there, that no adults knew about it. Teenagers obviously still thought the same thing. How many generations of young people had? No wonder my father knew where to look for me. "Go on," I urged.

"Well, I'd see her there. She sat on the big rock on the riverbank. Sometimes she'd be reading. Once I heard her singing, some old song I don't remember now. Singing, all to herself."

"Did you ever see her here at the house with Myles?" I asked.

"Nah," he said. "Never did. But I know they were friends, 'cause once when I saw her at the river, he was there, too, sitting next to her, talking."

"When was that?" I asked.

"Months back," Scotty said. "I can't say how long ago."

I considered how much I didn't know about Laurel Johansson's life, and how even the smallest details could make a difference. We'd searched around Myles's land earlier but hadn't been able to get into the cabin. I wondered what could be inside that might answer some of those questions.

"Scotty, since Myles left you in charge, I would like to ask for your help," I said. "This is a serious matter, multiple murder victims, and we need your assistance with the case."

"What d'ya want?" he asked. "I can't let you do anything with the dogs. Myles is really particular about those animals. It's his livelihood."

"No, nothing with the dogs." I thought about how to phrase this. I needed Scotty to agree to a search. "As the person Myles put in charge of his property, you have the legal authority to allow us to enter the cabin. I'd just like to see if anything in there might help us. It could be that Myles left a map or a note showing where he's gone. People do that sometimes when they go off alone. I need to find him. I'm hoping he has information that might help us solve the murder case."

Scotty sucked in a healthy dose of oxygen and thought it through. "Why would you think Myles might be able to help you?"

"Because he knew Laurel. As you said, they were friends. We need to find Myles as quickly as possible, Scotty," I said.

The man looked unsure, and Conroy moved forward and said, "You know, Scotty, I'm thinking Myles will want us to find him. He'll want to know what happened to his friend."

Scotty chewed on that for a few moments and then nodded. "I think you're right. I could tell he had a lot of feelings for that woman. I think he'd want to know what happened to her and to help if he could."

"So, it's okay if I go inside?" I asked. "I have your permission to go into the cabin and look for anything that may be connected to the case or that could help us find Myles?"

"Sure," he said. "I know Myles. He won't have anything to hide."

"Why don't you two stay here? We don't need all of us inside," I said to Conroy. While I would have liked his help, I wanted him to distract Scotty so he didn't change his mind.

The men agreed, and I left them and headed toward the house. Once inside, I clicked off my flashlight, since Scotty had the lamps on. I scanned the well-worn desk, Myles's collection of books on the wall, a pipe in an ashtray on an end table near an overstuffed chair. I walked through the kitchen and everything shined. Nothing looked new, but it all appeared well cared for. In his bedroom, I found a photo of Laurel, her high school graduation picture I guessed, in a silver frame beside the bed. Her hair in a topknot, her eyes glistening, she looked happy and excited about the future. I snapped the photo with my cell, and my chest filled with anger when I thought of her defaced body on the bed at the ranch.

It was then that I spotted a pair of dark brown high-top boots neatly placed just outside the closet door. I stooped down and picked the left one up, turned it over. Dirty but nothing remarkable. I picked up the right one and did the same. This time I saw something on the sole near the toe, something that had dried brown and looked like it might be blood. I took out my phone and clicked through the photos I'd taken at the crime scene until I found the ones in the kitchen. I enlarged the one of the bloody print on the tile floor and compared it to the tread on the boot I held in my hand. The same bowling pin semicircle ringed the outside with the chubby crosses in the center.

The manufacturer's mark was on the heel: a 'W' for Wilderness.

Before I walked back outside, I called Max. "I'm at Myles Thompkins' cabin. He's not here, but he put his neighbor in charge of watching the place and caring for the dogs. The guy gave me permission to look around inside."

"Did you find anything?" Max asked.

"We need the CSI unit," I said. "Call Judge Crockett and get a warrant. When he asks for probable cause, tell him that it looks like we've got the bloody boot."

CHAPTER NINETEEN

"Explain to me how and when Myles got in touch with you," I asked Scotty. "Everything you can remember."

The guy looked flustered, regretting having given me permission to enter the house, I assumed. "I told you what I know, which isn't anything much," he said. "What'd you find in there?"

Conroy had retrieved crime scene tape out of his trunk, and Scotty watched my fellow officer string the yellow and black plastic from one tree to the next, cordoning off the cabin and barn. Each foot of tape that unrolled increased Scotty's discomfort. "I don't know why you're doing that," he said. The temperature kept dropping, a frigid night ahead, and the wind had started to blow. I had my parka on, and Conroy was bundled up tight, but Scotty had on only an insulated plaid wool shirt. The guy kept shivering.

"Look, Myles didn't do nothin' wrong. I know him, and he's a good guy," he insisted.

"You're a true friend, and I bet he'll appreciate hearing that you said that," I said. "But there are some things inside that we need to get the crime scene folks out here to look at. I've got a search warrant being drawn up, and we'll be taking a closer look. But it's nothing for you to worry about."

"Shit," Scotty looked at me with something akin to terror in his eyes. "Is Myles going to be pissed with me?"

"Why should he?" I asked. "If it's like you said, he's not the kind of guy to do anything wrong, right?"

"Yeah," Scotty said. "That's right. Not Myles."

"Tell me, when did he get in touch and exactly what did he say?"

Scotty thought for a minute. "I guess it was middle of the night some time. I got a text. He said that he'd be gone for a while."

"You said earlier that he was going up the mountain," I said. "That he was doing some hunting."

"Well, he didn't actually say that. At least, I don't think he said that," Scotty said. "I think I kind of guessed at that. Myles just said that he was going to be gone for a while and he needed me to watch the cabin and the dogs. Usually when I do that, it's because he's hunting."

"Okay, I see. How about showing me the text? That might make it easier."

Scotty looked doubtful at first, but then pulled out his cell phone. He maneuvered through his text messages, then opened one and handed me the phone. It had been sent just after 3 a.m. It read:

This is Myles. I left and won't be back for a while. Please feed the dogs and take care of my place. Thanks.

"He wasn't specific about how long he'd be gone or where he was going. Did you have any other communication from Myles?"

Scotty screwed up his face, thinking. "Nope. I don't think so. I don't remember any calls or anything. Like I said, I just figured he went hunting again."

"Does Myles have any other vehicle, or just that red pickup?" I asked, gesturing toward the truck parked near the house.

"Just that one," Scotty said.

"But he has a horse?"

"Yeah, Homer," Scotty answered. "He usually takes the horse when he goes hunting. That's another reason I figure he's up on the mountain, 'cause Homer is gone. Plus, it's bow hunting season on deer right now, and Myles usually goes right about this time. I didn't see his bow and arrows around the place."

"Describe Homer."

"A bay stallion," he said. "Big-shouldered, maybe sixteen hands with the typical black points, mane and tail."

"Okay, great. One more time, please think about this: Did you hear from Myles after that text at all?" I asked. "Any other texts you might have deleted by accident? Any other communication?"

"Not that I remember. But I gotta admit that I'm a little fuzzy. I stayed up kind of late last night drinking with a buddy, and this afternoon I smoked a couple of joints." He looked at me and shrugged, like maybe he shouldn't have mentioned the marijuana. "I get a little forgetful when I've been indulging."

I chuckled, tried to put the guy at ease. I didn't care about a little weed. We had a killer to find.

"Okay," I said. "Now tell me again about the times you saw Laurel with Myles."

At that, Scotty said much of what he had before, except that he remembered something else, that Myles had once told him that he sometimes spent time with Laurel, and that Scotty shouldn't ever mention it to anyone. "Her being married, Myles didn't want her husband to think anything wrong was going on. Myles said it wasn't," Scotty said. "I didn't think much of it. They were just good friends."

"You never saw her here at the cabin though?" I asked again.

"No. Never," he said.

About then, we heard the sound of wheels on gravel. Max drove up first, followed by the county's CSI trailer. He got out of the car, stopped to talk to Conroy for just a moment, and then came over to where I stood with Scotty. "I've got the search warrant," Max said, presenting Scotty with the paperwork. Then to make sure if he was ever asked he could verify that I hadn't conducted an illegal search, Max said, "Scotty, thank you for giving Chief Jefferies permission to go inside the cabin. We appreciate it."

"Why're you mentioning that?" he said.

"I just wanted to personally thank you for helping us. We have an important case to investigate. Like I said, we appreciate the help. It was you who gave permission, right?"

At that, Scotty beamed with pride. "Yeah. Glad I could help."

"Okay, well, let's get going then," I said.

The CSI trailer's doors opened, and the techs immediately went to work. A couple of them looked bushed. The bison ranch. Carl's trailer. Now Myles's cabin. This was the third scene we'd called them to process in the past fifteen hours. They started by setting up a generator with lights outside, shining them toward the barn and house. Once that was done, a cameraman videotaped the area, the land and the barn. I followed next to him, guiding him, since I'd been the one to do the initial walk-through. There wasn't much to document outside, but then we went inside, he recorded the way the house looked when we first entered, and I led him to the bedroom.

"Get the boots," I said.

The videographer did as I'd instructed. Another tech trailed him holding a yellow tent with the number one on it. When they stopped filming, the ID tech placed the marker. That done, they shot still photos and then bagged the boots and took them into evidence. The boots would be shipped to the state lab. First, they'd pull DNA from the dry blood on the sole. Once that was done, they'd be sent to the ID section, where the tread would be compared to the kitchen print. I had no doubt that we had a match.

While the techs worked, I went outside to stay out of everyone's way. Max and I stood back and watched. "Anything else in there that stands out?" he asked.

"A photo of Laurel near the bed."

Max heaved a heavy sigh. "Myles really does love her, huh?"

"I guess," I said. "Sad that it turned out this way."

"Are we sure he has to be the one?" Max asked. "Is there any other possible explanation for his boot leaving the kitchen print?"

"I don't know," I admitted. "I don't think we can be sure until we piece all this together, maybe find his fingerprints on that knife or gun, or something else tying him to the murders. But it doesn't look good for him, does it?"

"No, it doesn't."

At that point, Lieutenant Mueller walked out. He'd been inside the cabin, overseeing the search. "We found something in a desk drawer," he said. "I think you'll want to see these."

He had an evidence bag, and inside was a four-inch stack of envelopes. Each one was addressed in a flowing, handwritten script to "My Dearest Myles."

"Letters inside?" Max asked.

"Yup," Mueller said. "Love letters."

"Who signed them?" I inquired, although I certainly suspected that I knew.

"Laurel Johansson," Mueller said.

I frowned, thinking about how the day had unfolded. This morning Mullins had been convinced that Carl was our killer. When I found the evidence that he was stalking Laurel, I tended to agree. Partly, I still did. But so much was coming together with Myles that seemed to suggest we were wrong about Carl. Yet I wasn't ready to rule out Jacob's buddy. *Poor Laurel,* I thought. I wondered if she knew how much jeopardy she was in and from whom. Maybe I hoped that she didn't know. I didn't like the thought that she may have spent her final days living in fear.

"We need copies, ASAP," I said. "There could be something in one of those letters that would answer all our questions." The originals would have to be preserved to be fingerprinted and logged into evidence, but I had to know what Laurel wrote.

"I'll send someone to the office with them. We'll have duplicates for you in an hour," Mueller said.

"Good," then I turned to Max. "Have we issued a be-on-the-lookout for Myles yet?"

"I did it on the way over here," he said. "State troopers, everyone should be getting the BOLO as we speak."

"Add to the alert that we think he's on a bay stallion," I said. "We need to get everyone looking for this guy. If it's him, I want him behind bars pronto. If not, we need to rule him out and find the real killer."

"You're not convinced, despite the boot? You're thinking about Carl, aren't you?" Max asked.

"We still have more questions than answers," I said. "But whoever is behind this, we need to figure it out fast. Max, we have no reason to be sure that this killer is done. Maybe this monster intended to massacre everyone in that house, and Jacob, even little Jeremy, are still in grave danger."

"I've been..." Max said.

"Thinking of that, too?" I asked, and he nodded.

CHAPTER TWENTY

Max stayed to watch over the search of the cabin, but I left as soon as the copies arrived. At the shelter, the closest thing I had to a home in Alber, Hannah and most of the women were sleeping. The only ones still up were a small group of night owls in the parlor, talking and hand-sewing squares for a quilt. Hannah had started working with some of the families in town that sold to gift shops, mostly in Salt Lake, to make money for the shelter. I'd been intrigued by all the ingenuity she used to pay the bills and buy food and supplies to keep the place functioning. Most of the donations came from mainstream Mormons, who gave generously to help the shelter, although they didn't condone or practice polygamy. The hallways were dark as I walked quietly by the parlor, staying in the shadows. I paused at the foot of the stairs when I realized the quilters were talking about the Johansson case.

"I know what you're saying. Bad things do happen everywhere. That's true. But it's so sad to think someone would do that to Anna and Laurel, those two innocent children," a slightly built woman sitting on the couch said. "What will happen to Jacob now, and that poor little baby?"

"I heard that Naomi Jefferies found the bodies. Folks in town are saying that she's been hanging around at the hospital with the family ever since it happened," another woman said, her voice laced with just a bit of sarcasm. There was a titter among the group, and then the woman said, "I think she has eyes for Jacob."

"Oh, no!" the first woman protested. "She's years older than he is, and she has a bunch of kids. Why would he—"

"You watch and see," a third woman answered. "You know, even before this happened, Naomi was interested in Jacob. I saw them whispering together at worship services a couple of weeks ago, and Naomi wasn't looking at him like a neighbor, more like a woman intent on becoming his third wife."

"Well, now she'd be his first, since Anna and Laurel are out of the way," the woman on the couch said. "How convenient is that?"

"Very convenient," someone answered with a short laugh.

"Oh, you don't think—" yet another woman said.

"All I know is that I'm sure Naomi wouldn't mind being first wife to a man with property and status," the woman on the couch insisted. "If Jacob survives, that is. I hear he's in bad shape. If she's got marriage on her mind, Naomi might be wasting her time courting the Johansson family. He might not live long enough for a wedding."

I considered walking into the parlor and defending Naomi, telling the women that she was only concerned with his welfare. But I thought about her at the hospital, twice on this one day, and that moment when I thought Jacob was awake and talking to her. I wondered yet again what was going on inside Naomi. And I considered what the one woman had said, that even before the murders, Naomi might have been interested in Jacob. As a child, I'd seen Naomi through the eyes of a daughter; she'd always appeared virtuous in the extreme. But she was also a woman, and since Father's death one without a husband. Could it be true that even before the killings Naomi had her cap set for Jacob Johansson?

"I'm getting pretty sick of this," the woman on the couch complained. The others murmured, and she said, "There's a lot of violence in this town, bad things that happen that no one talks about."

"That's true," someone said. "Way too much that gets swept under the rug."

"Lots of the women here have had bad stuff happen," the first woman continued. "Now Laurel and Anna, those two little kids are dead. You think that police chief, that woman from Dallas, cares? You think she's going to find the killer? She left here. She's an apostate. A lot of the people in town shun her, won't even talk to her, like the prophet decreed."

"She's not one of us," someone hissed.

"That's true," another agreed. "I've heard people say they don't want her here, and I've heard some of them say that they'd like to force her out."

"You know Ardeth Jefferies is her mother," someone said. "I hear she told this Clara woman to leave. Even her own family doesn't want anything to do with her."

At that, one of the women shushed the others. "She's a friend of Hannah's. She lives here, you know."

"I don't care," the woman who'd made the charge said. "I'm thinking some woman shows up from Dallas, someone who ran off and deserted her family, and suddenly she's in charge. And then two of us get murdered, two little children, and what's she doing? Out digging for bodies this morning, I heard, like some kind of a loon. All the while a maniac is running around killing folks."

In my room, I thought about what was said, how I was an outsider, not to be trusted, and one who hadn't proven herself. They were right. I was rejected by many in town, even my own family. Why should they trust me?

I took a deep breath, a few more, while I tried to calm down. Yes, I'd run away, but I'd had no choice. No one cared about what had pushed me to leave. Instead, they blindly followed the prophet's orders and turned their backs on me. As much as that hurt, and it did, I reminded myself that none of what they'd said mattered. They might never want me here. But all that truly counted was that four people were dead, murdered, one gravely injured. Again, I thought about the two survivors. For all I knew, while I wasted time nursing my bruised feelings, little Jeremy and Jacob were in danger.

I pulled on a pair of old gray sweatpants and a white T-shirt, then sat on the bed and took out the copies of the letters Mueller's men found at the log cabin. I'd noticed when Mueller showed me the envelopes that they weren't addressed and had no postmarks. They'd been hand-delivered, somehow. I wondered if Laurel had an intermediary who passed the letters to Myles. Or, did she give them to him herself, when they spent time together? Maybe Laurel had a place where she left the letters for Myles to claim.

Each letter had a date in the upper right-hand corner, and I arranged them with the most recent letter on top. They were written precisely one week apart, each Sunday. The final one was dated eight days before the murders. It started: "My Dearest Myles," just like the inscription on the envelope.

Laurel's handwriting was flowing and really quite beautiful, and she wrote passionately about her concern for Jeremy and that he had barely regained his birth weight in the two months since his birth:

He's such a sweet child. I hold him on my lap, and he smiles up at me. But I worry. Will he be healthy? Anna helps me. She's wonderful with children. We sit together in the afternoons, our housework done, dinner filling the air with the scent of the bison roast in the oven, and she helps me nurse, trying to get the baby to latch on and feed the way he should. But the child seems disinterested. Perhaps it is too hard for him. Perhaps I am not a good mother, as much as I pray to be.

Here at home, things are not good between Jacob and me. He seems disinterested in me and does not want to be bothered with his newest son. Perhaps I am a disappointment to him.

He dotes on Anna and plays with Benjamin and Sybille, and I wonder if when Jeremy is older Jacob will be as drawn to our child. Some men aren't as good with babies as they are with children who can run and play, throw a ball. It's possible that my husband is such a man. I must admit that despite this year of marriage, I don't know him well. He is a mystery to me in many ways. Those years in Mexico, I think, haunt him. He told me once of the violence he saw in the sect in El Pueblo de Elijah, the thirst for retribution.

My love, I wonder how different my life would be if the prophet hadn't ordered me to marry Jacob but allowed us to be together as we planned, as we should be. I think of you each day. I feel Jacob's arms around me, and I wish they were yours. His lips against mine are familiar but not the ones I crave.

If my parents had not commanded me to consent to the prophet's orders, I would be your wife and Jeremy your son.

I put the letter down on my lap and recalled again how Laurel looked on her deathbed, and my anger built. I thought of those I knew who used religion to control the lives of others and the unfairness of a world where so many have no power and no voice.

Since the letters were written on Sundays, I wondered if perhaps she'd composed them during her afternoon prayer times, when she'd be alone. Once a week, she wrote of her life, brought Myles up to date, and professed her love for him. On page after page, she grieved for the loss of the life they'd planned. Looking down at the pile of letters, something occurred to me. I picked up my cell and called Mueller, still at the log cabin. "Did you go through all of Laurel's possessions at the ranch?" I asked.

"Of course," he said. "What are you looking for?"

"We have Laurel's letters to Myles. He kept them," I said. "I'm thinking that somewhere she must have his letters to her. She'd probably have them hidden to make sure that Jacob never found them, but I don't believe she would have thrown them away."

The phone quiet, I assumed Mueller was thinking that through, wondering if they might have missed something. "Chief, we'll head back over there first thing in the morning, once we have daylight, and take another look," Mueller said. "Now that we know what we're looking for, maybe we'll have ideas about where she could have them."

"How much longer will you be there?" I looked at my watch—it was well after midnight.

"Finishing up," he said.

I thanked him, hung up and went back to my reading.

A few months before Jeremy's birth, Laurel wrote of her pregnancy, the feeling of the baby moving within her. "Life, a life I am bringing into the world. I want my child to have a happy one. Happier than I've been given. One with more freedom, so he or she can pick a future, chart a course."

Twice, Laurel mentioned meeting Myles, but she never said where that took place. I thought of the spot on the river, wondered if that might be their special place, as it had once been mine with Max. "We never have more than minutes together," she wrote. "Stolen seconds, and then we have to part. I know we can't risk more, yet I want so much more time with you. I know it is sinful of me to think this way, but I want days, weeks, and years. I want a lifetime."

I continued to read, trailing further back in time as the letters grew older. Their correspondence, it seemed, started about the time that Laurel was ordered to marry Jacob. Perhaps it was then that their ability to openly see each other ended, and they had little opportunity to communicate in person.

My father forces me to marry Jacob, even though I object. I have refused to eat for days now, but to no avail. Mother,

too, has told me that I have no choice. I get thinner and
weaker, and I woke up this morning feeling faint. But they
ignore my plight. Each morning, one of my mothers fixes a
plate for me and puts it before me at the breakfast table. I
sit, hands crossed, surrounded by my brothers and sisters.
Across the table, my father eats his bacon and eggs, all the
while staring at me, daring me to eat again. When I don't,
he shouts and orders me back to my room.

I thought of Laurel's father, of my own father, so determined
that they rule the household, so unwilling to listen to their children,
so intent on having us obey. I felt my resentment build, until I
had to remind myself that the father Laurel spoke of was one of
my detectives, Jeff Mullins, and that despite what I read, I knew
he was a decent man who was following his religion's dictates. But
then, my father was a good person, as well, and that didn't stop
him from standing idly by, refusing to interfere when he had to
know the hell my life had become.

Gradually, I nodded off, the copies of Laurel's letters stacked
beside me, one open on my lap. My dreams took me back to my
own past. I was so young, only seventeen. Max had been forced
out of Alber the year before, banished by the town elders as one of
the lost boys, and I plotted to find him. But then, in that fateful
meeting with my parents, I was told that the prophet had a vision,
and that I should be honored, because it involved me. I was to
be married in three days to a man not of my choosing, a man I
didn't want. I cried. I begged. I refused. My father forced me to
obey, as Mullins did Laurel. I, too, felt as if my life were ending.
In a way, that day, it did.

In my slumber I traveled back in time.

Mother fussed, straightening the folds in the pure white dress she'd
sewn for me, the skirt billowing around me. Her dark hair twisted
in the back and anchored in curls, she hummed as she took a stitch

at the neckline to tighten the thick lace. My hair and face covered by a sheet of netting, I should have felt like a princess. Instead, a fist of fear and anger opened and closed in my chest and I worried that it might rip out my insides.

"Ardeth, is she ready?" Father asked, as he poked his head into the bedroom I shared with my sisters. "We don't have much time, you know."

"She will be in just a moment, Abe," Mother answered. "Doesn't she look beautiful?"

Father walked into the room. "Clara, you are a vision, one any father would be proud of, any husband would cherish," he said. "Daughter, today is an important day, but what is more important is the future, that as a wife you strive for perfect obedience, to be in harmony with the desires and needs of your husband. One day soon you will become a mother whose children will give your husband honor."

"Yes, Father," I said. "But, Father, I don't want to—"

"Be sweet, daughter," Mother said. "Don't trouble your father this way. The prophet has had a revelation from God that told him you must have your future sealed to this man."

"Mother, please. Father, I… don't… please don't… don't make me—" I didn't trust my voice to continue. Tears flooded my eyes, beginning to stream onto my cheeks.

"Stop that, girl. You'll smear your makeup," Mother reached over with a tissue and soaked up my tears while she tsk-tsked and then said, "We have been through this, Clara. There is no more to discuss. You will obey. This man will be your husband. You should be honored to have such a prominent, such a righteous man as your husband. All of Alber knows how the prophet relies on him."

The sobs came, the heavy weight of emotion crushing against my chest, my heart aching as if it would surely split into two and I would die. I thought of Max. I wondered if he knew of the troubles that had befallen me.

"Come now, girl," Father ordered. "We must go for the ceremony."

My bedroom dissolved, and I stood in a room surrounded by family, all adults, those in the hierarchy of our community. My father's chest expanded inside his suitcoat with pride, and my mother glowed with excitement. A daughter becoming one of the wives of a man so high up in Elijah's People would give my parents great standing. This was a momentous occasion.

On the walls, two mirrors hung directly across from each other multiplied their reflections endlessly, identical images inside of images, each successively smaller, until it seemed that they echoed into eternity. The mirrors were symbols of the bond that would be forged during the ceremony as we became husband and wife. Father had explained that our sealing would bind us not just during our lifetimes but after death into the hereafter.

Candles flickered and the room swam with light and color. Mother's heavy perfume surrounded me. I tried not to look at the gray-haired man, older than my father by more than a decade, who stood across the altar from me. I didn't want to see the excitement in his rheumy eyes. When I could avoid him no longer and he took my hand in his, my body recoiled. A lifetime, I thought. An eternity, I'd been told. His smile grew, my pulse quickened, and I wished I had somewhere, anywhere to run.

CHAPTER TWENTY-ONE

I had a restless night, the nightmare of my wedding running through my mind, keeping me from fully giving myself over to sleep. Years ago, those images had come often, but not recently, and I thought about how Laurel's story was becoming interwoven with my own, and how it was bringing back pain I'd fought to bury. I woke early, foraged around in the refrigerator and found a plate of biscuits and gravy. Hannah had left a note on top: *Clara, please, eat before you leave. You're getting thinner than a walking stick.*

I popped the plate in the microwave, warming the gravy so that it went from a solid to a liquid. While I munched on a biscuit, I put in a call to Max, still thinking about the dream. It seemed to haunt me. I heard his voice, and it comforted me. "Did you find anything else I should know about at Myles's cabin?" I asked.

"We found his cell in a drawer," Max said. "Seems odd that he'd leave it there when he was going out to the woods. Mueller has the phone at his office. His IT guy is trying to open it. I wrote a subpoena for the records and sent it to Judge Crockett last night. He'll sign it this morning."

"Good," I said. "Anything else?"

"Nothing important. The only real pieces of evidence are the boots and those letters. Although we did take the photograph of Laurel with us, too. And Mueller took the computer, so the IT guys can search it," he said. "Did you read the letters? Did Laurel write anything that might help us?"

"No help there either, except that they confirm the relationship. They're love letters to Myles from Laurel, passionate, but they say nothing about feeling threatened or give any clue that she was afraid of Myles, Carl or anyone else."

"That's disappointing. Lieutenant Mueller is going back to the ranch today to try to find Myles's letters to Laurel as you asked," Max said. "I'll check on the evidence as soon as I get to the office, make sure it's being expedited at the labs, try to light a fire under the state guys and push it through faster. Have you got a plan?"

"I'm going over to see Doc Wiley, check on the autopsies. Then I'm heading into the office," I said. "Mullins texted me this morning saying he'll be there about nine and wants to talk to me."

"What do you think he has on his mind?" Max said.

"He probably wants a heads-up on how the investigation is going," I speculated.

"Sure, well, don't blame him. If Laurel were my daughter…" Max didn't finish that sentence. "I'll check in when I have news."

"Same here," I said.

The morgue was on the ground floor of Smith County Memorial, hidden behind an unmarked door far at the back. I'd called ahead and made sure that Doc Wiley would be there, and he was in the autopsy room working on Anna when I arrived. I glanced at the six coolers in the wall, and felt a surge of sadness when I saw Benjamin's and Sybille's names written on tape on two of the stainless-steel doors. At the far end, a woman's body lay on a second autopsy table covered by an evidence sheet. I walked over and checked the name on the toe tag: LAUREL JOHANSSON.

"Looks like you haven't gotten to Laurel yet," I commented.

Either Doc was in a bad mood, or I sounded as if I were complaining. He pulled the scalpel out of Anna's body, gazed over at me and gave me an annoyed frown. "I know you're in a hurry, Clara. We all are. We all want the murders solved. But I had a tricky delivery yesterday. Almost lost the baby. I think Max explained that to you, and—"

"Sorry, Doc. Yes, Max explained," I interrupted. "I'm just wondering where things stand."

Doc shook his head. "Not on the best footing, I'd say. This is pretty treacherous territory."

"Are you planning to elaborate?" I asked.

"Heck, Clara." He looked perturbed and as angry as I felt. "When I took this job, I never thought I'd have a case like this. Two little kids. These two women. You'd think people wouldn't do such a thing."

"Unfortunately, we can never predict what people are capable of." I knew we shared the same feelings of betrayal; these types of killings weren't supposed to happen, not in bucolic mountain towns. Doc glowered, and I said, "I don't want to be abrupt, but I have to get to the station. I'm here for a quick rundown. Where are we?"

Doc gave me another peeved glare. "Toxicology samples on the children are on the way to the lab, but won't be back for a week. I'm not expecting to find anything surprising. I think that the causes of death will be the gunshot wounds we saw at the scene," he said. "Manner of death, of course, is homicide on both."

I had a notebook out and wrote Doc's findings on the children. "And Laurel? Any thoughts on her yet?"

"I'll get to her next and call you with results later, but I looked the body over and didn't see anything surprising there either. The cut neck is the only wound, and my guess is that the cause of her death is blood loss. I'll send off toxicology, but, again, that'll take a while to get back."

"Okay," I said. "Thanks."

Doc looked down at Anna on the table, and then he closed his eyes and shuddered. I thought when he opened them that I saw tears welling up in the corners. The case was getting to him, and at his age, he had a hard time hiding it. Maybe he was beyond the point of caring if I saw his pain. Personally, I wasn't far behind him. Anna's long dark hair spread out around her head, and Doc had shut her eyelids, so that if it wasn't for the Y-incision he'd cut in her body, shoulders to the chest then straight down to her pelvis, she might have looked as if she were sleeping. "I'm doing all the usual lab tests, of course," he said. "But I'm not expecting any surprises with Anna either. It's clear that she had the likelihood of a long life ahead of her, until some coward pulled a trigger and shot her in the back."

"You're still thinking that time of death was early yesterday morning? About seven or so? About an hour before Naomi found them?" I drew a timeline starting from Sunday evening through Monday morning, when Naomi called 911. Anna had a short incision in her upper right abdomen where I figured Doc had inserted a thermometer to check her liver temp. A core organ, well protected, livers were routinely used to gauge cooling and estimate time of death.

"On these three victims, the children and their mother, I do think that's right. I did the readings about eleven yesterday morning, before I got called for the delivery. At that time, their temps were all down about seven degrees, but a little of that must have been due to the ambient temperature, since they were outside and it was a chilly morning," he explained. "The one that doesn't fit is Laurel."

I looked at him, puzzled. "Explain."

"I'm not sure, Clara." Doc had a habit of gesturing with the scalpel while we talked, and he used it to point at her on the table. "First off, Laurel was inside the house where it was warmer, so her body should have had a slightly warmer temp than the others if they were all murdered in close succession."

"But Laurel's wasn't?"

Doc shook his head. He walked me over and pulled the sheet off of Laurel, and she had the same incision where he'd checked her liver temp. I looked again at the strange circle of red lipstick around her mouth. "Laurel's body had cooled substantially more than the others," Doc said. "Nine degrees more, sixteen degrees in all, to just a little more than eighty-two degrees. If we use the standard measurement of one point five degrees per hour, when we took her temp at eleven yesterday morning, she'd been dead for—"

"Eleven hours," I said, finishing the sentence for him.

"Although that is, of course, nothing more than an estimate," he said. "But it's my best guess, and it is a rough guess, you know. These methods are never precise. But I'm thinking that Laurel died around midnight."

That didn't make a lot of sense. If Doc was right, whoever killed Laurel did so in the middle of the night and then came back at dawn and murdered Anna and the children and tried to kill Jacob. I wrote it all out in my notebook, the approximate times, the scenario as Doc thought it unfolded.

"Why would someone do that?" I asked.

"What?" Doc responded, as if not following me.

"Kill Laurel then return to murder the rest of the family?"

Doc smiled at me. "You know, Clara, that's your problem to figure out. I've always been grateful that I do the autopsies, and you police officers have to solve the crimes."

CHAPTER TWENTY-TWO

Mulling over what Doc had told me, I headed to my office. I didn't expect to see what I did when I drove past the front of the building—a small group of women carrying signs, at least a couple I recognized from the shelter the night before, the ones who'd expressed doubt that I was the right choice for police chief. One sign read, FIRE THE APOSTATE! Another: OUTSIDERS WON'T PROTECT US! And a third: TAKE OUR TOWN BACK!

I considered the irony that, after all I'd been through in my short time back in Alber, someone would question that I wanted to help not hurt the town. I entered through the back door. Kellie stood behind the front desk, staring out at the protesters on the street. "Did you see them?" she asked. After I nodded, she asked, "Why are they doing that?"

"Because there have been four brutal murders. They're worried and scared. That can bring out the worst in people," I explained. "And because I was once one of them, but no longer. In this town, this culture, although I grew up a few miles from this police station, I am considered an outsider. And from childhood on, they've been taught that they can't trust those who aren't like them."

A pause, and I thought for a moment about the day I left Alber, bruised and sore, tired and frightened. Was there another way? Should I have tried to find a different option? Did I have any choice other than to turn my back on my entire family? And didn't I deserve some of what I was getting, since I'd run out on them without even saying goodbye?

Kellie got up and walked to the window. She stared wide-eyed at the women marching past the building. "But this is four people killed. It's not something you can solve overnight. And you are working the case. Working hard. Why are they saying those things?"

I took a deep breath, thinking about how young she was, only nineteen. She had much to learn about life, about people.

"We know that I'm doing my best, but they don't," I said. "And the truth is that I don't blame them for being worried. *I* haven't, but this police department has buried cases in the past. We have stacks of unsolved cases to attest to that. By the way, did the night guys go through the backroom files looking for anything on Myles Thompkins and Carl Shipley as I asked?"

"Yeah," Kellie said. "They skimmed through them. They left me a note this morning."

"Saying?" I prodded.

"No luck," she said, with a shrug. "They found a few nuisance complaints and a petty theft charge against Carl, juvenile stuff, but nothing else, nothing violent or big. Not a single file on anything involving Myles."

It had been a long shot, but I was still disappointed. "Okay, well, any calls?" I asked.

"A few," she said. "And Detective Mullins is waiting for you."

"I know," I said. "I'll be right with him."

I grabbed my message slips and headed to my office. Apparently, Mullins had been on the lookout for my arrival. Before I could get more than a dozen steps, he'd fallen in next to me. "We need to talk," he said, the tone of his voice leaving no room for argument.

Conroy was sitting at his desk reading a case file, and the younger officer's head had snapped up, curious, when he'd heard Mullins' voice.

"Mullins, it can keep until we get to my office," I said. "Not here."

"Sheesh, I…" he started grousing, but then clenched his lips and fell into a lockstep behind me.

In my office, I hung my parka on the coat rack and strapped my old brown leather bag onto the back of my chair. Then I sat down and leafed through the message slips, just to make sure there wasn't anything important. At the bottom of the stack was a small pink envelope that smelled of vanilla, with my name printed across the front. I opened it. *LEAVE NOW. YOU AREN'T WELCOME IN ALBER*, it read. I stared at it for a few moments, wondering who wrote it. For just a second, I considered that perhaps Mother was behind it, but I shrugged that off. She didn't want me here, I knew, but Mother had no problem telling me that to my face. Did she have faults? Sure. But she wasn't the kind of woman who'd send an anonymous note.

"Just a minute, Mullins," I said. "I'll be right back."

I walked out a little way and held up the envelope. "Kellie, did someone drop this off?"

"It was on the desk when I got here this morning. The night dispatcher said she found it on the floor, just inside the door."

"She didn't see who dropped it off? Not on the waiting room cameras?" I asked.

"No," Kellie said, with a shake of her head. "All she could see was someone cracking the door open wide enough to slip it in."

"Okay," I said. "Thanks."

I turned back to Mullins, then thought of something. "Oh, Kellie, one more thing," I said. She looked up, expectantly. "Let's get a price on putting a camera on the front of the building, like the ones we have out back on the parking lot door."

"Sure," she said. "I'll make a few calls."

Nothing more to be done about the note, I returned to my office and threw it in my desk drawer. Then I turned my full attention on my lead detective, who had enough nervous energy to fuel a power plant. "Why don't you sit down," I suggested, gesturing toward the chair across the desk from me.

"I'll stand," he said, arms folded across his chest. "You want to tell me why you're wasting time looking for Myles Thompkins? Because that's what looking at him is, a waste of time."

"Jeff—" I started, but Mullins wasn't in a listening frame of mind.

"Damn it, Chief, I solved this case for you. I know who murdered my Laurel. Her mothers and me, we're sure it had to be Carl Shipley. Couldn't be anyone else."

I got up and closed the door. Mullins didn't move, so I pointed at the chair and said, "Detective, sit." He ignored me and stayed stationary, watching me while I sat down behind my desk. I leaned back in the chair, crossed my arms, stared up at him and waited. One of the first things I'd learned as a cop is that silence can be unnerving to the person across the desk from me, and it was often the best way to get what I wanted.

Mullins fumed. A minute passed. I remained resolutely quiet. He finally took one step over and plopped down where I'd told him to. He dropped his head and ran his fingers through his thinning salt-and-pepper hair. I thought about what he and his family must be going through, and as irritated as I was, I felt deeply sorry for him. But I couldn't let him sway the investigation.

"Jeff, listen," I said. "A few people, including Jacob's parents, mentioned the relationship between Myles and Laurel, how they'd been in love since high school. And—"

At that, he apparently couldn't hold back. He dropped both hands and they fell as fists on his knees. "You think I don't know she was in love with Myles? You think that's some kind of surprise?"

"No, I don't. I know that you were well aware of their relationship," I said. "But, Jeff, what I'm saying is—"

"Girl almost starved herself to death over that boy," Mullins said. "Would've died if we'd let her. She was so in love with that young guy that her mothers and me thought she'd run away."

"But she didn't," I said.

A long sigh, and when it ended Mullins' eyes filled with tears. I grabbed a tissue out of the box on the gray metal credenza behind me, but by the time I had it ready to hand to him, Mullins had a well-used white cotton handkerchief he'd pulled out of his pocket. He ran it over his cheeks, wiped his nose and upper lip, and looked like a man who'd lost everything he loved in the world. "Chief, you've gotta listen to me. Myles is a dead end."

"How do you know?" I asked. "You heard about the boot print?"

"Yeah, I heard," he said. "I can't explain that, but…"

A beaten man, he stopped talking. Mullins was a veteran officer, one who'd had years of experience at another department before coming to Alber PD nearly a decade earlier. I wondered how many parents and spouses, how many family members and loved ones had sat across from him over the years in similar situations. It must feel like the oncologist who gets cancer, the lawyer who becomes the defendant. I thought about how fickle life could be, and how quickly it could change.

"Mullins, we've got the blood evidence on Myles, and that's powerful. We've got a motive, that he loved Laurel," I said.

"That's why he couldn't have done it," Mullins said, the tears flowing hard, but his jaw anchored in determination.

"Sadly, people kill those they love way too often," I said. "How does that clear Myles Thompkins?"

"Because he truly loved Laurel," Mullins said. "Myles loved her like no man I've ever seen love a woman. And she loved him as passionately in return."

"But she married—" I started.

"Yes, she married Jacob Johansson," he bellowed. I would have bet that he'd thought about this often in the preceding twenty-four hours, and as he talked, it sounded almost as if he were trying to work his way through it, to reassure himself that he and his wives had done the right thing when they forced Laurel to marry Jacob.

"Laurel married Jacob not because we wanted her to. She married him because the prophet commanded it." Mullins talked to me as if I were one of the uninitiated, someone who didn't understand the laws that governed Elijah's People. "Emil Barstow had a revelation, a sign from God that told him that Laurel had to be sealed to Jacob. When that happened, her mothers and me, we couldn't do anything else. We weren't in control. We knew Myles and Laurel loved each other, but they weren't destined to be together. It wasn't…"

Mullins stopped talking. He sat back as if unable to go on. I thought of my father, my mother, the day they announced who I would marry. I thought of the way those in charge ran Max out of Alber to keep him away from me.

"It wasn't what?" I asked.

"It wasn't ours to decide," Mullins said, his hands turned over, palms up, as if pleading for understanding. "It was the prophet's call, Chief, not ours. And we had to follow it, and we trusted that if we did, Laurel would have a good life and glory in the afterlife."

It could have been my father's voice, my parents' reasoning, but it wasn't. I felt anger at Mullins, at his wives for not listening to Laurel, just as my parents ignored my wishes. But this wasn't about me. None of it. It was about the young mother lying on Doc Wiley's autopsy table, perhaps at this very moment having her organs removed, the slit in her throat examined to determine what type of knife was used to slice through her neck. It was about Anna and her innocent children. It was about Jacob, unconscious in the ICU, and keeping Jeremy, little Jeremy, safe.

As tied up as my emotions were, I looked at Mullins with sympathy. He was, after all, grieving a terrible loss. "Jeff, listen," I said, my voice softer. "You explained why it had to be Carl Shipley yesterday, but—"

"The cut throat!" he shouted. "Myles would never mutilate Laurel that way. He'd never do that. But Carl, those people he used to live with, they're brutal. They—"

"Believe in blood atonement," I said. "Yes, the way Laurel was killed and Jacob was attacked does seem to fit blood atonement."

"We had a case here in town once, Chief, did anyone tell you that?" Mullins asked. When I shook my head, he explained. "About six years ago. Someone from the southern sect showed up in town. He hadn't left the faith but he'd left El Pueblo de Elijah and came to Alber, wanting to get away. He didn't have permission from the folks in charge in that town to leave. We were never able to prove anything, but he was found dead out in a cattle field about a week after he got here."

"Throat cut?" I asked.

"Yeah," Mullins confirmed. "Throat cut."

I hesitated, deciding how to answer. "I do understand, Jeff. I'm not discounting what you're saying, but we have to consider the forensic evidence against Myles. Listen, we don't know who did this yet, but we'll figure it out. The last thing Max and I want is to go after the wrong person. You don't want that, do you?"

"No, but... Well, I think, I mean, I don't think..." he murmured. He seemed preoccupied now, lost in his thoughts, his emotions carrying him back, perhaps to those weeks when Laurel begged for her future, and he and his wives took it away from her.

"You know how tunnel vision can doom an investigation, right?" I asked. "You know that we have to follow the evidence, and right now the evidence leads to Myles Thompkins. The bloody footprint is—"

"Compelling," Mullins said.

"Yes, it is," I said. "If Myles wasn't on the scene, if it was Carl, why is the bloody boot in Myles's log cabin?"

Mullins sat back, incredible sadness deepening the substantial wrinkles across his forehead, the scar on his cheek, the deep creases webbing out from his clenched lips. My heart ached for him, and yet, he had to understand that this wasn't his case. This time, he was the family, not the investigator.

"Listen, Jeff," I said, as calmly and sympathetically as I could, "we haven't decided Myles is the killer. We haven't taken Carl off our list of suspects. We don't know yet. We're still figuring this out."

Mullins ticked his head a notch in slight agreement. Maybe he was beginning to understand.

"Jeff, you need to trust that Max and I have every intention of solving this case. And that we will solve this case. That we'll figure out who murdered your daughter, Anna and her children. Who cut Jacob's throat."

Mullins nodded, but not as if he truly believed what I was saying. He looked up at me, his face a mask of agony. "But you know what, Chief?"

"What?" I asked.

"Sometimes these cases, the bad ones like this, they get all screwed up, don't they?" he said. "We've all seen it. They get so convoluted, so crazy, they're never solved."

"Mullins, you can't think that way," I said. "It's just one day, twenty-four hours, and we're working this. We—"

"Sometimes, the wrong guy does end up in prison," Mullins said, almost as if he were talking to himself and I wasn't in the room. "And sometimes the real killers live their lives like they never did anything wrong, never killed anyone. And they're never punished."

I wasn't sure what to say, but I settled on, "Jeff, you need to go home, be with your family, your wives and children. That's where you belong right now. And you have to believe that in the end, all will be known. You have to have trust in Max and in me that we're going to do all we can."

At that, Detective Jeff Mullins stood up and towered over me. I gazed up at him and frowned. He looked every bit as single-minded as when he walked through my office door.

"Chief, I don't doubt that you and Max will do your best," he said. "But I know Carl Shipley did this. And I intend to see him pay for it. One way or another."

Although I suspected he didn't mean it as a threat, that wasn't what I wanted to hear. "Jeff, we've got this. You don't need to do anything, understand? And you need to be careful what you say."

"Don't worry about me," Mullins said. "But I'm watching. I've got my eyes on all of you. And I'm going to make sure this is done right." With that he turned toward the door.

I scowled at him. "Jeff, sit back down. Let's talk this through."

Mullins didn't respond. Instead, he slammed my office door behind him so hard that the walls shook with his anger.

After Mullins stormed out, I sat for a few moments and collected my thoughts. I considered what he'd said, that Myles had cared for Laurel too much to murder her. But there'd been so many cases in my decade as a cop where a life was ended in violence by someone the victim loved who had loved them in return. Mullins had similar experiences, I'm sure, yet for some reason he believed that the love between his daughter and Myles Thompkins was special. I thought again about Laurel's letters. Those, too, made their dedication to one another seem exceptional. I picked up my phone and called Max. "How's the evidence coming?" I asked.

"It's all on its way to the state lab. We got everything processed on our end," he said. "I personally talked to the lab supervisor, explained that we have multiple homicides and we need the results ASAP to find the murderer. He promised to rush it but warned that it may still take a day or two. The DNA evidence longer. They're hoping to do ballistics on the gun this morning, though. We may have those answers soon."

"Okay. That's good," I said. "Thank you."

"Clara, I got a call from Doc Wiley," Max said. "He said you two discussed the timeline. He went through it with me, too. That's odd about Laurel dying so much earlier, isn't it?"

"Very strange. I'm not sure what to make of it." I told Max about my conversation with Mullins, his certainty that despite the bloody print, Myles Thompkins wouldn't murder his daughter and the others, and how he repeated his assertions that it had to be Carl.

"Maybe Mullins subconsciously fears that if Myles is the killer, that means Laurel is dead because she married Jacob," Max suggested. "And if that's true, that this tragedy happened because Mullins and his wives forced the marriage. If Myles is the killer, maybe Mullins is worried that he shares some of the blame?"

I took a minute to consider that. "I hadn't thought of that angle," I said. "Could be."

"Mullins does have a point about Carl though. There's a lot there with the stalking, the photos, and the history with the splinter group in Mexico."

"Yes, Mullins makes good points," I said. We could have pondered the possibilities all day, but it wasn't getting us anywhere. "Anything from your informant inside El Pueblo de Elijah?"

"No," he said. "I've given up on my contact inside the cult. About half an hour ago, I put in a call to local authorities. I hope I'll have some info for us later today."

"Good," I said. "Anything from Mueller about the letters?"

"They're still looking, but so far no luck," Max said.

"I'll head over to the ranch and help," I said. "I can be another set of eyes."

"You think there's an answer in those letters, don't you?" Max said.

"I think they'll tell us a lot about Myles Thompkins," I said. "I'm assuming we've had no sign of him yet?"

"No sightings," Max said. "The BOLO is out and every cop in the state should be looking for him. We've notified the forest rangers, too, in case they see a campfire in the mountains and follow up on it, happen upon Myles on a hunting trip. You think we should put out a general bulletin to the public, alert the media?"

"Sure, let's get everyone looking for him," I said.

"Okay, I'll get my office on it right away. We'll describe Myles as a person of interest."

"Yes, that sounds good," I said.

"Okay. Well, I'm going to head over to the hospital then and check on Jacob. I'll give you a call when I have more info on his condition," Max said.

"Good idea." We were both quiet for a moment. "Max, have you thought about how..." I started, but my voice trailed off.

Max's voice became quiet. "Thought about what, Clara?"

"Oh... nothing..." I gulped down a lump in my throat and tried to pull myself together. None of this was about me, and I shouldn't make it about me, I scolded myself. None of it. "Max, I need to go. I have to find those letters."

CHAPTER TWENTY-THREE

On the short drive from the sheriff's department to the hospital, Max rehashed the end of his conversation with Clara. The word that stuck in his head was "how." *What was she going to say?* he wondered.

Could it have been: How life flips like a tossed coin? How we have so little control over our destinies? How different our lives would be today if we hadn't been torn apart all those years ago? How our story is eerily similar to what happened to Myles and Laurel?

If she'd asked that final question, Max would have admitted that he had thought about it, often actually, in the past day. The night before when he finally finished at the cabin and went home to sleep for a few hours, he had peeked in at Brooke, such a sweet sight sleeping peacefully in her forget-me-not lavender room. Afterward, he had tossed and turned in bed, unable to clear his thoughts. He'd wondered if brooding over having been torn away from Clara was disloyal to Miriam's memory. To Brooke, who wouldn't exist if his life had taken the path he'd hoped for.

I can't know these things, Max thought as he pulled into the hospital parking lot. *Maybe Clara and I would have broken apart without the prophet's interference. Maybe we would have gone separate ways on our own. How can we ever know?*

Yet at moments, he still felt so close to Clara, and he suspected she did to him.

I have to convince her that it isn't over, that we aren't over, that we didn't miss our only opportunity, he decided. *Life has given us a second chance. As afraid as she is, we have to grab it.*

*

As he walked into the intensive care unit, Max tried to table his ruminations and become all cop again. He followed the signs to Jacob's room and found Michael and Reba Johansson seated in the hallway with Carl Shipley between them. The drapes inside pulled shut, Max couldn't see into the room.

"How is Jacob?" Max asked.

"The same," Reba said. "No change."

Both of Jacob's parents had eyes marbled with bright red veins, and they looked as if they hadn't had a nod of sleep. "I'm sorry about Anna and Laurel and the children, Jacob's condition, all you and your family are going through," Max said. "I want you to know that Chief Jefferies and I are working hard to—"

"I hear you're going to arrest Myles Thompkins, found evidence in his cabin," Reba said, taking stock of Max as coldly as if he were an unwanted trespasser. "I told Clara Jefferies that he was the one behind it, you know."

Max wasn't surprised that Reba had already heard. News traveled fast in Alber. Soon it would hit the radio and television stations and all of Alber would know why they were looking for Myles, that he was more than a person of interest, a suspect. "We want to talk to him, yes, but we haven't made plans for an arrest warrant," Max explained. "We have a lot to investigate before—"

"Well, you should," Carl griped, giving Max a sideways stare. "You ought to for sure, because he did it, I bet."

"Carl, we—" Max started.

"Why the hell were you bothering me about this? It's ridiculous," Carl said, spitting mad. "Good thing Jacob's mom led you and that Jefferies woman to the real killer, so you wouldn't come after me anymore."

"We knew you wouldn't hurt Jacob, Carl," Reba said, staring defiantly at Max as she affectionately patted Carl's hand. "Why,

Carl and Jacob are as close as brothers. Carl grew up in our home. He ate dinners most nights at our table." Reba glared at Max, not even attempting to disguise her anger. "How dare you suspect Carl?"

Max's frown stretched until it scrunched his upper lip and tied up his chin. He stared at Carl and said nothing. The situation bristled with tension, and Max didn't see how it would accomplish anything to rile up Reba more than she already was. Instead of answering her, Max looked over at Michael, who had a lost expression on his face, as if he hadn't heard a word the others had said. Max wondered what so occupied the old man and tried to get his attention: "Mr. Johansson?"

When he got no reaction, Max said it louder: "Mr. Johansson."

Still no response, until Reba reached across Carl and grabbed her husband's arm. "Michael, he's talking to you."

"Yes." Michael jerked to attention. "Oh, Max, it's you."

"You looked as if you were in another world," Max said.

Michael's white hair was flattened at the back from resting his head against the wall as he sat in the chair, and he had tears gathering in his eyes that he wasn't bothering to wipe away. "I was remembering how just last Wednesday, six days ago, we went to the ranch and had dinner with all of them." He sniffled a bit, and Reba handed him a handkerchief. "Jacob, the women, they were all content, the children playing. Reba held Jeremy while Anna and Laurel cooked. Jacob and I talked about expanding one of the feed lots, buying more bison. It was... a good time... peaceful."

Max thought about that. "Carl mentioned that this past Sunday, the evening before the murders, Jacob appeared upset. Carl said it appeared something wasn't right at the ranch. Enough so that he didn't stay for dinner."

"It wasn't anything big—" Carl started to object.

Max shot him a look to quiet him. "Mr. and Mrs. Johansson, do you have any idea what that was about?" he asked.

Michael chewed on the inside of his mouth, apparently thinking, and then said, "Nah, nothing I know of. They were fine. A happy family. Couldn't have been anything at all."

Max turned to Reba, who stared down at her hands. "Mrs. Johansson, what about you?" Max asked. "Do you know what was wrong?"

She pursed her lips far to the right, as if deciding how to answer. "No, not really, but I bet it was about Myles."

"Why?" Max asked.

"I don't know what Jacob could be upset about. That's the truth," Reba admitted. "But I never trusted Myles. As much as he loved Laurel, I never thought he was going to let things be. That's why I told Clara Jefferies about him, because he had to be the one who did it."

As if uncomfortable, Michael squirmed in his chair, and it made a squeaking noise. Max thought about how Reba seemed hell-bent on the idea it had to be Myles Thompkins who murdered their family, and looking at Michael, well, Max had the impression that Jacob's father wasn't anywhere near as convinced.

Wondering what it all meant, Max looked over at Carl, who stared back at him, a look of contempt on his face.

As their eyes met, Max reconsidered Mullins' allegations and the album with the photos of Laurel. He wondered if Reba Johansson could be offering up Myles to push the blame off Carl. A son critically injured, Reba could be protecting a man she considered nearly another son. *I should get Carl off by himself and see if he'll talk more,* Max thought. *Maybe now that he thinks Myles is the prime suspect, he'll open up.*

"Carl, I—" Max started.

At that moment, a red warning light on the wall above their heads lit up and an alarm blared. The Johanssons jumped up, and Max followed them into the room. The machines beeped, the lights flashed, and Max was stunned to see Naomi Jefferies at Jacob's bedside with the call button in her hand.

"He's awake," she cried. "Praise the Almighty! Jacob's awake."

Taking in the scene, Max had the strangest feeling. Jacob, eyes wide, struggling to breathe through the slit in his throat, stared up at Naomi with admiration. Something about the way he looked at her, something about the connection between the two of them, struck Max as peculiar.

A pack of nurses and a doctor dressed in scrubs dashed in through the door. "Everyone outside," the doctor ordered. "Everyone out, now, so we can examine our patient."

"I need to talk to Jacob, to find out—" Max objected.

"Cops. Everyone. Get out!" the doctor shouted. "All of you. Now!"

Jacob's parents bustled out of the room followed by Carl, but before Max turned to go, he glanced back one more time at Naomi. She lingered, and when he looked down at the bed, he saw that she'd dropped the call button and held Jacob's hand.

Moments after the Johanssons and Max left the room, Naomi joined them in the hallway. For a few minutes the family peppered her with questions, and she smiled graciously and answered, "I was whispering a prayer to the heavens to heal Jacob, when all of a sudden I realized that his eyes had opened. I was so excited that I thought my heart might stop." Naomi looked nearly giddy with the memory. "That very second, I cried, 'Thank you, Lord, for answering my prayers to bring Jacob back to us!' Then I hit the call button for the doctor."

Michael and Reba extolled Naomi for all she'd done, from saving their son the morning before by calling for help to bringing down the curative powers of the Almighty. As they talked, Carl wrapped his arms over Reba's and Michael's shoulders and gathered them to him.

The Johanssons preoccupied, Max asked, "Naomi, let's walk over a little ways and talk. I have a couple of questions."

Naomi studied him, her face glowing with excitement. Her voice filled with a grand benevolence, she said, "Of course, Max."

Once they'd put a little distance between them and the family, he asked: "Did Jacob say anything?"

"No," she answered.

"Did he try to say anything?"

She shook her head.

"Did Jacob indicate anything in any way about what happened at the ranch and who was responsible?"

"No. Nothing. As I said, as soon as I thanked the heavens, I pushed the call button. I didn't talk to him. And he made no attempt to speak."

Just then, the doctor walked out of the room.

"Mr. and Mrs. Johansson," he said. Michael and Reba shuffled toward the man, and Max and the others followed suit. Once surrounded, the physician explained, "We've given Jacob a sedative, and he's gone back to sleep. I've just examined him, and I don't see any damage to his airway other than the wound, so we're going to take him into surgery and repair his trachea."

"He'll be all right?" Reba asked. "His chances are good?"

"We believe so," the doctor said. "He was extremely lucky in the position of the cut, that it didn't damage his vocal cords. The odds are with him. He should make a complete recovery."

At that, Naomi let loose a small scream and fell to her knees. She clasped her palms in prayer. "Lord, thank you for this wonderful blessing," she cried out. "Praise you for your kindness for saving Jacob and bringing him back to his family."

Reba and Michael dropped down on their knees beside her. They shouted their gratitude to God, while Max noticed Carl amble off a short distance down the hall. Max turned to the doctor. "When will Jacob be able to communicate with us?"

"The operation will take a couple of hours," he said. "Jacob probably won't be able to talk for a while, a day or two, but you should be able to get some type of response from him, a nod of the head or finger signs, he can write things down for you, late this afternoon."

"That's good, very good," Max said, feeling his first sense of hope about the case's prospects.

"I know Jacob's injuries look terrible, but the truth is that this isn't a tough operation," the doctor explained. "If Jacob swallows well enough, he may be released as soon as tomorrow or the day after."

At that, Max thanked the physician and turned to where Carl had walked, intent on striking up a conversation. Yet when he gazed down the hallway, Max saw only a solitary nurse pushing a medicine cart.

Carl was gone.

CHAPTER TWENTY-FOUR

The assembly of protesters in front of my office had grown while I worked on the case. As I drove out of the parking lot, I counted eleven. A few men but mainly women with homemade signs hefted high over their heads, calling out to passersby. As I watched, a car pulled over and rolled down a window, the family inside apparently asking what the hubbub was about. I wondered what the demonstrators said, what they thought they knew about me that made them decide that I was unfit to be the town's police chief.

A short drive, and I arrived at the MRJ ranch. As I climbed out of the Suburban, a male bison lumbered toward me. Its massive body ground to a halt at the fence. I walked over, curious, and stared into its dark, blank eyes, wondering what it knew, what it saw. As if it could read my thoughts, the bull threw its massive head back and released a long, deep bellow that vibrated the air surrounding me and sent a shiver through my body.

Outside the house, little remained that hinted at the horror that had transpired there.

The evidence markers had all been removed, the bloody sheet, every telltale sign gone. The vultures had moved on, undoubtedly looking for other carrion. I thought of the scene the day before, the blood spatter on the clothes hanging on the line, the bloody holes the birds pecked in the sheet that covered the bodies. *If Mother Naomi hadn't come...* I willed myself not to finish the thought.

"Chief Jefferies," someone called out, and Lieutenant Mueller trudged out of the barn. "You dropping in to check on us?"

"I'm hoping I can help," I said. "Max said no luck so far, unless you've had a recent discovery?"

"No. Can't say that we have, although we're continuing to search," he said. Mueller looked as worn out as I felt, and we weren't even a day and a half out from the killings.

"Tell me where you've looked," I suggested.

"All through the house," he said. "We're checking out the barn now."

"Okay," I said. "I'm going to nose around inside, see if anything occurs to me."

"I hope it does," Mueller said. "If not, we're out of here when we're done with the barn, without finding those letters you're after."

I signaled that I understood and then started off for the house. At the door, I turned and looked back at the yard again, where Anna's and the children's bodies had been. Sadness washed over me. I pushed it back and went inside.

In the kitchen, two floor tiles had been removed, those that had the bloody footprint. They should have arrived at the state crime lab along with the knife, the gun, everything the CSI unit had collected at the ranch the day before, and the boot we'd found at the cabin.

Sooty fingerprint dust soiled the cabinets, their doors gaping open. The techs had pulled out utensils and pots and pans, plates and glasses and piled them on the table. From the looks of it, it was a thorough search. I doubted that I'd find anything they'd missed in the kitchen, so I moved on. I stopped and scouted around the living room, lifted the couch cushions and found nothing. In the dining room, I looked through the china cabinet, then at the long table ringed by chairs, a high chair on one side for little Jeremy. I wondered if he was big enough to sit in it yet. I didn't think so. I thought how sad that Laurel would never see her son crawl or walk, hear him say his first words.

At the bottom of the steps I inspected the ceiling, wondering about the heating ducts, ultimately deciding Laurel would never have stashed the letters where they'd be dried out and destroyed by the heat over the winter. Examining the walls with each step I took, I moved upstairs. The most likely location had to be Laurel's room. If I were her, with something to hide, that would be the only place I wouldn't be seen taking the letters out to read or putting them away. Yet in Laurel's room, too, Mueller's unit had done a thorough search. All her long prairie dresses, her cotton nightclothes, were out of the closet. The drawers were empty, and they'd been turned upside down and checked for false bottoms. The bedsheets were gone, sent to the crime lab to check for fibers and hairs. I inspected the spindled headboard, looked under the mattress, and then lay on my back and slid under the box spring and examined the bottom, hoping to find the letters taped beneath.

Nothing.

I rolled up the rugs and checked the floor, board by board. Slow going, it began to feel fruitless. *But she must have kept them,* I thought. *They were too precious to throw away.*

Frustrated, I sat on the edge of the bed. It appeared such a normal room. *How could something so horrific have happened here? Where are the letters?*

In Jeremy's nursery, I inspected each corner, hoping to find something, anything that looked odd or out of place. They weren't stashed under the crib, or in the small dresser. I didn't find them concealed in the wicker changing stand. The closet still had Jeremy's tiny clothes hanging inside. Hand-me-downs, lightly worn and carefully kept, intermingled with a scattering of newer things: a tiny set of coveralls, a blue cardigan with a hood, and onesies with trains and airplanes. I'd sent a bag of the baby's things with him the day before, but I thought perhaps I should take more, so Jacob's family could have them for him. I grabbed a plaid vinyl bag off a closet shelf and stuffed the rest of the clothes inside.

The bag slung over my shoulder, I peeked in the other rooms. They all appeared to have been searched. Anna's clothes, those of her children, still hung in their closets. Nothing stood out. Nothing suggested the location of the letters.

Before I abandoned the upstairs, I stood in the doorway to Laurel's room one last time. I envisioned her body on the bed. I thought about Mullins at the office that morning, explaining to me that old man Barstow had to be obeyed, and that Laurel's life wasn't her own to live. Then, just as I contemplated admitting defeat, something caught my attention: the drapes. The fabric matched the pale blue duvet we'd found over Laurel's body, but the drapes were lined, opaque, and it seemed to me that they hung a touch askew.

I felt around the bottom. Nothing seemed odd until I pulled one panel away from the window and noticed a thread line about ten inches from the top. Neat, tidy stitches, done by hand, like those used to hem a skirt, they didn't show from the front. They were so small, so precise, they were nearly invisible. I slipped my phone from my pocket and called Lieutenant Mueller.

"I'm in Laurel's room. Bring up a stepladder," I said.

"Find something?"

"Not sure."

Moments later, Mueller and one of his men walked in with a folded aluminum ladder off the CSI trailer. "Over here, the curtains," I said. They positioned the ladder in front of the window, and I climbed up. The house old, the windows high, I had to stand on the second rung from the top. I touched the curtain near the top, and I felt something crinkle inside. I pulled the curtains' edges back and gathered all the fabric on the rod. Then I popped the wooden rod up, freeing it from the wall. Heavy, it momentarily threw me off balance, and I wobbled.

"You want help with that?" Mueller asked, reaching up to hold the ladder steady.

"No, I'm okay. Just take this." I dropped the curtains on the rod down to Mueller. Once he had it, I clambered off the ladder. We laid the curtains out on the bed, and Mueller and I pulled out the rod. Immediately, I noticed pockets gaping near the top, slight openings between the fabric and the thick lining above the row of stitches.

Mueller must have noticed them too. "I think you've got them," he said.

He handed me a pair of latex evidence gloves. Once I had them on, I slipped my hand inside the opening and felt something thin and papery. One after another, I pulled out envelopes, twenty-four in all, with TO MY LOVE hand-printed on the front.

Mueller bumped one of his techs on his radio: "Bring evidence folders to the victim's bedroom, second floor. We've got what we came for."

I gave them room, and Mueller and his tech took over the task of processing the evidence. Two more CSI officers rushed in, and I went downstairs.

I waited in the kitchen to talk to Mueller when they finished. Meanwhile, I stared down at the removed tiles, thinking about the boots we found at Thompkins' cabin, convinced they would be a match, and wondering: *Why am I so unsure of his guilt?* Then I noticed a calendar hanging on the wall. Open to November, it had a photograph of dried leaves and pumpkins in a field. Someone had scrawled reminders of activities for the two older children. I felt a particular sadness when I saw the notation of a dinner scheduled for the coming week with Mullins and the rest of Laurel's family.

On each day next to the date, someone had alternated writing in a capital 'A' or an 'L.' Having grown up in a polygamous house, I understood what I was looking at; it was Jacob's schedule, the one that kept track of which nights he slept with which of his two wives. When the date had an 'A' he slept with Anna. On those marked 'L' he slept in Laurel's bed. I checked the previous Sunday, and that date was marked with an 'A'.

That means that the night of Laurel's killing, Jacob was in bed with Anna. Laurel slept alone, I thought. *And Carl would have known that because he was at the ranch that evening, and it's documented right here out in the open on this calendar.*

I took out my phone and snapped a few photos of the calendar, just as Mueller walked into the kitchen. "Great find, Chief," he said. "I don't know how you spotted these, but I'm glad you did."

"When can I have copies?" I asked. "I need to read them."

"Give me ninety minutes, and I'll have them at your office," he said. "I'll send one of the guys right over with them."

"You've got it," I said. "And log this calendar into evidence, too, okay?"

"Sure," Mueller said. He looked as relieved as I felt that we were done at the scene and had found what we'd come for.

As I turned to leave, my cell rang. My heart immediately sped up a bit when I saw Max's name on the screen, and I made a conscious effort to slow it down. "Hey, what have you got for me?"

"Good news," he said.

Max explained that Jacob had come out of the coma and was in surgery, that he'd be out in a couple of hours, and that the doctor thought we might be able to communicate with him late that afternoon.

"That's great news," I said, hopeful that we might have a big break in the case. "And they think he'll recover well?"

"The doctor says he thinks so," Max said. "Thinks he'll be able to talk and breathe normally again. Said the same thing the paramedic did, that Jacob was lucky."

"I still have a hard time seeing him that way," I admitted. "But good news here, too. We found the letters. I'll have copies in an hour and a half. Want to meet me at the office so we can read through them?"

"You bet," Max said. "How about we grab lunch and then head to your office? I'll buy."

I hesitated, wondering if that was a good idea. Dinner at his house the evening before, now lunch? We were spending a lot of time together. Yet I couldn't deny that I wanted to see him. An hour off to talk about the case, but more than that, to just talk, was appealing.

"Okay," I said. "Lunch and then we'll head over to my office to read the letters."

We agreed to meet at the diner, but then Max said something, and our plans changed. "You know, Clara, what's really peculiar is that Naomi was at the hospital again."

"She was?"

"Yup. As a matter of fact, she was in the room with Jacob when he woke up. She hit the call button for the doctor," Max said. "And what seemed even odder, at one point, she was holding Jacob's hand."

For a moment, I was silent. I thought about what I'd overheard at the shelter, the woman who said that even before the killings Naomi appeared interested in Jacob. Then I considered that brief moment the previous day when she'd been in the room alone with Jacob and I thought I saw her talking to him. I wondered what was going on. I'd never known her to be secretive, but I wondered if she was hiding something. If Naomi wouldn't tell me the truth about their relationship, who would?

Then I knew. It was a long shot that she'd cooperate, but maybe I could convince her?

"Max, I can't make lunch. I'll meet you at the station, but I'm going out to the trailer first," I said. "I need to have a talk with my mother."

CHAPTER TWENTY-FIVE

Three months in Alber, and after I finished the case that brought me home, I'd only driven to my family's trailer once. A few weeks after I signed on as police chief, I had tried just dropping in. I'd knocked on the door on a Sunday afternoon and one of my half-sisters, twelve-year-old Delilah of the auburn hair and freckled nose, spotted me. She'd screamed my name and run to me. "Clara! Clara! I was hoping that you'd come." Jabbering so fast I could barely understand her, she'd said, "I ask my mom all the time if I can see you, but she won't let me!" Delilah giggled, excited and happy, and I'd laughed and wrapped my arms around her.

"I wanted to see you so much." Delilah scrunched up her nose. "And now you're here."

The news of my arrival had spread and the other children swarmed me. I'd thought my heart might burst. This is what I'd wanted more than anything: to spend time with my family, to get to know my brothers and sisters. But before I'd said more than hello, Mother Sariah rushed over and gathered Delilah up, pulled my arms from around her waist and walked her off. In a split second, Mother Naomi had corralled the rest of the children and had whisked them away.

Ardeth, my biological mother, then suggested she and I talk outside. She'd taken my arm and explained that she was grateful for what I'd done, that I'd helped reunite the family. As she'd talked, she'd kept guiding me toward the road. When we reached my Suburban, she'd smiled at me and said, "Clara, as I have explained to you before, you aren't welcome here. We can't have you influence the children."

In my mid-thirties, I wasn't a child, and cops get pretty good at hiding their feelings, but I'd felt crestfallen. I'd fought the tears that threatened to spill from my eyes. Maybe I should have expected this reception. Maybe I had. But the disappointment felt like a slap across the face. "Why? Are you afraid that by seeing me they'll realize that there's another life and a big world out there? That they'll want the freedom to choose their own futures?"

Mother had assessed me as if I were a spoiled bowl of milk.

"Clara, I'm worried that you'll put false ideas in their heads, ones that will make them question their faith and our ways." With that, Mother had dropped her hand from my arm, and I'd thought I'd seen sadness in her eyes. I was, after all, still her daughter. Perhaps she hadn't completely forgotten that? "In another world, it might be possible for you to visit. But not in this one. Not when you're a deserter who has turned your back on our faith, all our beliefs," she'd said. "This very moment, by talking with you, I am disobeying our prophet and committing a grave sin."

I had no argument to counter that. As a child, much of what mother taught me revolved around the faith of Elijah's People, about the importance of adhering to our strict ways. I've understood for nearly all of my life that her religious beliefs ruled Mother's world. That they were more important to her than my father or any of us children. Despite it all, I loved her. On that afternoon, I'd leaned forward, and before she could stop me, given her a peck on the cheek. While Mother had looked surprised, she didn't pull back. Then, I did as she had asked; I'd left and never gone back.

As I drove through town, I passed the police station again, and the protesters had multiplied. I noticed the crowd had become predominantly men, with only a half dozen or so women, in all counting maybe thirty or more, most carrying some kind of poster-board sign. The women had started it, but it didn't surprise me that the men had taken over. As a wife who'd defied her husband and run away, I was a threat to the men more than to the women. The sight of them milling about in their heavy coats reminded me of a meeting of the faithful from my childhood, when I'd seen groups of men congregate intent on a common cause. Usually it involved driving someone from the community—a wayward woman, a teenage boy, a man who they judged as not living up to the standards of the faith. I stopped reading the placards after the first: OUTSIDER GO HOME!

My pulse sped up, and I cleared my throat. It felt as if something had lodged there. Then I put my head down and kept driving. I willed myself not to consider the men with their bitter signs. Not now. Later would be time enough. More to prove to myself that I wasn't rattled than because I was hungry, I stopped at the diner and grabbed a ham and cheese sandwich to go. I ate it behind the wheel as I drove past the big, two-story house I'd grown up in. The sun not yet high, it still had frost on the roof. I thought about how I'd come home, but not really home. That might never happen. Maybe I should leave, but was that the answer? At least I understood Alber. Strange to the rest of the world, no doubt, the town and its way of life were familiar to me. For the first twenty-four years of my life, until I fled, it was my normal.

I kept driving toward the mountains, heading to the trailer park that lay at the foot of Samuel's Peak. I passed under the gate with a horn-blowing angel at the top and turned to the right on the final road, the one that backed up to the cornfield. The stalks had been cut down and hauled away, and it lay plowed under for the winter. At the weatherworn double-wide, I got out of the Suburban and wrapped my parka tighter to ward off the bitter cold.

I trudged toward the back, passed the outhouse, and then turned toward the door. I still found it hard to believe that my three mothers and more than a dozen of my siblings lived in such close quarters. After father's death, everything had become hard for the family. I scurried up the cement steps to the screen door. A Tuesday, all the children should have been in school, but before I could knock, my fourteen-year-old sister, Lily, opened the door, her cheeks flushed and her dark hair, so like mine, pulled back into a loose ponytail. "Clara!" She lowered her voice, I assumed fearful that Mother might hear. "Are you supposed to be here?"

I chuckled just a bit. "Let me in. I need to talk to our mother."

Lily glanced over her shoulder and carefully opened the door. She had a long apron on over a well-worn green-flowered prairie dress that had probably been handed down for fifteen years from sister to sister. Two steps into the trailer, and I heard Mother banging around in the kitchen. I whispered to Lily, "Are you sick? Why aren't you in school?"

She leaned forward and put her lips to my ear, her hand cupped to muffle her voice. "I only go to classes two days a week and do the rest of my lessons at home. Three days a week I help Mother."

I frowned. "Go to your room while I talk to her."

Lily nodded, turned and trudged off, just as our Mother shouted from the kitchen, "Lily, come here, girl. I need you."

Mother had on her work clothes as well, topped by her own ragged, stained apron. Ever since I could remember, Mother had conjured up and sold herbal remedies, poultices, tinctures and the like for everything from gallstones to heart conditions. Only in dire situations, like Jacob's, did members of Elijah's People go to Gentile doctors. For nearly all maladies, we were told that our faith would heal us. Mother had a special place in our community as something of a healer. When Father was alive, the money Mother made bought extras; my assumption was that now it was sorely needed to pay living expenses.

Her steel-gray hair knotted on top of her head, Mother looked thinner and more fragile every time I saw her. On the table, she had dozens of small amber bottles lined up and a pile of caps with droppers. On the counter, a mixture that resembled weeds floating in dirty water filled a metal bucket. I caught a whiff and recognized Mother's sleep potion, a tincture of alcohol, passionflower and valerian root. In her hands she held a strainer.

"Lily, come help. I only have two hands," she said, not looking up.

I walked over and took the strainer from her. "Clara!" she said, startled. "What are you doing here?"

"We need to talk," I said. "While we do, I'll help."

"You're not supposed to be here," she said, irritated. "I told you not to come to the trailer, that you're not welcome. Where is Lily?"

"I sent her to her room to study. She tells me she isn't going to school three days a week," I said.

Mother frowned, forming sharp arches in her dark brows. I thought she'd tell me this was none of my business, and perhaps she considered saying that, but I sensed the situation troubled her. Instead, she admitted, "Clara, this isn't what I want, but I need help with my work. We have many to feed and clothe. We have bills to pay. And the prophet has said that girls really only need to go through the eighth grade. Lily is in the ninth." At that Mother pursed her lips. "I don't know why I'm explaining to you."

"Probably because you know how bright Lily is, how gifted, and that it is wrong to keep her from her classes." I held the strainer over a large pitcher, as I had often as a young girl when I'd helped her, and Mother poured the mixture through, filtering out the debris. The herbs had been sitting in the alcohol for six weeks, turning the clear liquid amber. "Lily needs to go to school, Mother. She's smart enough to go to college, to get a real job."

"Like you did?" Mother said pointedly. "So she can abandon her family?"

"A job that would help support the family," I said.

"I provide for the family with my work," Mother said, standing taller. In the last years, she'd become stooped, looking more like an old woman than she should at fifty-five. "Your three mothers work hard, Clara. Sariah makes beautiful quilt skirts she sells through the gift shop. And Naomi bottles her honey and sells it. We take care of our children."

"Yes, I understand, but Lily—"

"Is that why you've come?" Mother demanded, her voice shrill. "To chastise me about Lily?"

"No, I... I'm here to talk about Mother Naomi and what happened at the Johansson house," I said. "I'm working on the investigation, and I've been hearing some things."

Mother finished filtering the tincture into the pitcher and glowered as she picked up a funnel and handed it to me. I inserted it into the neck of the first of the small amber bottles, and mother remained silent as she carefully poured in enough to nearly fill it. She put down the pitcher and capped the bottle with one of the droppers, then smoothed on a label that read: SLEEPING TINCTURE. MIX 3 DROPS IN WATER AND DRINK 45 MINUTES BEFORE BED.

We moved on to the next bottle.

"What have you been hearing? Gossip, I assume?" Mother asked, her voice dripping with annoyance.

"About Mother Naomi's interest in Jacob Johansson," I said.

Mother didn't look surprised. Filling the second vial, she repeated the process, screwed on the cap and pasted on the label. "Clara, Naomi is one of your mothers. You're not to question her actions or her motives. To you she is above reproach," she said.

"I am not questioning her as her daughter, but as the Alber police chief," I said, as matter-of-factly as I could muster. "I take it that you were aware of her interest in Jacob?"

Mother shot me a suspicious glance, her dark eyes flickering over my own. "I know that Naomi saved Jacob by finding him and calling for help before he bled to death. I know that she visits him to pray for his recovery, and she tells me that his family is very grateful."

"People in town say that Mother Naomi showed interest in Jacob even before all of this," I said, and then I waited. She didn't comment, so I went on. "I've seen some things that make me wonder if that's true."

For a moment, Mother remained quiet, then she looked over at me, narrowed her eyes and asked, "What if it is?"

"I don't know what it would mean to the case, if it means anything," I admitted. "But it is important for any investigation to understand the truth about all those involved, about their relationships. So, I need to know about Mother Naomi and Jacob."

"The truth? You want to understand the truth?" Mother's voice sounded strained as she placed the pitcher on the table, careful not to spill a drop. "Clara, look around. Do you see how we live?"

I bit my lip. I'd thought about this often, how far the family had fallen. "I do, Mother, but that's not what this is about."

"It's not?" she challenged.

"No, it's not. This is about my job. I need to understand how Naomi fits into the puzzle. If there was a relationship before the killings between her and Jacob, that could make a difference."

"Clara, have you forgotten who we are? What we stand for?" Mother looked at me with disappointment. "Naomi isn't involved in any killings, you know that."

"But how do we—" I started.

"Clara, this is simple." Mother cut me off, twisting to look at me through the corners of her eyes. "I am getting older, but Sariah and Naomi are young yet."

"I realize that they're younger women," I said. "I'm thirty-five, which means that Naomi is in her mid-forties?"

"Yes, she is. And I've noticed for months that Naomi is interested in Jacob. I assumed that she hoped to become one of his wives, and I didn't discourage that. We are too crowded in this old trailer and have too many to support," she said. "If Naomi leaves and takes her children with her to a new household, it improves all our lives."

"Of course," I said, aware of the fragile walls of the trailer that protected my mothers and siblings from the world. "But, again, this isn't about that. It's just that I'm—"

"You are what?" Mother asked, her voice rising.

This time, I stood straighter and looked down at her. "Mother, it's important for the investigation that I understand Naomi's relationship with Jacob."

"You've said that," Mother reminded me. "And I've told you what you asked."

"But not everything I need to know. What did you see pass between them?" Mother didn't answer, just glowered at me. I sensed that she believed she'd told me enough. When Mother got like this, it had always felt to me as a girl that she threw up an invisible wall between us, one I couldn't break through. But this time, I wasn't going to be denied. I had to find a way around her blockade. "You can help the investigation, Mother," I said, my voice soft, urging. "Help me understand so I can see the big picture here."

"And I would do that because…?" she queried.

"Because Laurel, Anna and two beautiful children are dead, murdered," I said. "And because I'm not sure who killed them, or if Jacob and his baby son, Jeremy, are still in jeopardy."

Uncertain, Mother sighed. "Clara, I don't know. To gossip is to sin."

"I need to know what you know, Mother," I said. "It's important."

Mother stood, lips tight, silent, then, biting off each word, she said, "I don't know a lot. But off and on, I saw Naomi talk to Jacob after services, smiling at him, giggling like a young girl at his jokes."

"How did he respond?" I asked.

"I saw interest in Jacob's eyes as well, which I interpreted as a clue that perhaps one day Naomi might escape what our lives have become," Mother said, weary. "He is a wealthy man, with a big house and a successful business. I was hopeful for Naomi. I said nothing to her about this, and she probably doesn't know that I am in favor of her aspirations, but I am."

"You who have always been so firm about the family staying together," I noted.

Mother shook her head. "I am older now, Clara, and tired. I am working too hard since your father died. We all are."

Seeing the dark shadows under her eyes, I felt sorry for Mother. Life had treated her harshly. Yet I didn't try to console her. I knew my mother, and she wouldn't have accepted my sympathy. "Anything else I should know about Naomi and Jacob?" I asked. Mother remained silent, and I pushed. "Think of those dead children mother, Benjamin and Sybille. Think of Anna and Laurel. I need to know."

Mother hesitated, but then said, "It was only once."

"What was?" I asked.

Although she appeared reluctant, Mother explained, "You can tell no one I've told you this, Clara. Do you understand?"

I nodded.

"Once when Naomi and I were at services, I heard Jacob whisper to her," Mother said.

"What did he say?" I asked.

This was hard for Mother. That I knew. "Jacob said that he would see her the next day at the bee shack."

"At the bee shack? That was all?" I asked, and Mother nodded. "Okay. Thank you. That does help." I prepared to leave, but then turned back to her. I had another matter to discuss. "Mother, Lily needs to go to school," I said. "I can help you and the family financially. I have my salary, and I live at the shelter so I have very few expenses. I have savings from my years in Dallas. Perhaps some extra money would make it possible for Lily to go to school and concentrate on her studies and also make life easier for all of you."

"No, Clara—" she protested.

"I would like to help."

Mother appeared exhausted, but she shook her head. "Clara, you make a good point, and I will try to get Lily to school three days a week instead of two," she said. "But I will not take your money."

"Why turn me down when it would help all of you?" I asked. "Accept my offer, if not for you, for the others."

Mother shook her head. "That will not happen. You are no longer one of us, and it would be wrong for me to act as if that were not true."

Her words cut into my heart. "I'm not asking for anything in return," I said, trying to hide the disappointment and hurt that had crept into my voice. "I can have the money deposited automatically into an account for the family. You won't need to have anything to do with me."

Mother didn't hesitate. "It would still be sinful of me to take money from you," she said, her eyes firmly on mine. "Clara, you must leave. I have work to do, and you should not be here. I've explained before that you're not welcome."

I returned Mother's gaze, swallowed my disappointment and wondered how far I could push her. She'd been more helpful than I'd anticipated. Could I get her to say more?

"One more question," I said. This wasn't about the case or about Lily but about me. My life. It was about the horror that had forced me to flee. "After I ran away, did you and Father ever regret making me marry as you did?"

Her eyes flickered wide, and Mother appeared startled, as if that had never occurred to her. "Why would we have anything to regret, Clara?" she asked. "Did we not do what the prophet ordered?"

CHAPTER TWENTY-SIX

The street overflowed with protesters when I drove up to the station. I figured there had to be fifty people or more milling about. Some stood around talking, animatedly waving their arms, I assumed debating my place in the community and whether or not I was fit for my job. I saw old friends, a few from my school years. They looked resolutely away from me. I waited for the crowd to clear on the side street so I could drive into the parking lot. Angry faces shouted at me, and I stared straight ahead and kept driving. The group parted, and I drove through without incident, but I felt shaken.

"Heck of a crowd out there," Max said when I walked in. He put his hands on my shoulders and looked into my eyes. "You safe with all that going on?"

I felt a wave of gratitude, and I wanted to lay my head against his chest and rest against him, to feel the warmth of him. It would have been a relief to let go and let him protect me. But I couldn't take that step. Not yet. None of this was over. "Thanks, but nothing to be concerned about," I said, conjuring up a rather slim smile. "Once we solve this case, they'll get over it."

"You had your meeting? How did it go?" Familiar with the gulf between my mother and me, Max understood she might not cooperate. He knew that any conversation with my family automatically carried an eighteen-wheeler full of emotional cargo. I was considering how to respond when Kellie glanced up from behind the front desk, interested.

"How did what go?" she asked.

"Nothing important," I said. "Have those protesters been causing any problems?"

"Not really," she said. "But I wish they'd give up and leave."

"Probably won't for a while. Looks like they're enjoying it," I said. "Any messages?"

Kellie handed me a pile of a dozen or so, and I rifled through them. One was from the state lab's ballistics section. I turned to Max. "Let's go to the conference room. We can call them back, and then I can fill you in on my conversation with Mother."

Once I threw my leather bag down, I slipped my phone out, placed the call, and put it on speaker so Max could hear. "What'd you find out?" I asked the tech who answered. "Is the gun the murder weapon?"

"Yes, it is," he said. "It's been recently fired. We fingerprinted it, but it's been wiped clean. No prints. We typed some blood found on the barrel, a very small amount, and we think it's either Benjamin or Anna Johansson's. We've sent it out for DNA to make sure it's a match, but of the five victims, it's their blood type."

"Okay, good," I said. "And you did ballistics?"

"And we did ballistics, fired it and retrieved the bullets. The rifling marks match a bullet removed during autopsy from the body of Anna Johansson."

"Were there any bullets left in the magazine?" I asked.

"There were five remaining. The magazine holds ten," the guy said.

"So, the killer could have shot all five victims if he'd wanted to," I said, looking at Max. "But he chose to cut Laurel's and Jacob's throats."

"Yeah," Max said. He then asked the tech an important question: "Who is the gun registered to?"

"Not the killer," the guy said, and Max and I looked at each other in disappointment. "While I worked on ballistics, another tech ran the serial number. This gun was originally sold nine years ago to a guy in Colorado Springs. The registration never changed. We tracked him and interviewed him via phone. He says he sold that particular gun about six years ago through a private sale at a gun show."

"No background check?" I said.

"Right," the tech responded. "It fell under the private sale exclusion to the gun laws. The seller has an alibi. He's seventy-eight and has been in the hospital for the past few days, just getting out this morning. He had heart surgery."

"Send us the registration form and anything you have on this guy," I said. "Doesn't sound like he's our killer, but I want to verify that he has nothing to do with this."

"Will do," the tech said.

"You think the seller might recognize a photo of the person he sold the gun to?" Max asked. "We could get together a couple of photo lineups, put our suspects in, email them to his local PD and ask them to go over them with him."

"We asked that. The guy says no chance. He buys and sells guns like a hardware store owner flips hammers, dozens every year," the tech said. "Sometimes, he buys new, gets tired of them and sells them, like he did with this gun. Other times he buys used, repairs and marks them up, then sells them for a profit. He says he keeps no records."

This wasn't good. We'd just lost what could have been a valuable lead. "Thanks," I said. "Anything on the knife?"

"We sent photos of the blade over to Doc Wiley," the tech said. "He says it could be the weapon used to murder Laurel Johansson. The serration of the blade is consistent with the cut in her throat. We've sent samples of the blood found on the knife for DNA."

"Fingerprints?" Max asked.

"Nada," the tech said. "Like the gun, the knife handle has been wiped clean."

"What about Jacob's wound?" I asked. "Does it match that, too?"

"Not sure yet," the tech said. "We're waiting on photos and X-rays from the hospital to compare. We should have that for you soon."

"Okay, and the bloody print and the boot, anything there yet?" Max asked.

"Not sure. I'll check and email it over when it's ready," the tech said. "I know they're working on it. I saw a colleague scanning the print into the system."

"We'd appreciate that," I said as I plopped down in the chair, thinking.

"We'll watch for it," Max said. "And thanks again for turning all this around so fast."

As we hung up, Kellie walked in with the copies of the letters I'd found sewn into Laurel's curtains. Max took a stack and I grabbed the rest. We started shuffling, the earliest letters top left on the conference room table, the most recent bottom right. We had three rows, twenty-one letters in all. Unlike Laurel's letters, which were sent religiously once a week, Myles sometimes skipped a week, even two. While hers were written on Sundays, Myles dated his on Wednesdays. None of his was terribly long, just a page or two, a couple at the most three pages, and we read them in order, starting with one that was written shortly after Laurel was promised to Jacob. At the top, he addressed each TO THE WOMAN I LOVE.

WHY WOULD THE PROPHET DO THIS TO US? Myles wrote. The letters were block printed in a precise hand. *DOESN'T HE UNDERSTAND LOVE? HOW CAN THIS BE A REVELATION FROM GOD, WHEN GOD IS LOVE? HE WOULD KNOW THAT WE AREN'T TO BE SEPARATED, WOULDN'T HE? I CAN'T ENVISION A GOD WHO WOULD DENY OUR LOVE FOR EACH OTHER.*

The letters were heartfelt and kind. Myles inquired about Laurel's health and urged her to stop her hunger strike and eat:

I WANT YOU ALIVE MORE THAN WITH ME. I WANT YOU TO LIVE, LAUREL, MORE THAN ANYTHING ELSE. IF YOU DIE, I WILL, TOO. FOR HOW COULD I LIVE WITHOUT YOU IN THIS WORLD? THAT WOULD BE IMPOSSIBLE.

Laurel had written little about Jacob in her letters to Myles, and he ignored him as well, rarely calling him by name. At times, when Myles had to, he referred to Jacob as "your husband."

YOUR HUSBAND SHOULD NOT MAKE YOU DO SUCH HARD WORK, LAUREL, he wrote a few months after she married. *DOESN'T HE HAVE WORKERS TO FEED THE BISON? THEY'RE POWERFUL ANIMALS, AND UNPREDICTABLE. IT WORRIES ME THAT HE SENDS YOU OUT INTO THE FIELDS WITH THEM. WHAT IF ONE WERE TO CHARGE YOU?*

I turned to Max. "Just a minute," I said. "I'm going to get the copies of Laurel's letters."

I hurried to my office and claimed them off my desk, whisked them back to the conference room and we laid them out also based on date, intermingling them with Jacob's letters. When we read them in succession, we quickly realized that they rarely flowed one to the other. Laurel and Myles weren't answering each other's questions or concerns from the previous letter in their own. "Look at this," I said to Max. "There's nothing in Laurel's letter before this about feeding the bison."

"So, he didn't get that out of a letter?" Max inquired. "Then how?"

"In two of the letters, Laurel mentions that they met. Maybe they did this often, or whenever they could." I then mentioned what had occurred to me earlier, when I'd first read Laurel's letters. "That time that Scotty said he saw them at the river, maybe that was their meeting place."

"It could be. Or they may have been talking on the phone," Max pointed out. "Jacob might not have been able to tell. The house phone is a landline, a wall phone, one of the old Trimline models without caller ID."

"So, Jacob wouldn't have known," I said.

"Probably not," Max said. "Maybe she called Myles while Jacob was in town or out in the fields, when he was somewhere with Anna and the children."

"Or late at night, when Jacob was in Anna's bed, not hers," I said.

Max sighed. "Not a lot of answers here."

"That could be true. They may have been able to hide the phone calls. Unless there's a detail on the phone bills." I picked up the phone. "Let me check something."

Moments later, Mueller picked up. "Lieutenant, did you happen to find any bills at the crime scene at the ranch, especially phone bills?" I asked.

"Yes, we did," he answered. "I'm pretty sure they're in the desk in the downstairs study. I could probably find them. Do you want me to swing out there and get them, log them in and bring them to you? It shouldn't take long."

"That would be great," I said.

When I hung up, Max said, "What if Laurel had a cell phone?"

"Good thought." I nodded. This time I called Mullins. When he answered, his voice sounded subdued and hoarse, thick with sadness. "How're you doing, Jeff?" I asked.

"Best we can," he answered. "Have you found Myles yet?"

"No, but we have Conroy back out at the cabin watching for him, a BOLO out to law enforcement, and it should be on the news tonight," I said. "And I don't want you to fret about Jeremy. We have a squad watching Jacob's sister's house, where he's being kept, just in case whoever did this isn't finished."

"I wondered about that," Mullins said. "Almost called you and asked about it."

"We're covering it all, Jeff. Try not to worry," I said.

"Shit, Chief, I really think you and Max are wrong about Myles," he said. "And it frosts me because you're wasting time. Have you looked any more into Carl?"

"We're following that lead, too," I said. "But right now, the evidence is pointing at Myles."

"Hell," Mullins groused. "If it's him, I'm going to be flat-out stunned. I just don't believe it."

"Jeff, listen, did Laurel have a cell phone while she was married to Jacob? Do you know?" I asked.

"No cell, just the house phone. I asked him a couple of times to get her one, didn't like her not having one to call if she had a flat tire and such, but he never would. Said she didn't need it," he answered. "Why?"

"Just trying to piece some things together," I answered. "Gotta go. We're working. We'll be in touch soon."

"No cell," I relayed to Max.

At that, Max's phone rang. He talked to someone, then hung up. "The lab says it appears the knife found on the scene is consistent with the one used to cut Jacob's throat."

"Good," I said. "That's one more question answered."

While we waited for the phone bills, we returned to the letters. In many of them, Myles tried to comfort Laurel. She must have complained about her husband's sexual attentions, for Myles told her to try to train her mind to think of other things until it was over:

YOU CAN'T REBUFF HIM. LAUREL, HE WILL
COMPLAIN TO THE PROPHET AND THE MESSAGE
WILL COME DOWN THAT YOU ARE DISOBEDIENT.
IT'S BETTER TO TOLERATE HIM. YOU SAY WHEN
YOU ARE WITH HIM YOU THINK OF ME. I THINK
OF YOU EVERY NIGHT. PERHAPS OUR MINDS
CAN CONNECT ON SOME OTHER PLANE, IN A
PLACE WHERE YOU CAN BE WITH ME IN SPIRIT
ALTHOUGH NOT IN BODY.

At no time did Myles grumble. It seemed that he understood, perhaps better than Laurel did, that this wasn't a war they could win. At one point, Laurel must have suggested they run away together, for Myles advised her to forget such thoughts:

LAUREL, YOUR HUSBAND WOULD COME FOR
YOU. HE WOULDN'T JUST LET YOU LEAVE. AND
WE WOULD NEVER BE ABLE TO LIVE IN PEACE.
I CAN'T ASK YOU TO SPEND YOUR LIFE IN FEAR.

An hour after we began, we were reading the most recent of the letters. In them, Myles talked of Jeremy. Laurel must have brought the baby to meet Myles:

I HOPED ONE DAY YOU WOULD BEAR MY CHILD,
MY LOVE. BUT THAT ISN'T TO BE. STILL, IT FILLS
MY HEART WITH SUCH HAPPINESS TO SEE YOU
WITH JEREMY. YOU HAVE A SON, LAUREL. A SON,
WHO WILL BRING YOU JOY.

The final letter was only a week old, dated the Wednesday before the murders, and it ended with the only hint of anything unusual happening:

I'M DISMAYED BY WHAT YOU SO RECENTLY TOLD ME, AND I AM FEARFUL FOR YOU. WE MUST TALK SOON. VERY SOON. I WILL NOT HAVE YOU SUFFER. LAUREL, I WILL ALWAYS PROTECT YOU.

Max read that paragraph twice out loud and then asked, "What do you make of that?"

"That something was brewing," I said. "But what?"

"Who was Myles offering to protect her from?" Max asked. "Carl?"

"It could be," I said. "If Laurel knew Carl was stalking her, maybe even knew that he was taking the photos, she could have told Myles. But this is too sketchy. It could be something else. You know what's odd?" Max shrugged, and I explained, "Myles doesn't have a letter from Laurel dated this past Sunday. There should have been one, if they kept to their usual pattern."

"You're right," Max said. "But maybe she simply didn't write that last Sunday."

"That would seem odd. She did every other week," I said. "But then they'd met the day before, and Naomi said it appeared that they might have been arguing."

At that moment, Kellie popped the door open. "Lieutenant Mueller dropped this off for you," she said, as she placed an envelope on the table.

"The phone bills," Max said. "Let's have a look."

I opened them. No detail of the calls. Jacob used a small local phone company, one that didn't supply itemized bills. "I'll call the company," I said. "Let's find out if they can run a report that includes the phone numbers for us."

Minutes later, I had a billing clerk on the phone. "Don't you need a subpoena?" she asked.

"I can get one, but that's going to take time," I said. "We have five victims, four murdered and the fifth gravely injured. Time's important here. We have a killer walking around free who might go after the two survivors, one a small infant. We have to move fast on this."

The woman went quiet for a minute. "I'd like to help, but is this going to get me fired?"

I looked at Max. "We'll get a subpoena to cover you. It'll be in your office within the hour," I said. "But meet us halfway and email what you have ASAP, okay?"

A moment's hesitation and she agreed.

I hung up and turned to Max. "You want to track down Judge Crockett and get the subpoena while I wait here for the phone bills?"

He agreed, and fifteen minutes later, I had print-outs of the itemized bills in front of me. There weren't a lot, maybe thirty on each bill. What I was looking for were calls between Laurel and Myles. At this point, I drew a faint pencil line through all those to Mexico. If a lead popped up that suggested those should be looked into, we could do that later. The remaining phone numbers, I called.

"Who's this?" a woman asked.

"Police Chief Clara Jefferies," I said. "Who am I talking to?"

That woman identified herself as a friend of Laurel's from high school. We talked briefly, but she knew nothing that could help us. I continued down the list that way, confirming who had each number, until Max came in. The subpoena was on its way to the phone company, and I gave him the prior month's bill and he started the same drill.

In the end, more friends of Laurel's, Jacob's parents and other members of the Johansson family answered their phones. Carl's voicemail picked up when we dialed his number. I didn't leave a message but circled that one and went on. Mullins answered his home phone along with others in Laurel's family.

"All the numbers on this list are accounted for," I said, when I finished.

"I'm done, too," Max said. "No calls to Myles."

"Which means that they weren't communicating by phone," I said.

"No, they had to be meeting in person," Max said.

"At the river?"

Max looked at me and smiled. "We do have a lot in common with these two, Clara," he said.

Suddenly self-conscious, I felt my face flush. I looked into his eyes and pictured him that day at the river. In many ways, he hadn't changed. "We were so young, weren't we?" I said.

Max walked toward me, took my hands in his, and this time I gave in. I rested my head against his chest, and he held me close. I felt his lips on the center part of my dark hair, the warmth of his breath, and I listened to his strong, regular, dependable heart. I gave myself—gave us—that moment, then, without moving away, I said, "Max, you know, there's just something really off here."

"How so?" he asked.

Although I would have liked to remain as we were, I stood straight again, moved away, dropped his hands and said, "Reading these letters, how protective Myles was of Laurel, how could he be the one who murdered her, who so coldly shot Anna and the children?"

"I don't know Myles, so I can't say," Max responded. "But what you said yesterday about love sometimes turning violent is true. And we both know that people can have two sides. They're not always who they pretend to be."

Could my instincts be that far off about Myles Thompkins? Maybe. Every investigator had a story about misjudging a suspect. In my first year as a cop, I wrote off a sixteen-year-old as the perp in a homicide, just couldn't believe such a polite, smart kid would have raped the girl and beaten her to death. Turned out to be him, and I learned a valuable lesson, one I needed to remember while we wove our way through this case.

"Any news from the hospital on Jacob's condition?" I asked.

"I heard from them a little while ago," Max said. "He's out of surgery but still in recovery. The surgeon said it went very well. It'll be a couple more hours before we can try to communicate with him."

"Okay, that's good," I said. "And we still have Jeremy under surveillance, so that's covered. We know he's safe."

"What do we do while we're waiting to talk to Jacob? What are you thinking?" Max asked.

"We have the world on notice to watch for Myles, so I'd like another shot at Carl. Any idea where to find him?"

"Ah, yeah, well, I was going to mention that. He disappeared from the hospital pretty quickly after Jacob woke up," Max said. "Which, to be honest, I thought was strange at the time. While I talked to the doctor, Carl was standing in the hallway. A minute later, he was gone."

"You know, I got his voicemail when we were going through the phone numbers. He didn't answer," I said. "How about we drive out to his trailer? Let's have another go at him."

Just then, Kellie stuck her head in the door. In her hand she had four sheets of paper stapled together. "From the state lab, about the boots," she said. "I thought you'd want to see this."

She left, and Max and I skimmed the report. There was a scan of a photo of the boot's sole and another of the print found on the kitchen floor. The ID specialist had inserted lines and numbered corresponding points on both. I read the conclusion out loud: "Twenty-three match points have been identified between the boot found at Myles Thompkins' home and the bloody print found at the crime scene. It is the opinion of this analyst that the boot in question is the one that left the print at the crime scene."

"Things aren't looking good for Myles." Max grimaced. "Still think we should try to rustle up Carl? Even with this?"

I hesitated, thinking it through. The report hadn't changed anything really. We still couldn't find Myles. My suspicions weren't quieted when it came to Carl.

"Yup," I said. "Let's go."

CHAPTER TWENTY-SEVEN

We exited out the back door to avoid the crowd of demonstrators. As we walked to my car, we heard them chanting, "Go home! Go home!" Max paused to get a good look at the crowd. He had a frown that encompassed his entire face, his eyes locked on the signs and those carrying them. I did my best not to show any reaction, but their voices rang in my ears, and a fist of anger squeezed my chest. I hurried to the SUV, but Max took his time, a pensive expression on his face. We left the lot, and I took a side street, heading toward the highway.

As if choosing his words with great care, Max spoke slowly and deliberately. "Clara, this may be getting out of hand. I don't like what's happening in Alber. These protests. The signs. Maybe we need to do something to quiet things down." I heard the worry in his voice, fear for me, I knew, but I shook my head, dismissing his concerns.

"Just some disgruntled folks," I said. "They're upset about the murders, wondering if I'm up to the job. They'll be okay, once we solve this."

"You think that'll do it?" he asked, sounding dubious. We'd both grown up in Alber, and Max understood the town's unshakable rules, that when I'd fled Elijah's People, I'd become considered a pariah.

I glanced over at him and shrugged. "If not, maybe this isn't the right place for me."

At that, I felt Max tense in the seat beside me.

"Maybe that's part of the problem. You can't have one foot here and one on the road out. Maybe these folks sense that you haven't committed to the job or to the town," Max complained. "Maybe they don't trust you because they can see that your heart's not here."

I had a suspicion that this conversation was more personal than Max portrayed it. "Is that really what we're talking about? The protesters?" Looking over at him, I softened my voice but asked, "Max, is this only about the protesters, or is this about you and me? Is it that I haven't committed to the town, or to you?"

"Maybe both," he admitted. For a moment, the SUV's interior fell uncomfortably quiet. "Clara, when we embraced in your office, I…" Another pause, and when he spoke again, his throat was tight with emotion: "You know, you and I have history. And your roots are in Alber. These are your people."

We were picking our way across a field of emotional landmines. I didn't want to hurt Max, but I knew I needed to be honest. Nothing good would come of promises that I couldn't keep. "I'm not sure what's ahead for me," I confessed, fighting to keep my voice steady. "We both know that I'm not wanted here. Not by those people carrying their signs demanding I leave, or by my mother who has repeatedly ordered me to stay away from my family. And as for us, Max, sure I have feelings for you. I don't deny that. But I'm… I'm not sure I can…"

Max waited for me to finish, but I went silent. I couldn't explain what I wasn't sure I truly understood.

He glanced over at me, his face etched in sadness. "Clara, maybe you should think about what you want out of life," he said. "As for me, I know: I want to give us a real shot, the one that was stolen from us all those years ago."

"But how can we—" I started.

"We can if you want to," he said. "As for the others, Ardeth will come around. The folks in town will come around, maybe not all of them but most of them. And you're probably right—solving the case would be a big step toward getting that done."

"It will." I heard uncertainty in my voice, as if I were trying to convince myself. Still, I insisted, "I believe that."

"Good." Max sighed, and when I glanced over, he looked relieved. The thought occurred to me that he'd been wanting to say those words to me for a very long time. "What worries me is how to calm things down in the interim," he said.

"People have the right to protest."

"I know, but—"

"Max, let's just work the case," I said, determined to keep focused. "I promise that we'll figure the rest out later. Okay?"

That didn't appear to put his concerns to rest. "I don't like these demonstrations. They could get out of hand."

I didn't like them either, but I swallowed my feelings and changed the subject. "You didn't say if you heard anything from your guy in Mexico? Did he get back to you about Carl?"

Max pulled out his phone and checked emails. "Not yet. They're busy with their own work, I'm sure. Whenever I've dealt with them before, it's been pretty hit-and-miss."

"Maybe give him a call," I suggested.

Max sat quietly for a moment, and I wondered if he wanted to say more about us and the decision I hadn't yet made, or if he was still worried about the protesters. But instead he placed the call. "*Hola, señor,*" he said, when the guy answered. "*Tienes algunas información para mí sobre los amigos Jacob Johansson y Carl Shipley?*"

While the guy talked, Max kept nodding and going, "*Si… si…*" I didn't know Max spoke Spanish, and I was impressed. Although I wouldn't have understood all of it, most likely just snatches, I wished I could have listened in. Max focused intently, and I had the sense it could be important. The conversation went on for ten minutes or so.

"Spill it," I said when he hung up, eager to hear.

"Well, that was pretty interesting. The guy I was talking to works for the local cop shop in the town down the mountain from El Pueblo de Elijah. He's the top guy in the station." Max stopped talking and shook his head. "This is all pretty crazy."

"And he said?" I prodded.

"They've had a lot of problems with the folks living in El Pueblo over the years. Infighting within the sect has sometimes led to violence. Some of it against women and families. The local cops tend to ignore it, because they get no cooperation when they do try to investigate. The town is clannish, circles the wagons when anything happens and won't assist local authorities," Max said.

"That sound like any of the folks we know?" I asked, the question rhetorical. "Any of the violence tied to the Johansson family?"

"Not that the guy knows of," Max said. "They had no issues with Jacob, but Carl Shipley was a frequent problem. He left El Pueblo and drove down to the town, often on his own, where he drank and harassed people. Multiple women complained that he hassled them. He got into a couple of bar fights. They locked Carl up one time, kept him for a few days before Jacob showed up with money to get Carl out."

"He paid a fine?" I asked.

"I think the guy was suggesting that Jacob paid a bribe," Max said. "Anyway, things really blew up about a year ago, when Carl started pestering a woman named Señora Maria Sanchez Mendoza. Turns out this señora is the wife of a powerful local politician. Her husband noticed Carl watching the house from the street, taking photos through the windows."

"This all sure sounds eerily familiar," I remarked. "What happened?"

"The politician stormed the police station demanding Carl's arrest. This time they couldn't ignore the charges. The police drove up the mountain to the pueblo, but when they got there, Carl, Jacob and his family, they were all gone. The folks in the pueblo said that Carl and the Johanssons had moved back to *El Norte* and assured the local cops that none of them would return."

"Maybe that was the reason Jacob agreed to return, not Michael and Reba's need for someone to run the bison ranch, but Carl's need to get out of Mexico?" I speculated.

"Sounds like it," Max agreed. "The timing is pretty definitive, I would think."

I considered what we'd just learned. "So, we know that Laurel wasn't Carl's first obsession," I said. "But your contact didn't say anything about him going past the photographs, beyond pestering the women?"

"No," Max said. "That's it. No assaults or other types of harassment."

"That would be a big jump, from stalking to committing four murders," I said. "But it's not unheard of."

"No," Max agreed. "Unfortunately, it's not."

I'd turned off the highway and was headed toward Carl's trailer, but as I drove by the MRJ Ranch, I noticed one of my department's squad cars parked out on the road watching the house. I wondered what was up, until I saw the long white van with shaded windows in the driveway: the van my family owned. "Who do you think is at the ranch?" I asked Max, although I had my own suspicions.

"Naomi, maybe? That's odd," he said. "Is that the squad you have watching over Jeremy? You think she has the baby inside with her?"

"Yup," I said. "I think that's exactly what's going on."

I turned in, waved at the officer in the squad, and parked next to the van. Out of the back seat, I grabbed the bag I'd filled with Jeremy's things. At the front door, I knocked. We waited. No one answered. I knocked again, this time shouting, "Mother Naomi, you need to open the door. It's Clara and Max Anderson."

Nothing. "You think she's in there?" Max asked.

I took another look at the van. It had to be her. "Let's try the side door."

The third time I pounded, the door eased open so gradually that I didn't realize it was moving until the hinges squeaked. I saw a thin slice of her face. "Mother Naomi," I said. "I know you're in there, now please, open this door."

"What do you want?" she asked.

"We want to know what you're doing here," I said. "And why do you have Jeremy? He's supposed to be with Jacob's sister and her family."

Naomi sighed and opened the door all the way. She had on an old dress and big rubber boots and gloves. "They're busy planning the funerals. I offered to babysit and get the house ready for Jacob to come home." Naomi looked piqued, one eyebrow higher than the other. "How is this any business of yours, Clara?"

"This is a crime scene, and although it's been released, everything that happens at this house right now is our concern," I said. "Why are you the one cleaning?"

"I wanted to be of service to Jacob and his parents, and I offered," she said. "The doctor said that maybe Jacob can come home tomorrow. I didn't want him returning to an untidy house. Clara, your officers left this place in a mess. I wish they'd cleaned up. The blood was all over the kitchen and Laurel's room."

Max gave her a strange look and then came right out and said it: "Naomi, how is this any of *your* business?"

"Well…" She stopped talking and frowned, her lower lip protruding as testimony to how irritating she found the question. "Because I care about Jacob and his family, and I want to help. I'm being a good neighbor."

I didn't believe that for a blink of an eye. "Let us in. We need to talk."

At first, I thought she'd refuse, but she slipped back and opened the door all the way. Right about then, I heard a whimper coming from the kitchen. I pushed forward. Except for the gap left by the missing tiles, the kitchen sparkled. The dishes had all been returned to the cabinets, and on the table sat an infant carrier with a squirming baby. "And here's Jeremy," I said, walking over. The little guy scrunched his pug nose, twisted and turned, and I leaned down toward him. He had a dumbbell-shaped rattle in one hand and was kicking his legs and hitting his skinny thighs with it. The poor little guy did look a bit undernourished. "What's going on?" I asked. "Why are you the one babysitting? Jacob has a whole pack of family. Someone must be able to help out."

"None of this is yours to worry about, Clara," Naomi insisted. "You and Max need to leave me to finish my work."

"These are Jeremy's clothes. I'd planned to have them dropped off with his sister, but I gather there's no need," I said as I put the bag down on the table. That settled, I stared at her and said: "What's the deal here? Half of Alber is gossiping that you've set your sights on Jacob, planning to pull him into a marriage. That true, Mother Naomi? Is that where this is going?"

Behind her, Max smiled. I had the distinct impression he thought this was more than a little amusing.

"Well, I just thought I could be of service," Naomi sputtered. "You know, Clara, the family is having a rough time and—"

"I understand that this has been going on for some time, starting before the killings. I hear that Jacob has visited you at the bee shed," I said.

"Who would tell you such a thing?" Her eyes flashed wide and her mouth dropped open, as if in shock.

"It's true, isn't it?" I asked.

"No, well yes, but only once," she admitted.

"Why was he there?" I demanded.

Her voice got quiet, and she gave me a cold stare, as if challenging me. "He came to buy honey. That's all. How dare you insinuate anything else!"

From behind her, Max said, "Naomi, if you two have a relationship, there's nothing wrong with that. But we need to know. We're trying to put all the pieces of the case together."

"What does anything I do have to do with the murders?" she asked. "I don't have to answer these questions. I have a right to my privacy."

I shook my head. "That's the thing about a criminal investigation. We don't know what does and doesn't matter until things start to link up, so no one has any privacy. Right now, you need to tell the truth. What's up with you and Jacob Johansson?"

Naomi peeled off the gloves and threw them into the sink, the drain missing. The CSI unit had taken the pipes out to have them tested for blood. "I don't know why you had to do so much damage to the house," Naomi groused again. "Jacob is going to have to do a lot of repairing to make this place livable again."

"Rather inconvenient if you're planning to move in," I commented.

Her lips parted, and she appeared ready to chastise me, when she stopped.

I gave her a suspicious glance. "Why aren't you talking? What are you hiding?" I asked.

She averted her eyes, began picking at her sleeve, pulling off a piece of lint. "Nothing. Nothing."

"Sit down," I told her, pointing at a chair. "We're getting to the bottom of this."

She hesitated, gave me another of her judgmental looks, but then did as told.

The three of us spent about half an hour talking. Although I tried to get her to open up, Naomi didn't offer any information. But when I confronted her with what I knew, she confirmed it was true. She'd had her eye on Jacob for months. She saw him as a catch with his big house and the farm, and he seemed interested in her. At least, that was the way she interpreted it when he called her a few times at the house.

"We didn't see your house number on his phone records," I mentioned, curious. "But he called you?"

"Always from the car," Naomi said with a shrug. "It must have been on his cell phone."

I nodded, and Max asked, "What did he talk to you about?"

"Mainly advice about the children, how to train them to mind and such. Nothing really, but I thought maybe he was feeling me out, trying to decide what kind of wife I would be and if I would fit into the family. I hoped that he'd ask the prophet for me," Naomi said. "I was encouraging that, trying to show him how helpful I would be to have around, that a wife who was a little older would be more attuned to caring for him and the children. I thought I'd be a good influence on Anna and Laurel, I could teach them how to run the house."

Naomi lowered her head as if embarrassed. Good Alber women weren't supposed to pursue men; they were raised to be modest and compliant, not brazen enough to set their sights on a man and go after him.

"Since you two talked, you must know more about Jacob than you've let on," I said. "What haven't you told us?"

"Nothing, really," she said.

"Did Jacob seem upset in the days before the murders? Was he complaining to you about anyone or anything?" I asked.

Naomi squirmed a bit in the chair. "Well, I guess. Maybe a little."

Max moved to the edge of the couch, listening intently. "What about?"

"This is so personal," she said. "I don't think I should be telling anyone what Jacob confided in me. That would be—"

"Talk," I ordered. "Now."

Naomi took a long breath.

"Are you going to tell me, or do you want to have to call the Johanssons to get someone here to take Jeremy, because Max and I are taking you to the station for questioning?" I asked.

At that, Naomi squinted at me, spitting mad. I still didn't think she'd open up, but she finally acquiesced. "Laurel complained that she suspected Carl sometimes followed her. She saw him peeking at her through the windows at the house and once watching her from behind a display in the grocery store in town. Jacob said that Laurel was upset about it and making things miserable at the house."

"Was Jacob angry at Carl?" I asked.

"I don't… I'm not sure," Naomi stuttered. "Jacob didn't like it. He said that Carl needed to back off, but I don't think Jacob was really mad. It was more that he was annoyed about Laurel complaining."

"It didn't bother Jacob that his friend was watching Laurel?" Max asked. "After all, Laurel was Jacob's wife. That would seem to be crossing a line."

Naomi thought about that for a few minutes, then shook her head. "I don't know, but I think what bothered him was that Carl was causing discord at home. That the women—Anna and Laurel—were upset."

Nothing about this smelled right. "Mother Naomi, when I arrived at the hospital and you were in the room with Jacob, I was right, wasn't I? He was awake and you were talking to him."

At that, her eyes flashed round. She shook her head. "No, Clara. No. He didn't wake up."

I couldn't prove she wasn't cooperating, but all my senses said she was holding back. There had to be more she wasn't saying. I looked at her and wondered. At that moment, the baby cried, and Naomi jumped up to get him, I suspected grateful for the distraction. "I have no more time," she said. "I need to feed Jeremy and finish my work. You two need to go."

Knowing I wouldn't get more from her, I agreed. Outside, Max turned to me. "What do you think?"

"Well, she confirmed that there was tension in the house before the murders," I said. "But it wasn't about the kids. It was because the women were fed up with Carl."

Max nodded. "Any other takeaways?"

"Yes," I said. "I think Naomi is still lying. I can't help but believe that she knows more than she's telling."

From the ranch, we drove to Carl's trailer, where everything looked much as it had when we were there the day before. But this time his pickup wasn't out front, the door was locked—I tried it to be sure—and he didn't answer when we knocked or when we called out into the woods for him.

"Should we look around?" I asked.

"I don't think he's here," Max said. He looked as confused as I felt.

"What are you thinking?" I asked.

"That the evidence is piling up against Myles," Max said. "But that Carl's the one who looks increasingly suspicious."

"You're still thinking about the way Carl disappeared as soon as Jacob woke up, aren't you?" I asked.

"It was really odd," Max said. "It was like he couldn't leave fast enough."

"Maybe he just wanted to let Jacob's parents spend time with him. Maybe he didn't want to get in the way."

"Could be," Max said.

"Speaking of Jacob, it must be about time for him to be heading back to his room after surgery," I pointed out. I glanced at my watch and decided we'd been spinning our wheels long enough. It was time to talk to our best witness. "We can look for Carl later, after we find out what Jacob knows."

CHAPTER TWENTY-EIGHT

Jacob's parents appeared to be growing into the chairs they'd occupied outside his room for the past two days. Reba had her knitting spread out, aquamarine yarn she twisted and pulled around two of the biggest needles I'd ever seen. She was making some kind of a loopy scarf. When she saw us, she frowned, shook her head and let out an abrupt huff.

"Clara, I hear you've got a heck of a stew boiling over in front of the police station," she said, sounding delighted at the notion. "Folks aren't happy that you haven't arrested whoever murdered our grandkids and daughters-in-law, are they? Maybe you need to get busy looking for the real killer instead of bothering Carl. I heard you were at his trailer again this afternoon."

"Who told you that?" I asked.

"Naomi called to check on Jacob and she mentioned it. She said you headed off in Carl's direction from the ranch," Reba said. "Why are you looking for Carl? Aren't you onto Myles yet? Even after I gave you all the dirt on him and Laurel?"

"Reba, please," Michael said, looking genuinely upset by her ranting. "You know what the prophet says about a rude woman meeting her end."

"Do you know where Carl is?" Max asked. "He wasn't at the trailer."

"Haven't seen him," Michael said, and Reba shook her head. "Not since Jacob woke up. For some reason, Carl just took off."

"How is your son?" I asked.

"He's shaky, but he's coming around. He'll recover, praise the Lord," Reba said. "Naomi's prayers have brought a miracle. She's been a godsend."

This time her husband agreed. "God has smiled on us," Michael said. "Our son has come back to us."

"Has he said anything about the murders?" I asked. "Communicated with you in some way about what happened?"

"No. He's only been awake from the anesthetic for an hour or so and he's foggy. We asked him about what happened, but he didn't appear to understand what we were talking about. Michael and I told him how upset we are about Anna and Laurel, Sybille and Benjamin. But it was strange. Jacob's face went blank. He didn't react," Reba said. "I mentioned it again, told our son how heartbroken we are, and that time Jacob got agitated. The doctor walked in, and he made us leave the room. He didn't want Jacob upset."

"Jacob didn't indicate at all what had happened on the ranch? Who was responsible?" I said, disappointed when they shook their heads.

"No," Reba said. "He seemed... confused."

I thought about that. "Well, maybe he's more awake now. Max and I will talk to him."

As we headed toward the ICU room's door, the Johanssons stood to follow. We turned, and they halted inches behind us. "We need to talk to Jacob alone," I said. "We can't have him distracted."

"But he's so weak. We should be there to—" Reba started.

"We'll be patient with him. We understand what he's been through," Max assured them. "But you two can't come in. You need to stay out here."

Reba looked at her husband and scowled. "Naomi warned us to watch you two," she said, assessing me as if I might attack at any moment. "She said you in particular, Clara, shouldn't be alone with Jacob."

Naomi interfering again, I thought. *What is she up to?*

"Reba, Michael, we don't know who did this or why," I explained. "The person who committed these murders is still out there and may try again. We don't know if Jacob will be in danger once he leaves the hospital. Max and I are concerned enough that I have officers watching over Jeremy. But we can't protect them forever. So, we need to get this solved quickly, and Jacob is our best hope to put an end to it all. He's the only survivor able to tell us what happened. You need to let us do our jobs."

They looked at each other, unsure, but then Michael took his wife's hand. "Reba, let's sit here and wait. We can go in and visit with Jacob once they're done."

Reba appeared uncertain but followed her husband's lead. Then she turned back toward us. "Jacob can't talk yet, you know. You'll have to communicate some other way."

"Sure. We'll write it down," I said. Reba let loose a long sigh and shook her head again just as a nurse walked by and noticed us.

"Are you two going in there?" she asked. When I nodded, the nurse said, "Only five minutes. And don't upset him."

"We heard you'll be releasing him as early as tomorrow. Is that right?" Max asked.

"If he's eating soft foods and drinking okay," she said. "We like to free up the beds, get people out of the hospital."

"When will he be able to speak?" I asked.

The nurse shrugged. "It could be a day or two. There's no way of telling."

As the nurse ambled off, Max and I walked into the room. Some of the machines had been carted away, but a monitor flashed Jacob's blood pressure and heart rate. He was sitting up, the head of the bed raised. The slit in his neck stitched up and bandaged, he was breathing normally, albeit with a nasal cannula delivering extra oxygen. When Max closed the door, Jacob turned toward us.

"Hello. Good to see that you're awake and getting better," Max said, and Jacob gave a twisted half-smile. "I'm with the sheriff's department, Chief Deputy Max Anderson, and this is Alber Police Chief Clara Jefferies. We need to talk to you about what happened at the ranch Monday morning. Can you please tell us what you remember?"

His light blond hair disheveled, Jacob brought his hand without the IV up to his neck and shook his head, as if to say, "I can't talk."

Out of my bag, I pulled a notebook and pen. I opened to a blank page, placed it on the bed tray and then swiveled it in front of him. He smiled, ever so slightly, wincing as he picked up the pen. It appeared that even the smallest movements caused pain.

As we waited, Jacob, awkward and slow, wrote something down on the notebook, and then held it up: *WHY ARE YOU HERE?*

This time I tried. "As Max explained, we need to know what happened on Monday morning at your ranch." Jacob looked confused, and I went on and said, "We need to know who attacked you."

Jacob's eyes narrowed, and he wrote something on the open page.

He turned it toward us. I'd had such hope, and when I read the six words on the blue-lined paper it came crashing down on me: *IS THAT HOW I GOT HURT?*

He doesn't remember, I thought. *But he must remember something.*

"Okay, let's rewind," I said, hoping we could lead up to it and refresh his memory. "Sunday evening, do you remember Carl coming for dinner?"

A big man, Jacob filled the bed. A few days' worth of stubble covered his chin, and he dropped the pen back on the tray, and then glanced, confused, at the two of us before scanning the room as if looking for someone to help him. He made no move to pick the pen back up, and before long he rested his head against the pillow and stared at the ceiling as if we weren't there.

"Jacob, who attacked you?" I asked. When he didn't respond, I waited a heartbeat and then tried to keep my voice level but firm. "We need information. Tell me who came to the ranch on Monday morning. Who hurt you?"

Jacob's head rolled back down, and he lowered his chin toward his chest, but then jerked it back. His face twisted in agony.

"Was your friend at the ranch Monday morning? Carl Shipley?" I asked.

Jacob showed no emotion and little interest.

"What about Myles Thompkins? Did you see him there?" Max asked.

Suddenly, Jacob had a glimmer of recognition. Concern flashed across his eyes and he had a visceral reaction, his body tensing. But he wrote nothing down. He didn't nod or shake his head.

"If Myles was there, give me a thumbs up," I said, demonstrating with my right hand.

Instead, Jacob picked up the pen and wrote: *WAS HE SUP-POSED TO BE THERE? WHY?* As soon as he showed it to us, he dropped the pen.

I watched him, worried, and before long I felt the long, thin fingers of a headache unwind behind my eyes. I felt suddenly weary, spent. This wasn't going as we'd hoped, not at all. Not ready to give up, I picked up the ballpoint and placed it back in Jacob's hand, wrapped his fingers around it. "Please write down the last thing you remember before waking up here in the hospital. Whatever it is."

I counted off the minutes on my watch as Jacob toyed with the notebook and pen. Then, it appeared that something occurred to him. As we watched, he wrote: *OUR FAMILY WENT TO SUNDAY SERVICES AND ANNA MADE SPANISH OMELETS FOR LUNCH.*

Max and I smiled, encouraging. "Yes, that's it," Max said. "Now, Jacob, write down what you remember after that."

I tried so hard to be patient, but I wanted to shake him, to shout, "Tell us what happened!" But I bit my lip, smiled, and did my best to be calm. I thought about what the man in the hospital bed had been through, and I told myself that he deserved time to digest it. I took a step back, letting Max take over.

Jacob held the notebook by the metal spiral, making a triangle-shaped tent of it, but he made no attempt to write anything. I wondered if this could be a reaction to the anesthetic, that it wasn't completely out of Jacob's system yet. Max reminded him: "Jacob, please, think hard. Write down the first thing you remember after Sunday services and lunch."

Jacob swallowed and his face convulsed. I couldn't imagine how much the severed muscles in his throat must hurt. My hopes rose as he once more picked up the pen. They plummeted when he wrote: *I REMEMBER SEEING NAOMI JEFFERIES STANDING NEXT TO MY BED SMILING AT ME.*

Nothing, I thought, *from Sunday lunch until he woke up in the hospital and saw Mother Naomi at his bedside.*

Max shook his head, and I drew in my lips to stop myself from scowling, struggling to hide my disappointment. The headache intensified, and I wondered if I could talk the nurse into giving me an aspirin. I wondered how far we dare push this man, in his condition. We needed answers. "Jacob," I pleaded. "Please, think hard and tell us who hurt you and your family."

At that, he sat up higher in the bed, and I had the feeling every nerve stood at attention. He glanced from me to Max, then back at me again. He picked up the pen and wrote: *SOMEONE HURT MY FAMILY?*

Michael and Reba had said that they'd tried to tell Jacob about Anna and Laurel, the two children, but the look on their son's face was one of utter confusion. Did Jacob truly not remember? Could his mind be blocking the horror of what he saw, protecting him from the pain of watching his family slaughtered?

Max and I shared a glance, and he said, "We're going to let your parents come in now and talk to you. We'll be gone for a while, but we may try to stop by later."

Worry lines etched across Jacob's brow. Then he wrote on the notepad: *PLEASE SEND IN LAUREL AND ANNA. I WANT TO SEE THEM. I WANT TO SEE MY CHILDREN.*

I read the note and felt as if someone had punched me in the chest.

Jacob couldn't tell us who'd murdered the women and those two precious children. He'd be no help. Although we could hope that his memory would return, it might not. Disappointment weighed me down like a sodden wool cape; Max and I were on our own. All we could do was keep trying. Then I thought about what Naomi had said, and I turned back to Jacob one more time. "Were you upset with Carl at all? Do you remember if the women were upset with him?"

At that, Jacob shrugged. He wrote: *WOMEN ARE ALWAYS UPSET AT CARL.*

Max and I had arrived with such hope, but he glanced at me, and I saw my disappointment mirrored in his eyes. Jacob would have to be told yet again, perhaps multiple times before he understood, that his wives and children had been murdered. But that painful duty wasn't ours. It rested with his family. "We'll send your parents in." Max patted Jacob's shoulder while I picked up the notebook and pen.

Max smiled and said, "Get better."

We barely had the door open when Michael and Reba rushed us. "Did he tell you anything about the killings?" Michael asked.

"It was Myles Thompkins, right?" Reba said. "It has to be."

Max frowned. "Your son doesn't seem to remember anything about what happened. You did say that you'd told him about his family?"

"We tried to, but like we said, he got kind of a strange expression on his face, like he didn't absorb what we were saying," Michael said, looking warily at his wife.

"Well, it appears he doesn't remember anything that happened at the ranch yesterday morning," I said. "Did the doctor say that this might happen, that he might not have a memory of the killings?"

Jacob's parents looked at one another, and his mother turned away as she pulled a handkerchief from her purse. Her husband put his hand on her back to comfort her. "Yes. The doctor brought that up with us yesterday. He said Jacob could have post-traumatic stress disorder or some type of hysterical amnesia," Michael said. "He said that's not unheard of after such a shock and so much blood loss."

"We didn't tell Jacob about the murders," I explained. "We thought that would be better coming from the two of you, maybe with the doctors to help you."

Michael nodded, and Reba buried her head in his shoulder.

The moment awkward, we hesitated, but then Max asked, "Did the doctor say if he expects that Jacob will eventually remember?"

His wife by then openly sobbing, Michael held her close. His voice broke with pain when he said, "The doc didn't give any guarantees one way or the other. He warned us that if Jacob didn't remember the killings, his memory might never come back. Or one day, something, anything, could bring it all flooding back. Reba and I discussed that. She's upset that Jacob can't tell us what happened."

"Not you, though?" I asked.

Michael shrugged. "Maybe forgetting would be a blessing."

Max sighed. "It may be better for Jacob's mental health," he said. "It's not for the investigation."

CHAPTER TWENTY-NINE

As they walked away from Jacob's room, Clara cornered a nurse. "I have such a headache. Splitting," she said, putting her hand on her forehead. "May I have an aspirin?"

"Not without a prescription," the nurse said. "I'm sorry, but it's not allowed."

"Of all the ridiculous—" Clara started.

Max thought she was about to lose her temper with the woman. He touched her arm and said, "Let's stop at the drug store. There's one on the first floor."

"Oh, of course." Clara nodded. She appeared embarrassed and apologized to the nurse as they turned to leave.

After she started the engine, Clara took two tablets with a gulp of water and closed her eyes for just a moment. "I'm sorry I was short with that nurse," she said. "It's just that... well... that turned out to be a waste of time."

"Very true," Max agreed. "But no reason to give up hope. We'll figure it out."

At first, she said nothing. Then as they pulled out of the lot, he heard her murmur, "God, I hope so."

Her mood worried Max. They were both upset, but Clara had taken Jacob's inability to help them hard. She frowned behind the Suburban's wheel and mumbled to herself. Max considered how wrapped up she'd become in solving the murders. She invested so much in her work, but in some cases, like this one, a cop had to keep perspective. Answers often didn't come overnight. But he had to admit he, too, felt devastated when Jacob had been unable to finger the killer. Every time Max thought about Benjamin and Sybille, their small lifeless bodies under the sheet, he felt sickened.

Nearly thirty-three hours since Naomi's 911 call, and they didn't have a lot of answers.

True: they had two suspects. Max again wondered where Carl was and mulled over the possibility that he'd gone into hiding. Why would he do that if he wasn't involved? And Myles? Nearly a full day had passed since they'd put out the BOLO asking law enforcement officers all over the state to be on the lookout for him, and nothing. The news stations in the area and as far away as Salt Lake were displaying his driver's license photo and asking anyone who saw him to report in, but no one had called. Where was Myles Thompkins? It was as if the guy had vanished.

On top of that, something needled at Max.

Earlier that afternoon, he and Clara had read the letters together, and Max couldn't get them out of his head. The emotions Myles and Laurel expressed brought back memories of a time when he and Clara were young and he would have given up anything and everything to be with her. In fact, he did give up everything when the prophet's henchmen ran him out of Alber. That was a terrifying time. Just seventeen, Max was left to fend for himself in the middle of downtown St. George. Only two hundred dollars in his pocket, he had no one to call for help. Max's heart filled with rage remembering how his own father abandoned him at the direction of the prophet.

While Clara fretted about the case, Max considered the girl he'd known. Sometimes he caught glimpses of her in the new Clara, the woman she'd become. Like the teenager she'd been, her long black hair never managed to stay in a bun. Instead, wisps habitually curled at the nape of her neck. Max recalled their kiss the evening before. He felt his chest warm as he remembered her head pressed against it at her office that afternoon. Stolen moments, that was all they had. He wanted much more. Lost to his thoughts, he reached over and wrapped an errant strand of her hair around his finger.

Caught by surprise, Clara shivered.

"I'm sorry," he apologized. "I didn't mean to—"

"No, it's okay, Max," she responded. "I just wasn't expecting it."

"I should have given you a warning." He hesitated, but then, since he had her attention, he ran his fingers down her arm, until he cupped her hand on the steering wheel. She smiled, not appearing to mind the attention. There'd been something he'd wanted to ask her for a week or more. It had been gnawing at him. Was this the time?

"Clara," he said. "Neither one of us has a place where we can be alone together. I have Brooke, and you're living at the shelter. Everything we do in Alber is... watched."

"As I've recently found out," she acknowledged.

He didn't ask what she meant, but continued. "A friend offered me a cabin in the mountains. Assuming we've wrapped this case up, I'm heading there on Thursday. Alice is keeping Brooke for the weekend. I'd like you to come."

"To the cabin?" she asked.

"Yes," he said. "I'm hoping... well... it might be a good place for us to figure this out."

"Figure this out?" she murmured, as if unsure what he was saying.

"Figure us out," he answered. Her frown grew longer, and Max paused, considering what to say next. "Clara, like I said earlier, I want to give us a try. I do. But I also have Brooke to consider. And my own feelings. The thing is: I need to know where this is going. If it is going anywhere."

"Max—" she started.

"No pressure. I promise. But if this *isn't* going to work out..." He knew she was skittish. He understood that he couldn't push her. She hadn't explained what she'd been through, but Max sensed that her marriage had been traumatic, and that something truly bad must have happened to convince her to leave her family and her home. But he'd been hurt, too. He'd lost Miriam, nearly lost Brooke. And as much as he wanted to be with Clara, he couldn't endure that kind of pain ever again. Last time, it had sent him reeling to the bottle, cost him his job and nearly his sanity. If that happened again, he wondered if he could survive it. "You don't have to answer me now. Just think about it."

For a moment, Clara was quiet. Then she asked, "Where's the cabin?"

At least she hadn't said no. "Outside Salt Lake. He's always offering it to me as a getaway, and I decided to say yes, this time. Mountain views. The cottage is cozy. A stone fireplace. There's a stream nearby. It may be too cold for trout fishing, but we can go hiking."

She glanced over at him and gave him the hint of a smile. Max wondered what he'd do if she said no. He felt an overwhelming relief when she said, "I'll think about it. Okay?"

"Good. Yes. Okay," he said. "We can—"

Before Max could finish his sentence, Kellie's voice on the radio filled the Suburban: "Chief, you there?"

"Yup. Chief Deputy Anderson is with me," Clara answered. "What have you got for us? Have any more lab results come in?"

"No, not yet."

"What is it then?" Clara asked.

"Conroy needs you over at Myles Thompkins' place," Kellie said.

"Is this good news? Did Thompkins turn up?"

"Conroy didn't say. He just said he needs you ASAP," she explained.

Instead of turning off the highway toward Alber, Clara flipped on the siren and lights and headed in the direction of the mountains. They might finally have a break in the case, and Max heard relief in Clara's voice, optimism that had evaporated in the ICU room with Jacob, when she said to Kellie: "Tell Conroy we're on our way."

CHAPTER THIRTY

The sun sets early in November in the mountains, and it was low in the sky when Max and I arrived at the cabin. We found Conroy with Thompkins' neighbor, Scotty, near the barn. Both men had their arms folded across their chests, and they were jabbering away as if they had a lot to discuss. The dogs barking in the background, we walked up and Conroy, who never seemed to waste a single word, said: "Homer is back."

"Homer?" I repeated.

"Thompkins' horse."

"But no sign of his owner?" I said, simply to verify.

"No," Conroy confirmed.

Inside the barn, the penned-up dogs kicked up the noise level, while Homer nonchalantly munched on a pile of hay. He looked just as Scotty had described him: a big-shouldered bay with black points. It wasn't hard to believe that he measured a full sixteen hands. Homer had a colorful blanket on his back topped by a thick strap that ended in stirrups and a worn saddle.

"When did he arrive?" I asked.

"Not sure, but I found him here about half an hour ago. Gave Officer Conroy a call to let him know," Scotty said. The guy looked clearer than at our last meeting. Maybe he'd sworn off the pot for a day. "I came over to feed the dogs, and I found Homer nosing around in his empty oat sack. Hungry, I guess, so I fed him."

I wondered how to handle this. I hadn't had any experience searching a horse. I suggested, "Max, let's get some gloves on and take that saddle off, check out the pockets and the blanket."

"Instead of that, let's get the CSI folks out here," Max said. "No telling what secrets this horse might reveal. There could be prints on the saddle that might help."

I considered balking, not wanting to waste any time, but Max made sense. While he put in the call to Lieutenant Mueller and the CSI unit, I clicked on my radio. "Kellie, tell Stef to come out here ASAP. I want her in on this."

"Will do, Chief," she said.

The sun kept getting lower, the light dimmer. While we waited, we searched the property, trying to figure out what direction the horse had come from. We had given up by the time the forensic trailer pulled in, followed by Stef in her Alber PD squad car. Soon we had eight folks including Mueller and two of his team staring at the horse. Stef and the CSI folks gathered round and whispered, concocting a plan. Mueller was the one who announced: "We're going to treat Homer like he's a crime scene, okay?"

"You bet," I said.

Max and I stood back with Conroy and Scotty, while the CSI folks carefully removed Homer's hardware, his saddle, canteen, all the rest, and laid them out on a table they popped open just outside the barn door. Stef helped the techs bag the blanket and the reins. They inspected the saddle but decided to wait to test it for prints until they got it to the lab.

"You know, it's funny," Scotty commented as we watched.

"What is?" Max asked.

"I figured Myles was out hunting. One reason was that I didn't see his bow and arrows in the barn," the guy explained. "But they're not on the horse either."

Stef chewed on that a minute and then said, "They're probably somewhere in the woods. Wherever he was when he got off the horse?"

"I wonder where that was." I looked at the horse and wished there was a way to tell. "We need to look through those saddle pockets," I said to Mueller. "Here, not wait for the lab."

"We'd have better control in the lab," Mueller pointed out. "We don't want to mess up any latent prints."

"You can be careful, but we can't wait," I said. "We need to know if there's anything in there that can help us find him."

Mueller sighed but did as I asked. The saddle glowed in the light emanating from the barn's interior as he used a small tool to pop the pockets open and a hook to search inside. Out came a stash of energy bars and a wallet. We found Myles's driver's license with the same photo we'd been showing on TV, those inquisitive blue eyes I remembered, dark hair and a pilgrim beard to match that covered his neck. Mueller closed the wallet and slipped it, as he had the energy bars, into evidence bags to go in for fingerprinting.

Meanwhile, the rest of us waited while one of the techs continued searching the saddle. At first, nothing, but then she found something in a small inner pocket—an envelope. On the front, someone had typed: *LAST WILL AND TESTAMENT.*

Inside she found a single sheet of folded paper dated the previous day, Monday, the day of the killings. The tech laid it out on the table and we gathered around. There were three short paragraphs and a typed signature at the bottom. I picked it up in my gloved hands, Max shined his flashlight on it, and I read aloud to the others:

To whom it may concern:
Point One: Being of sound mind, I, Myles Thompkins, want my cabin and all I possess liquidated. All funds are to be put into a trust for Jeremy Johansson, the son of Laurel and Jacob Johansson.

I paused. Before I went on, something immediately bothered me. I looked at the faces of the others. "Does this seem real to you?" I asked them. "Isn't it odd that it's typed?"

"I'd feel better if it were handwritten," Max said. "Why would Myles type this when he hand-printed all the letters to Laurel?"

At that, Mueller spoke up. "Also, we didn't come across this document when our tech guys examined the computer we found in his cabin. If Myles didn't write this on his computer, where did he write it? All we found on his desktop were old tax returns, financial records, and emails to buyers about the dogs he was selling."

"That does seem strange," I agreed.

"Is it possible that Myles had a second computer? A laptop?" Max asked.

"We didn't find any," Mueller pointed out. "And no evidence of one, no cords sitting around, laptop cases, anything like that."

"Well, let's send Myles's printer in for analysis, see if the characters in this document match the printer," I suggested. "At least we might be able to figure out if this letter was printed on his equipment."

"Good idea," Mueller said. He looked up, called out to one of his techs and said, "Get the printer boxed and logged in." The guy nodded and ran off toward the cabin.

That done, I returned my attention to the paper in my hands. "Okay, well, let's keep going," I said, and I started reading the second paragraph to those of us gathered:

Point Two: I, Myles Thompkins, confess that I murdered Jacob, Laurel, Anna, Benjamin and Sybille Johansson. I did this out of jealousy. I went to the bison ranch to take Laurel away with me, but she refused me. I didn't mean to kill anyone, but my anger took over. I killed them all. All except Jeremy.

I paused. I felt stunned. Reading his letters, I'd come to think I knew Myles, that I could see inside his heart. Despite the evidence of the boot's sole matching the print on the scene, part of me didn't believe—or didn't want to believe—that he could have been the murderer. Yet, here it was, typed out for all to see, his confession.

I mentally clicked through Doc's timeline that indicated Laurel died six or seven hours before the others. It didn't seem logical in the context of the confession I held in my gloved hands. How could Myles have gone to the ranch to claim Laurel and been rebuffed, killed her around midnight but then waited all those hours to murder the others? Why would he do that? It made no sense. But then, maybe, I just didn't want to see it?

"Does this sound right to you?" I asked Max. "What do you think?"

Max's frown stretched tight. "No way to tell for sure, but no… I'm thinking the same thing you probably are, that this scenario doesn't fit the autopsy evidence."

"Not that I can tell," I said. "Maybe we're misinterpreting something?"

Max thought for a minute, then said, "Keep reading. What does he write next?"

I did as Max requested, and the letter became even more alarming:

Although I understand that bequeathing him my money and property will not make up for all the harm I have done to Jeremy, all I have taken from him, it is all I have to leave him. I am unable to live with what I have done. I ask God's forgiveness as I prepare to meet my end in the place where Laurel and I shared our happiest memories.

And then there was the strange document's most suspect element—the typed "signature."

Mueller took the paper from me and slipped it, along with the envelope, into an evidence folder. "We'll work on the printer and do fingerprinting and trace evidence," he suggested. "That might help."

"Thanks, sure. Good idea," I said. I thought about that phrase "as I prepare to meet my end." I turned to Max. "What are you thinking? What's he planning to do?"

"Suicide note," Max said. "Plain and clear. Every indication."

Mueller walked off to take the envelope with the letter to the CSI trailer, and a few of the others returned to examining the horse. I glanced over and saw Stef petting the animal, murmuring to it. We all felt the sadness, I figured. So many lives lost, so much tragedy.

"He says, 'where Laurel and I shared our happiest memories,'" I pointed out.

"Are you thinking what I am?" Max asked.

I called over to Scotty, who was petting one of the dogs, just to be certain I hadn't misunderstood. "One more time, where did you say you saw Myles and Laurel together?"

"Along the river, where the kids go to hide from their parents. The clearing where there's a big boulder right on the bank," he said. "Only saw them together there the one time, but, like I said, I saw Laurel off and on sitting next to the water."

Max and I exchanged worried glances. "You finish up here," I said to Mueller. "But don't head back to your office until you check in with us. We may need you."

CHAPTER THIRTY-ONE

Driving back down the highway west of Alber, I turned off on the dirt road Naomi had taken days earlier. I thought about how she'd seen Laurel and Myles talking, and that she said Laurel seemed upset. Max and I got out of the SUV, and we walked down the dirt path that wound through the woods. Nineteen years earlier, we'd taken this path together. Now gray speckled Max's hair and the stubble on his dimpled chin. All those years ago, his cheeks were soft and boyish, and I remembered the fluttering of my heart that accompanied our first kiss. I could almost hear my father emerging from the trees and shouting: "Stop!"

In the growing darkness, our flashlights lit the way as we trudged through the trees. Surrounded by the scents of pine and the river, I felt a stiff chill in the air. I wondered what we'd find. Perhaps Myles Thompkins' dead body against a tree trunk, a gunshot wound to the head, his gun at his side. From the tone of his note, if it were genuine, that didn't seem improbable.

The grass was winter yellow and brown, and dead leaves crunched beneath our feet as we scouted around the riverbank, wandering off in different directions into the forest, looking for Myles. I privately hoped we wouldn't find him. I thought of the man who wrote the letters, the one who seemed to love Laurel more than he loved himself, who wanted her happiness above his, and I wished that in the midst of so much death, he'd survived. I wished that the confession wasn't true.

An hour later, Max and I stood in the dark with our flashlights not far from where we did the day of our kiss, alongside the big boulder where Scotty had seen Laurel alone, singing.

"So, neither one of us found a single sign that he's been here," Max said. "The note's a lie?"

"Could be," I said. "But maybe not. Maybe they had another favorite place?"

A wave of anxiety flooded through me, and I felt unsettled. Raw. Being there with Max brought back too many memories. I looked over at him, so close I could have reached out and touched him. I considered my years in Dallas, how I'd spent a decade alone trying to restart my life, training to be the best cop, never letting anyone close, all the while keeping the world at arm's length. Being home these few months, I'd realized how much I missed my family, how much I'd grieved for the connection I once had with Max. He was offering to rekindle what we had. Was I too scared to accept it, in case it got taken away again?

I needed to be alone for just a moment, to collect my thoughts.

Wandering off, I again walked the bank, watching the river lap against the land. Something scurried by in the woods, and I shined my flashlight on a gray wolf fleeing, eager to get away from me. I stopped and looked back. When I did, I saw Max's silhouette illuminated by moonlight. He was sitting on the rock, looking out over the water. His profile achingly familiar, I thought about all I'd never told him, about the bad turn my life had taken in Alber, why I fled, and about how during those long years we'd been apart, he came to mind often. In the quiet moments, I'd wondered where he was and if he was happy.

As I began pacing yet again, those thoughts from the past left me. Instead, I caught flashes of images from the murder scene the day before, the bodies of the women and the two precious children; my heart ached so that I thought I might scream.

Pulling myself together, I turned to eye the shoreline, the water, the river's rocky bottom visible along the bank. I searched the woods around me. In my flashlight's glow, I saw something just ahead of me, a black shape on the ground. Part of it had caught the light. I rustled over, crunching the leaves beneath my boots. When Scotty mentioned that Myles hunted deer with a bow and arrow, I'd pictured a high-tech fiberglass device, probably finished in camo print. But the one that lay in the woods was old-fashioned, made from wood polished to a fine dark sheen. Beside it lay three arrows, broken in half. I bent down and took a closer look at the craftsmanship, so fine, the feathers skillfully anchored in hand-cut notches.

Not far from where I stood, I noticed grooves in the mud leading to the river. A fallen branch lay across them.

"Max, come here!" I shouted.

Not asking why, he rushed toward me.

"The bow and arrows are over there," I said, pointing into the woods. "And look over here. These marks look like someone either slid into the water or was dragged in."

"You think?" he asked, then he looked up and my eyes followed his flashlight's beam. Where the branch had broken or been ripped off the tree, the cut looked relatively fresh. "I'll call Mueller."

It took less than half an hour for Mueller to reach us, and by then he'd made calls of his own. One went out to a local guy with a boat who volunteered to do water searches for the sheriff's department, another to a trained recovery diver.

"You think he went in right about here?" Mueller asked, looking at the branch a couple of his guys were logging into evidence under the glare of the team's portable lights. It would be examined for fingerprints, although the rough bark made it unlikely that we'd find any.

"Well, it could be," I said. "We're thinking maybe he slipped on mud along the bank, and instinctively gripped the branch and tore it off while getting in the river. Or, if it wasn't his idea to get into the water, he might have grabbed the branch when someone forced him in."

"Knowing where he might have gone in gives us a place to start," Mueller said.

Not long after, the guy with the boat showed up. We helped him unload the trailer, and then we pulled the drag bar he'd brought with him off his pickup's roof. A triangle, five feet wide at the base, it had evenly spaced treble hooks hanging from chains.

"Any idea how deep the river is here?" the boat's owner asked.

Mueller and Max considered that, and they figured around twenty feet. "Maybe some deeper. There are rapids about a mile down, but the current's pretty calm here," Max said. "If he's here, we think he's been in the water for at least twenty-four hours, most likely longer. Do we need to move downriver and look?"

"No, he should be close around here," the guy said. "Bodies drop like stones when folks drown. They don't usually drift until they float. We'll start here. We can always move if we don't find him."

"We have dogs coming?" Max asked Mueller.

The boat guy gave him a sideways glance. "I'd call and tell them not to bother if you do," he said.

Mueller nodded in agreement. "The water's cold, Max. There won't be any decomp going on this soon. No way for them to get a scent. As a matter of fact, the bacteria probably aren't even growing yet in these water temps." He turned back to the boatman. "Diver's on his way."

"Good. Him we can use," the guy said. "I'll get started."

In Dallas, we would have had our own water recovery unit on the scene with a sonar unit that would have lit up with images of the bottom, a body showing up as bright red bumps. Out here in the sticks, we didn't have access to such expensive high-tech equipment, and none of us wanted to wait for the state guys to fly or truck some in.

The first thing the boat guy did was set out a grid, to keep track of where he searched. He started at the point nearest the skid marks on the shore. He moved slowly, methodically, the hooks dragging on the rocky river bottom. At times, they snagged something and he backed up, waited, tried to lift whatever it was, but the object broke free. "A rock or something. Not for us," he'd shout. "Don't get your hopes up."

He judged by touch. The rocks didn't give way. Underwater, bodies were light. If they weren't weighed down somehow or latched onto anything, just clipping onto clothes often would be enough to bring one up.

The diver arrived, pulled on his wetsuit, and joined the guy in the boat. We waited on the riverbank, anxious and wary. "Do you think we should call Doc Wiley, to be ready?" Max asked.

I shook my head. "Odds are we won't find anything. This is a real long shot."

The night grew darker and the temperatures dropped. We kept going, the buoy markers floating on the river, marking off each section as the grid expanded. At times, the boat overlapped areas it had already searched, its skipper intent on feeling what lay submerged in the water.

"This is torture," I said to Max. He understood that I meant the waiting.

"It's getting late. They may want to abandon this soon," he whispered. "We may have to try again in the morning."

I didn't want to consider that.

The search continued, and the sky grew darker as the air turned colder. We had a few false alarms; we pulled up a tree limb and an old boot, but no luck. Finally, Max and I were talking about calling it a night when the boatman shouted: "I think we've got him!"

The diver disappeared under water that shone like ink in the moonlight. As he broke the surface again, we saw a head emerge with him; dark hair, a pale face with a pilgrim beard. They attached floats to the body, and the boat dragged it to the shore. By then, I'd put in a call for Doc Wiley.

We laid Myles Thompkins out on the brittle grass and turned the lights directly on him. His blue eyes were open. Something in the water had nibbled away at his eyelids and his lips, giving them a ruffled look. Otherwise, the body, as Mueller and the boat guy had predicted, showed no signs of decomp. His skin was wrinkled, especially on his hands. He had a bruise on his forehead.

It didn't take long for Doc to arrive. He looked tired—had probably been about to head to bed when I called—and he trudged toward us limping. "Bursitis," he said when I inquired. "My knee acts up off and on."

He winced when he knelt to give Myles a once-over. There was a bloodless gash among the bruising on his forehead.

"What do you think?" I asked.

Doc shook his head. "Can't tell. We need to get him to the morgue. I'll do the autopsy tonight."

Max pointed above Myles's eye. "That bruise and the cut, from an altercation, you think?"

"Could be from somebody hitting him," Doc said. "Or could be from the rocks when he fell in, or those at the bottom. I've read that drowned bodies look pretty much like they're crawling until decomp sets in and they start to rise. I'll need to take a look."

"We were lucky to find him," Mueller said.

"Yes, you were," Doc agreed. "Cold water like this? He wouldn't have floated until April."

"Will you be able to tell if it was suicide?" Max asked Doc. "Or homicide?"

Doc looked wary. "That can be hard with a drowning. Water destroys a lot of evidence," he admitted. "And I'm not an expert in these types of deaths. I've only seen a couple in my career. But let's not get ahead of ourselves. Give me a chance to get him on the table."

"I'm going to follow you to the morgue," I told Doc. "Max can head back to his office with the CSI crew."

"No," Doc said. "I'm going to have a cup of coffee at home first, explain to my wife what's happening, and then I'll get on this. I'll call you when I'm done. I don't need you looking over my shoulder, distracting me and hurrying me along."

CHAPTER THIRTY-TWO

From the river, we headed back to the station, where Max had left his car. We saw the street glowing from a block away. It looked beautiful, sparkling like fallen stars. All along Main Street, folks were lined up holding candles: women, children, men. The signs were still there, and some held a candle in one hand and a placard in the other. Although the scene shimmered, the signs screamed: Apostate Leave! Another: Outsiders Not Wanted Here!

"Clara, they're—" Max started.

"Voicing their heartfelt appreciation for all I've done," I said, not sparing the sarcasm. "I understand."

My Suburban with Alber PD on the side wasn't hard to spot, and I thought about taking a side road again but decided to hell with it. I pulled up right in front of the station and put on my blinker to turn toward the parking lot. When a sea of the protesters flooded in front of the SUV, I decided I'd probably made a bad choice. But I was tired of backing away. I hadn't done anything wrong, and I resented this. Being as careful as I could, I drove slowly. The sea of faces and flickering lights parted, and eventually I drove past them. As we got out of the SUV, Max said, "I'm going to head home and look in on Brooke. Call me when you hear from Doc."

There'd been murmurs, but at that point the crowd called out: "Go home! Go home! Go home!"

"Sure, I'll call," I said. Max looked worried, and he started to walk toward me as if he was going to guard me as I walked into the office. I mouthed "No."

I couldn't have the people in town thinking that I was afraid, that I needed Max, any man, to protect me. He reluctantly turned and walked to his car, glancing back a couple of times to check on me while I made my way to the building. The crowd continued their chant but didn't approach me. I keyed in the access code, and as the door slammed behind me, something flew in my direction from the crowd. I turned to see something blood red on the glass. I glanced down at the asphalt outside and realized that someone had thrown a tomato.

Inside the station, the night dispatcher had replaced Kellie. Except for her absence, it looked like afternoon in the office; Conroy was at his desk and Stef sat on the couch in the waiting area reading a textbook entitled *Death Investigation.*

"Stef, haven't you had enough for today? Shouldn't you be home?" I looked over at Conroy. "You too. You're both done for the night. Time to go off duty."

They shared a glance, and Stef gave me one of her half-apologizing expressions. "We don't think it's safe for you to be alone here with just the dispatcher, Chief. The night shift is all out on patrol. Conroy and I are staying until the protesters leave."

"No," I said. "There's no need to—"

"Chief, I'm sorry, but it's not up for discussion," he said. "We're not leaving. Plus, we both have work to do. You don't have to pay us overtime. Don't worry."

I chuckled at the reference to overtime. Everyone knew the department's budget was habitually tight. Maybe I was glad they were staying. I did appreciate the concern. Still, I wasn't sure it was a good idea for my officers to think they had to protect me. "You should both go home," I said again. "Really, I'm fine here. You don't have to worry."

"Too late," Stef said. "Mullins is on his way, and he's bringing all of us dinner."

"Mullins? He should be home with his family," I said. "His daughter—"

"He heard about the crowd," Conroy said. "He didn't ask. He said he was coming."

It was at that moment that Detective Jeff Mullins, carrying sacks from the diner, bustled in the front door shouting behind him: "I told you folks to go the hell home. Now get out of here!" He was about to slam the door, but held it open for a moment longer and yelled out: "The chief's working hard on my daughter's murder, the others, figuring out who killed them all. Chief Jefferies doesn't need the distraction of all of you being so ridiculous. So, go the hell home!"

Mullins walked in mad, glowering at no one in particular. "Mullins, you didn't have to do this," I said.

"I wanted to be here," he said, squirreling his cheeks high while he clenched his mouth into a decidedly unhappy frown. "I'm not here because of those folks out there. I want to hear what happened with Myles. Where we stand on the case."

The crowd outside thinned and then disbanded as we ate our burgers from the diner. Stef and Conroy finally took off for the night, but Mullins and I sat in the station's meager breakroom at a table with a cracked Formica finish.

"Do you think Myles did it?" Mullins asked.

"I don't know," I admitted. "Max and I have doubts about the confession. We're not convinced."

Mullins looked relieved. "You still have the squad protecting my grandson, right?" he asked. "In case it's not Myles and the killer comes back?"

"Yes, I do," I assured him. "We're not going to leave Jeremy unguarded until we're sure this is over."

Apparently satisfied, Mullins began playing with an onion ring he'd peeled off his burger. It was filling the air with a heavy odor. "I can't get my mind around it, that there's any chance he did it," he said. "I'm not going to believe Myles killed Laurel until I see that note myself and read the autopsy that says he committed suicide."

At that moment, my cell went off. Doc Wiley's number displayed on the screen, and I considered putting him on speaker so Mullins could hear, but decided not to.

"Doc, you finished the autopsy, I take it?" I asked.

"No," he said. "I'm not going to be able to come up with a determination on manner of death until morning."

"Doc, I know you're tired. It's been a long couple of days for all of us, but we really need to know how Myles died tonight," I said. "What's the problem?"

"I think I know what happened here, but I'm not sure," he said, sounding irritated. "Sometimes I need help. I'm an internist first, not really a pathologist, remember?"

That was true. He had been pressed to take over the medical examiner's responsibilities for the county when his predecessor retired, but Doc Wiley was more comfortable stitching up a wound, delivering a baby, or prescribing antibiotics for a sinus infection than issuing rulings on cause and manner of death.

"Doc, why not tell me what you do know?" I suggested. "Time is important and waiting until morning—"

At that, my lead detective grabbed my phone and put it on speaker: "Mullins here, Doc. What's the hang-up? What did you find?"

"I'm not going to go into it tonight, Jeff," Doc said. He let out an aggravated sigh, as if we were trying his patience. "I've contacted a pathologist who specializes in drownings, based in Nebraska of all places. Took forever for me to find such a guy, but he's agreed to look over the photos and my notes first thing tomorrow, so I'll have what you're waiting for then. Right now, I can't do more for the night. And all of us could use a good night's sleep."

Mullins' shoulders sagged, and he looked beaten. "You know, Doc, this is my girl who got murdered. My Laurel. You should tell me what you're thinking, not hold anything back."

Doc didn't answer.

I looked at Mullins, how fragile he appeared, and I fought two urges—one to help him push Doc so we could both get the answers we were looking for. The other? To tell him to go home and be with his family. He didn't belong in the investigation. I considered how he'd cornered Carl Shipley, and how easily Mullins' emotions could tip him over the edge.

"The doc's right, Jeff," I said. "We don't want speculation. We need to hear the truth about how Myles died. The morning will come soon enough."

"You're sure you'll know then?" Mullins asked Doc.

"Tomorrow morning, first thing," Doc said. "Chief Jefferies will get back to me, and I'll have answers for her then."

CHAPTER THIRTY-THREE

I lay in bed for what felt like hours, awake, going over the evidence, thinking it all through and coming up with no new answers. When I finally closed my eyes, I was in the woods at night, running, from what, I didn't know. I wasn't sure who chased me, but as I glanced back, I saw the flames from their torches bright against the darkness, the way the protesters' candles had rippled in the breeze. Why I was running, that I understood: someone chased me. I had to escape, to flee as fast as I was able. I needed to get away, because if I failed, if they caught me, I would die.

In my dream, I left the woods and fell into the river. The water rushed up around me, pulling me down. I flailed around underwater, unable to breathe, unable to swim back up to the surface. Suddenly, Myles Thompkins floated beside me, his unseeing eyes locked on me. I tried to grab for him, but he slipped through my hands. Then, his head dropped, and when he looked up again, my heart beat like a base drum in my chest. Instead of Myles staring at me, it was Max. I reached out again, and again I couldn't grab him. Max slipped past my fingers and drifted farther and farther down until he disappeared.

Total darkness. And then I stood at the window in Laurel Johansson's bedroom. The blue drapes were gone from when we removed them to find the letters. Below me, outside near the clothesline, Anna and the children swirled like dancers on a stage. They appeared happy and playful, but they wore white nightshirts stained with patches of red like the sheet had been. Benjamin saw me in the window and told his mother and sister. Soon, all three stared up at me, their hands waving as if to make sure I saw them. The bison in the field filled the air with mournful groans, and my pulse raced. I shouted that I was trying, that I was doing all I could for them, but they couldn't hear me. I stepped away from the window and Laurel sat up in the bed, that hideous ring of red surrounding her mouth dripping like fresh blood.

Her eyes opened. She saw me and screamed.

The dream rushed through me the next morning while I pulled on a clean uniform. I thought about Myles, about Max. Our stories were becoming interconnected. In the dream, Max had taken Myles's place. I wondered if my subconscious was trying to tell me that could have been us. That my fate and Max's could have been as dark and final. I thought of the day I'd heard that Max had been driven from Alber. Father came into my room to tell me.

"You are never to see him again, ever. And you will make no attempt to ever seek him out. You will keep your thoughts pure. From now until the day you die, Clara, Max Anderson is not to enter your mind," Father had said, a stern look in his eyes. I'd been on house arrest for months, ever since the river kiss. After school, I went to my room and studied, and I only came out to help prepare dinners or tend to the younger children. My brothers and sisters looked at me warily. They had all understood that our parents were unhappy with me. Mother rarely looked at me, except for those moments when I glanced over and caught her staring at me with a visceral disappointment.

I rarely talked back to Father; none of us children dared. It wasn't that he was mean or violent in any way, but that his manner welcomed no dissent. This time, I had no choice. I needed him to understand that Max and I hadn't sinned, that there was no reason for Max to be forced out of town or banned from my life. "We didn't do anything wrong, Father. I've told you before, nothing happened beyond a kiss," I'd pleaded. "Max and I, we're… he's… you don't understand, I am…"

Silence, as Father glared at me.

"Was it my fault, Father?" I'd begged. "Please, tell me. Was it because of me that Max was sent away?"

Again, Father didn't speak. Instead, he'd looked into my eyes, bored deep inside me, working his way into my heart until it ached so that I felt a sharp pain cut through me. Then he turned toward the door. He stopped with one hand on the doorknob and looked back at me. "Pray, Clara," he said. "Ask God and the prophet for forgiveness for your indiscretion."

I tried Doc's number twice before I left the shelter at six that morning. No answer. I decided he was probably not ready to talk and avoiding me, and I headed to the hospital instead of the office, to pin him down. I needed to know what he knew. But when I got there, the morgue door was locked, and no one responded when I rang the bell. I tried Doc's cell again, and this time he picked up. "I'm at the sheriff's office," he said. "Just got here. Come over. I have something to show you and Max."

The sheriff's office was on the first floor of the Smith County Courthouse, a short drive from the hospital, so I made it there in ten minutes or less and rushed inside. Max and Doc were in the conference room, autopsy photos of Myles spread across the table. I looked over at Max and again thought of that day with my father.

"Good, Clara, you're here," Doc said. "Come take a look."

There were images of the body, his clothing on in some, in others his clothes removed. Nude, it was easy to see bruising not only on his forehead but other parts of his body, especially his chest. "Is this what you're showing us, the bruises?" I asked.

"Yes," Doc said. "They're perimortem, moments before or coincidental with the time of death, but with most of them, I can't tell if they're from a struggle or from the fall into the water and the body sinking down to the rocky bottom."

"What then?" I demanded. I had little patience, it seemed.

"Clara, Doc's trying to explain," Max said. "Give him a chance."

"Sorry, I didn't mean to…" I took a deep breath and pulled myself together. It wasn't just Max and the memories of my father that had resurfaced—the dream had stayed with me. I felt as if I'd brought Anna and Laurel, the children, with me, and that there were things that they needed to explain to me. But they had no means, other than Myles Thompkins' dead body.

Doc went silent, and I prodded, "Doc, just tell us what you think happened here. Okay?"

He gave me a worried frown. "This isn't like you to be so impatient, Clara. It's been a long couple of days. Are you okay?"

I almost didn't admit it, but I suspected we all felt the same way. "Again, I'm sorry. This case is getting to me. Whenever I think of those two women, those two little kids, I want to…" Overcome by emotion, not trusting my voice, I couldn't finish.

The two men nodded. They understood. Max cast his eyes down, as if upset by the memory. Doc cleared his throat.

"Looking over the body, it's these bruises right here that are important," he said, pointing at the tops of Myles's shoulders, where contusions stood out in stark contrast to the pale, lifeless skin surrounding them.

"Why those?" Max asked.

"They suggested something to me, but I wasn't sure," Doc explained. "That's an unlikely place for bruises, and for there to be similar discolorations on the tops of *both* shoulders? That struck me as very odd."

"What does it mean?" Max asked.

"Well, I had a theory, but I wasn't sure," Doc said. "Like I said yesterday, I don't see a lot of drownings. Unsure of my hypothesis, I decided to look for an expert. That's how I found the physician in Nebraska, sent him everything I have on the case, and he got back with me this morning. He concurred with my suspicions."

"Good. What's the verdict here?" I coaxed.

Doc shook his head, as if he hated to deliver the news. "We both believe that these particular bruises occurred when Myles was pushed on both shoulders to force his body underwater."

We were silent, digesting the news, when Max spoke up. "Just to be clear—you're saying Myles Thompkins didn't commit suicide."

"Yes. That's what we're saying," Doc said, looking from Max to me. "The autopsy will read homicide."

Stunned, I sat down in a chair at the table. I'd of course considered this outcome, thought it probable, but hearing it made it real. Another murder. "You okay?" Max asked.

"Sure," I said, although I felt my mind spinning. Nothing was as it should be in this case. Nothing seemed clear-cut. "Just thinking."

"Considering who we look at for this?" Max suggested, and I nodded. "I've been going over the same question. I've only come up with one name."

"Carl Shipley," I said. "He has the motive. Carl had a thing for Laurel. He knew of Myles and Laurel's relationship, that they'd been in love. Carl was jealous."

"Yes," Max said. "That's my best guess, too."

"Max, when we searched Carl's trailer, did we take his computer?" I asked.

"No. We weren't authorized to do that. It wasn't covered by the warrant," he said. "All we were allowed to take was anything that appeared to have blood on it, that was tied to the crime scene, Jacob Johansson or his family."

The room grew quiet, the only sound Doc shuffling through the photos, putting them back in the file. When he finished, Max and I thanked Doc, and he hurried out the door to attend to the patients he had waiting in his office.

Once we were alone, I said to Max, "What have we got to justify a warrant to get Carl's computer?"

In the conference room, Max and I laid out all the files, everything we had. "I don't think there's enough here," Max said. "I don't think the judge will buy it."

"He has to," I said. "Not getting Carl's computer isn't an option. We have to find out if Myles's suicide note is on it."

To work through it, we started debating it all. I took one side. He played the judge. I argued for the warrant, and he assessed the evidence as the judge would. "Based on the autopsy, we have reason to believe Myles Thompkins was murdered—forcibly submerged in the river," I explained to Judge Max. "We have a suicide note that was not typed on Thompkins' computer. We checked with the lab this morning, and it was also not printed on his printer. We're looking for the computer and printer where the note was generated."

"But what evidence do you have that it was Shipley who wrote the note and murdered the guy?" Max as the judge asked.

"We have motive. Carl Shipley was stalking one of the Johansson murder victims," I explained. "Myles was Laurel's true love. They'd continued to be close after the marriage to Jacob Johansson. But Carl Shipley had a thing for Laurel."

Max paused, then he frowned. "This isn't enough, Clara. The judge won't go for it."

"Jeez, Max!" I said it so loud I figured everyone in the sheriff's offices could hear me, so I lowered my voice. "Ease up here. Don't make this hard."

"This is hard. We don't have a lot but conjecture going for us. We need enough justification or Judge Crockett will turn us down," Max countered. "What else do we have?"

"I don't know, you tell me," I snapped. Max shot me an irritated frown, and I backed off a bit. Not an excuse, but my mood wasn't improving; I was on edge and frustrated. "We have to think of something. There has to be a way to get that warrant!"

"We need to look at all of this again," Max said. "There must be something we know that the judge would accept as sufficient probable cause. We need to find it and bring it to him. We need that warrant."

For half an hour we threw out idea after idea, batting around possibilities but getting pretty much nowhere. In a last-ditch effort, I called the lab, hoping they had more of our test results and that there was something there that we could use. Some things were still missing, mainly the fiber and hair evidence. They said that they were backlogged and it could be days for some of it, another week if we were lucky for the DNA.

"That's not fast enough," I shouted into the phone. "Come on. You can turn it around faster than that. We've got a killer out there somewhere."

"Chief Jefferies," the clerk started, as Max put his hand on my arm to try to calm me. "We are doing the best we can. We have cases in the lab from all over the state."

I hung up in a snit. Max looked like he was trying to come up with something to say, but hadn't settled on anything before my phone rang. "I hear Myles didn't kill himself. He was murdered," Mullins said, his voice whisky rough. He sounded like he was burning fumes, as if he hadn't slept in a week.

"Who told you?" I asked, irritated. We'd only gotten the autopsy results a little more than an hour earlier. Who else would have known? I doubted that Doc would have told Mullins. Maybe someone at the office heard and let it slip?

"I have sources," Mullins said. "I've worked law enforcement for a long time, Chief. I don't need to hear it from you, although I'd hoped to."

My pulse speeding, I was irritated beyond words. I took a deep breath. "I'm sorry, Jeff, but this isn't your case. Unfortunately, this time around you're the victim's family, not the investigator," I reminded him yet again, my voice leaving no room for argument. "You've got to back off."

"That sounds like what we told you last summer when your sister was missing. It didn't stop you, and it's a good thing, or that case might never have been cracked," Mullins pointed out. I didn't answer. It did no good to bring up the past, plus he was right. Mullins didn't wait for my response, but said, "I figure Carl killed Myles. It's gotta be him. He knew Myles and Laurel still had feelings for one another, and he couldn't abide that. He's behind all of this. All of the murders."

"Jeff, let's not get ahead of ourselves," I said. "We can't assume—"

"Don't tell me what I can or can't assume. What I do or don't know. I've known from the beginning that Carl is the killer, and I just hung up with that SOB and told him so," Mullins railed, spitting mad. "I told him we knew Myles didn't commit suicide, that he was murdered. And I told that piece of human debris that we're gunning for him. Told him it's only a matter of time before we slip the cuffs on and make an arrest."

"You told him all that? Do you realize what you've done? You've warned him!" I shouted, unsuccessfully trying to dial down my own anger. "Jeff, you're tired and grieving. I understand that. But you're not thinking clearly. You just told our main suspect that we're focusing on him. I wanted Carl Shipley calm and collected, not worrying that we'd knock on his door. That's not good. You know better than that."

"Chief, I…" he started, but then he grew quiet. "Shit. I didn't think—"

"It's like I said, your judgment isn't good right now, Mullins," I said, softer. "Your instincts are off because Laurel's one of the victims. Your love for her is making you—"

"A liability," Mullins said, and I didn't contradict him. Silence, until he said, "Chief, you're right. I shouldn't have tipped him off."

"It's okay, Jeff. I understand," I said, thinking back to those days a few months earlier when I crossed the line more often than I liked to admit while searching for my sister. "But you're out of this. We can't have you interfering. Be with your family and make arrangements to bury your daughter tomorrow. Leave the investigation to us."

Silence again, then a grudging agreement.

As I hung up the phone, I griped, "Damn it."

Max had heard my half of the conversation, enough to understand our predicament. "If Carl knows we're coming, we need to act fast," he said. "We don't have any time to waste."

Judge Alec Crockett had his full robe on and was seated behind the bench when we walked into the courtroom. Max whispered in the ear of the coordinator, who was in the process of calling the cases. She wrote a short note that she put in the judge's hand. The old man shot us an irritated gaze and ordered: "My office. Now."

Once we got there, the judge lit a cigarette, the tip glowing bright red. He had an overflowing ashtray next to him, despite the fact that the laws banned smoking in any public building. He didn't look happy. Max and I detailed the evidence, went over a bullet list of the murders, Myles's supposed suicide letter, the results of Doc's autopsy, and explained why we needed Carl's computer. We laid out our theory that Carl had staged Myles's suicide and written the note, most likely on his desktop computer.

The judge looked from Max to me and back again, clearly disappointed, and said, "You need more evidence."

"This is what we've got. We know it's a little sketchy," Max explained. "But Judge, we need the warrant now. This minute. We can't wait."

"And why is that?" he said, giving us a suspicious eye.

This time I answered: "Carl Shipley knows we're coming for him. He's been told that the autopsy will read murder as Myles Thompkins' manner of death. If we don't act quickly, he'll destroy any evidence on that computer."

"Who warned him?" the judge bellowed. Known for having something of a short temper, the judge got red-faced and sputtered, "Chief Jefferies, goddamn it, why haven't you got control of your department?"

I'd never seen him so angry. "It doesn't help to go into who talked. There was a mistake made," I admitted. "But we need that warrant."

"Just the computer equipment, Judge. That's all we want," Max said. "We're requesting a really limited warrant. Any computers and printers. That's it."

When the judge frowned, his unruly white eyebrows peaked in the center and twisted into a question mark. He sighed, but his face was still as flushed as an overripe peach. "Okay," he said. "I'll sign your blasted warrant. But if this goes to trial and you lose the evidence on appeal because we didn't have enough probable cause to justify this damn warrant, you're going to have to live with it. Because you're on thin ice here, I want you to know."

"Absolutely," I said, putting the typed warrant down on the judge's cluttered desk. We watched as he signed it, then he picked it up and handed it to me.

"Now get out of here," he said. "I've got a courtroom to get back to."

CHAPTER THIRTY-FOUR

Twenty minutes later, we were at Carl Shipley's trailer, loaded with a list of questions for him and the warrant for the computer equipment. The CSI folks were on their way, but Max and I had a head start. I didn't see Carl outside, but this time the trailer's front door stood open. "Carl, it's Chief Jefferies and Chief Deputy Anderson," I shouted. "We need to talk."

Silence. Max stayed back, but I saw him pull out his handgun. I was surprised, but then thought maybe he sensed something. I grabbed mine out of my holster. We waited. We heard insects chirping and buzzing in the woods around us, nothing out of place. That said, it felt strange, unsettling, and, I can't explain why, but my nerves bristled. I walked up, peeked inside the trailer and saw that it looked as we had left it after the last search, disheveled but not in bad condition. "No Carl," I said to Max. "What do you think?"

"His pickup's here. He must be somewhere nearby," Max said. "Let's look."

I nodded.

"Carl Shipley!" Max shouted, as loud as his lungs would allow, toward the woods. "It's Chief Deputy Max Anderson. Chief Jefferies is with me. We need to talk to you. This minute. Come out!"

Again, silence.

"Damn," I whispered. "Where the hell is he?"

Max tucked his mouth into a nub, then unfolded it and suggested, "Let's spread out." He nodded toward the woods past the trailer indicating I should take that direction, and he began easing off onto an opposite track. It was 11 a.m., and although the air felt fall-crisp, the sun was high, beaming down on us. I didn't much like walking into the woods alone, weaving through the brush with no one to cover our backs, but we needed to find Carl. As I trekked in, I speculated about whether or not he'd lawyer up like he'd threatened to, or if we could coax him to talk.

Mostly, I wondered what we'd find on his computer's hard drive.

Keeping my focus on the area surrounding me, I wove between the trees on the path where the grass was worn down. I stared off as far into the distance as I could and saw nothing but trees and brush, slivers of sunlight beaming between them. The trail before me clear, I moved forward, thinking about the Day of the Dead tree we'd seen last time we searched these woods. I worked my way in that direction, passing Carl's horse in the corral. I wondered if Carl might be at the oak tree, perhaps taking down his decorations or sitting around eating lunch and drinking a beer while he enjoyed the view, but as I approached, I stopped. Even from a distance, I knew that the tree wasn't as I'd last seen it.

"Max, can you hear me?" I shouted. When he didn't answer, I tried again, calling out, "Max, I need you here."

"Coming!" he answered.

I picked my way forward, still scanning the woods, but with my attention increasingly drawn straight ahead. By the time Max arrived, I stood at the base of the tree, looking up, my stomach roiling. Max moved in beside me, and we said nothing until he got on his phone and asked for his boss. A black-winged vulture swooped overhead, circling above us. As Max talked, another arrived, mimicking the first. It reminded me of our arrival at the ranch two days earlier, the vultures in the trees staring at the bodies under the bloodstained sheet.

"I need to talk to Sheriff Holmes," Max said into his phone. A moment passed, and I assumed the sheriff responded. "Sheriff,

Lieutenant Mueller is already on his way with the CSI folks, but we need Doc Wiley again, this time out at Carl Shipley's trailer, past Old Sawyer Creek. You know where it is?"

Silence while I assumed the sheriff said that he did. The vultures were gathering, more coming, and the sight of them repulsed me. I aimed my gun, took a shot toward one, not really wanting to hit it. The gunshot rang through the woods, and the scavengers scattered.

"That was nothing," Max said. "Chief Jefferies just discharged her weapon to scare the buzzards away."

A brief silence, and then Max explained to the sheriff: "It's a bizarre turn of events to be sure." Max hesitated and cleared his throat. This was sticking in his gullet, too. "You know that tree I told you about, the one that's all trussed up with string and covered with skulls and skeletons?" Max cleared his throat a second time. "Well, Carl Shipley is hanging from it."

CHAPTER THIRTY-FIVE

The others arrived quickly. Lieutenant Mueller, Doc, Max, and I examined the route from the house to the tree for footprints and saw some, but Mueller thought they'd all come from Carl's boots. Still, he snapped a bunch of photos. One of his team taped off the area with the prints and mixed up materials for castings to preserve them. Meanwhile the rest of us kept working our way toward the body hanging in the tree. We were trying to determine if anyone else had walked on that path that day besides Max, me, and Carl.

"This looks interesting," Max said, pointing out a place where a patch of grass had been uprooted. It wasn't large, just a couple of inches wide and a few inches long. "That could be from something or someone being dragged. Don't you think?"

"Could be," Mueller said. "Or Carl could have dragged his toe for a couple of inches. How can you tell?"

Doc ambled over and put his hands on his hips. "You think?"

"Yeah, I do," Mueller said. "We'll take a cast and photograph that, but I'm not sure it really tells us anything."

"I see what you're saying. It's not very deep," Doc agreed, adjusting his glasses. "I sometimes don't raise my foot as I should and scuff it. Of course, at my age…"

"Gentlemen, we need to focus and figure out what happened here," I said, stating the obvious. The question we were attempting to answer was the same one we'd just put to bed on Myles Thompkins' drowning that morning. "We need to know if this really is a suicide, or if we've got another homicide."

The problem was that while we'd found a hand-printed note hanging on another tree, one just twenty feet or so away, the scene suggested a lynching. Not that we could find any signs of a struggle. The inside of his trailer didn't look disturbed. We couldn't find any evidence of anyone else having been in the area. On one level it didn't seem out of the question that Carl walked out to the tree with the rope and did himself in.

"We think he killed himself because?" I asked. "What's his motive?"

"He knew we were closing in on him. Mullins told him," Max replied. "Maybe Carl figured his time was up, and he wanted to make amends. So, he wrote the note."

"Sure. Could be. But explain that." I pointed at the corpse still hanging from the tree. His skin a ghostly pale, Carl's jaw was clenched, and his head lolled to the right at an unnatural angle. A thick foam encircled his mouth, along with blood. I guessed the latter might have happened when he bit down on his protruding tongue. Doc had climbed on a ladder and taken a look, and Carl's open eyes were speckled with petechial hemorrhages, tiny blood vessels that are a sign of asphyxiation.

The hard thing to explain was that Carl's wrists were bound with rope.

"It doesn't scream suicide, does it?" Lieutenant Mueller said. "But sometimes things have more than one explanation. Could he have done that to himself?"

We all looked at Doc, who shrugged. "Well, it's not unheard of. There have been cases like this in the literature," he said. "Suicides where the victim wanted to make sure he didn't back out, so he tied himself up before he jumped."

We all stared at the body, wondering.

"Will you be able to tell during the autopsy?" I asked. "Is there usually telltale evidence of some kind?"

"Not sure. I've never had anything like this before," Doc admitted. "But I'll look into it."

I thought about that, wondered who else might be able to help. "Listen, I know this guy in Texas who is an expert in knots and bindings," I said. "How about we take photos of those ropes on his wrists, get some good ones of the knots and the position of the rope. Maybe he'll have some insight."

"It's worth a shot," Mueller said.

While the others worked on the photos, I walked over to the tree. Someone had pounded a roofing nail into the piece of paper to keep it from falling. For what wasn't the first time, I gave it a read. All it said was: *TELL JACOB I'M SORRY*

CHAPTER THIRTY-SIX

While the others helped Doc lower Carl's body out of the tree, I circled back to the trailer with the CSI unit's IT expert, a guy named Randy Nader, a scrawny fellow who had the long, straight hair of his Navajo mother and the aquiline profile of his Armenian father. Once he had the computer on, Nader played around for a while, tried out a few common passwords to unlock it. Nothing worked. Then he picked up the keyboard and looked underneath it. Nothing there. No cheat notes with the code.

"Try Laurel," I suggested.

He did, and it didn't work. "Any more ideas?" Nader asked.

"Hmm. Not sure," I said. I looked around the trailer, didn't see anything that spurred any thoughts. I pulled up Carl's info on my phone through the state website. We tried his driver's license number without luck. His birthdate didn't work either. I opened his NCIC profile on the national database and looked at his arrest on the bar fight. I gave Nader the name of the guy Carl beat up, and that did nothing. It turned out that the last four digits of Carl's social security number did the trick, and we were on.

"What are we looking for?" Nader asked, as he loaded a program that examined the hard drive.

"Anything associated with any of the victims," I said, then recited their names slowly while Nader keyed them in. "And in particular anything that includes the name Myles Thompkins."

The screen filled, line after line of documents and photos. Nader flipped through, loading one after another. There were images of

Jacob Johansson and his family, some posed, others candid shots, and some that resembled those in the album of Laurel, like they were taken with a telephoto lens from a distance, in secret. While Anna, her children and Jacob were in many, the majority seemed to be of Laurel.

Half an hour into the search, Nader opened a file dated the previous Saturday, two days before the murders, and images of Laurel and Myles together at the river popped up on the screen. In some, Laurel appeared despondent, holding her infant son and sitting on the rock, looking as if she were crying. Myles stood above her, his arms folded as if angry, closed off to her, glaring. "That's the argument Naomi caught the tail end of," I murmured.

"What?" Nader asked, but I brushed him off.

"Keep scrolling through those," I said, and he did. Carl photographed them as they embraced, Laurel's head on Myles's shoulder. They walked to their cars, and Carl shot a photo of Naomi getting out of the van with little Kyle. Then Naomi staring down the dirt road at Myles and Laurel. The final photo was of Laurel holding Jeremy, not in his car seat, as she drove away.

Just like Mother Naomi described it, I thought. Then I said to Nader, "What we're really looking for is a text file, a suicide note. It would have Myles's name and was probably written very recently."

Nader continued scrolling, then clicked on a short file. The suicide note popped up. I didn't have the original with me, but I saw no differences from the one we'd found in the saddle pocket. It seemed evident that Carl was Thompkins' killer.

"When and at what time was this note written?" I asked.

Nader opened the file info: it had been created Monday, the day of the murders at the ranch. I looked at the time: 02:11:59 AM.

I pulled a notebook out of my bag, the one where I'd jotted down Doc's timeline. Around midnight, Laurel was murdered. According to what we'd uncovered on the computer, two hours or so later, Carl wrote a suicide note for Myles. Just past three, someone texted Scotty on Myles's phone and asked him to feed the dogs and watch over his place. Four hours later, Anna, Benjamin, and Sybille were all murdered, and someone slashed Jacob's throat. The timeline seemed to fit.

"Thanks," I said. "Make sure you log all of it into evidence, the entire hard drive, and look through it, see if anything else is connected to the Johanssons or Myles Thompkins. And take the printer, so we can be sure that the note was printed on it."

"Will do," Nader said.

I left Nader working and followed the path through the woods to rejoin the others. It seemed that the case was falling into place, but loose ends kept circling through my mind. I felt unsettled, ill at ease, not at all the way I'd come to expect as a case wound to a close. Usually, I'd have a sense that all was becoming right with the world. That wasn't happening this time. Why not?

Walking farther on, I thought about Jeremy. Was it time to pull the guard off? That brought to mind Sybille and Benjamin, their still bodies on the cold ground. I couldn't let that happen to Jeremy. I still wasn't sure I'd kept my promise to him.

Not yet, I decided. The guard stays until I have it all figured out.

I reached the Day of the Dead tree—the vultures were back, perched on tree limbs around the clearing, I assumed waiting for an opening. A racket above, and I saw one soar over me and swoop down. It flew off, its muscular wings rustling the air. As I lowered my eyes, I focused on one of the ornaments dangling from the tree, a brightly painted skull, mouth wide open, as if it were laughing at something uproariously funny.

At the tree's base, the men had Carl's body laid out in the bag. They were all standing around, looking down at the dead man, murmuring. Max had a sour look on his face, like he wanted to shake the deceased awake. "What's wrong?" I asked.

"We were just saying that we all feel cheated," Max said.

"Cheated?" I echoed.

"Madder than a wet hen," Doc said. "It's just not fair."

"Because he's not here to answer questions?" I wondered if that could be what bothered me, why it didn't feel final. For a moment, I thought maybe. But then, that didn't sit right either. There was something else.

"Well… yeah, that too. We'd like to know the details," Max swallowed hard, and I could see anger in his eyes. "But mostly it's that this stiff is responsible for a lot of carnage, those two dead little kids, the two women. And now we can't tell him what garbage he is. We'll never be able to throw him in a jail cell."

I understood but didn't comment. My mind was elsewhere. It seemed odd that with so much death surrounding me, so much pain, when I took a deep breath, I caught the scent of fresh pine from the trees and the mountain breeze. Life held such contradictions. People died, and the next morning others woke and started a new day. Carl Shipley's dead body lay at our feet, and it wasn't enough. We wanted him to suffer. We still ached for revenge.

I bent down and helped Doc zip up the body bag, shutting Carl away in the darkness in which he'd lived his life. At that moment, my message alert pinged, and I opened it and saw a text from my friend in Dallas, the expert in bindings and knots:

If other evidence supports suicide, hand bindings don't disprove it. The angle of the knots and the way the rope is wrapped isn't inconsistent with having been done by the victim. It is entirely possible that he did this to himself, and this is far from unheard of in a self-hanging.

I handed Max my phone, and he read it, too. "What did you find on Carl's computer?" he asked.

"The suicide note," I said. "Nader is logging everything in to take it to the lab to get a better look, but it appears that Carl wrote the note. We have more photos of Laurel and Myles, too.

Many taken that Saturday before the murders, of the two of them together at the river."

"Everything fits then?" Max asked.

I showed him the timeline in my notebook, starting at midnight and ending around 8:05 a.m. when Naomi arrived at the ranch and found the bodies. "Well," Max said. "It does all appear to match the evidence. So, Carl murdered Laurel, then killed Myles and staged it to look like a suicide. He then returned to the ranch, and when the family got up at seven, he slit his best friend's throat and shot Anna and the children."

I frowned and shook my head, then semi-agreed. "I guess."

"Clara, it looks like this is over. Carl's our guy, and he's dead. No chance he'll hurt anyone ever again," Max asked. "What bothers you?"

"Some of this doesn't make sense to me. I don't understand why he murdered Anna and the children, or attacked Jacob," I said. "If Laurel's upstairs, her throat slashed, and the rest of the family's asleep. Why didn't Carl just make Myles look like the killer and go on with his life? What did he gain by killing the others?"

We stood silent as Max thought that through. "Maybe Carl blamed them all? Maybe he was jealous of Jacob, too, and he couldn't kill him without killing Anna and the children?" he speculated. "But the sticking point here is that Carl's dead. We can't ask him. Maybe we'll never know for sure why he did any of it other than that he was obsessed with Laurel."

"I don't like not knowing," I said.

"Me either," he agreed. "But sometimes cases don't end up with every question answered."

Max was right, of course. Sometimes we never did uncover all the circumstances, the blow-by-blow details that laid out the intricacies of human behavior. We liked to think that we could analyze others, figure out what drove them, know for certain why things happened. But people were often mysteries, especially those like Carl whose brains weren't wired the way the rest of ours were. To do what he did, he had no empathy.

"We need to get to the hospital," I said. "We have to explain all of this to the Johanssons before the town rumor mill delivers the news."

When we got off the elevator, none of the family was in the hallway. I'd grown so accustomed to seeing Michael and Reba there that I wondered what was wrong. Instead, as we walked toward Jacob's room the curtains were pulled back and we saw him with his parents. The machines were gone. He was dressed in jeans and a T-shirt, and they were packing a bag. Mother Naomi stood just inside the doorway, grinning so wide I wondered if it would make her cheeks sore.

"Clara, you're here just on time for the good news," Michael said when I walked in. "You too, Max. Jacob is released. Going home."

"So soon?" I asked.

"No solid food for a while," Reba said. "Lots of liquids, ice cream and malted milks, but he swallows like a champ. The doctors said he'll do as well at home as here."

"And the house is ready for him," Naomi said. "Ready for him to move back home with his son."

"That is good news," Max said.

I smiled at Jacob, and he tried to reciprocate, but it came off as more of a grimace, so the healing wasn't quite miraculous. The bandages covering the wound on the front of his throat moved up and down as he swallowed.

"Jacob, do you remember any more about what happened at the ranch last Sunday and Monday?" I asked.

Jacob dropped his head and shook it ever so slightly as he gave me a half-hearted thumbs down.

Michael, who moments earlier had been smiling at his son, teared up. He walked over and wrapped his arms around Jacob, who stood at least half a foot taller. At the same time, Reba rubbed Jacob's arm. "We've explained to Jacob everything we know," she said. "He doesn't remember what happened, but he knows about Anna and the children, about Laurel's death."

"We're sorry, Jacob," I said. "Very sorry about your family."

A slight nod, and tears filled Jacob's eyes.

"Did you make any more progress on the case?" Michael asked, and at that, Max suggested they sit down and listen while we explained.

We went over it all, not in detail but the big picture. It didn't take long before Reba jumped back up. "Not Carl!" she shouted. "Not after all we did for that boy, raising him like a son. It's not possible that he'd do this to hurt us. Jacob treated him like a brother."

But as we laid out more of what we'd uncovered, slowly they came to agree that it had to be Carl. All the evidence pointed to him. Everyone but Reba, who couldn't seem to make that jump, appeared to accept it.

The room dissolved into a mixture of tears and cries, shouts of anger and pain. Michael tried to calm his wife as he asked us more questions, Reba in the background swearing that the only one responsible for her family's horrific tragedy had to be Myles Thompkins and that we'd failed the family by not focusing on him.

Jacob remained quiet, until he grabbed a pen and paper off the bed tray and wrote: *CARL WAS MY FRIEND*

I then told him about Carl's suicide note, and that he'd asked us to tell Jacob that he was sorry.

Jacob dropped his head, and Naomi slipped between the older Johanssons to put her arms around him. She whispered in Jacob's ear, and he closed his eyes, as if to shut out the world.

*

As Max and I left the hospital, I phoned Mullins. It went right to voicemail, so I got in touch with dispatch. "I just hung up with Detective Mullins. He's on his way here to talk to you," Kellie said. "He knows about Carl Shipley. The detective sounded kind of relieved."

I dropped Max off on my way. Only a handful of protesters congregated on the sidewalk outside the station, and they seemed less dedicated, not bothering to shout at me. When I walked in the back door, Mullins was sitting at his desk. He had his head propped up on his fist, and he looked like he'd been to war. Maybe he had. I approached him, and he stood, and tears flushed his eyes as he threw his arms around me. "Thank you, Chief," he said. "I am sorry that I kept interfering. I knew you two would solve the case, but Laurel was my little girl, and I worried that..."

Overwhelmed, he couldn't seem to form the next words.

"Let's go in my office," I whispered.

Mullins never asked me what had happened when we arrived at Carl Shipley's trailer, what we saw. He seemed to know about the hanging and the note, probably from someone at Max's office or mine. It appeared that he had closed that chapter; the angry father of a murder victim role was gone. Now, for the first time, he gave himself permission to grieve.

"Chief, let me tell you about my girl," he whispered, his voice breaking with the deepest of pains. "From the beginning, Laurel was special..." The rest of the day dissolved in memories.

CHAPTER THIRTY-SEVEN

My sleepless nights endured. I lay in bed well past midnight, my mind roiling. By four, I was again awake, the lights out in my room, staring into the darkness, troubled. Everyone else considered the case over, but I couldn't get there. Was I being compulsive, hanging on when it was time to put it to rest? Maybe Mother Naomi's assessment of me was right; perhaps I simply didn't understand when to let things be.

An hour after sunrise, I walked through Alber's cemetery. The headstones at the front were obelisks and flat panels so worn by the decades, some more than a century, that the names were barely legible. A scattered dozen or more were sanded off by the winds and rains until whoever lay below would remain anonymous for eternity. With time to spare before the funerals began, I lingered at the graves of my sister Sadie and one of my four mothers, Constance, who'd passed away years earlier. In an area where clusters of Jefferies were laid, I was surrounded by family history: great-grandparents, aunts, uncles, a few cousins, many of whom I'd never known.

For a long time, I sat on the ground at the foot of my father's grave. No one around, I whispered, "Did you ever regret what you did to me, Father? Giving me away to such a man, when I was little more than a child?"

I waited, as if my father might answer, although I knew that he never would. I thought of Max's words, how even when cases are closed, we don't always have all the answers. Life was much the same way. But I couldn't deny that I wanted to hear my father's response, just as I wanted to know how events unfolded that horrible day at the bison ranch. I didn't like mysteries. If I could have revived Carl Shipley long enough to interrogate him, I would have.

Overhead the sky formed a hazy gray tent, and the ground beneath me chilled me until I shivered. There'd been another freeze the night before, and the sun hadn't yet warmed it. The forecast included snow for the coming weekend, and I thought of that morning at the ranch, the frost on the rooftops and the mountains' snowcaps, the breeze that shivered through me as I looked at the bodies of Anna and her children under the bloodstained sheet.

The hearses paraded into the cemetery, four in all, and Jacob and his parents arrived in a limousine. After they crawled out, someone handed Jacob his only surviving child, baby Jeremy. The woman tending him clambered out, and I saw that it was Mother Naomi. Jacob handed the baby back to her, and they walked to the graves together.

Another car pulled up, one with Mullins and his two wives, followed by a pack of their children. One of the daughters resembled Laurel. I saw the similarities in her patrician features. Mullins nodded at me, and I responded. He tried to smile, but in the end simply turned away. At the graveside, my lead detective and his wives joined Jacob and his parents. Tears flowed, and Jacob singled out Mullins to stand with him at the head of Laurel's casket.

Around them the mourners congregated, the men wearing dark suits and coats and the women with the skirts of their long dresses flowing from beneath woolen wraps. Some carried flowers to place on top of the four sad coffins, two so small they squeezed the breath from my lungs.

"Heavenly Father, we are here today to entrust to you two dutiful women, wives and mothers, and two innocent children," the ceremony began.

I didn't listen to the consecration of the burial plots, or when the officiate asked God to comfort Jacob, Mullins, and their families. My thoughts drifted to the river, to Myles and Laurel on that final Saturday. I wondered yet again, as I had so often, why they appeared so agitated. I thought of Carl's photos, of Myles with his arms crossed and Laurel rushing away when she saw Naomi arrive.

Max and the sheriff came to the services and stood beside me. We were silent, somber like all the others, and as the crowd disbursed, the three of us walked off together. We left the sheriff at his car, and then Max escorted me to my SUV.

"Have you decided about the cabin?" Max asked. "Brooke is staying at Alice's, so she's taken care of. I'm leaving in about an hour."

"Well, I'm still…" I fumbled, unsure what to say.

"Clara, there's no pressure here beyond that I want to be with you." I knew he was trying hard to put me at ease. "We can take this slow. I promise. Nothing has to happen other than that we have the freedom to be together without others watching."

I understood what he was asking, why he wanted the time alone without the town, his daughter overseeing us. My pulse quickened and I felt unsure. I thought of Myles and Laurel—their story had ended, and despite my fears, I didn't want that for us.

"Sure. I'll meet you there, but I have some work to clean up. Text me the directions, and I'll join you tomorrow morning."

Max grinned at me, happy, and I thought he might grab me in his arms, but I saw a clutch of townsfolk watching, and I hurried away.

From the cemetery, I drove into town to the station. I felt on edge about the weekend with Max. I wanted the time with him, but I still had fears. I wondered if I should be honest, tell him about my past? It was such an odd tale. What would he think?

My desk had a pile of reports on it. The last of the fingerprints, fiber and hair evidence had arrived in manila envelopes from the state lab. A note said that the DNA was a few days out. Still troubled that so much didn't make sense to me, I paged carefully through each report, looking for something, anything, that signaled the case wasn't over. In the end, nothing appeared surprising. Everything pointed to Carl as the killer. The lab even discovered one of his fingerprints on the suicide note found in Myles's saddle.

At lunchtime, I drove down Main Street toward the diner. At least on the surface, Alber had returned to normal. The case solved, the demonstrations outside the police station had stopped. But I knew that just under the surface the tension remained; I had to accept the fact that I wasn't wanted. I might never be wanted. Later that afternoon, perhaps as a reminder, I received another personally addressed note that someone had wedged into a gap in the station door's window. A pink envelope, it smelled of vanilla like the first one. I assumed both had come from the same woman. When I opened it, I read:

GO BACK TO DALLAS WHERE YOU BELONG. YOU AREN'T ONE OF US ANYMORE. YOU DON'T BELONG HERE. LEAVE BEFORE WE MAKE YOU GO!

I wondered if she wanted me to interpret that as a threat.

"Where do I belong?" I whispered. I glanced at my shirtsleeve and thought of what it covered—my eagle tattoo, my homage to my home, to my past. I thought of my mother who wanted nothing to do with me, the siblings I had yet to meet, and I questioned yet again: did home still exist? If it did, was it Alber? Was this where I belonged?

On the way out the door, I stopped to talk to Kellie. "Did you inquire into adding a surveillance camera to the front of the building?"

"They said they'll send someone out next week," she said. "Is that soon enough?"

I thought of the note in the pink envelope and wondered when I'd receive another, then decided that I wasn't going to let anyone spook me. "Sure, that'll be fine."

At that, Kellie mentioned that Alber's rumor mill was churning. Somehow, Jacob had finagled a rushed approval from the prophet, and he and Naomi planned to be married the next day. I hadn't heard, and I was surprised. Kellie appeared to be, too. She lowered her voice and whispered, "So fast. Anna and Laurel, the two children just buried this morning. Lots of folks think it's disrespectful."

It did seem hasty, yet I wondered, as short as life was, as uncertain, if maybe they were wise not to wait. And I felt a glimmer of hope for Mother Naomi. Maybe marrying Jacob would bring her peace and happiness. I wanted that for her. "You shouldn't gossip," I scolded. "Jacob and Naomi have both lost spouses, so maybe they're just a good fit and need to go on with their lives."

Kellie seemed to consider that, but then dismissed it. "All I can say is that folks are wondering why so fast."

That brought up Jeremy. "Do you still want the squad guarding him?" Kellie asked. "Can't we take it off now?"

I nearly said yes, but I couldn't get there. "Give it a few more days," I said. "Just to be sure."

"But the case is over." Kellie looked surprised. "Isn't it?"

I didn't answer.

Early the next morning, Friday, I packed to join Max at the cabin. Although nervous, I was committed to keeping my promise. When I texted that I was on my way, Max said he planned to go fishing, and that he hoped we'd have fresh-caught trout for lunch. I remembered a long-ago town gathering after my father caught us kissing. We'd both been ordered to have no contact with the other, so we had only furtive glances and rare stolen moments. That day at a picnic in the park, each family brought their own lunch, and Max and one of his brothers fried fish for their family. When no one watched, Max walked up behind me and whispered: "Clara," so softly I barely heard him.

He held a paper plate with a small fillet and a dab of tartar sauce. "Saved this for you," he said, smiling so wide I could see his back teeth. "I caught it yesterday on the river." His voice even quieter, he said, "Near our spot."

Months later, on his seventeenth birthday, Max was banished. As I grabbed my battered roll-on suitcase and clomped down the stairs, I thought about how I ached for him when he was gone, how I thought I caught glimpses of him at school, at town functions. When I took a second look, he was never there.

We've found each other again, I thought. *I can't throw it away. Why am I so afraid?*

On the way out the shelter door, I saw Hannah talking to a small group of residents. In front of the women, I explained that I was talking a short trip. I hoped that having them all hear me might tamp down the gossip a bit, in case anyone realized Max and I were both gone over the same weekend. "I'm visiting old friends in Salt Lake," I said. "I haven't seen them in such a long time. I can't wait. I'll be back Sunday."

"That's great. Have fun," Hannah said, drawing me in for a hug. "Clara, you deserve the time off. You work so hard. What a wonderful thing you did solving the Johansson murders."

I watched the faces of the women behind her. None of them smiled or echoed Hannah's praise.

Another chilly morning, I raised the liftgate to load my suitcase in the Suburban. On the highway, I drove past the Johanssons' bison grazing in a field and thought about Mother Naomi and Jacob, their wedding planned for that afternoon. I wondered if they had considered inviting me. Probably not. As an apostate, I wasn't allowed to attend such ceremonies. I was, after all, no longer a member in good standing of Elijah's People.

Telling myself it didn't matter, I drove on, intending to head directly to the cabin. I thought about Max waiting for me there. What would we be like together? This would be the first time we'd truly be alone. I glanced at the clock. Nine a.m. I should arrive at the cabin by noon.

I picked up speed on the highway, and I thought about how I'd pass the road that went to the river, to the place where Myles and Laurel spent their final time together. Again, I had an overwhelming sense of matters not put to rest. That brought to mind the lingering doubts that bothered me about the case. The first point on the list: that we'd never found Laurel's final letter. She'd written so faithfully, right up until a week before the murders. Then, that final Sunday: nothing.

Old unanswered questions filled my mind: *How did they pass the letters to each other?* I wondered. *Did someone do it for them?*

I didn't think so. There'd been no evidence of that. *How then?* I wondered. I thought of the river, of the big rock where Laurel sat, and when the time came, instead of continuing on to the cabin, I called Max.

"You're not coming," he said, deep disappointment in his voice.

"I am," I said. "But I'll be a little late. I'm stopping at the river on the way."

"Why?" he asked. "Old times' sake?"

"Not because of us," I said, although I might have added, I do think of you—of us—there. "I want to take one more look around, see if I can find Laurel's last letter."

"The letter?" Max said. "I'd forgotten about that. What makes you think she even wrote one? And if she did, why would it be there?"

"I don't know," I said. "Except that so much happened at the river. That's where they were together. That's where we found Myles's body."

Silence for a moment, and then Max gently asked: "Clara, the case is closed. We solved it. What do you hope the letter will tell you?"

"The answers," I said. "To all of the questions."

CHAPTER THIRTY-EIGHT

Despite it appearing that much of Alber knew of the secluded spot, I had never run into anyone else there. This time, too, I was alone. The water on the bank undulated in gentle waves, and the air smelled of the fall forest. The river was about seventy feet across—I could stand on one bank and stare through the trees at the other side. I wondered where Carl hid to take the photos of Laurel and Myles on that final Saturday. I focused on a rock outcropping nestled in the trees and speculated that he'd peered at them from behind the brush. I shuddered when I thought of Laurel and Myles arguing, unaware that Carl watched them from the shadows.

Looking out at the water, I sat where Scotty had seen Laurel, on the big rock on the shore. I thought of Max in that exact place the evening we found Myles's body, and then I turned and looked at the spot where so many years ago, I brushed my hand against his dimpled chin and kissed him.

So many ghosts haunted me as I glanced from water to rock to earth and back again. I began to pace off the area. I started tracing the bank from one end of the clearing to the other. I watched for a hidden cranny, someplace a letter could be secreted away to wait for an eager hand to claim it. Nothing jumped out at me on the shoreline. I walked inland about a dozen feet, then turned back in the opposite direction, hoping to find what I'd come for. Nothing again, and I repeated the drill on the other side of the clearing.

While I searched, I thought again about Jacob and Naomi, about the wedding that would be unfolding that very day. A small service—only family and those in the church hierarchy would be invited to the ceremony. Afterward, I assumed there would be a larger reception at the ranch. I wondered if anyone had replaced the missing tiles in the kitchen floor, if all traces of the atrocity were wiped away. Even if they had, I doubted that anyone could ever forget what happened there.

I quickened my pace. Where would Laurel have left a final note for Myles? Maybe this was all in vain. Maybe there was no final letter. Maybe they'd said their goodbyes on Saturday. Maybe that was the explanation for their emotional meeting.

From somewhere far away, I heard the call of an owl, a long, haunting cry that echoed through the forest into the clearing and seemed to bounce off the cold earth. An hour after I started, I faced defeat. I reluctantly headed toward the road where I'd left the Suburban. *How foolish I've been,* I thought. *How obsessed. Why can't I stop digging for bodies? Why can't I accept that this case is over and done with?*

In that instant, everything changed.

I would have missed it except for the fawn-gray squirrel that scurried past and ran up the side of a box elder tree. I stopped to watch, laughed when it jumped from one limb to another, and at first, I didn't recognize what I was looking at pinned to the trunk maybe ten feet up. In the summer, foliage would have hidden it. Even with the leaves fallen, it was barely visible.

A large rock at the base of the tree had a flat top, and I climbed up. I thought about Laurel doing the same wearing her long prairie dress, how she must have held the skirt up or she would have tripped. I had to stretch to reach the weathered wooden board and push it to the side. The nail the board hung from resisted, but I shifted it out of the way and uncovered a hole in the tree, one that a bird might nest in. Instead, I saw something white inside. While still standing on the rock I read the front of the envelope: *My Dearest Myles.*

The writing was familiar—I knew it had to be written by the same hand as the letters I'd read that night at the shelter in which Laurel recounted how she'd been torn from Myles and given, assigned as one might property, to Jacob. Only this letter differed in many ways. This was an apology, and a plea.

> *I am sorry for our argument. I should have understood your point of view, that I wasn't free to leave with you, and that you had to go. It must be hard for you to have only these few stolen minutes together, the two of us separated by days and even weeks at times. I understand that you need more in life. I understand that you have to make plans to leave Alber.*
>
> *While I say that, I plead with you one last time to take me with you. I tell you that it isn't safe for me here. It is only a matter of time before he tells. I know you hope your leaving will protect me, but I fear that isn't true. I know he has been watching me. I know he knows about us. And I know that he will not keep our secret. Myles, I am in grave danger. Please, don't leave without me.*
>
> *My love, each night, I say my final prayer: that somehow, some way, we can be together.*

The letter went on for three pages, Laurel pleading with Myles to meet her at the river the following day, that fateful Monday afternoon, to make plans for their escape. I thought about how if Myles had gotten the letter and agreed, they might have run away together. But the letter was never retrieved from the tree, because in the middle of the night, Myles and Laurel both died.

While Laurel had confided in her father that Carl stalked her, the new letter spelled out that she'd discovered that Carl knew about her and Myles, and that she feared Carl would tell her husband. I thought about Jacob lying on the kitchen floor struggling for life, and again I wondered why Carl did what he did. He was angry with

Laurel, perhaps, that I understood. But why did he attempt to kill his best friend? Why did he murder Anna and the two children?

As I walked toward the Suburban, I clicked through the evidence, compiled a mental inventory. A thought occurred to me, and I called Stef at the station. "I need you to do something for me," I said. "I just realized that a document was missing when I went through the Johansson files yesterday. We need to check on it. I'm looking for the response to a subpoena."

I gave Stef the information, and she promised to track it down and call me ASAP. When I reached the Suburban and climbed inside, I placed Laurel's letter on the passenger seat. Time clicked by. I thought of Max waiting at the cabin. He would be expecting me. I thought of Naomi and Jacob. I wondered where they'd marry. Probably at the ward house in town where Jacob's father used to be bishop. I looked at my watch and decided that it wouldn't be long before the wedding.

"Chief," Stef said. "I've got it. And this is odd…"

When I pulled up at the ward house, the parking lot looked nearly full, and the squad car I had guarding Jeremy was parked out front. I was relieved to see Conroy behind the wheel. He looked surprised to see me, but I didn't take time to explain. "Come with me," I said. "We're going inside."

"What are we—" he started to ask.

"Just follow my lead," I ordered.

It turned out that I was arriving with the guests attending the wedding, not truly dressed for the event in my black jeans and white shirt, my parka over the top. No one appeared to notice me, however, and I worked my way through the small crowd with Conroy trailing behind me.

I spotted her easily, in the center of the hive of women tittering around her. Mother Naomi looked lovely in an off-white dress with lace ruffles at the neckline. I wondered if it was the same dress she'd worn to marry my father, or if she'd made it for the occasion. Naomi always had been exceptionally talented with a sewing machine, and she'd covered the buttons that ran down the front. Holding Jeremy, she bounced him to keep him quiet, as she had that day at the ranch while she told me what she'd found when she arrived. It had only been a few days since he'd started on formula, but he looked as if he'd picked up a little weight. I had the fleeting thought that Laurel would be pleased. When Naomi saw me, she stormed toward me, still holding the infant to her chest.

"Clara, it is nice of you to want to attend the wedding, but you're not supposed to be here," she said. "You know that only members of Elijah's People in good standing are allowed at the ceremony."

"Oh, no worries. I'm not staying," I said, flashing her a smile. "I just wanted to give my congratulations to the groom, tell him how lucky he is to marry you." I looked around the room. "Where is Jacob?"

Naomi seemed taken aback by that. She glanced around. "Well, that's nice, I suppose. But again, you aren't supposed to be here," she said. Moving closer to me, she whispered as if we were conspiring: "You'd better make it fast. Your mother should be arriving soon, and she won't be as even-tempered as I am."

I gave Naomi a smile that said not to worry. "I'll only be here for a moment. Again, where's Jacob? He's not chickening out, is he?"

"Of course not! We're both so excited," she said, but then she cast her eyes down, as if she realized it could be construed as unfitting at such a time. "I mean, he's still grieving, of course. Poor Anna and Laurel, those two beautiful children."

"Yes," I said. "Poor Anna and Laurel, Benjamin and Sybille. Such a terrible loss."

"Of course." She leaned close and whispered, "Clara, do you suppose it's too soon? Are people talking?"

I wondered how she couldn't know, if Mother and Mother Sariah hadn't told her that all of Alber was abuzz about the hurried nuptials. "I don't know, Mother Naomi. I'm an apostate," I said. "You know that no one talks to me."

At that, she put her hand to her lips. "Oh, of course," she said with a brisk nod. Then she seemed to remember why I was there. She pointed toward the far corner of the room, where Jacob stood surrounded by a group of dour-looking men. His second day out of the hospital, he looked remarkably well. "There's my husband-to-be," she said, bustling with pride. "Right over there. Say what you want quickly, and leave. The sealing ceremony will start soon."

At that moment, I saw my mother walk in the door with Mother Sariah. The two women spotted me almost immediately, and mother barreled toward me like a train picking up steam on a track. Intent on reaching me, she wove through those gathered. Conroy followed me as I moved away from Mother, toward the corner, and when Jacob saw me, he beamed as if he couldn't have been happier.

"Gentlemen, I need to talk to this lady," he said, his voice gravelly and barely above a whisper. Some of the bandage had been removed, but he had a gauze pad taped over the stitches. "Without Chief Jefferies, the tragedy that befell my family never would have been solved."

The men scowled at me, unmoved by his testimonial, but they stepped back, and I walked through. As surreptitiously as possible, in one smooth movement, I pulled a pair of handcuffs out of my pocket. Before Jacob understood what was happening, I had him cuffed.

Michael and Reba walked over just in time to hear me say, "Jacob Johansson, you are under arrest for the murders of Anna, Benjamin, Sybille and Laurel Johansson. You have the right to remain silent. Anything you say can be used against you in a court…"

As I finished reciting Miranda to Jacob, his mother shouted, "Lord, woman, have you lost your mind!"

From the center of the room, Naomi let loose the type of scream that warns of impending catastrophe. "Clara, no!" she bellowed. "I am one of your mothers, and I order you to stop this right now."

For his part, Jacob appeared stunned. "What is this?" he asked. "Why are you doing this?"

"The charges are four counts of murder and one charge of conspiracy to commit murder, because you killed your family," I explained. "And you had your best friend murder Myles Thompkins."

Jacob's eyes widened. He looked at me in wonder and shook his head. "I can't... why would you think... this isn't possible. Stop her, Father," he said, turning to Michael. "Tell this woman that it's not true."

The old man's frown dripped down both sides of his face nearly to the edge of his chin, and his eyebrows collapsed one into the other, but he didn't utter a word of objection. I looked at him and shook my head. *Now that's a surprise.* I thought about how Jacob's father had supported Myles when his wife brought up his name, how he never offered any theories on the killings, and a thought formed: *Michael Johansson suspected his son all along.*

When his father didn't jump to his defense, Jacob started to say something. "I didn't—" Then he abruptly stopped.

"Didn't what? Murder two women you were supposed to love, two children who loved and trusted you as their father." I pointed at Jeremy clutched in Naomi's arms. "If that baby had been old enough to talk and tell what happened, you would have murdered him, too."

Jacob shook his head. "This is ridiculous."

At that, I shouted, "Everyone back. We need to get through to the door!"

For a brief moment, no one moved, but then Conroy walked in front of me and the crowd split wide. When we passed my mother, she looked at me as if I were a stranger and then turned away.

CHAPTER THIRTY-NINE

"What is this all about?" Jacob asked. He winced when he spoke. We were at the police station in interrogation room three, the farthest from the dispatch desk and waiting area, but, every once in a while, I heard Reba shouting, other times Naomi. I wasn't sure which one was more upset about Jacob's arrest, his mother or his bride-to-be. Noticeably absent was the voice of Jacob's father.

"You want to tell me what you did, Jacob? Lay it all out there. I bet it would be a relief to get it off your chest. I'm here to listen," I said. "Confession is good for the soul, you know."

"I haven't got anything to confess." At the table, he fanned his hands out, palms up, as if pleading with me to be reasonable. "I don't know what you think you know, but there's nothing *to* know."

"Well, that's not true," I countered. "Is it?"

"Chief Jefferies, you solved this case, all four murders, the attempt on my life," he argued. "I heard about all the demonstrators in town, demanding you leave. Instead of riling people up, why not take credit for your hard work? You've earned it. If you do, maybe folks won't hate you anymore."

I crumpled my lips and frowned. "I'm not feeling much like listening to praise I don't deserve," I said. "Because we didn't get it right, did we?"

"You did," he said, his voice thin with strain. "And my family will vouch for you, tell everyone how you figured out who murdered my wives and children. They'll believe us, because they know us. We're of them, in high standing in the community."

"I solved your case, did I?" I asked, leaning back in the chair and staring at him.

"Yes, absolutely," he said, with a slight grin, the kind that's meant to be reassuring. "You got Carl. You proved that he massacred my family."

I considered the man seated across from me. "Carl was your best friend, wasn't he?"

"I thought he was," Jacob replied with an irritated shrug.

"Then why did you agree so quickly that he was the one behind it? As soon as we said Carl did it, you embraced it. You never put up an argument that it couldn't have been him."

"You had evidence," he said, his voice rising, incredulous. "You explained what you knew."

"And you accepted it without question," I said.

"Well, I, I meant to talk to you about that. You see, I haven't been totally honest with you." He focused on me, his eyes centered on mine but timid, as if reluctantly confiding about a great transgression.

"You haven't?"

"Well, no. I have been remembering some. Off and on, I've had flashbacks." Jacob's frown curved ever farther down. "I was having them all along, I guess, but after you told me about Carl, it became clear. With what you and Max told me, I understood what the flashbacks meant."

"What flashbacks?" I asked.

Jacob hunched forward, his shelf of thick blond hair falling over his eyes, his smoothly shaven face slightly flushed. His eyes narrowed as he implored me to listen. "You understand, I'm sure, that this has been hard on me. Carl was my *compadre*. We were like that," he said, holding up his right hand with the first two fingers entwined. I noticed the bandage was gone. The cut on his hand not deep, it had already begun to heal. "But sometimes I've seen Carl in nightmares and such, or just off and on in flickers of memories as it came back to me."

"And what happens in these nightmares, these flickers of memories?"

"Someone comes at me from behind, and I feel the knife at my throat."

"And you think that was Carl?" I asked.

"I know it was. It was hazy at first, but the memories get clearer all the time. In the last couple of days, I've seen his face," he said, his words coming fast and urgent. "Sometimes I even feel a searing pain in my throat." He reached up and put his cuffed hands to his neck, covering the bandage. "I remember falling to the floor, and when I looked up, Carl was standing over me, a look like a crazy man on his face, blood dripping from the knife."

I stared at him and said nothing. Jacob shifted in the metal chair, the aluminum seat squeaking as it rubbed a table leg. A cloud of Old Spice surrounded us, a favorite of the men in town. Jacob had applied it heavily, and I thought about how he'd fussed for his wedding, four days after his wives and children were murdered.

Once he appeared sufficiently uncomfortable, I smiled at him. "I'm glad you're getting your memory back. That will make it easier to clear all this up." I glanced at the ceiling and verified that the red record light was lit on the camera mounted on the wall. I'd told Jacob that we were making a video of our conversation, but when people get tense, they tend to forget such warnings. The more they talk, the more they try to convince me, and pretty soon they forget that every word they utter can someday come back as nails in their coffins. "Do you remember anything else?" I asked.

"Well, not much," he said. "But I remember that vision of Carl standing over me with the knife and the blood dripping down."

Done saying his piece, he appeared unconcerned, I assumed convinced that he'd swayed me.

"It's odd," I said, purposely keeping my expression blank.

Jacob gave me a half-shrug and asked, "What is?"

"When someone is standing like that, blood falls off the knife straight down in round drops, splats on the floor."

"Yeah," he said. "So what?"

"There weren't any round drops anywhere near your body," I said. "Actually, not on the entire kitchen floor."

Jacob squirmed ever so slightly in the chair. "Maybe they got smudged when I fell on them."

"Well, it's all pretty strange," I said, keeping my voice even, as matter-of-fact as I could manage. "I noticed it at the time, but it didn't strike me as important until now, but there were no blood drops from anyone holding the knife high, like an assailant would have done if he stood over you. How do you explain that?"

A slight flush crawled out of Jacob's shirt collar, white to go with his dark gray suit. He had on a blue tie for the wedding.

"I don't know anything about things like that," he said.

"I don't think you planned very well," I said. "Despite that, it was rather convincing for a while."

Jacob scooted back just a bit in his chair, put some space between us. It didn't worry me. The video camera covered the entire area.

"The blood evidence actually suggests something else." I waited for him to ask what, but his lips were tight, his jaw clenched. "There were smears on the floor, blood that rubbed off the knife's handle and blade, between your body and where we found the knife, under the kitchen table."

This time he spit out the words. "So what?"

"So, whoever threw the knife was low, close to the floor. I thought at the time that the killer was kneeling over you. But now I'm thinking that he was lying down." I placed my arm across the rickety table between us. "It's like my arm is your body, and the knife was flung out across the floor. Jacob, when I think about it, it's like you threw it there while you lay bleeding."

"Why would I do that?" he asked, for the first time his brow lowering as if growing angry.

"To get the knife away from you after you cut your own throat," I said.

At that, Jacob curled back his lips, revealing a slice of teeth, and released a short burst of laughter, as if I'd just told the most amusing joke. When he did, he flinched again. His voice growing increasingly rough, he asked, "You think I cut my own throat?"

"Yes, I do," I said. "And I didn't know this until today, but the doctor at the hospital thought you did, too. He hadn't mentioned it to me because he assumed it was preposterous. But I contacted him on my way to your wedding. The doctor said that from the angle of the cut, that it curved up just a little, the entire time you were in the ICU, he wondered off and on if you'd done it to yourself."

"Oh, come on," Jacob scoffed. "Why the hell? I almost died."

"At the house, the EMT told me that you were lucky," I said. "But it was really that you were smart. You knew you could cut your windpipe and survive, as long as you didn't sever any arteries."

"That's crazy," Jacob snickered. "How can you say that? I almost bled to death. Didn't the doctor tell you that?"

"Well, everything didn't go as you planned it, did it?" I said. "Naomi promised you and Laurel at Sunday services that she'd come over first thing Monday morning, seven thirty at the latest. What you couldn't know was that she'd be late. That was why you almost bled to death."

"Carl—"

"Killed Myles for you, didn't he?" I asked. "Then, when he realized it was all unraveling, that we'd figured out that Myles wasn't the killer, he panicked and hung himself."

Jacob sucked in a deep breath, I supposed trying to calm the pounding in his chest.

"I'm figuring that this whole thing started on Sunday when Carl told you about Laurel and Myles, that he saw them together on Saturday afternoon," I said. "You were mad, felt betrayed, cuckolded. That's why things were tense at the ranch that evening, why Carl didn't stay for dinner. After he told you what he'd seen, you were angry."

"I wasn't…" Jacob started but didn't finish his denial.

"According to the kitchen calendar, you slept with Anna that night, but around midnight, you got up and killed Laurel, took that lipstick and branded her as a harlot."

"No! No! I didn't," he objected, his voice growing weaker, more strained. "I wouldn't…"

His words trailed off, and I said, "I should have figured this out earlier. There were clues all along. Like I couldn't figure out why Carl would have murdered Anna and the children. It didn't make sense."

I paused, and Jacob glared at me, so much hate in his eyes that I had no doubt that he wanted to lunge at me from across the table. But he was helpless, and he knew he was trapped like a rattler I once ran into up in the mountains. It was hiding under a rock and nearly bit me when I surprised it. That time, I backed off, retreated. That wasn't my plan with Jacob. I felt my pulse hasten as I went in for the kill. "It didn't make any sense for Carl to have murdered all of your family, to have cut your throat."

"But you think it makes sense for me to murder my family?" Jacob jeered, his hand pressing on the bandage, I guessed to try to ease the pain. "That's ridiculous."

"Not if Anna knew what you'd done, walked in on you while you stood over Laurel's body, or saw the body and knew you had to be responsible," I said. "You would have worried that you didn't have control of her. She probably said she wouldn't tell anyone, but she might have eventually, if you'd let her live. And since you panicked and killed their mother in front of the children, you had to sacrifice Sybille and Benjamin."

Jacob turned in the chair and crossed his legs. "You don't have any evidence for all this," he said. I'd thought that maybe he'd cry and profess his innocence, but instead he smiled at me. "Not a lick of it."

"Well, there are your boots," I said.

The look on Jacob's face transformed, and I saw the beginnings of fear. It crawled over his eyes and froze his mouth in a straight line.

"You shouldn't have used your own boots to make the print," I said. "That must have been why you cut your hand. I figure you called Carl after you murdered Laurel, asked him to frame and murder Myles for you. By the time he got to your house that night, you had it all planned out. A bloody footprint on the kitchen floor to tie Myles to the crime scene. The boots that made the print found at his house with your blood on one. A fake suicide."

"You're mistaken," Jacob said. He cleared his throat. "Those aren't my boots."

I waited, smiled at him, in no hurry.

"We sent Wilderness Shoe a subpoena, and I just got the information a short time before I showed up at your wedding."

Jacob didn't respond, just stared at me, his eyes freezer-cold.

"You really should have used shoes you'd paid cash for in a store, not ones you ordered from a website. They keep a record of those purchases. The right style. The right size. And I'm betting the report coming early next week will list your DNA as having been found on the inside. I'm sure you left traces when you wore them, probably on the inside of the high-tops where your leg rubbed, and on the shoelaces when you tied them," I said. "But I don't suppose you had time to think everything through, since you planned this in such a hurry."

Jacob's head dropped, and he cringed and again brought his hands up to the bandage on his neck.

"Hurts, huh?" I commented. "Of course, it's nothing compared to what you did to your family. Think about how Laurel felt when she saw you wielding that knife. What Anna and the children went through when you killed them one by one. Who died last, Jacob? Little Benjamin? I bet he worshipped you, followed you around like a shadow. How terrified he must have been as he watched his father murder his mother, his sister. Or was it Sybille, that precious little girl? Then you wiped off the grip, the trigger and threw the gun out into the woods. You went in the kitchen, cut your own throat and waited for Naomi to arrive. It was a gamble, but you were betting that she'd call for an ambulance and save you."

Jacob's hands trembled ever so slightly. "No one will believe you," he whispered. "No one."

"Are you willing to bet your life on that? We have the death penalty in Utah. Four murders, terrible murders, you'll certainly be a prime candidate." I let that sink in for a little while. Then I whispered, "Are you willing to take that risk?"

I hesitated to let him stew, then said, "Or would you rather make a deal?"

For a moment, nothing. Then Jacob slowly brought his head around until he faced me straight on. He took a few deep breaths, thinking it all over, I figured. I didn't rush him. Minutes passed before he asked, "What are you offering?"

CHAPTER FORTY

"I couldn't have proven any of it, except that those were his boots," Clara said.

Despite the three-hour drive to the cabin, she'd arrived a bale of nervous energy. Max was cooking a very late dinner. His fishing trip successful, he had two good-size trout sizzling in a cast-iron pan. Outside, the icy winds were beginning to howl. They still had one full day and part of Sunday for their stolen interlude, but weather reports predicted that they would be spending most of it indoors. The impending gale carried up to a foot of snow, and Max secretly wondered if they'd be able to dig out to go home. But then again, he didn't really care. Perhaps the storm would give them a day or two more. After waiting so long to have Clara to himself, extra hours carried the promise of more time to sort through their emotions.

"You should have called me," Max said. "I would have come."

Clara smiled. "I didn't want you there."

"You didn't want me? Why—"

She shook her head and gestured as if to wipe away what she'd just said. "Not that I didn't want you there, more that I didn't think I should have you there," she explained. "I needed to do this on my own, to show the locals that I didn't need your help or anyone else's to do my job."

"Oh, the protesters?" Max said. "They're just a bunch of disgruntled folks who are mad at the world about how the town is changing."

"Yes, them, but not just them," Clara said.

Max flipped the trout, the two-bedroom cabin filling with the heavy scent of the hot oil browning the cornmeal coating the fish. He'd mixed together homemade tartar sauce, and he had French fries baking in the oven. Salads were already on the table. The place defined the word "cozy" for Max. Small but comfortable, chintz curtains and hand-stitched quilts on the beds. A sign out front read: THE HIDEAWAY, and Max understood why his friend named it that, secluded as the cabin was on ten acres and backing up to a forest.

"Okay, I understand why you didn't wait for me," he said. "But what would you have done if Jacob hadn't agreed to the plea deal? If he hadn't admitted his guilt?"

A half-hearted shrug, Clara curled her lips into a bow. "I didn't let myself think about that," she admitted. "I figured there wasn't going to be any more definitive evidence than what I already had. When Stef told me that the shoe company said the boots belonged to Jacob, that pointed in a direction. I thought about what that could mean and called the doctor. He sounded surprised, but then he admitted that he'd had suspicions about Jacob's injuries. Before long, I thought I had it pretty well figured out. I knew the little evidence I had would never stand up in court. I don't think I could have gotten the DA to take charges with it, but I thought that spun right, what I did know might be enough to get Jacob worried about the death chamber. If he was innocent, he'd tell me to go to hell. If I was right, I figured I had a shot."

"And it worked," Max said. "He opened right up."

"Opened his mouth and let it all stream out like a convert making his first confession," she said. "Once he talked to the DA, had a paper in front of him signed by her that said she wouldn't pursue the death penalty, he unraveled every secret."

"Why, do you think?" Max asked.

"Jacob did a horrible thing, but it was on impulse," she said. "I think, as cool as he was about it, it needled at his conscience. Not enough so he was going to voluntarily accept blame, but enough so that once we struck the deal, he wanted to let it out in the daylight."

Max nodded. They'd both been cops long enough to have encountered this before, the need of some killers to unburden themselves.

"So, Carl was the one who murdered Myles, but none of the others?" Max asked.

"Yes," she said. "After Jacob killed Laurel, he called Carl and told him how to set up Myles."

"So, Jacob planned the entire cover-up?"

I nodded. "Carl wrote the suicide note as Jacob told him to. Then Carl went to Myles's cabin on horseback. He had a gun. Carl forced Myles to text Scotty to tell him to look after the cabin and the dogs. He left Myles's phone at the cabin because Jacob had warned that it could be traced."

"Smart," Max said. "Why did he bother to have him text Scotty?"

"Jacob thought it was more believable that Myles left voluntarily if he made provisions for his dogs."

"That makes sense," Max said. "And then…"

"Carl planted the boots in the bedroom. Then he forced Myles to saddle up Homer. Carl tied Myles up, and used the horse to lead him to the river. Once they got there, Carl cut off the bindings and forced Myles into the river. Then Carl let Homer loose with the suicide note in the saddle. He rode that old mare of his home to the trailer, and it was over."

"Carl murdered for Jacob. He was willing to do that?" Max shook his head, a look of great sorrow on his face. "Friendship is one thing, but this…"

"As Carl and Jacob both put it, they were *compadres, amigos,*" Clara said. "The odd thing is, I think Carl almost told me that he'd done it at one point. Early on, he said that Jacob knew he would do *anything* for him."

Max shook his head. "What about Naomi? You thought she was lying to you. Was she involved somehow?"

At this, Clara let loose an exasperated sigh. "Not in the murders, but my hunch was right. Jacob was awake that day I saw her talking to him. He had signaled her not to tell anyone. So, she lied and told me he was still unconscious. Jacob didn't want to have to start answering questions yet. He wanted to pretend to be out of it for a while longer, to give us time to land on Myles and discover the horse and the suicide note."

After dinner, Max stacked more logs in the fireplace. The blaze spread and the room grew warm and welcoming. He turned off the lamps, and the only light came from the flames. Max wanted to curl up on the couch with Clara, but she stood up.

"Let's go outside," she said.

"It's freezing out there," he protested.

"Just for a few minutes," she said. "I want to see the stars."

Moments later, wrapped in their heavy parkas, they stood on the front deck, looking out at the shadowy mountains in the distance and the navy sky above. "You never see stars like this in the city," Max said. "Salt Lake always gave off too much light."

"Dallas, too," she agreed. Moments passed, and she confessed, "I missed this."

Max wondered if this was the time to bring it up, to talk at last about the future, about them. "Have you missed it enough to stay?" he asked. "To put down roots?"

"I don't know," she admitted. "I'm still not really wanted. The folks in town are working hard to make that clear to me."

"It's a small minority. They're just angry that Alber is changing, that the old ways are dying," he tried to explain. "You're handy to take it out on, an apostate in a position of power. Time passes, and they'll regret what they've done. You're too good at your job for them not to realize how much they need you."

The temperatures dropping quickly, with each breath Max felt his lungs burn ever so slightly. To keep Clara warm, he wrapped his arms around her shoulders. Clara nestled into him, nuzzled against his chest.

"You know, Max, I'm tired of trying to win people over," she confided. "Mother doesn't want me around either. She tells me that every time I see her. And Mother Naomi was spitting mad when we booked Jacob. I think, despite it all, she still saw him as her only chance out of poverty."

"No," Max said. "She was just confused. I'm sure once she thinks it through, she'll understand that you saved her from a terrible marriage. Any man who could do what Jacob did? When she realizes that he was such a man, she'll be grateful."

Clara thought about that and wondered. "Maybe."

"How did Mullins take it?" Max asked, his voice edged in worry.

"He blustered at first and didn't believe me." Clara thought back to her detective's visceral reaction, his fury as he refused to accept that the man he'd given his daughter to had savagely murdered her. "Telling Mullins was one of the hardest things I've ever done," she admitted. "We both knew that Laurel didn't want Jacob. Mullins finally watched the video of Jacob's confession. When it ended, Mullins got deathly quiet, thanked me and rushed off."

"Pretty broken up, I bet," Max said.

"I think he needed to be alone," she whispered. "I don't think he wanted me to see him cry."

They leaned into one another in silence, and then Clara looked up at the stars again and asked, "Max, do you think that although not here on earth, Laurel's final prayer was answered?"

He held her tighter. "Was that in her last letter?" Clara nodded, and he asked, "What was it?"

"That she and Myles would someday be together," Clara said, staring out at the vast landscape, the heavens above them.

Max rubbed her shoulders to keep her warm. "I'd like to think the afterlife works that way. I hope it does."

She smiled up at him. "I do, too."

At that, he suggested they go back inside.

They shed their jackets and hung them on hooks near the door. Clara returned to her spot on the couch, and Max walked over. "Okay if I sit next to you?"

She looked up at him, smiled, and patted the cushion beside her. "I'm counting on it."

The fire flickered, and he held her close. She tilted her face up to his, and as she had so many years earlier at the river, she placed her hand on his cheek and drew him to her. Their lips met and didn't part for long minutes. Then she turned away again and watched the fire.

"You know that first time we kissed?" she asked.

"I'll never forget it," he said.

"We were children," she said. "Just really children, who had our lives ahead of us."

For a minute, Max remained quiet and considered what she'd just said. "We still have much of our lives ahead of us, Clara, don't you think?" When she didn't answer, he lowered his voice and murmured, "The question is if we'll spend those years together."

Quiet moments passed, and Clara stroked his arm and settled on his hand. She took hold and held it, and she thought about how warm he felt, how inviting. She wondered if this was the time to explain and again if he'd understand. "The man they gave me to, his hands were like ice," Clara said. "So cold. As cold as his heart."

She'd never brought up her marriage before, and Max wanted to ask questions, but didn't. Instead, he waited, and moments later, she said, "On the day my parents delivered me to him I was seventeen, and my husband was sixty-four. He could have been my grandfather."

Max had asked about Clara over the years. He'd never been able to find out what caused her to flee, but he'd heard about the marriage to one of the prophet's brothers, a man with many wives and children.

"You never had kids?" he whispered.

She shook her head. "No, I…" at that, she hesitated, then she focused on him with such intensity that he understood what she'd say next was something she held close. "Max, my husband told everyone I wasn't a good woman, that I wasn't in communion with him, of like mind, and God had punished me by making me barren. Even my own mother believed him."

Max thought he understood where she was heading. "But that wasn't the truth? It wasn't you?"

"No, it wasn't," she said. "It's that… well… he was so much older, not in the best health, and… I was young, but he was past the point where he was able to…"

"He couldn't…" Max said.

Clara shook her head. "He blamed it on me," she said. "He said I was ugly and unlovable. He said that no man would ever desire me."

Clara fell silent, and Max waited, unsure what to say. He thought she'd talk more about her past, but instead she asked about his. "We both have ghosts that haunt us," she said. "At times, I've had the feeling that you're still carrying Miriam around with you."

That struck him, and his heart ached. It often did at the mention of his late wife's name.

"At times, I am," Max whispered. As she had, he fought to find the right words, and the courage to say them. "I've always felt responsible for Miriam's death, for Brooke's injuries."

"No!" Clara said, turning toward him, shaking her head.

"That night, when Miriam decided to go home, not stay at her aunt's house until the morning, I should have driven through the mountains. But I'd had a tough case, and I'd been working long hours all week. I felt sleepy, and she insisted she would drive. I knew Miriam had problems seeing at night, but when I brought that up, she swore she would be fine. I shouldn't have given in, but I did. I should have at least stayed awake to keep watch. But I nodded off. If I'd been awake to see the truck overturned on the road..."

Max's eyes filled, and he pulled Clara closer. She used the tips of her fingers to wipe away his tears.

"Oh, Max, I'm so sorry," she said. "I didn't mean to upset—"

"I don't talk about it," Max murmured. "I haven't been able to get to the point yet where it doesn't rip me apart when I think of it. But I've wanted to tell you. I've tried to a couple of times."

For a while, silence. Then she said, "I wonder if either one of us will ever be free of our pasts. Do you think so?"

Max hesitated, but then said, "Our pasts are part of who we are. The pain will always be with us. But maybe we don't have to let it define the rest of our lives."

Clara nodded, and then they kissed again, a long, familiar coming together, this time at his urging. When their lips finally parted, he asked, "Clara, you know what you said earlier, what that old man you married said to you?"

"Yes," she said. "What about it?"

He gazed deep into her dark eyes, and she felt the years fade away, all the hurt, all the pain, all the loneliness she'd endured. Maybe she'd been wrong when she assumed that she would always be alone, and that she'd never find a place to call home. All these years after they'd parted, she still felt as if she belonged in his arms.

His voice husky with emotion, he said, "No matter what, there is something you should never doubt." She brushed her lips against his cheek, burrowed into his warm, soft neck. He put his hand on her chin and tilted her face up to his, then whispered, "I assure you that you are a highly desirable woman."

At that, Max smiled at Clara, his eyes reflecting the deep emotions flooding his heart. She reached for him, and he pressed his lips to her hair, her ear and whispered so quietly she could barely hear him: "One more thing: I don't give a damn about your mother or any of those people carrying their ridiculous signs. They may not realize it, but they need you."

"They do?" Her lips hovered so close to his that it was as if they shared a breath.

"They do," he whispered. "They absolutely do."

A LETTER FROM KATHRYN

I want to say a huge thank you to you for choosing to read *Her Final Prayer*. If you enjoyed it and want to keep up to date with coming books in the series, just sign up at the following link. Your email address will never be shared and you can unsubscribe at any time.

www.bookouture.com/kathryn-casey

For those of you who haven't read the first book in the series—*The Fallen Girls*—it introduces Clara Jefferies and explains her journey, from growing up in the fictional polygamous enclave of Alber, to fleeing afraid for her life, to returning to find her missing sister.

People often ask about how I've ended up writing such books, where the inspiration comes from.

While I've turned to fiction, my journey began as a journalist, and for years I covered sensational murders first for magazines then in true crime books. As a crime writer, I spent decades delving into dramatic murder cases, interviewing prosecutors and defense attorneys, forensic psychologists and medical examiners, victims' families and killers. Over thirty-five years, these experiences gave me an extensive education in the psychology of such cases as well as an entrée into the inner circles of law enforcement. The result is that I've spent many months inside courtrooms, and I've traveled from victims' living rooms to death row.

While the settings, characters and events depicted in my fiction aren't real, they represent no one who actually exists and no actual cases, those experiences have given me a rich foundation for my work.

In closing, I hope you loved *Her Final Prayer*. If you did, I would be grateful if you would write a review. I'd appreciate hearing what you think, and it makes such a difference helping readers discover my books. I truly enjoy hearing from readers, and you can get in touch on my Facebook page, through Twitter, Goodreads or my website, or at kc@kathryncasey.com.

Thank you again, and happy reading,
Kathryn

 kathryn.casey.509

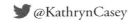 @KathrynCasey

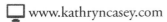 www.kathryncasey.com

ACKNOWLEDGMENTS

There are always so many to thank when I finish a book. Regarding *Her Final Prayer*, I'm very grateful for the assistance of the following people:

Retired detective Tracy Shipley, Texas Ranger Lt. Wende Wakeman, and forensic pathologist Elizabeth Peacock, M.D., for sharing their expertise.

Retired prosecutor Edward Porter for his support and advice.

Bethany Shadid, R.N., for her medical insights.

Sue Behnke, who read the manuscript and gave me feedback.

My literary agent, Anne-Lise Spitzer.

All the wonderful people at Bookouture: my editor, Jennifer Hunt, who took such great interest in the Clara Jefferies series. She's been there from the very beginning. Also: Alexandra Holmes, Fraser Crichton, Jenny Page, Hannah Bond, Lucy Dauman, Jenny Geras, Alex Crow, Kim Nash, Noelle Holten and Sarah Hardy.

As always, I thank my husband and my entire family for their constant support. I love all of you.

Finally, I am very grateful to all of you who read my books. Without you, I wouldn't be able to do what I love. And a special note of appreciation to those of you who recommend my books to others. You make a world of difference.

You've just finished reading the second book in the Clara Jefferies series. I've loved writing it, and I look forward to many books to follow.

Printed in Great Britain
by Amazon